BRILLIANT

Book One of the StarCruiser Brilliant Series

RICK LAKIN

iCrew
digital publishing

Library of Congress Control Number: 2018904198
ISBN 978-1946739025

Printed in the United States of America

Published by iCrew Digital Publishing
Website: icrewdigitalpublishing.com
e-mail: icrewdigital@gmail.com

Cover Design by Renata Lechner
thelemadreamsart.deviantart.com/

iCrew Digital Publishing is an independent publisher of digital works. We support the efforts of authors who wish to publish in the digital world.

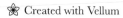 Created with Vellum

To all my kids who inspired me to believe that Jennifer is real.

Contents

Praise for Brilliant

Jennifer Gallagher is a truly unforgettable character, of this world, yet out of this world, an extraordinary young woman who is, in many ways, the best of us.

Richard Lederer, *New York Times*
best-selling language author

This is two hundred and sixty-plus pages of mostly sheer action.

Jim Bennett

The Virtual Copa was a tour-de-force.

Pendleton C. Wallace, Author of the
Ted Higuera Thrillers

Our world even in this time needs heroes we can walk beside. Brilliant isn't just about the heroine's talents or a unique spaceship. It is about good people in general and what they do with what they have. In Hollywood, you are only limited by your imagination.

Sarah Char, executive producer

Introduction

Gentle Readers, *Brilliant* is set fifty years in the future. Scenes that do not indicate a different year will refer to the events beginning in late May of the year 2067.

Prologue

O n a cool day in late Spring, 2067, the temperature was in the low nineties in the dry arid climate of the San Fernando Valley. Harry Ford Academy of the Arts educated children and grandchildren of the Hollywood elite plus a select group of scholarship students from the valley.

Jennifer Gallagher and Tayla Mendoza ambled down the path to the parking lot as other excited students ran past them in a rush to begin their summer.

Jennifer tilted her head back and surveyed the aerial panorama that circled the valley. "School's finally out, girlfriend."

Tayla sighed. "I'm graduating Sunday. After that, I never plan to set foot on this campus again."

"Someday you'll miss it."

"Seriously, Jen, you should've graduated with me."

"Early graduation sounds good, but I still want to walk with my class next year."

"At least you get to follow your dream this summer."

"I'm worried," Jennifer said. "Maybe I won't get in."

"Not even. You're way over-qualified. You had a great interview." Tayla smiled at her friend. "You'll be starting that internship before you know it."

Jennifer bit her lip. "Assuming Mom agrees."

"Your mom understands you and trusts you. She'll let you go."

"I miss my dad."

"You never met him."

Jennifer stopped. "I'm going to find him."

"You think he's alive?"

"I know he is," Jennifer said.

"The vision thing?" Tayla asked.

"Yes."

They got to Tayla's car. "Wanna ride?"

"I need to think this through. The walk home will give me time to do it," Jennifer patted the car's fender. "Love you, Tay."

"Love you more, Jen."

Jennifer's thoughts took her mind in the zone as her legs autopiloted down Valley Center Boulevard and the shortcut through the tree farm. Jennifer was the only one who strode past the chauffeurs and helicopter parents to walk the short distance to the gated community.

Kalim Kone was the only occupant of Patrol Ship *Mendex* of the Hoclarth Alliance on a routine patrol to monitor the third planet from the star called Earth.

"We'll begin our patrol at the fourth planet and circle around to Earth."

The computer navigation system said, "Predex, I'm detecting a rogue ship heading towards the third planet. It has a stardrive."

"Disengage the stardrive. On display."

Kalim again saw his nemesis on the main screen. He knew this ship. It was *StarCruiser Brilliant*.

"Pursue!" ordered the Predex.

As Jennifer entered Hidden Hills on Long Valley Road, she greeted the Irish gateman, "How's yer onions, Sean?"

"Arseways, Jennifer. How Ye?" Sean said.

"Alright, Boyo," Jennifer said.

"Tear your hole off the Haggart."

Sean and Jennifer traded Irish slang when she passed the gate. Sean shared the wisdom he gained before coming to America. Her favorite was his old saying, "Knowledge becomes wisdom when experience becomes the teacher."

STARCRUISER BRILLIANT WAS RETURNING TO EARTH FROM NEAR Saturn after a three-day mission to Comet 2943.

Blonde and fit at sixty years old, Captain Jack Masing occupied the center seat. He was twenty pounds lighter than when he had quarterbacked for Navy his sophomore year against Army. His nineteen-year-old son David sat in the pilot's chair, and Riley McMaster sat behind at the Engineer Console. In addition to the ship's crew, five NASA Engineers and three members of a film crew from Tovar Studios, home of the motion picture franchise *StarCruiser Brilliant*, were aboard.

On final approach to Earth, David prepared the starship for re-entry.

Yellow alarm lights flashed, and tones sounded, "Sensor alert."

"Ani, report?" Jack asked.

Ani, short for Artificial Navigation Intelligence, was the heart and brain of *Brilliant*. "There is an object twenty-degrees above the Mars Ecliptic."

"Ballistic track?"

"It's decelerating from one-point-one light-speed."

"Not natural," Jack said. "Can you identify?"

"It's a Hoclarth Patrol Ship bound for Earth Space," Ani said.

"Deploy shields and activate Owwie," Jack called up the Artificial Weapons Intelligence. "What've we got?"

"Owwie activated. Tracking bogey. Identity: Menday class Hoclarth Patrol ship. Close-in plasma weapons and medium-range Meteor Cannon without AI Guidance. This Menday is not in my database. Maintaining Track," Owwie said.

"Does he have us yet?"

"He's turning to pursue."

"What is our weapons load, Owwie?" Jack asked.

"Captain, we're light. Only close-in energy weapons."

"Evasion it is," said Jack. "Ani, deploy the HoloDrone and release to Owwie!"

"Aye, Captain. HoloDrone deployed, right echelon under weapons control."

"Time to re-entry?"

"Eleven minutes to re-entry. Seven until we're in Hoclarth weapons range," Ani said. "We can delay that by two minutes if we duck behind the moon."

"Execute! Find us some lunar shade," Jack said.

"I've lost the bogey," Owwie said. "Reacquisition in less than a minute."

Ani reported, "Three minutes to re-entry after reacquisition."

"Captain, detecting an active scan. He has us," Owwie said.

"The Hoclarth is hailing us, Captain," said Ani.

"Let's see who we're dealing with."

"*StarCruiser Brilliant*, I'm Predex Kalim Kone of the Hoclarth Alliance ship *Mendex*. Heave to and make ready to be boarded. If I'm happy with what you have to offer, I'll leave you with your lives and your ship," the pirate said.

"Sorry, *Mendex*, we're hungry and homebound. You'll have to save your visit for another time," Jack said. "Secure coms."

"*Mendex* is locking Meteor Cannon," Owwie said.

"Owwie, turn the HoloClone to attack the *Mendex*. Position, so the Meteor shot passes Earth."

"*Mendex* is tracking the clone. He took the bait."

"Ani, dive the gravity well. We're going to have to go in very steep and wake up Southern California."

"*Mendex* has fired on the clone."

"What is the track?"

"Captain, the meteoroid will enter Earth's atmosphere at a high angle," Owwie said. "It will reach the ground."

"Thirty-five seconds to re-entry," Ani said.

"Owwie, fire a plasma salvo at the Meteor to break it up."

"Engaging. Three shots on the mass," Owwie said. "It has broken up. Captain, a three-ton mass will reach the Earth's surface."

"Damn!"

The forward display screen turned red as Brilliant entered the atmosphere.

As Jennifer walked along Long Valley Road towards home, she paused. *The letter will be there, or it won't. I'll get the internship, or I won't,* she thought. *But Dandy Lion depends on me for a treat every day.*

She walked back half a block and clapped her hands. The light-orange Tabby strutted out into the front yard with a regal air. Dandy thought, *how dare you force me to wait for my treat!*

It's almost as if I can read his mind, she thought. Jennifer presented Dandy Lion with his treat. The cat sniffed then consumed the gift with royal relish.

"Captain, we entered the atmosphere southbound over Vandenberg Air Force Base. We're putting on quite a show," David said.

"Make your turn and contact SoCal Air Traffic Control."

CLAP!

Dandy jumped, Jennifer jumped, and windows rattled. The sound echoed off the nearby hills. *I know that sound. Sonic boom!* She looked to the Northwest sky, and she saw a red ionization trail. And then it turned toward her. She spoke a single word, "Impossible!"

The red trail faded.

"THE FAA WILL BE BUSY EXPLAINING THIS ONE. OWWIE, WHAT WAS the trajectory of the mass?" Jack asked.

"The mass entered at a thirty-five-degree angle from north to south," Owwie said.

"Will it make it to the ocean?"

"No, sir."

"Where?"

"The valley, sir. It is going to hit somewhere in Hidden Hills."

Jack slumped. A tragic end to a successful mission. The Hoclarth Alliance was now in Earth Space. Jack thought, *why did that Hoclarth captain look so familiar?*

BOOM!

Another sonic boom. Jennifer looked North and saw a fireball coming toward her and Dandy. She knew it wasn't going to turn away.

Dandy jumped into her arms and Jennifer ran straight west. She made it three houses, took a right turn behind a house and the neighborhood exploded. Her ears rang. After the echoes from the nearby hills faded, all she could hear were car alarms. A fireball shot skyward. It was the Nesbitt house, Dandy's home.

Jennifer walked back toward the blaze. In an empty lot that used to be a house, there were only raging flames. Residents came out of their homes.

Before the fire trucks, the Battalion Supervisor arrived in a red SUV and got out, "Did you see what happened, young lady?"

"Yes. A supersonic fireball came from the north. I ran west before it hit," Jennifer said.

"Was there anyone inside the house?"

"The Nesbitt family gets home later. The house was probably empty — Dandy's their cat. I was feeding him a treat like I always do," Jennifer said.

"The house is a total loss," the fireman said. "What's the tabby's name?"

"Dandy Lion, but everyone calls him Dandy."

The fireman rubbed the head of the regal yellow tabby, "Well,

Dandy, you can credit one of your nine lives to this nice young lady. What's your name; we might need more information?"

"Jennifer Gallagher," she said. "Kailyn and Kamryn Nesbitt will be devastated. At least they'll have Dandy."

ABOARD THE MENDEX, THE HOCLARTH PREDEX CURSED. "Bacnaath!" The Meteor shot missed. He tracked the rock to a fiery hole in the ground. The bearded captain focused his blue-green eyes on the display to a crimson-haired girl holding a yellow animal. *Why does she look so familiar?* he thought.

THREE FIRE TRUCKS ARRIVED, KNOCKED DOWN THE HOUSE FIRE, AND watered-down adjacent properties. Two distraught parents came to the Police Line clutching their screaming twins. They saw the yellow bundle in Jennifer's arms.

"Dandy!"

Dandy jumped from Jennifer's arms and ran to the girls.

"You saved Dandy Lion. Are you okay? What happened?" Mrs. Nesbitt asked.

"I stopped to give Dandy a treat. I heard multiple sonic booms and saw a fireball headed our way. I picked up Dandy and ran." Jennifer explained.

"Thank goodness, you're okay," Mrs. Nesbitt said. "The girls will never forget this."

"I always give Dandy a treat on the way home from school," Jennifer said. "If I don't, he reminds me."

Jennifer resumed her walk home. Her mind buzzed. The sonic booms. The fireball. The explosion. Her mind went into overdrive trying to figure it all out until her mind returned to the letter.

Jennifer thought, It's important, but the studio will say yes. My father would say yes. Now, if only mother will agree....

Navvy

ONE

Brilliant's Arrival

Navilek Kelrithian, Chairman and CEO of Tovar Studios, sat at a large oak desk that was entirely empty save for a foldup computer display and a scale model of *StarCruiser Brilliant*. The awards that adorned the walls of the third-floor office reflected the accomplishments of the most successful and longstanding studio executive in Hollywood. The walls contained photos of Navvy with actors of note often with one or both holding a gold statue. A large picture window displayed the busy lot with the stunning Angeles National Forest framing the sky. In a display case were numerous awards, including four for Best Picture. The clutter in the office reflected one who was extremely busy yet well-organized.

Navvy Kelrithian and Jack Masing were sharing an adult beverage after a long day. Riley McMaster and David Masing were drinking iced caramel macchiatos.

"The Hoclarth came from nowhere and jumped us. *Brilliant* was just not ready," Jack said. "We weren't carrying the weapons we needed. We weren't carrying the crew we needed."

"You can't blame yourself, Jack. You couldn't have foreseen the *Mendex* coming in right at that moment," Navvy said.

"Dad, you always said that a successful landing means you had a good day," David said.

"David, you're as good a pilot as I ever was," Jack said. Riley, you are the best engineer we've ever had, but I need a solid tactician. I need a First Officer who can see the big picture, plan out a mission, and see what's coming. I need you, Navvy. No one died today, but it was close."

"Jack, I'm seventy-four years old. I'm too worn out to be a space warrior," Navvy said.

"Seriously, old Friend, with you on board, *Brilliant* was always one step ahead of any disaster."

"We wouldn't be here if I hadn't made that one mistake."

"Yes, there is that."

"I've only heard bits and pieces of that story," Riley said.

"Dad, I've only heard your version," David said. "Navvy, could you tell the story of how you and Brilliant got here?"

"David, your dad, Hanna and I were born in a much different timeline," Navvy said. "When we took off that day, May twenty-third of 2227, the Great Energy Wars were two-hundred years in the past."

"Did it go nuclear?" Riley asked.

"It did. There were still areas that were blocked off because of high radiation. During the dark times, the world's population declined due to disease, starvation, and conflict." But the Second Renaissance brought a century of progress and recovery. *StarCruiser Brilliant* was the crown jewel of the reawakening."

"You designed her," David said

"Me, Hanna, and a team of Naval Engineers at the United Space Exploration Academy. It was the first ship to have both stardrive and gravity drive."

"That's all in the *Brilliant Tech Manual*," Riley said. "Tell us about the flight."

"*Brilliant* was a prototype," Jack said. "We were on a shakedown cruise that would take us deep in the Sun's gravity well to test the gravity drive. Hanna was the engineer and Jack was the pilot."

Navvy sipped his scotch. "I hate this story. Failure brings back bad memories."

David and Riley spoke together. "Tell the story."

Navvy settled in and looked at the model on his desk. "We were an hour out from Earth inside the orbit of Mercury accelerating toward the sun on the em drive. we expected to be back for dinner...."

"JACK, START THE OUTBOUND TURN INSIDE MERCURY'S ORBIT AT MY mark. Engage the gravity drive to point-one light-speed outbound." Navvy said. "Engineer, report systems status."

"Em drive nominal. Gravity drive indicates ready. Stardrive available," Hanna said.

"Five seconds to turn." Navvy looked at all the indicators, "Make your turn and engage the gravity drive."

The sun appeared as a giant yellow ball on the view screen. It moved to the left off screen, and Jack said, "Engaging." He pushed the t-bar with his right hand to mid-range.

Red lights flashed; audio signals blared. Hanna's eyebrows went upward, "Navvy, the main gravity drive relay has failed!"

"Engage the em drive!"

"Em drive at full power!"

The navigation computer said, "Alert. Decaying orbit. Collision with the surface of the sun in 47 minutes."

"Hanna, can you fix it?"

"It will take me three hours to replace the relay."

"Navvy, we need to engage the stardrive!" Jack said.

"The stardrive is untested; we don't know what will happen."

"I can't repair the relay in time, Nav!" Hanna said.

Navvy and Hanna went down a deck to the gravity drive and inspected the failed relay and returned five minutes later. "The main relay is fried."

"Alert. Decaying orbit. Collision with the surface of the sun in 40 minutes," Navigation said.

"Navvy, we need to save our child!"

Navvy turned his chair, and his eyes were wide open. "Hanna?"

"I woke up sick this morning. I tested. We're pregnant," Hanna said.

Navvy turned back with clenched fists and leaned forward, "Jack, set your course to engage the stardrive!"

Navvy pressed the com button on his chair. "Academy, this is *Brilliant*. Our main gravity drive relay has failed. I'm sending a complete data dump. We will engage the stardrive to escape the gravity well. We may not see you again, so hug our families for us and tell our parents that they will be grandparents. *Brilliant* out."

"Alert. Decaying orbit. Collision with the surface of the sun in 35 minutes."

"Navvy, the stardrive is ready in all respects."

"Very well. Engage!"

There was a flash on the screen. The starfield blurred and shifted.

Two minutes later, "Disengage stardrive!"

"Disengaged."

"Navigation, report position."

"We're six astronomical units from the sun." *Brilliant* was outside the orbit of Jupiter.

Navvy pressed the communicator, "Academy, this is *Brilliant*. Com check."

"There are no space wave frequencies active," the coms computer said.

"That's not good," Navvy said. "Navigation, evaluate celestial positions and compute the exact time."

"It is 2:37 p.m."

"We've gone back two hours. We should be able to contact the Academy." Navvy thought for a moment. "Navigation, what is the exact date?"

"The current date is October 15, 2027."

"Omigod, two centuries?" Hanna said. "That's just two years after the nuclear wars."

Navvy said, "Let's repair the gravity drive and go back and see what's left of Earth."

"I RECOGNIZE THAT SCENARIO," RILEY SAID.

"I suspect that you do," Navvy said.

"There's more to the story, though," David said.

"You two don't want to sit around with a couple of old guys drinking too much, do you?"

"Nav, ya did kind of leave the story on a cliff hanger," Jack said. "I'd like to hear this story again."

"Fill my glass, will you, Jack?"

Jack poured more scotch into Navvy's glass and his own. David and Riley held their empty coffee mugs out. "No way I'm pouring sixty-year-old scotch into a coffee mug.

David jumped up and retrieved two cocktail glasses from the sidebar.

Jack poured each of the youngsters a shot. "Autodrive, got it?"

"Yes, captain," David said.

"IT TOOK HANNA, JACK AND ME THREE HOURS TO FABRICATE THE NEW gravity drive relay and install it," Navvy said. "We were still at point-six lightspeed when we went beyond the orbit of Neptune."

"That's just a day trip now," Riley said.

"In the other timeline a trip to the rings of Saturn still took months." Navvy took a sip. "We didn't know what we would find so we continued the shakedown to test the gravity drive."

His eyes lost focus as he continued the story.

"JACK, SET A COURSE TO EARTH AND ENGAGE THE GRAVITY DRIVE AT point-one light-speed. Hanna, report status as we accelerate."

Jack slowly advanced the t-bar that controlled acceleration. "Point-one lightspeed, Captain."

"Performance is nominal, Captain," Hanna reported.

"Point-two lightspeed, Jack."

Jack continued to increase speed a bit at a time. "We're now at our maximum of point-four light-speed."

"Navigation, set course to approach Earth. We will decelerate inside lunar orbit."

The computer voice replied, "Three hours and twenty minutes to lunar orbit."

As they made the transit, Hanna asked, "What are we going to find on Earth?"

Navvy quoted from Google. "History says that there were wars and starvation after the war in 2025. The nuclear conflict is over, but there are still cities that are uninhabitable due to contamination. There's still excessive carbon dioxide in the atmosphere, and global warming is still accelerating. Economic globalization has ground to a halt. Even the countries that were not targeted with nuclear weapons have suffered economic collapse. Complex systems like the Internet, global commerce, food, and energy production, and, of course, the national governments no longer exist," Navvy said. "The greatest tragedy is that the expansion of human knowledge has come to a halt. Major universities cannot exist without the complex systems that existed before the wars."

"So, we get some parts and supplies and then find our way back home?" Jack said.

"Not quite. Einstein was half right. Time travel forward is not possible. We're stuck in this timeline two hundred years before our time. Hopefully, we find a new life on a hospitable planet, but the chances are not in our favor. Jack, you have the ship. I will be in my ready room," Navvy said.

Three hours later, the three were back at their bridge stations.

"Alert, the ship will be inside lunar orbit in five minutes," the computer voice said.

"Pilot, decrease to one-percent light-speed. Hanna, monitor communications. Let's see what they're talking about."

"Aye, Captain." Hanna's looked up in surprise. "Navvy, I am receiving communications traffic originating on the moon. You need to hear this."

"Audio on."

"HOUSTON, THIS IS ARMSTRONG COLONY. A DECELERATING VEHICLE bound for Earth just passed us. We measured its maximum speed more than one-tenth of light speed."

"Armstrong, Houston, We're tracking it as well. I hope they're friendly. "

"THAT'S NOT POSSIBLE," NAVVY SAID. "ON THIS DATE, EARTH IS supposed to be headed for the stone age. Engage the deceptors. That will prevent any further detection."

"HOUSTON, THE BOGEY HAS DISAPPEARED. HOW DO WE LOG THIS one?"

"Armstrong, Houston, we lost him, too. Log it like the others. They will let us know they're here when they want to. Let's hope their first contact is friendly."

"NAVVY, WE DIDN'T RETURN TO THE MOON FOR ANOTHER 125 years," Jack said.

"It's possible we traveled back two hundred years to an alternate timeline," Navvy said. "And it looks like we're not the only ones visiting Earth."

"It's getting curiouser and curiouser," Hanna said.

"Einstein proposed quantum entanglement in 1935, but it wasn't until 2198 that Pedaranko theorized that sustained faster-than-light travel near a heavy body could land a ship in an alternate dimension," Navvy said.

"I guess we should write a letter to the Academy and ask them to congratulate the Russian and let him know we proved his theory," Hanna said.

"Jack, put us in a low-Earth orbit at 150 miles covering sixty degrees latitude north and south," Navvy ordered.

"Decelerating to 18,300 miles per hour," Jack said. "In orbit. Perigee 125 miles."

"Very well. We have enough food for a day. Let's see if we can find a drive-through," Navvy said. "Secure from powered flight. Everyone on science consoles. Looks like we're on a timeline where Earth made it through the Energy Wars. Let's find out why. Jack, monitor the environment. Hanna, monitor broadcast networks. Look for landing spots where we can keep a low profile. I'll try to hook into the Internet."

They sat at the port and starboard science stations. "Standard network news chatter. Lots of talking over each other and accusing each other of fake news," Hanna reported. "There are no discussions of energy shortages or talk of war. Same as our networks at home."

Jack said, "No radiation in the atmosphere. There were no recent nuclear explosions. Carbon dioxide in the atmosphere is not as high as it was in our 2227. The amount of CO_2 going into the atmosphere is about a third of the peak from our timeline. Navvy, is it possible that they found an alternative energy source?"

"They have data networks originating from a satellite. I'm googling information," Navvy said.

"Nav, their entire transportation system is electrical," Hanna said. "Electrical production seems to originate from neighborhood facilities about the size of convenience stores. There is no carbon coming from these facilities."

The three continued to explore their new home. About an hour later: "Bingo," Navvy said. "I have the timeline diversion. I compared our two timelines, and it's incredibly fascinating, but there is a single event in 1997 that diverted their timeline from ours. A nuclear engineer with a Berkeley doctorate named John Mitchell Scott made a single decision that caused the new timeline."

"In our timeline, Dr. Scott spent a year studying fusion at Livermore Labs. He then gave up on fusion and moved to Los Alamos National Laboratory. He supervised the maintenance of nuclear weapons until the Energy Wars. In this timeline, Dr. Scott stayed with fusion after 1997 and participated in building a large containment fusion power generation reactor that successfully connected to the grid in 2010. Those reactors are incredibly difficult and expensive to build."

"The butterfly effect," Hanna said.

"Exactly. But, get this. Dr. Scott published a paper proposing a scalable soft containment fusion reactor. The first Scott Reactor went online in 2015. That one was huge and unwieldy, but they have since been scaled down to the point where they fit in a large jetliner," Navvy said.

"Just like our timeline, only sooner," Jack said. "This timeline began a renaissance of carbon-free air travel. In 2025, instead of a nuclear holocaust, Dr. John Mitchell Scott received the Nobel Prize in Physics. His net worth is nearly one hundred billion dollars. The Earth that we have come to has unlimited clean and affordable energy."

"What about *Brilliant?*" Jack asked.

"I estimate that at the rate of growth in technology, they will build a spacecraft comparable to *Brilliant* in forty years."

"So, what's the plan?" Hanna asked.

"We find a place to lay low until...."

"Navvy, I just took a picture of something on the ground that you have to see," Jack said.

"On Screen."

The screen showed a spacecraft in the middle of Southern California's Imperial Sand Dunes surrounded by many people working. It looked like an early drawing of *Brilliant*. "Navvy, they jumped the gun on your forty years."

"Jack, circle back. Let's enter quietly, drop down, and see that spacecraft."

Brilliant slowly entered the atmosphere without breaking the sound barrier. "Keep the sun behind us."

"Blind them, aye," Jack responded.

"It looks like they are filming a movie," Jack said. "They see us."

"The ship is made of wood. It's a movie prop," Hanna said.

"They say movie sets are good feeders."

"I'm hungry, too," Hanna said. I'm eating for two."

"Ground the ship, and I will fire anyone who says, 'Take me to your leader,'" Navvy said.

"I'll put us down about a hundred yards away," Jack said. He set the starship down on the soft sand dune.

"Captain, they are running and hiding," Hanna said.

"Hanna, put the ship in standby and lower the ramp," Navvy said. "Let's see if these filmmakers will invite us to lunch."

"So, you landed a starship from two centuries in the future on a movie set and invited yourselves to lunch?" David asked.

"We were hungry, son."

"This was effectively a First Contact," Riley said. "You violated all the rules and guidelines."

"This *was* the First Contact," Navvy said. "We kinda figured out the rest along the way."

"We kind of know the story because of Bill Mason's book," David said. "So, what really happened?"

"When they saw *Brilliant*, most of the movie crew scattered. But the producer and the consultant, a former NASA designer, met us."

Navvy told it from Bill Mason's perspective.

I looked at the consultant, "Is this one of yours?"

The consultant said, "I left NASA five years ago. I assure you we had nothing like this on the drawing boards. It has to be a black op."

A thirty-something man with an unmistakable air of command spoke to us, "I'm Navvy Kelrithian, this is my wife, Hanna, and our pilot, Jack Masing. Is it possible that we could meet the person in charge?"

Hanna gave Navvy a quick look of amazement and then just shook her head.

"I'm Bill Mason, producer of *The Lost Starship* from Tovar Studios, and this is John Nascimento, a former NASA designer, who is acting as our consultant."

Nascimento was a bit rude that day, "What agency built your ship? You're not from NASA. It must have taken a lot of funding from our programs to build that ship."

"Why don't we hold those questions?" Navvy said. "We got sidetracked from our shakedown mission, and we happened to run out of supplies. Is it possible that we could impose on you for lunch? Then we can give you a tour of *Brilliant*.

John interrupted, "You're obviously from a secret organization, and you might be a threat. We need to see your identification...."

He saw a conspiracy theory, and I saw an opportunity. "John, these travelers are hungry. They left their ray guns on their ship. Why don't we have lunch? Navvy, call me Bill. Craft Services are over here." The other crew members emerged from cover. Bill called the Assistant Director over. "Tell the crew to break for lunch."

"WAS THE FOOD AS GOOD AS OUR CRAFT SERVICES," RILEY ASKED.

"It was adequate, but you have to remember they were on a tight budget," Navvy said. I sat down at the picnic table across from Bill Mason. "So, tell me about this film that you're making."

"Navvy, I'll be honest. We risked a lot on this picture with Tovar Studios near bankruptcy. I discovered this science fiction property and ran the numbers. Unfortunately, we are way over budget. We may have to close down unless we can convince our money people that we can make a profitable film."

"What kind of problems are you facing?" Navvy asked.

"Our star is ready to leave the film because we can't pay him. We have no idea how we're going to shoot the space exteriors. Paramount has premiered a film with a new 3D process, and we can't afford the technology."

"Again, speaking for NASA, I must insist that you identify yourselves and the government agency that built that ship," John said.

Navvy looked annoyed and then said, "Okay, NASA, I can't tell you where we are from but if I promise to share some, not all, of our tech with NASA, will you be happy? We'll give you a walk-through of our ship and then you can call your buddies in Houston." The consultant relaxed and nodded. "Bill, let's introduce you to *StarCruiser Brilliant*."

"StarCruiser? That's preposterous," John said.

"Nascimento, you're my employee," Bill said. "You signed a non-disclosure agreement. You keep your mouth shut, or I'll sue your ass right out of this business."

After they finished lunch, I asked Hanna, "Hanna, please take our NASA designer through the lower decks. I'll take Bill to the bridge. Jack, stand by the ramp and answer questions."

We arrived on the bridge and Bill looked around. "Navvy, I've been around space technology for years. You're not from around here, are you?"

Navvy looked at the small viewport at the forward end of the bridge and nodded. "I was born in Philadelphia, but yes, the date on my birth certificate has the year 2193."

Bill gasped.

"*Brilliant is* a brand-new ship. We had an engineering casualty on our shakedown cruise, and we jumped back two-hundred years."

"Can you get back to your home?" Bill asked.

"Nope, we're stuck here. My wife, Hanna, is pregnant and Jack has left his parents behind. So, let's discuss how we can mutually benefit from this."

"Have you ever thought of becoming a filmmaker?"

"I'm a fast learner," Navvy said. "Where do I start?"

"Here's a laptop that has a large library of screenplays," Bill said. "Look at the classics and then follow up to the space operas like the genre we are shooting."

"That's a good beginning."

"So, THAT'S HOW YOU GOT IN THIS BUSINESS?" DAVID ASKED. "I WAS born into it, but dad has always reminded me that the people on our set had to work hard and sacrifice."

"You said you are a fast learner?" Riley asked. "What's your IQ?"

"I think it's pretty high but who counts?"

"You said you hired me partly because of my 204," Riley said. "C'mon, Navvy."

"This guy clocked a 211 on his academy entrance exam," Jack said.

"I had a good breakfast."

"So, Tovar was broke," David said. "How did you overcome that.

"I pulled a couple of all-nighters like we used to do on a project and put it all together."

Navvy continued the story.

"BILL, I HAVE ANALYZED THE BUDGET, THE SHOTS YOU HAVE ALREADY, the problems with your actors and your screenplay. Let's throw it all out."

"Navvy, you know nothing about this. Your idea would cost the studio one-hundred million dollars," Bill said. "We've already shot our entire budget."

"Read this." Navvy handed Bill a one-hundred-fifteen-page document titled, *StarCruiser Brilliant, The Lost Starship.* "We can do it with a hundred-and-fifty-million-dollar capital investment."

"Where the hell are we going to get a hundred-and-fifty million dollars?!" Bill asked.

"You read my screenplay; I'll take care of the money," Navvy said.

"I TALKED TO THE NASA CONSULTANT. WHAT DO YOU THINK OF *StarCruiser Brilliant?*"

"None of this technology is known to me," John said. "First of all, why won't you tell me who built this ship?"

"John, can we stipulate that, right now, I cannot tell you from where or when we came?"

"Yes, I suppose."

"The technology on your ship is impossible. It's science fiction. If it weren't for my non-disclosure agreement, I would have NASA out here in a heartbeat," John said.

"Can we further stipulate that the technology on *Brilliant is* real, not fiction?"

"That's a reach but yes, for argument's sake."

"Do you understand that I cannot release all of the technology at one time because it would disrupt too many industries?"

"That's reasonable."

"Finally, can we agree that you would like to become a rich man?"

The NASA engineer rubbed his face and throat. "Yes, of course."

"Here's what I have in mind," Navvy said. "You set up a

company with me at the top. You can be chief technology officer. You would act as the intermediary between me, as ship designer, and the large aerospace technology firms, and the government."

"This will be worth billions of dollars," John said.

"All I need is a couple of hundred million in three months," Navvy said. "Can you do it?"

"I'd need staff, location, patent attorneys…."

"I'll be the senior partner and give you all of the advice you need."

"I can do it."

"Let's start by getting a high-powered corporate attorney in here to write this up."

"I'll start right now."

"Within two years, Navvy and Tovar were in the Forbes 100," Jack said.

"Weren't you making money off the work of others?" Riley said.

"Yes, but they wouldn't be born for another century," Navvy said, "and in a different timeline."

"Boys, don't let Navvy kid you," Jack said. "His and Hanna's name were at the top of every patent that we took off with that day."

"So, you learned to write screenplays in a day?" David asked.

"I dabbled in writing at the academy and I had seen most of the movies he referenced."

"And he could quote every line from every movie he ever watched," Jack said.

"There is that," Navvy said. "So, I rewrote the screenplay and handed it to Bill Mason. He ducked in his trailer and came out two hours later."

"This is the best sci-fi screenplay that I have ever read, but there's one major problem. You use the term 'SFX TBD,' which I assume means special effects to be determined. Those details make the budget half-a-billion dollars. How are we going to afford all of the outer space shots with expensive models and the interiors with all of the exotic technology?" Bill said.

Navvy pointed to the ship he designed.

"Omigod."

"I have a device on board called a fabricator. Hanna and I can design and create spaceborne cinedrones that can capture *Brilliant* at any angle. We can place cameras anywhere you want and generate any view that you need."

"We will have to recast the entire picture," Bill said. "The only actor you kept was Ellie Johansen. She has no experience. Who can we use as the captain and crew?"

"How about Jack Masing as the captain? He has the looks and the starship experience. I think he and Ellie can develop some chemistry. Hanna and I can fill in the crew. You can cast the rest."

He took another long look at the ship. "Omigod, this will be…."

"Brilliant, *StarCruiser Brilliant*," Navvy said.

———

"That's how you met mom."

"Yep," Jack said. "We opened eight months later to the highest opening gross of 2028. StarCruiser Brilliant, the Lost *StarShip* was the first picture to gross three billion dollars. Bill Mason got Best Picture and Navvy won Best Original Screenplay."

"And Ellie her first Best Supporting," Riley said.

"It was the beginning of a beautiful friendship," Navvy said.

"Navvy, this is really good scotch," Riley said.

"How would you know?" Jack said. "You're not legal for another year."

"After my dad died," Riley said," my mom and I used to share a glass of his favorite scotch on his birthday."

"Is this a special occasion?" David asked.

"Jack and I break this out after a difficult mission."

"What's the worst mission you ever had?" Riley asked.

"This one is too hard for me," Navvy said. "Jack, tell this one."

TWO

Anthen

"We were on a four-day mission to explore Gliese 832c," Jack said. "I was aboard *Brilliant* and my First Officer Anthen, Navvy's son, accompanied a NASA exoplanet exploration crew. Maiara was in charge belowdecks. The NASA scientists tested for water and found massive deposits of ice just below the surface."

"Sounds like one of those milk runs you talk about," David said.

"Not this time, son."

Jack continued the story:

"I'm going to climb to the top of this hill and see what's around," Anthen said.

"Don't lose eye contact with the mission scientists," Jack said.

"Aye, sir."

Anthen climbed to the top of the promontory that overlooked the ancient lakebed.

"Jack, I see something in the next valley over," Anthen said. "It's not natural. It looks like a large hangar. I'm going to walk down and get a closer look."

"Anthen, let's get everyone aboard and we'll do a flyover."

"It looks like it's a thousand years old. There is no one around."

"NASA, we may be making a quick getaway," Jack said. "Prepare to return to *Brilliant*."

"Acknowledge," the lead NASA scientist said.

Anthen walked around the large building. "It's made of a metal composite that I haven't seen." He saw an opening. "Jack, there is a ship in here. There are lights. Jack, we need to get out of here...." The last thing he saw was the flash of a stun gun in the hands of a humanoid.

"Anthen, return to *Brilliant*."

No response.

"NASA, return to the ship immediately. First Lieutenant, report when all the scientists are aboard."

"Sensor Alert. Unknown spacecraft launching from the surface," the Artificial Navigation Interface said. Ani was aboard *Brilliant* for her first mission. "There are two life signs aboard. One has an Earth DNA signature. It's Anthen, sir."

"All scientists aboard, Captain," Maiara reported.

"Ani, raise ship and pursue the bogey."

Sand scattered on the ground, and *Brilliant* rose from the desert surface.

"Sir, We're clear of the atmosphere. Gravity Drive engaged at point-five lightspeed," Ani said.

"Can we catch them?"

"No, Captain, they are traveling at point-eight light-speed. That is above our maximum speed. They are now beyond our long-range sensors."

"Damn."

─────────

ANTHEN WOKE UP ABOARD AN ALIEN SHIP. HE WAS IN AN OPEN enclosure surrounded by a force field. A bearded humanoid observed him from outside the field. "I'm Predex Kalea Komdor of the Hoclarth Patrol Ship *Maldex*."

"You speak English?" Anthen said.

"You hear in your language. Your enclosure has a translator. You see, Earthman, we have been monitoring your system for a long time, we recorded your radio emissions since you achieved that technology, and we decoded your language. Our scientists predicted that you wouldn't achieve faster than light travel for another two hundred of your years. Our scientists are curious. You're coming with me so that we can find out how you advanced so fast."

"Will I be able to return to my ship?"

"That won't be possible. You have seen our technology. You're now a part of the Hoclarth Alliance," Kalea said.

"My son was a bit of cowboy at times," Navvy said. "I miss him."

Jack refilled the four glasses and they raised them.

"To Anthen," Jack said.

"Wherever he may be," Navvy said.

"Dad said this scotch is sixty years old," David said. "Is that true?"

"Give or take a couple hundred years," Navvy said.

"You said you didn't carry any supplies that day."

"Son," Navvy said. "A starship captain never leaves home without a couple of cases of scotch."

Growing Up Jennifer

THREE

Seventeen Years Earlier

S heila Gallagher sat at the family table as her mother served roast beef and candied yams. Sunday evening dinners were a Gallagher family tradition. Her father, Sean Gallagher, helped her mother, Ciara, prepare and serve the meal. She and her older brother, Aiden, set the table. Her Aunt Joanne, the family historian sat opposite her brother.

"Those sons-of-bitches at Tovar blame GGG for the accident that killed that actor, Anthen. They canceled all our contracts," Sean said. "There's no evidence and no body. I think they staged the fake accident to cover their asses. I don't think Navvy is in on it."

"Will GGG survive?" Aiden asked. "They're a big part of our business,"

"We'll be fine, son," Sean said. "Some of the other studio heads have been urging us to expand. But I hate to lose Tovar."

"It's too bad. They made it clear that we weren't even welcome at the funeral." Ciara noticed the wetness around Sheila's eyes, "Honey, were you dating him again?"

Sheila began to sob. Her mother hugged her. "We'll all miss him," Ciara said.

Sheila covered her face with her hands. "Mom, I'm pregnant!"

"Are you sure?" Sean said.

"Anthen and I planned to get married. I was going to tell him. And then…." More sobbing. "I loved him!"

"I know, honey. We're here for you. Have you seen the doctor?" Ciara asked.

"Yes. The baby's due in late June."

"You're on track to graduate," Sean said. "What about Stanford?"

"Sean, it is too early to talk about law school. Let's give her some time," Ciara said.

"Again, the Gallagher curse," Aunt Joanne said.

"Joanne, not now," Ciara said. Joanne often volunteered unspoken family truths.

"What's she saying?" Aiden asked.

"The first child in each Gallagher generation has been on the plane before the pilot and copilot filed the flight plan," Joanne said. "My mother was six months along with me at the altar. It goes back to Sean Senior."

"Joanne, you always bring such colorful context to our family dinners," Sean rolled his eyes and shook his head.

"I met our great-grandfather once," Joanne said. "Sean Senior is the one who started Gallagher Gaffers and Grips. He told me the story where he met Clark Gable. On his first day, Sean saw an actor moving one of his cables. He said, 'Hey, bud. Stay away from my cables. That's my effing job.'

The tall actor stood, and said, 'If you did your effing job right, people wouldn't be tripping over your cables and falling on their faces.' "

The wrinkles at the corner of her eye showed, "Great Grandfather never feared for his life like he did at that moment. He said, 'I'm very sorry, Mr. Gable. Let me get them out of the way.' He never made that mistake again."

"And he never used the word 'effing' either," Ciara said.

Aunt Joanne bit her lip and then said, "No, I don't think he did."

"Sis, we're all here for you," Aiden said. "I'm looking forward to be an uncle!"

"Why don't you take a gap year and work for GGG?"

. . .

A YEAR LATER, THEY SAT AT THEIR WEEKLY FAMILY DINNER, SHEILA held the infant Jennifer. Grandpa Sean filled in as much as possible for Jennifer's father, and Grandma Ciara was always there to support her daughter. A year after graduation, Sheila Gallagher was an unmarried widow and a single working mother at GGG. She was going through the motions as she dealt with the grief and anger of loss.

"Before this happened, you had your acceptance at Stanford Law," Ciara said. "We feel you need to get away from the business and clear your mind."

Her father continued, "Your mother and I will take care of your tuition, childcare, and living expenses. We expect you to bring our granddaughter home often, but we agree that you need to get away from the valley for a while."

Sheila replied, "Who will handle my clients?"

Her brother, Aiden, spoke, "C'mon sis, we can handle things without you. And when you come back, you can form the Legal Services division we've always planned."

Sheila smiled for the first time in quite a while. "It does seem to be the right way to start over."

Three years later, Sheila returned to the valley and started the legal services division at GGG with the title of General Counsel.

JENNIFER GREW UP IN THE VALLEY WHERE ALL HER FRIENDS HAD STARS in their eyes. Each one expected someday to either marry a movie star or become one. At seven years old, Jennifer knew that she was much smarter than her classmates as well as being five inches taller.

One day when she came home from school with scrapes and bruises. Sheila said, "Did you hurt yourself today?"

"Mom, I try as hard as I can. I play hard. I try to be as good at sports like other kids, but I keep falling. I'm uncoordinated. And then the kids laugh and call me a nerd."

Sheila squatted down and looked directly at her, "Jen, you're tall for your age, and the kids are a little bit scared of how smart you are. But never quit trying. Never give up on meeting your standards."

Jennifer knew that her superpower was her fantastic intellect. She knew this long before her mother told her about the phone call. "Jen, the school psychologist called, and you hit a high number on her test."

Jennifer stood up straight, "What was my IQ?"

"Are you sure you want to know?" Sheila frowned as she deliberated whether to share the information.

"I've taken IQ tests on the web, and I always ace them."

"That's just what you did. You got a 175, but the psychologist recommends that we take you to UVN for more testing. Do you want to be a lab rat?" It wasn't the first time that Sheila Gallagher had an adult conversation with her precocious preteen.

"I don't know," Jennifer said. "It sounds fun."

"Jen, do you want to go through a battery of tests in a laboratory with people in white coats?"

At the age of seven, Jennifer said, "Why not? It sounds interesting, and I'm curious." Her mother was happy and proud of her daughter's standard answer when asked if she would like to participate in new and different experiences.

Dr. Allen Goldstein was a practicing neurosurgeon at the University of Van Nuys Hospital with a second doctorate in Child Psychology. He was a friend and mentor of the psychologist who tested Jennifer at school. He was very interested when she told him about the seven-year-old prodigy. Dr. Goldstein received the referral and arranged to spend a day with Jennifer the summer after second grade. A few days later, he called her mother

"Ms. Gallagher, we analyzed the results from last Tuesday and found that Jennifer scored an IQ of two hundred and six, the highest score ever tabulated. Statistically, it means if she were in a room with all twelve point eight billion people in the world, she would likely be the smartest person in the room," he said.

"Two hundred and six?"

"Also, we believe that Jennifer has an extremely rare form of eidetic memory we've never seen before. We believe that your daughter can remember one hundred percent of all that she sees, hears, and feels. You must understand that this is a blessing and a curse. You might consider enrolling your daughter in specialized counseling to check in and help Jennifer handle ongoing bad memories especially if she is experiencing nightmares. Also, Jennifer learns all that she can remember, and when she learns something new, she automatically integrates it into her thought processes. We'd like you to bring your daughter down for three days of tests so that we can measure her intellectual capabilities more accurately."

At that point, Sheila made a prescient decision. "Dr. Goldstein, I don't believe that my daughter wants to become a lab rat, so I'll decline at this time. But, let's keep in touch. If, after a couple of years of my daughter just being a kid, UVN is willing to offer Jennifer some enrichment activities which will fulfill her curiosity, I'll allow you to participate and do your evaluations as a part of that."

Dr. Goldstein replied, "That's a deal, and it will give me a chance to formulate a grant for my colleagues in the psychology department. From here out, call me Allen. I look forward to chatting with you and, of course, Jennifer."

"Allen, call me Sheila. Over time, my daughter's precocity has forced me to look for more interesting outlets to occupy her mind. Her outgoing curiosity and friendly personality don't lend themselves to boredom, but I know that it's just a matter of time before friends, school, and our activities won't be enough to keep her challenged."

"I'll work with our psychology department members and the university to develop a plan to keep her engaged as well as give us an opportunity to work with the unique mind that your daughter possesses."

Over the next few months, Dr. Goldstein developed a friendship with Sheila that led to periodic dinners.

THE SUMMER AFTER THIRD GRADE, JENNIFER'S MOTHER SAT DOWN with Jennifer. "Dr. Allen called me to let you know that UVN has opened their undergraduate online course library to you. Some courses are off-limits because of your age, and you must take some courses at the same time as the course on campus. The university will keep me informed of your progress and let me know of any problems. Otherwise, you will do this on your own. He said that the online catalog includes some college courses for advanced high school students and some courses that can be taken by regular high school students. Are you interested?"

With a broad smile and gleaming eyes, Jennifer said, "Sure, Mom. When can I start?"

"Dr. Allen sent me the link so you can start right after dinner for a couple of hours before bedtime. But, remember, I don't want you to become obsessed and not take part in the summer activities that we planned," her mother instructed. "And remember, you can browse as many courses as you want but don't enroll unless you intend to complete it. And…no more than two at a time. Dr. Allen asked in exchange that I take you down for a couple of days each summer for some poking and prodding."

"That works, Mom, I'll participate as LabRat One," Jennifer said.

"Dr. Goldstein said that you would only have to eat rat pellets while you're in the cage."

"Eww, Mom," Jennifer squinted her eyes harshly. "There is one more thing," Jennifer tilted her head towards the garden. "My friends are starting to tease me sometimes. The kids are starting to notice that I'm a lot smarter than they are. I know that you want me to get all A's, and I do, but sometimes in class and on homework, I make dumb mistakes so that the other kids believe that I'm only a little bit smarter than they are."

Her mother raised her eyebrows, "You've thought about this a lot, haven't you?"

"Yes, I know that my mind is my superpower, but I don't want to use it around my friends because they might not understand it and it might make them feel afraid or like I'm different," Jennifer said.

"I'm guessing that you have a solution?" her mom winked.

"Mom, you know how, in the comic books, all of the superheroes have secret identities. Like, SuperGirl is Kara Danvers." Sheila nodded. "Well, I'd like to have a secret identity when I take classes at UVN. And that way none of my friends or teachers at school would know about my superpower. I wouldn't be totally stupid in class, but I might play the part from time to time. They would probably laugh at my mistakes, but they would be laughing with me. And…they wouldn't pick on me…much."

Her mom considered. "That's a good idea. Have you thought

about how incredibly difficult it is for a superhero, even in the comics, to keep their identity secret? I mean, this is reality, and it might be a lot harder than on paper."

Jennifer bit her lip. "I've thought about it, and I know that I might slip up and ruin it, but I like this idea better than becoming the intellectual supernerd."

Her mom was now almost laughing, partly from nervousness and partly from shock and awe at this cerebral superstar who was her daughter. "So, what shall we call my daughter, the intellectual supernerd college kid?"

"How about Jenna Seldon?" Jennifer replied.

"Is that an Asimov reference?" Sheila said.

"I started the Foundation Trilogy last week. I'm half-way through the second book."

"Hari would be proud."

"I'll call Dr. Allen at UVN and tell him you'll be the star of LabRat One starring Jenna Seldon," Sheila said. "Explain to me again how you figured this out."

"Ok, I was starting to get teased at school, and I knew that it was going to be a problem that would get bigger. So, I reviewed all of my memories, all of the things I read about kids growing up, and the comic books as well. I built several dreams. They played like movies in my head, and I tried to figure out which solution would work the best, and the secret identity was the best," Jennifer explained. "I guess I call it the vision thing."

The next day Sheila called Dr. Allen at UVN and chronicled the discussion that she had had with her precocious eight-year-old.

"Sheila, there aren't many children who have the gifts Jennifer has, and all of them suffer the teasing and abuse from other children to some degree. Jen's solution is certainly original, mature, and just might work." Dr. Allen continued, "But 'the vision thing' is a unique and stunning revelation that warrants further study in the field of psychology. Imagine being able to conduct detailed computer simulations in your mind without a computer."

"Dr. Goldstein, Jen and I agreed to two days each summer when she's willing to play the lab rat in a cage for you. She calls it LabRat

One. I promise you and her that the rest of the summer belongs to her."

"Sheila, I understand and will comply with your concerns. May I make a suggestion that might benefit both Jennifer and our scientific community? Could you suggest to Jennifer that she keep a journal? She already understands that many of her own experiences are unique and it would help her reflect on her capabilities and her growth as she learns to cope with her gift, especially 'the vision thing.'" He continued, "Give me an hour, and I'll make the necessary changes with the Registrar to her identity. Should I create an email address in her name to accommodate the confidentiality issues with the Jenna persona?"

"That would be fine, and I'll discuss the journal with Jennifer. I think that is a great idea."

SOMETIMES, AS SHEILA CHATTED WITH HER DAUGHTER, SHE FORGOT that Jennifer was just a kid.

At dinner that evening, mother and daughter continued their discussion. "I spoke with Dr. Allen. He was impressed with your secret identity idea, how it was an incredibly mature decision and he wants to hear you explain it. He was amazed and enthusiastic to learn more about your vision thing. And he wants to put you in a cage and feed you rat pellets."

"Eww, Mom!"

"I told him no on the last part, but he did make a great suggestion. He'd like for you to keep a journal about your unique experiences as the cerebral superhero," said Sheila.

"Can I tell you a secret?"

"Another one?"

"Do you remember that time you took me to the library one spring? I think you were at Stanford Law."

"You mean the day you surprised the librarian and me with the fact that a two-year-old could read? How could I forget! It was your first trip, and the moment you entered the Palo Alto library, I could see your eyes get huge as you looked around."

Sheila took a drink of tea and continued, "You walked out that morning with a library card. So, tell me your secret."

"It took me about a year before I got bored with the chapter books. So, I started into the classics, Jack London, Rudyard Kipling, and Louisa May Alcott. I spent about a month on L. Frank Baum and all the Wizard of Oz books. The next month, I read all the Harry Potter books. When I was four, you asked me what I wanted to be when I grew up."

"I remember you wanted to be either an author or an astronaut," Sheila said.

Jennifer continued, "I thought about that, and then I came across some books about authors. As I read them, I found that all the successful authors started journaling at a young age. So, I started a journal, beginning with one hundred words a day. I've worked up to at least five hundred words a day since I was five-and-a-half. I write book reviews, I write about my friends and people I meet, and sometimes I write short stories. And, yes, I write a lot about me being me."

"How much have you written?" Sheila asked.

"Most of it is boring. It's my journal, so I brag a lot. It's over five-hundred-thousand words," Sheila brought her hand to her mouth and suppressed a nervous laugh.

"Do you touch type?" her mom asked.

Having grown up along with steveLearn, Sheila knew that the qwerty keyboard was still the fastest way to enter text into a computer. Voice entry never developed because it took way too much brain power and words to accommodate punctuation. It turned out that the good old keyboard invented in 1862, before the telephone, was still the most efficient tool.

Jennifer answered, "That was why I was so slow at the beginning. I found an online typing trainer app, and now I take the last fifteen minutes before bedtime and type in my journal. Thinking and typing slow me down to fifty words per minute."

Her mom was curious, "What about when you're away from the computer?"

"I use my memory and the vision thing. Last fifteen minutes

before I go to sleep, I type it in my head. When we returned from Hawaii last Christmas, it took me two hours to type it all in."

Sheila realized that day that her relationship with her daughter changed. "Jen, you're amazing and incredible. And you're turning into a fascinating friend. Dr. Allen said that your steveLearn identity would be set up by now. Go take a look at those online courses."

Jennifer said, "Thanks, Mom. It's nice to have a great mom, but it's also nice to have an adult friend."

Sheila reflected on all that she learned about her eight-year-old daughter that day. It was exhilarating but also a little bit intimidating.

LATER THAT EVENING, EIGHT-YEAR-OLD JENNIFER GALLAGHER A.K.A. Jenna Seldon entered steveLearn and logged into the UVN course catalog for the first time. She focused on writing and mathematics. She was interested in Enrichment Courses for Middle and High School Students.

An icon labeled "The Tutor" piqued her curiosity. She reached up and pressed the Tutor button to begin. She heard a tone and then audio.

"Welcome to the University of Van Nuys online steveLearn tutor assistant. I am your HoloBuddy called The Tutor. I notice that you are Jenna Seldon, a new student at UVN and my notes say that you're eight years old and your searches indicate an interest in enrichment activities for gifted students," The Tutor said. "My notes also say that Professor Allen Goldstein initiated your enrollment and that your mother, Sheila, has given permission for you to enroll in age-appropriate coursework. I am obligated to keep your mother, and Dr. Goldstein informed of your progress. Am I correct so far?"

Jennifer said, "Yes."

The Tutor continued, "Let me tell you about myself. I am a steveLearn Tutor hosted at UVN, and I will stay with you as your assistant, your tutor, your academic counselor, and hopefully your friend as you pursue your entire course of study at UVN. I will continually evaluate your progress, guide you through the maze of being a university student as a counselor, and recommend learning activities based on your progress, your academic needs, and your personal goals." The Tutor spoke in a serious tone, "I will be in contact with your mother. She has set down some time limits and wants to know your progress, but I will always keep what we say and what we do just between us unless you say or do something dangerous to yourself or others or that which is outside the law. Then I'll either tell your mother or the University. Do you understand this?"

Jennifer responded, "Sure."

"Next Jenna, we can interact through the keyboard, with audio only, or by full holograph tactile virtual reality interaction." The Tutor asked, "Which do you prefer?"

Jennifer said, "Full HTVR."

There was a slight pause, and then a middle-aged woman appeared in the room. She said, "Hello, Jenna, I am The Tutor. It is nice to meet you."

Jennifer replied, "Hello, what is your name?"

The Tutor replied, "Jenna, that is up to you. Right now, the person you see is a generic HoloBuddy. But steveLearn allows you to create an avatar and choose what I look like and what to call me."

"Cool. Could you be like a big sister."

"Of course. How much older?" The Tutor asked.

"How about four years?"

"Last thing. What is my name?" The Tutor asked.

Jennifer thought, "I like Samwise Gamgee. How about Samantha?"

There was another pause as the older woman morphed into a twelve-year-old girl. She had the same red-brown hair as Jennifer but with blonde highlights. Her high cheekbones sat under the same blue-green eyes that Jennifer had. Jennifer smiled when she saw the image of the big sister she always imagined.

"Hello, Jenna. I want to introduce myself. My name is Samantha, but you may call me Sami. You're only eight years old. Have you read The Lord of the Rings trilogy?"

Jennifer said, "I read it about a year ago."

"Who was your favorite character?" Sami asked.

"Gildor, the Elf Lord, who saved the Hobbits."

"I won't leave you, Frodo," Sami smiled, and they both laughed. "According to my notes, you're a very bright girl and you might benefit from this enrichment beyond elementary school. Let's start with this. What would you like to be when you're older?"

Jennifer tilted her head to the side. "I want to do several things. First, I've read two-hundred-thirty-four books. The more that I read, the more that I think I would be a good author. Secondly, I watched a lot of movies, and I think I could combine my writing with filmmaking. My mom works in the business. My favorites are the *StarCruiser Brilliant* series. Finally, I started to read *The Tech Manual* for *StarCruiser Brilliant*. I am finding that I don't know enough about math and science to understand The Manual, so I guess I think I need to start right now to become a mathematician and a scientist."

Sami said, "Jenna, that's an incredibly challenging course of study, but your profile indicates that you can handle it. It's a good idea for you to start with mathematics. How much math have you learned at school and how much have you taught yourself?"

"I've been in steveLearn my whole life. I finished all the elementary school math. I am starting to look at Algebra."

"Jenna, I recommend that you enroll in the Self-Paced Math Enrichment Course. The Math Tutor there will give you some tests to determine at what level you are performing, start filling in the holes, and then take you through the high school math sequence," Sami explained and pointed to an icon floating to her right labeled SPMath. "Jenna, your mom has set time limits on your time on our system. So, it's bedtime. We will chat some more tomorrow."

Jennifer remembered that she was starting tennis camp in the morning.

"Sami, when you showed up earlier tonight your picture looked like my mom but also how I believe my dad appears? Do you know who he is?"

Sami looked concerned, "Professor Goldstein has given me access to your medical record. I used your DNA profile to create my avatar. I do not know the identity of your father. Sorry."

FOUR

Tayla and Tennis

Jennifer's mom was not a tennis mom, so Jennifer entered the Ten-and-Under Girls Tennis Camp at the Calabasas Tennis Center alone. The camp was for beginners through advanced junior players. Jennifer avoided the girls who looked like they were in a group. She knew that girls at this age formed cliques. She wanted to find someone who knew what she was doing, and with whom she could become friends.

Assigned to the beginner group, the girls were practicing forehands. Jennifer concentrated on her shots until she heard a distinct pop from the advanced court. The beginner girls turned to look. On the next court over, she saw a tall Latina girl hit the ball again. POP. Her coach was almost unable to return it.

On Jennifer's court, the coach was ready to change the routine. "Okay, girls, you've got the basic form of a forehand. Remember racket preparation. You're going to have to chase these next balls." Jennifer was the youngest girl in the group but also the tallest. From experience, Jennifer knew that this was a recipe for disaster or, at least, a lot of laughing and teasing.

The first girl got a wide ball. She chased but gave up. So did the second girl. The third girl was able to pursue the ball and get a racket on it, but the return went wide. Jennifer was fourth, and she was determined to get the ball back. The coach delivered a soft volley just inside the doubles line. Jennifer cross-stepped to get the fastest start. She opened up and prepared her racket as she took two more steps. Her swing was textbook, and the ball went straight down the line and deep. Then Jennifer lost her footing. It was only because she turned her head to follow the ball that she didn't do a classic face plant. She was spread eagle, and her court mates were laughing hilariously.

IT HAD BEEN A WEEK SINCE TAYLA MENDOZA MOVED FROM THE Valley of the Sun to the valley of tennis divas. In Phoenix, she was the top nine-year-old on the courts. She knew she would have to prove herself again to get to the top against much stiffer competition.

Earlier that morning, Tayla joined a beginner group. Starting with the forehand, the instructor taught the girls how to grip the racket, prepare the swing, swing from low to high, and how to follow through to be ready for the next shot.

The instructor asked the girls to practice together without a ball. He said, "Good form, Tayla."

"Line up on the backline." He hit soft volleys from the net. One girl missed altogether, one hit the ball, but it went wild. The third girl thought she was lucky when she hit the ball across the net.

Tayla went last. Her form was graceful but powerful. But the sound when she struck the ball. POP. In an instant, the shot was low across the net, and the surprised young instructor was unprepared when it hit his belt buckle.

The instructor recovered and said, "Tayla, I don't think you belong here." He then took her to join the advanced group.

Tayla was getting into the pace of the clinic. Between balls, she glanced at the beginner group on the next court over. As expected, the play on that court was not serious and not competent, except for one tall girl with crimson hair, her attention riveted on the instructor and the ball. Tayla could see that she was the youngest member of the group.

Tayla attacked the next forehand with a satisfying sound. The instructor said, "Good shot, Pop Girl."

On the beginner court, Tayla noticed the tall girl chasing a wide ball into the alley. *Good first step. Good racket preparation. Good swing. Perfect placement. OUCH!* Tayla thought.

Tayla ran over to help Jennifer and saw her court mates making fun and pointing. "Why are you laughing? She's the youngest girl out here. She went after that ball harder than any of you, and she made a perfect shot. In a couple of weeks, this girl is going to be on the advanced court. Who're you going to laugh at then?" Pop Girl reached a hand out and helped Jennifer up. "I'm Tayla."

"I'm Jennifer."

"Wanna hit some balls after clinic?"

"Sure."

"Later."

Tayla went back to the advanced court, and Jennifer continued on her own court, but she stood taller and played with more confidence. The eight-year-old mean girls ignored her for the rest of the day.

JENNIFER FINISHED A FEW MINUTES EARLY AND WATCHED THE TALL, experienced Latina. Tayla had a nice racket, but unlike the valley girls, it was well-worn. She wasn't dressed tennis cute but more like someone going to work. After Tayla finished, Jennifer approached the girl who looked to be about a year older but only a little bit taller. "Thanks for helping me. It's my first day, and I'm new to tennis."

"I'm new to the valley, but I'm not new to tennis. I'd love to hit with you after clinic; I'll probably be in the advanced group during instruction."

"That works. Maybe you can show me a few things," Jennifer said.

"Sure, if you will admit to being the first person in the valley that I know," Tayla said.

THE CAMP ENDED AT THREE P.M. JENNIFER'S MOTHER CAME TO PICK her up and found the two new friends sitting together.

Jennifer said, "Hi, Mom, this is Tayla Mendoza. She's excellent at tennis."

"I'm glad you found a friend, Jen." Sheila offered her hand. "I'm Sheila Gallagher. Is your mom coming soon?"

"She'll be here at five."

"Her job?" Sheila asked.

"She's job-hunting," Tayla said. "We just moved here from Arizona. Jennifer is my first friend in the valley. My dad is an airplane designer. He works at some company in the valley that has a strange name like some smelly animal."

"SkunkWorks?" Sheila asked.

"That's it."

"Two hours is too long for a nine-year-old to wait alone," Sheila said. "Why don't you call her and let me talk to her. If she says yes, you can come and spend the time at our house."

"That would be cool." Tayla grabbed her phone out of her bag and called her mom. "Mom, tennis camp is over, and my new friend's mom wants me to come to their house for a couple of hours. She wants to talk to you." She handed the phone to Sheila.

"Hello, this is Sheila Gallagher. Apparently, our daughters have become good friends. Tayla was waiting alone so I figured she might want to spend the rest of the afternoon at our house."

"I'm Ana Mendoza. That is very generous of you Sheila. If you text me your address, I'll be there as soon as I finish my job interview."

"I'll have coffee on, and we can chat," Sheila said and then finished the call.

Ana arrived later, and the two moms discussed the challenges of being working mothers.

Sheila asked, "I heard that you're job-hunting. What are your skills?"

Ana said, "I worked my way through Arizona State working as a legal secretary with an aerospace firm while my husband worked as an aerospace engineer. I have now graduated as a paralegal, but there aren't that many jobs here in the valley for new graduates."

"Are you willing to work in the entertainment industry? I'm the general counsel at GGG Production Services, and we are expanding to provide legal services to more of our clients."

Sheila explained the kind of work that her firm did, and Ana talked about her qualifications.

"Let me send you my résumé and references. Could I come in for an interview?" Ana asked.

Sheila replied, "Yes and no. Yes, on the résumé and references and no on the interview because we just did it. And, if your references check out, you can start on Monday after you've had time to settle in to the valley."

"It would be an honor and thank you so much," Ana said.

"Ana, it'll be great to have you at GGG. You'll find that our company is very friendly to work, family, and school."

"Tayla, it's time to go. And good news, Ms. Gallagher has offered me a job!" They said their goodbyes and the Mendozas headed for home.

From there, the friendship between Jennifer and Tayla grew, and they shared their obsessions. Jennifer learned about tennis, acting, and dancing and Tayla learned about *StarCruiser Brilliant*.

THE TENNIS CAMP LASTED FIVE WEEKS FROM NINE TO THREE. JENNIFER and Tayla spent all their free time together from the moment they first met at tennis camp. One day they were hitting after the lessons ended. Tayla said, "You're getting pretty good, and I need a partner for doubles. They are having a camp tournament the last two days, and I'm entering singles. If you come with me, I'll also enter doubles."

"That sounds fun. Are you sure that I won't hold you back?" Jennifer asked.

"Singles for me is serious. Doubles with you should be fun."

Over the last few sessions, they worked with a coach who taught them doubles technique, and they played some sets against other campers. Tayla was junior championship quality, but Jennifer struggled to hit the ball accurately. She was starting to learn the importance of being in the right place at the right time, though. The tournament began on the next to the last session day. "Remember to watch me when you're in the back and listen when you're at the net. Keep your racket up for volleys and let's kick some valley butt," Tayla said.

"If we win, it is all you. I'll do the best I can to help."

Tayla and Jennifer were seeded second because of Tayla, so their first opponents were weaker and still learning doubles in the one-set match. Jennifer couldn't hold serve on two games but Tayla and Jennifer worked well for the other six, and they won their first match, 6-2.

Tayla said, "One down, two to go. Our next match is after lunch at one. My first singles match is at eleven."

"You'll be busy today. Can you win four matches today?" Jennifer asked.

"I'm seeded three in singles, so it's easy pickin's today. Tomorrow, I'll have the single semis and two finals. Let's steal a court and hit some balls. I want to show you how to do a kick serve," Tayla said.

Throughout the summer, Tayla had been helping not only Jennifer but some of the other beginners.

"As bad as my serve is, it might make sense for me to kick the ball over the net," Jennifer confessed.

Tayla laughed, "No, Jen, the kick means that the ball kicks up in front of the returner because you put topspin on it."

"That sounds difficult," Jennifer said.

"It's one of the hardest shots in tennis, but I haven't seen anyone at this camp that can handle a decent kick serve."

"Besides you."

"Besides me. And even if I get a return, it gives me a nice put-away at the net."

"Tell me what do," Jennifer said.

Tayla explained to Jennifer how to set her feet, how to rotate her hips and then, "The key is in your wrist. When you bring the racket up over your head, bend your wrist and point the racket toward the ground. If you do it right, the racket brushes upward on the ball and gives it a lot of topspin. When it lands in front of the returner, the ball kicks up high. The returner either hits it long, soft, or misses it altogether. Either way, we win the point."

Tayla demonstrated several times slowly, then at full speed. "You try it."

Jennifer tried three times and missed the ball altogether. "Ouch, this is hard."

"It's all about timing and building muscle memory."

"I have lots of memory in my brain." Jennifer touched her head. "But muscle memory, not so much."

"We have another twenty minutes. That's sixty serves. Keep at it."

Hard work and Tayla's good coaching started to pay off. By the time they finished, Jennifer was able to hit one successful serve out of three.

"That's not going to win any games today," Jennifer said.

"Probably not, but we'll win all my service games," Tayla said, "and the girls we are playing next don't serve well either. I have to go. My first singles match is on Court 5."

Jennifer watched her friend dominate the weaker opponent. Tayla put up a bagel, winning 6-0. The girls in the camp began talking about the sound made when Tayla's racket met the ball. Sitting in the stands, Jennifer joined the other girls as they called "Pop!" when Tayla connected. The sound of her shots drew so many spectators that by the end of her match, Tayla had the loudest gallery.

Jennifer and Tayla's lunch table got busy as even the ten-year-olds stopped by to talk to nine-year-old Tayla.

THEIR OPPONENTS IN THE SEMIFINAL WERE STRONGER THAN THEIR first opponents.

"Jen, don't worry about your serve, just practice the kick. We can beat these two on their serves. Your kick will be there tomorrow when we need it," Tayla said. Again, Tayla dominated on her serve, and again Jennifer lost two service games. As predicted, their opponents weren't strong servers. They only held one game; Jennifer and Tayla advanced, winning 6-3.

"Congrats, Pardner, we're in the finals," Tayla said, as they hugged before they walked to the net for the handshakes. "I'm up again on Court 7 in a few minutes."

Jennifer watched the singles round of eight, Tayla again faced a weak opponent. She struggled with one service game, but with her excellent defense, she still advanced to the semis, winning 6-1. Jennifer was amazed that Tayla drew the biggest crowd, all of whom shouted "Pop!" every time Tayla connected. Even after three previous matches, Tayla was gaining strength with her enthusiastic support.

The girls' mothers had coordinated car-pooling for Jennifer and Tayla, and on the ride home with Sheila, Tayla said, "Tomorrow may be tough for both of us. We face Rena and Chrissie Dale in doubles, and I'll probably face both in singles. They were runner-up and champion in the Under-Ten Valley Juniors tournament this past spring."

Sheila said, "Your mom and I are taking the afternoon off. Would you two like to go to the beach? They reconstructed a section of Malibu beach twenty feet higher."

Both girls screamed, "Yes!"

Tayla said, "I have never been to a real ocean beach. In Phoenix, we had the sand but not the sea."

Jennifer replied, "You'll love it. I will bring both of my boogie boards."

———————————

IT WAS A WARM AND WONDERFUL MALIBU BEACH AFTERNOON AFTER Tennis Camp. Jennifer and Tayla consumed hot dogs and sunscreen in almost equal volume. Jennifer relished the four-foot waves, and the athletic Tayla quickly established mastery as a boogie board surfer.

Sheila asked Ana, "Have you enrolled Tayla in school for the fall yet?"

"Steven and I have been looking at reasonable private schools. Tayla is good at math, and I want her to attend a school where there is a quality program for the gifted. Some of the high-end schools are out of our range."

"Have you looked at Warner? Jennifer loves it there," Sheila said.

"We looked at Warner, at least the price tag," Ana said. "Based on the tuition, it is probably the best in the valley. It's way beyond what we can afford."

"Ana, my grandfather was one of the founders of Warner Academy. I went there shortly after it opened. It's the best school in SoCal. GGG has always had a seat on the board, and we provide generous scholarships to GGG employees."

"In that case, let me call Steven and confirm. We share important decisions like this." Ana got her phone out, walked up the beach and came back a few minutes later. "Sheila, Steven is very excited and appreciative. We look forward to having Tayla at Warner this fall."

"Then we have some good news for the girls."

When the girls came back up the beach for a sugar fix, Ana said, "Girls, Ms. Gallagher has some news."

"Jennifer, would you like to have a good friend at school this fall?" Sheila asked.

Jennifer's eyes got huge, "Really! Cool!"

Tayla looked confused, "What's going on?"

Ana smiled and said, "Tayla, you're going to join Jennifer at Warner Academy this fall."

The girls screamed and hugged.

Sheila said, "Ladies, there is way too much sun in the sky for my fair Irish skin. Let's head home and let our future tennis champions relax."

ON FRIDAY MORNING AT HER USUAL FIVE A.M. WAKE-UP TIME, Jennifer logged in as Jenna Seldon and checked in with her Math Tutor. "Good Morning, Srinivasa."

"Good Morning, Miss Jenna," Srinivasa Ramanujan was the artificial intelligence avatar modeled after the Indian math whiz. "Last session, you finished up Pre-Algebra. Are you ready to move on to High School Algebra?"

"Yes, where do we start?" Jennifer asked.

"We'll start with equations and expressions," Srini said with the typical head nodding, and mouth closed accent that Jennifer knew to be part of his Indian heritage.

For the next hour, Srini explained a concept, let Jennifer practice each part, and then gave her problems. Periodically, Srini competed with Jenna in instructive games that built on the current topic and integrated previous learning. Jenna and Srini even manipulated concrete objects in the air.

"Srini, you always let me win," Jenna complained.

Srinivasa replied, "I am a computer, and you're a child."

"Don't let me win."

"If I try as hard as I can, I'll always win," Srinivasa said.

"Not always. If we tie, that means I'm perfect like you. I want to be perfect."

Srinivasa said, "There is a Hindu saying, 'Seek within first and find the perfection within and you will see the perfection without.' That means that you don't need to measure yourself against me to view yourself as perfect."

"I want to be as good as I possibly can."

Srini smiled, "That is a noble goal, Miss Jenna. Therefore, I'll try hard and set the measuring stick higher."

By the end of the hour, Jennifer was winning the same number she was losing. Srinivasa said, "You made much progress, but you have a big tennis match and only an hour to rest up. Remember, you can still be as good as you can be, but still lose."

"Srini, I know I'll be the best that I can, but I played the match several times in my mind. I know that we'll win."

"This is the 'vision thing' I heard about?" Srinivasa asked.

"Yes, Srini, but wish me luck anyway. Laters."

"Of course, good luck, Miss Jenna, and good morning."

WITH AN HOUR BEFORE TAYLA'S SINGLES SEMI, THEY WENT TO AN empty court and practiced Jennifer's kick serve. "Remember when it's good and forget when it's bad," Tayla said. "That way you'll build muscle memory. That's how I get in The Zone."

"The Zone?" Jennifer asked.

"Sometimes when I am in a tough match, I get so focused that everything slows down. A tough ball will come, I can feel each step, the racket preparation, and the swing. I know in my bones exactly where the ball is going off my racket. I have heard that pro athletes call it 'The Zone,'" Tayla said.

"I'm starting to feel it, but I'm just not consistent," Jennifer said.

"The good ones are getting better, and the bad ones are getting fewer," Tayla said.

"I need to tell you something. I worked this match out in my head, and it's going to depend all on me at the end. I know we'll win, but the reality part says I hope I don't screw up."

"What do you mean you worked it out?"

"I take my memories and my knowledge, and I build movies in my head. I call it 'the vision thing.'"

"Does it work?" Tayla asked.

"It does. But I've never done it with sports."

"I don't like to lose, and getting in The Zone usually works for me," Tayla said. "I've got Rena Dale in the semis. She's my age. I'll probably have her older sister Chrissie in the final. Watch closely. Maybe you can use the vision thing to figure out how to beat them."

"Good luck, Tay. I want you to win."

"Thanks, that's the first time you've ever called me that. I like it."

"Hey, we're BFFs. At least until I blow the final."

"Not gonna happen. Either way, though, Best Friends Forever." They hugged, and Tayla headed for Court 2.

RENA DALE WAS GOOD, AND BOTH GIRLS KNEW IT. SHE WAS fundamentally sound, but after watching her in practice and clinic over the last few days, Tayla knew she didn't recover from mistakes well, especially when her friendly rivals threw in some trash talk.

The two girls shook hands before the match and Tayla heard her say, "Watch out for Valley Power." Her opponent just made it okay to play the mental game.

The two girls traded quality serves until 3-3 when Rena was serving at 30-30. Rena's first serve went wide; then she sent a soft second serve floating across the net. Tayla jumped on the approach shot. The crowd heard the Pop and Rena saw the low forehand coming straight for her belly button on the bounce. Rena just wasn't prepared for the shot. She had a look of fear as the ball collided with her racket and went wild for an error. Tayla looked across the net and said, "Too hard, Rena?"

30-40. It was the first time in Rena's short tennis career she felt real pressure. Her first serve went long. She looked rattled but got it together for a decent second serve. Tayla was ready and returned hard. The two girls swapped groundies until Rena chased out too far and Tayla hit a winner to the open court.

Tayla was up a break. Tayla hit four powerful serves, 5-3. Rena's heart wasn't in it anymore, and Tayla broke Rena for the match.

The two girls met at the net to shake hands. Rena said, "That was mean."

"You told me to watch out for Valley Power. Tell your sister to watch out. I'm a valley girl now."

TAYLA AND JENNIFER ATE LUNCH AND RELAXED. AGAIN, OTHER players came to their table, congratulated Tayla, and wished the two luck. The other girls weren't big fans of 'Valley Power.'

As they walked toward their doubles showdown with Rena and Chrissie, Jennifer said, "I watched some of Chrissie's match during your match. Chrissie is a stronger player. Tayla, I think that they both cheat towards the center on the opponent's second serve. Could I have imagined that?"

"I saw that once or twice. They both do it?"

"They do. How can I take advantage?" Jennifer asked.

"It might be too tricky for you. You would have to adjust the timing of your kick serve," Tayla said.

"I want to beat these two. Let's try tricky."

"Okay, in the deuce court, when you throw the ball up, throw it a little forward and you will hit the ball a bit later. It will give the ball some sidespin, and if the sisters are cheating to the center, it will bounce high and wide and be harder to handle."

"Nothing to lose. I haven't held serve in our first two matches. I'll do my best. Tayla, we'll win, though. I know it."

. . .

ONE P.M. COURT 1. IT WAS THE FINAL AFTERNOON OF TENNIS CAMP. The parents were in the stands to see how far their daughters advanced. Jennifer and Tayla were facing Rena and Chrissie in the Doubles final with Sheila and Jen's grandparents, Jack and Ciara sitting in the bleachers. Steven and Ana Mendoza sat nearby.

On the court, handshakes were exchanged but no smiles, and this time no trash talk. Jennifer and Tayla hugged once more and took their places for Rena to serve. The younger sister looked as if she had recovered from the earlier loss. She served with power and attitude and held the first game.

Jennifer served at 0-1. She won a couple of points, but the sisters broke her. Chrissie served at 2-0. Jennifer and Tayla took her to deuce, but two points later, Tayla served from three games down.

"I can win my serve," Tayla said. "but it's all about defense from here out. We need to get back in this."

Tayla won her serve efficiently and put the two friends on the board.

Rena served at 3-1 with the same confidence as before, but Jennifer received and hit a solid cross-court return. Rena barely got to it, setting up a clean volley winner for Tayla. At Love-15, Rena served to Tayla. At the last moment, Tayla saw Chrissie cheat as if she was going to poach across and hit the volley return into the defenseless Jennifer. Tayla then hit a clean winner down the line past Chrissie.

At Love-30, Rena offered a strong serve that Jennifer couldn't handle. 15-30. Tayla then hit another strong return that was too wide for Rena to handle, so Rena was serving to Jennifer at 15-40.

"Get another nice return, and we can beat these girls. If Chrissie tries to poach again, take her down the line," Tayla said.

Jennifer settled to receive. Rena served. Chrissie moved to her right. Jennifer hit a great return into the empty alley. 2-3. The friends were back on serve.

Jennifer struggled again on her serve but won a couple of points before being broken.

Chrissie served to Tayla at 4-2. Chrissie and Tayla traded groundies in a powerful exchange. Tayla hit one wide, and Chrissie chased. Chrissie's return popped up right in front of Jennifer at the net. She was surprised, but she put away the volley. The girls traded points. At 30-40, Chrissie served, and Jennifer hit a soft return to Chrissie. The older sister charged but she made a mistake of over-confidence. She struck a powerful approach forehand directly at Tayla right across the net thinking that her nemesis was weaker and couldn't handle it. But Tayla was ready and volleyed right past Rena and Chrissie for the break of serve.

All the other matches were over, and the camp girls and their families heard about the drama on Court 1. The stands were quickly filling up.

The sisters looked at Jennifer and Tayla with new respect and now a bit of fear. They were way ahead before, and now Tayla could serve to even the match at 4-4. And she did.

The girls put their heads together, and Tayla said, "Defense. We got this." Jennifer nodded.

Rena's service game was strong, but she couldn't overcome the friends' building confidence. Rena was broken and Jennifer Gallagher, beginning tennis player, was serving for the set and the championship.

Jennifer served to Rena. They traded groundstrokes, and then Tayla was able to cross over and hit a winner at the net. Jennifer served to Chrissie, but Jennifer couldn't handle the hard return. 15-all.

Jennifer served to Rena. The two younger players traded groundstrokes again. Rena hit one too softly. Jennifer approached and hit it past the surprised Chrissie. 30-15.

Jennifer hit her first serve long. Chrissie was ready for her second serve. Rena was hugging the net. Jennifer saw it and served, and Chrissie hit a deep return. And then Jennifer did something entirely unexpected. She took the ball on the short hop and lobbed it over Rena. Chrissie chased the ball deep and to the alley but couldn't catch up. 40-15. The championship was on Jennifer's racket.

Jennifer looked at Tayla with a questioning look. Tayla stared right back, nodded her head and mouthed the word 'yes.' Jennifer shrugged. It was time to reach into the trick bag.

Rena settled for the return. Jennifer saw her cheat to the middle. She breathed and thought through all the things that Tayla coached her on. She served wide. It landed in the deepest corner and bounced high and away from Rena. Rena chased and swung. She only hit air. Ace. Game. Set. Championship. The new girl from Arizona. The Total Tennis beginner. Best friends forever. Champions!

There were cheers from the stands. Jennifer and Tayla celebrated. Jennifer looked at her mom who looked like she was crying.

The competitors came to the net. There were handshakes and, surprisingly, hugs as well. Chrissie said, "You two deserved this."

Tayla responded, "Good Luck, Chrissie."

"You too, Tayla."

THE SINGLES FINAL WAS POWER VS. POWER, BUT TAYLA HAD JUST A BIT more finesse, and she went on to win the singles title 6-3.

At the awards ceremony, Tayla and Jennifer got the doubles trophy, and Tayla got the singles trophy, Jennifer also got the Most Improved trophy, and Tayla got the Kid's Coach award for helping the younger players throughout the summer. The families took lots of pictures, and afterward, the girls ate lots of pizza. School was three weeks away. Jennifer and Tayla were inseparable.

After a morning on the tennis courts and afternoon on the beach with Tayla, she entered steveLearn.

"Good evening, Jenna. How did your math session with Srinivasa go? I heard that you covered a lot of ground."

"I like Srini. He said that I should take a break between sessions. Sounded like a good idea."

"So, what do you need?" Sami asked.

"Mom says I can take two courses at one time. I'm doing a math course, but I want to become an author someday. Do you have anything on writing or literature," Jennifer replied.

"You need an English Tutor, so why don't we make this more fun? I'll introduce you to someone who loves books and also loves mathematics."

"Send me the list of books you have read, and I will set up your English Tutor for the morning? Call up English Lit."

"Good idea. I am kind of tired. See you tomorrow."

In the morning, she entered steveLearn. "Open English Lit."

A figure appeared dressed in garb from the nineteenth century looking very confused.

"Who are you?" Jennifer asked.

The figure composed himself, "Who in the world am I? Ah, that is the great puzzle. To some, I am known as Charles Lutwidge Dodgson. I am an author and a mathematician."

Jennifer smiled, "And to others, you're known as Lewis Carroll, and you wrote about Alice in one of my favorite books."

"Correct, Miss Jenna, and you may call me Lewis. You're ten years old and very well read." Lewis continued, "If I may ask, how did you discover *The Faerie Queene* by Edmund Spenser. It's quite a mouthful for a youngster. It's one of my all-time favorites."

"I was reading poetry, and I read somewhere that Spenser was one of the first English poets."

Lewis Carroll said,

"Lo I the man, whose Muse whilome did maske,

As time her taught, in lowly Shepheards weeds,

Am now enforst a far unfitter taske,

For trumpets sterne to chaunge mine Oaten reeds,"

Jenna continued the verse,

"And sing of Knights and Ladies gentle deeds;

Whose prayses having slept in silence long,

Me, all too meane, the sacred Muse areeds

To blazon broade emongst her learned throng:

Fierce warres and faithfull loves shall moralize my song."

"How much of the poem have you memorized?" asked the tutor.

"All of it. I have an eidetic memory. It is my superpower. I can remember and recite all the books that I've read."

"Have you read The Bard?" asked the tutor.

"I intend to. Shakespeare's plays and sonnets are on my list for the future."

The Tutor quoted,

"... THAT WE WOULD DO

We should do when we would; for this 'would' changes

And hath abatements and delays as many

As there are tongues, are hands, are accidents;

And then this 'should' is like a spendthrift sigh,

That hurts by easing."

"THAT IS FROM A PLAY CALLED 'HAMLET,'" LEWIS SAID. "YOUR exploration of English Literature should begin with the Immortal Bard of Avon. 'Hamlet is a good starting point."

"I must start somewhere," Jennifer said.

"Begin at the beginning," Lewis Carroll said, very gravely, "and go on till you come to the end: then stop."

"Good advice from The King," Jennifer said, recognizing the reference. "I will see you in a few days."

"Good day, Miss Jenna."

Warner Academy

J ennifer began fourth grade at Warner Academy spending two to three hours a day with steveLearn. Tayla was a year ahead in fifth grade and it was her first exposure to steveLearn. After learning the system, she thrived.

Jennifer advanced quickly, spending part of her time on the UVN system with her tutors, Srinivasa and Lewis. The remainder of their time, they were in group activities and sports. Jennifer and Tayla were becoming known in local sports circles as the dynamic duo, not only in tennis but in basketball and soccer. Their rivalry with the Dale sisters became much more intense on the field but more friendly off.

As Tayla caught up and surpassed her classmates in math and science, Jennifer finished Algebra by the end of the first semester of fourth grade.

AROUND THANKSGIVING, SHEILA SPOKE WITH JENNIFER, "I HAVE OUR tickets to Hawaii for the two weeks after Christmas. And this time, they had two spots open for surfing lessons."

Jen said, "Cool, mom, are you going to learn to surf this year finally?"

"Not me. But I talked to Ana, and she says that Tayla wants to learn," said Sheila.

"Tayla is coming to Maui with us? Amazingly way cool." said Jen.

"Ana and Steven are coming too." Sheila got serious, "Jen, is it okay if Dr. Allen comes as well?"

"I like Dr. Allen, and yes, it is perfectly okay," Jen replied.

"One more thing. Your grandparents are coming over for the weekend for a special event."

Jen's eyes got huge, "Mom? Really? You're serious?" Sheila nodded. Jennifer screamed, "I'm gonna have a dad!"

"And he said you only have to spend every other weekend in the cage with the rat pellets."

"Eww, mom!"

ON CHRISTMAS DAY, TAYLA'S FAMILY JOINED JENNIFER'S. TAYLA GOT a new Serena Williams model tennis racket. Jennifer asked, "Who's Serena Williams?"

Tay lit up, "She is just the best women's singles player ever. She and her sister grew up in East LA in Compton."

When Jennifer's grandparents, Sean and Ciara, arrived, the three families had Christmas dinner.

Sean gave Jennifer a present, "I think this might keep you busy for a while."

Jen opened it and found a pad. "Thanks, grandpa. It is just like my other one."

Sean Grandholm said, "Why don't you start it up and see what it contains?"

Jennifer followed the instructions. Up popped a diagram of StarCruiser Brilliant. "Is this what I think it is?" She went faster paging through the contents. "Way cool, Grandpa. It's the *Brilliant Tech Manual.* I've wanted this for a long time. Thank you so much."

"It's all twelve volumes. Your mother said you were looking for something more advanced to study," Sean said.

. . .

One morning in steveLearn, Jennifer was chatting with Sami, "I think I'm ready to move on to Geometry. What do you have in mind?"

"I have a Tutor who can get you started from the very beginning of geometry. He invented it two thousand four hundred years ago.?

"May I meet him?" Jen asked.

"Press the button labeled Geometry," said Sami.

Jennifer pressed the button. After a few moments, she was seated in the grass on the slope of a hillside looking up at an immense white marble structure at the top of the hill. She felt a damp ocean breeze and smelled smoke coming from the cooking fires in the city below and just a hint of the smell she remembered from the time she went horse riding. She heard absolute silence beneath the peaceful sounds of birds. It was a stunning contrast to the constant din she heard from the Ventura Freeway less than a mile outside her window at home. She looked around at the beautiful city. Below and to her left were several large buildings with small dwellings nearby. There was a total absence of markings of a modern city like vehicles, utility poles and wires, signs, asphalt roads and most notably anything made of steel or metal.

A bearded gentleman approached wearing red robes and a hat that looked like a cross between a beanie and a turban. He spoke, "Welcome to Ancient Greece, Miss Jenna. I am known as Euclid." He carried a tablet and a hinged angular device and had a simple ruler sticking out of a pocket. The ruler had no markings.

"What is this beautiful place called?"

"You are sitting on a hill called the Acropolis. Before you is the Parthenon, it appears to you the way I saw it when I walked on this hill about 2,400 years before you were born. Behind you is the Temple of Athena Nike. Below you to the left is our city of Athens. The open space is our public area called the Agora."

"You invented geometry," said Jen.

"The truth of that is buried in the rubble that is Athens today or went up in smoke in the library of Alexandria in Egypt. What did survive to your time were the thirteen books of mine called the Elements. These books brought forward our ideas of geometry that took my name, how to find a square root, elementary number theory, a form of geometric algebra and most importantly the logic of deductive proof. These are the things that I hope to teach you in the coming months," said the ancient mathematician.

Jen asked, "What are the tools that you are carrying?"

"Of course, this is a tablet for recording our constructions. In my pocket is a straightedge," said Euclid.

Jen interrupted, "So you can draw a straight line."

The Greek man looked offended, "Young lady, you have stated a redundancy. A line extends in the same and opposite directions forever. A line that is not straight would most assuredly not be a part of MY geometry."

"What is that other thing?"

"This tool, Miss Jenna, is a compass."

"That thing will help you find your way out of the forest?" asked Jennifer.

Euclid laughed, "You are thinking of a magnetic compass in which the magnet always points in the same direction. This device measures a constant distance. One arm stays at a single point and the other traces on the paper."

Jen closed her eyes, "I am trying to visualize." She opened them, "A circle?"

"Excellent, Jenna. You will be a worthy student."

"Where did you go to school?" asked Jen.

"Like you, I went to an academy. It was the very first academy founded by a man called Plato," said Euclid.

"What is logic?" asked Jennifer.

"Let's explore. Pretend we know very little about math. What is two plus three?" asked Euclid.

"Five"

"Assume that two and three are old ideas that you already know, then what is five?" asked Euclid.

"Five would be a new idea," said Jen.

"Correct. That is the logic of numbers. Next, do you have a dog?"

"No, but if I get one, I am going to name him Pugsley."

"Okay let's pretend again by adding two things called premises together. The first premise is: A dog has four legs. The second premise is: Pugsley is a dog. Now, add those two together and tell me what you have?"

"Pugsley has four legs," answered Jennifer.

"You are correct, again. You have started with two premises, put them together, and you have come up with a conclusion. That is called a syllogism and is the root of logical reasoning," Euclid explained.

"But a cat has four legs. Is a cat a dog?"

Euclid responded, "You cannot go backward from the conclusion to a new premise. You must start with known assumptions and build forward."

"I see. Thank you, Euclid, sir," she said. "It is time for my next class."

Present Day

SIX

The Letter

J ennifer arrived home about an hour after the explosion. As she climbed the hill, she visualized the feeling of success when she opened the mailbox. The large envelope would contain her invitation to the internship.

She reviewed all steps it took to reach this point.

Jennifer filled out the web application for the summer internship at Tovar Studios in early March. She was able to do this behind the closed door of her bedroom. The next step was to fill out a written bio and essay in mid-April. The task became more difficult as she needed to intercept the mail before her mother got home. With her friend Tayla's help, she went to the studio for a thirty-minute interview with three studio executives in May. She told her mom she was going on an outing with her best friend Tayla and then took three buses into Hollywood and back without her mother becoming aware of the plan. The executives thanked her and said she would hear at the end of the month. Thus, on this 27th day of May, Jennifer envisioned that getting the internship was the easy part.

The most challenging step was getting the permission of her mother, chief legal counsel at GGG. When Jennifer proposed the venture, her mother had forbidden it in no uncertain terms. She pleaded with her daughter to be reasonable and not even consider applying to Tovar Studios. Sheila had gone so far as to offer her an internship at GGG working with the computer engineers who created special effects. Biting her lip, she worried how to convince her mom.

"So begins the rest of my life." She opened the mailbox. She found a large number of letters, but no large packet. She pulled out the stack and began sorting. Bill. Congratulations, you've been selected... Bill. Cremation Ad. Tovar Studios.

It was a simple white envelope from Tovar Studios that could only contain a very polite letter that will congratulate and thank the applicant in elegant business-like prose to soften the real message typed on the expensive cream-colored stationery: "REJECTED!!!"

Jennifer turned her head away and looked over the valley without expression. Her valley. Her company town.

Her hands were shaking as she held the mail. She struggled to get the keys out of her backpack, and, out of character, she fought back the tears.

Jennifer walked into the kitchen; her mother was already home and looking concerned. "Did you get held up by that explosion on Long Valley Road?" her mother asked.

"Yeah, I was close by when it happened. I watched for a bit and then had to take the long way around." Jennifer kept looking down. She didn't want her mother to see how she was feeling right now.

"The firemen say it might have been a gas explosion. They don't know the exact cause," said Sheila.

"Or it could have been a small meteorite," Jennifer said.

"You and your space-borne imagination," replied her mother. "You're way too obsessed with that *Brilliant* movie."

"You never know." But Jennifer did know. A spacecraft entered the atmosphere to the west and shortly after an object from the sky hit that house. She saw the rock coming straight for her and Dandy.

"Was there mail?" her mother asked.

Jennifer looked away from her mother, "Yeah, nothing important." She looked back to see if her mom knew she hadn't told the whole truth.

Jennifer went back to her room. The letter sat propped up on the lamp on her desk. She stood looking at it with her arms folded over her chest hoping that it would somehow turn into the package she expected. It didn't.

"Oh, well. It looks like we're stuck here alone this summer, Pugs."

She entered her steveLearn system and searched for information about the explosion and fire. She viewed the event from several news drones that arrived several seconds after the explosion. There she was on the sidewalk holding Dandy as the firetrucks arrived.

She searched the net for information about the cause. She googled the term "sonic boom." She found this, "The Federal Aviation Administration released a statement saying that two Air Force fighters flying southbound from Edwards Air Force Base exceeded the speed of sound over the San Fernando Valley. They were practicing air combat maneuvers."

Seriously? she thought.

She looked some more but found no more information connecting the sonic boom to the explosion. Then she remembered the letter and the discussion with Tayla after school.

WHEN SHE WAS TEN YEARS OLD, JENNIFER'S BEDROOM WAS PINK. SHE asked her mom to redecorate for her eleventh birthday. Her new mahogany desk with the latest HTVR Tech fit nicely in her larger room. The display behind showed scenes to inspire her writing. A walk-in closet, which contained her antique books, an abbreviated wardrobe, and her greatest fashion indulgence, her sneaker and boot collection. Her state-of-the-art steveLearn system provided a comfortable place to study and communicate.

When Jennifer published her first book, *Galaxy Warrior*, her mother let her buy a pet. She picked the adorable wrinkles and tongue of a brown pug, appropriately named Pugsley. Pugsley had the run of the house and yard but spent most of the day on his doggy pillow in his corner. When Jennifer got home, he remained in her sightline, on her lap, or next to her asleep on the bed.

Now, with Pugs on her lap, Jennifer stared at the letter leaning on the lamp on her desk. Part of her hoped it would disappear and part of her wished that it would turn into the acceptance letter she banked on. Jennifer heard a ring.

"Hi, Tay."

Tayla was in her steveLearn sitting across from her. "Hi, Jen, did you see the explosion on Long Valley Road?" Tayla said.

"I was there. It was the Nesbitt home, and I was feeding Dandy Lion." Jennifer said.

Tayla's hand flew to her chest. "That was you I saw on the sidewalk? Oh, my God! Are you okay? Is Dandy okay?"

"Everyone is okay, but the Nesbitt house is a hole in the ground. The meteorite destroyed everything. I heard the first sonic boom, saw the streak, heard the second, saw the fireball, and ran."

"The news said the sonic booms were fighters from Edwards and the house went up in a gas explosion."

Jennifer shook her head, "Fake News. I was there. I heard the first boom and looked northwest. I saw a red streak turning this way. It couldn't have been natural. After the second boom, there was a fireball headed straight at Dandy and me."

"You're right. Dad came home from work and said that there were no fighters over the valley today. What happened?"

"I don't know, but someone is keeping a secret."

"Did you get the letter?"

Jennifer's shoulders slumped. "I got rejected."

"Seriously. That's nasty. What did the letter say?" Tayla said.

"I haven't read it yet," Jennifer said.

"How do you know you didn't get in?" Tayla was almost shouting.

"It's a standard-sized letter. I was expecting a large packet with information about the internship. The envelope is only big enough for a rejection letter. I got rejected." Jennifer explained.

"You did that visualization thing, huh?" Tayla asked.

"Well, yeah."

"Sometimes your visions don't work the way you expect. Open the letter." Jennifer understood Tayla's urging, but she resisted.

"What if it is a rejection?"

"Then you can take the summer internship at GGG. Your vision thing doesn't always work. Open the letter."

Jennifer looked at the envelope and apprehensively rubbed her arms. Finally, she picked it up as if it were radioactive. Jennifer inspected it to figure out how to open it. She said nothing.

"Open the letter already!" Tayla knew her best friend well.

Jennifer cut open the envelope, held the folded letter, and unfolded the letter with her eyes closed. She opened her eyes and saw one word: Congratulations!

Jennifer shouted, "I GOT IN!!!"

Pugsley barked.

Tayla shouted, "Way Cool. Read the letter."

"Tay, do you know how long I waited for this? This letter is bucket-list-worthy."

"So, read the letter," Tayla said.

"Congratulations. Tovar Studios is happy to offer you a summer internship as a Production Assistant at our studios in Canoga Park. It is a paid internship, and you will receive five-hundred-dollars per week for the summer." Jennifer finally breathed. "Please report to our studios at eight a.m. on Tuesday, May 31. Present this letter to security and they will direct you to our offices for orientation."

"What is your mother going to say?" Tayla asked.

"She's going to say no...."

"Do you need me there?"

"I got this. It may involve my well-honed teenage skills of manipulation, but I can get my mom to say yes."

"The vision thing?"

"The vision thing."

"Call me."

"Soon as I can." They hung up. *Tayla is a good sister.*

JENNIFER HELD THE LETTER. SHE CLOSED HER EYES AND READ IT TO herself from memory. The black ink on white stationery made it all the more real. Since she had seen the first *StarCruiser Brilliant* movie when she was five, she wanted to be part of the production. She was a very realistic five-year-old. She knew that she could never be a star, but Jennifer knew that she could help make the films. Years later, there was another reason.

She called up a file from her hidden folder.

. . .

ACTOR KILLED AT TOVAR STUDIOS

(DECEMBER 10, 2049 - HOLLYWOOD) In a freak accident today, an actor appearing in the latest StarCruiser Brilliant *film was killed today when a massive camera crane failed. Anton Kazerian, a twenty-two-year-old graduate of UVN Film School …*

JENNIFER REMEMBERED THE DAY SHE FOUND THE FILE ON HER mother's computer. She was surprised that her mother would keep a news story that was many years old. Then she looked at the date. December 10, 2049. *Mom was pregnant with me then. Was he my father?*

For Jennifer, it became a mission: become a part of making her favorite movies and find her father.

JENNIFER WENT INTO HER MOM'S OFFICE AND STOOD NEXT TO HER. "Did you find out anything more about that explosion?" Sheila asked.

"The FAA says that the sonic boom was from fighter jets out of Edwards," Jennifer explained. "The firemen said a gas explosion destroyed the house. Mom, none of that is true."

"How do you know?"

"It was the Nesbitt home."

"You mean the family with the twins and the cat that you love?"

"Yeah, Dandy Lion."

Sheila reached out and took hold of Jennifer's shoulder, "Wait, you were there?"

"I was feeding Dandy a treat. I heard the first sonic boom, looked northwest and I saw a decelerating spacecraft. Then, after the second boom, a fireball was coming toward us. I grabbed Dandy and ran."

"You should've called me immediately," Sheila said. "Thank God you're safe. You saved Dandy. You're very brave but, goodness, Jen, you could've been killed."

"I'm safe, and I can take care of myself if you trust me."

Her mom turned her head and looked Jennifer in the eye. "This discussion isn't about the cat. Spill."

"I got the letter."

"Tovar?" Sheila shook her head.

Jennifer nodded.

"You aren't that good at sneaking around. You lied to me."

Jennifer lowered her eyes. "I wasn't sure I would get in."

"I told you that you couldn't apply for that internship. I told you I'd get you an internship in our CGI department."

"I got in at Tovar. This is my destiny. I can handle it. I can be successful if you let me."

"No, you can't go."

"Mom, you know this is my dream. I've been preparing for this since I was five."

"That studio is dangerous. People get killed there."

"Like my dad?"

Sheila looked straight at Jennifer. "What do you know about that?"

"A few years ago, you asked me to look something up on your computer. I found the news story about the actor who was killed at Tovar. I didn't think anything about it until I saw the date. You were pregnant."

"That was just a news story about GGG business."

"He was my father, wasn't he?"

There was a long pause. "Yes, honey, he was your father. They say he died when a huge crane fell on him. They blamed it on GGG equipment."

Jennifer could see the wetness gather in her mother's eyes. "They say?"

"The location was in a foreign country. The local officials investigated it and sent photos of the damaged equipment, but…."

"But what?"

"They never returned Anthen's body."

"I need to find out what happened. *We* need to find out."

Sheila looked at her daughter. "Your father was killed because he was working at Tovar Studios. I don't have your vision thing, but I know that you're going to wind up around that damned starship."

"There is no guarantee that I'll ever work on the *StarCruiser Brilliant* movies."

"GGG hasn't done business with Tovar for seventeen years."

Jennifer stood with her feet apart, and her arms crossed, "This is my life. I need to follow my career. My destiny."

"The valley is a lot smaller than you think. People will know that you're my daughter."

"I need this. We need this. It'll be closure for you. I believe that *StarCruiser Brilliant is* my future."

"The vision thing?"

"Yeah."

Sheila's head dropped, and her shoulders slumped in defeat. "You have your driver's test on Monday. When does the internship start?"

"I report Tuesday morning."

"You will tell me if something looks dangerous. And, you will stay clear of that damn ship."

Jennifer's face was lighting up. "Yes, Mom. Of course."

"We'll tell your step-dad when he gets home. Be careful."

"Thanks, Mom. I want this." They hugged.

On Saturday, Jennifer woke up at seven a.m. and was editing the next book in the Galaxy Warriors series. At ten, the front doorbell rang. Sheila answered and said, "Jennifer, can you come here?"

Jennifer got there, holding Pugsley. She saw the Nesbitt twins standing on the porch and Kailyn, the older twin, held Dandy. Pugsley barked.

Kamryn, the younger twin, said, "We have to stay in a hotel while they build our house and they won't let us keep Dandy Lion." Both girls were almost in tears now.

"I know it is asking a lot, but we know Dandy loves you. Could you keep him for the summer?" Ms. Nesbitt said.

"I think we can manage. Jennifer?" Sheila said.

"It's up to Pugs." Pugsley barked again and looked at Jennifer with his tongue hanging. "Pugs says yes, but only for the summer."

The twins shouted, "Yes, we want him back."

"Thank you so much," Mrs. Nesbitt said. "Here is a bag of the cat food that Dandy likes. He's very particular in his taste."

The girls hugged Dandy and then handed him over to Jennifer.

Jennifer had her hands full with two animals eyeing each other warily. Dandy reached out with a paw and lightly slapped Pugsley on the side of the head. "Dandy told Pugsley to calm down," Kailyn said. Jennifer furrowed her eyebrows as she observed this curious cat behavior.

On the way to her room, Jennifer said, "Let me go get a pet pillow for you, Dandy." When she came back, Dandy enthroned himself on Jennifer's bed where Pugsley usually slept. Pugsley was on the floor looking up with a forlorn look.

"I have heard of alpha dogs but an alpha cat?" Jennifer put the pillow down and coaxed the pug over. "Well, Pugs, it looks like we're going to have to make sacrifices for our displaced guest." She looked at Dandy. "Don't kill him. I have to get ready for tennis."

He is harmless and stupid, Dandy thought.

Jennifer had a confusing thought. It felt like it came from somewhere else.

CHRISSIE AND RENA DALE MET TAYLA AND JENNIFER AT THE Calabasas Tennis Center for doubles. All four hit with the "Pop" coming off their rackets. They quickly drew a gallery. The girls split two hard-fought sets and then hit the showers.

They went to the Topanga Table for lunch.

"Tayla, you and Chrissie get to fight it out in college singles matches next year," Rena said. "I'm jealous."

"You and Jennifer will have to learn not to run into each other when you party up for the doubles tournaments next year," Chrissie said.

"Didn't your baby sister take out both you and Tayla in the high school championships?" Jennifer said. "I may be the weakest link here, but I think Rena and I can hold our own."

They headed toward their cars.

"Have a good summer, folks," Jennifer said, "and let's try to play on weekends. I have a gig during the week."

Chrissie asked, "You got the dream job?"

Jennifer replied, "Yep, I start at Tovar on Tuesday."

"Try not to bite David's lip when you meet him," Rena said.

"Seriously, guys, I'm *not* obsessed," Jennifer said.

"Seriously, Jen, you are," Tayla replied and the four girls laughed. The girls hugged and promised to keep in touch.

"Whatcha got this weekend?" Tayla asked.

"I'm getting Dandy Lion settled," Jennifer said.

"Dandy? The Nesbitt cat that you saved?"

"Yeah, but I think there is something strange about him."

"All cats are strange."

"He rolled his eyes at me."

"Maybe he has the vision thing?"

"No way," Jennifer said. *Is it possible?*

"I'll pick you up on Saturday morning."

"Someday, I won't have to bum rides off my bestie," Jennifer said. "I've got my appointment Monday."

"Call me as soon as you get your license."

On Monday, Sheila drove Jennifer to the California DMV in Winnetka for her driver's test.

"Do you remember the rules? Will you be careful?"

"Yes, Mom. You know I'm a safe driver."

"On this test, you can't use AutoDrive. You have to press the pedals and steer the wheel."

"Been there. Done that. I got this." Jennifer drummed her fingers on her knee.

"Be nice to my Mercedes."

Sheila parked in the Examiner's lot. "I'm going to Starbucks across the street."

"I'll call WHEN I get my license."

"You and your vision thing. Good luck."

"Thanks, Mom."

Sheila crossed the street to Starbucks. She ordered a mocha and took a seat when her assistant, Susan, and Ana Mendoza walked in. "Is it parked where I told you?"

Ana said, "Yes, here are the keys."

"Thanks. Tayla doesn't know, right?"

"It's our secret."

Susan and Ana drove back to their office.

Sheila took out her phone and made the call that she was dreading.

"Tovar Studios, Navvy Kelrithian's office. How may I help you?" Kathy Sakai, Navvy's assistant answered.

"This is Sheila Gallagher from GGG. Does Navvy have a moment?" Sheila said.

"It's nice to speak with you again, Sheila. It's been a long time. Can you hold just a moment?"

Kathy dialed Navvy's intercom, "Yes?"

"Sheila Gallagher is calling from GGG. I think she is the General Counsel there. Are we doing business with them again?"

"God, it's been seventeen years," Navvy said. "Wait, did I hear we have an intern named Gallagher coming in?"

"That's correct," Kathy said.

"Put her on."

Kathy connected the call.

"Sheila, it's been forever. I remember when you and Anthen used to play together at the studio."

"Hello, Navvy. Thanks for taking my call."

"Is GGG doing business with us again? How can I help you?"

"It's about my daughter, Jennifer. She's an overly obsessed fan of your movies, and besides that, she is crushing on a certain young actor of yours. Unbeknownst to me, she applied for an internship at your studio and, unfortunately, got it."

"I remember reading her résumé. She's a brilliant girl, and very talented. She has a future in this business," Navvy said.

"You don't know the half of it. Navvy, I want you to promise me that you will keep her safe."

"Sheila, I might not even run into her on set."

"I need you to promise."

Now, he was starting to understand. "I know that you and your family still have bad feelings about Anthen's accident. I lost a son, and furthermore, I didn't have anything to do with the news that came out—"

"Navvy, she's your granddaughter."

Silence from Navvy. "How?"

"The last semester of my senior year at UVN, I ran into Anthen on set. We connected and started dating. It was getting serious. I missed my period, and before I could tell Anthen, the accident happened."

More silence. "All these years. You could have told Hanna and me," Navvy whispered.

"I was angry. Tovar blamed GGG for killing Anthen. And I blamed Tovar. By the time I came to grips with it, I was a lawyer at GGG and a single mom. There was no point in opening old wounds."

"Does Jennifer know?" Navvy asked.

"Jennifer thinks that her father might be an actor called Anton Kazerian. That was his stage name. She doesn't know about you and Hanna."

"A summer internship doesn't involve danger, but I'll certainly promise to look out for Jennifer. May I take the time to get to know her?"

"Yes, Navvy, but I'd like to wait until she is ready to hear the whole truth."

"I'm sorry about what happened to Anthen, and I'm sorry about the way we portrayed GGG. I wish I could tell you more."

"That's in the past."

"If Jennifer is as talented as her résumé suggests and as passionate as her mother, I hope that Tovar becomes her home."

"Jennifer is my daughter. All I want is for you to keep her safe and not drop anything on her," Sheila said.

"I'll do my best, and I look forward to getting to know my granddaughter."

The call ended.

JUST THEN, A SILVER MERCEDES PULLED INTO THE STARBUCKS parking lot. Sheila came out of the coffee shop. "I take it from the circumstances that 'Congratulations' are warranted?"

Jennifer pulled out her license. "Yep, all I need is a car now."

"Woah, you just got your license," Sheila said. "Can't you wait until you get home to be a needy teenager?"

"Get in the passenger seat. I need to concentrate on driving." When they turned the corner to their home, Jennifer saw a bright red Prius and said, "Cute car, but why is it blocking the driveway?"

Sheila stopped and reached into her purse, "Here are the keys. Move it up next to the garage."

Jennifer got out then did a double-take. "Mom, why do you have the keys?"

"I don't have the keys; you have the keys."

Jennifer hesitated. Then her blue-green eyes got huge. "Omigod, I love it. Is it mine? Thank you. Thank you!"

Jennifer jumped back into the car and hugged her mom. Sheila thought, *206 IQ my ass.*

"Can I take it over to show Tay?"

"After you call your grandparents and thank them. And, thank Allen as well."

"Oh, mom, it's so cute. I love it."

AT 7:45 A.M. ON TUESDAY, JENNIFER PRESENTED THE LETTER AT THE gate of Tovar Studios and was directed to a conference room in the Human Relations Building. There, she met the five other summer interns.

A thirty-something woman introduced herself, "I'm Emily Hudson, Vice President of Human Relations here at Tovar. Welcome to the motion picture industry. We're happy and proud to have young and talented future professionals with us. We hope that you learn from us and more importantly, we hope to learn from you."

"For the next two hours, you will fill out the boring but necessary paperwork to get paid and get your security and parking credentials. At ten a.m., you will attend an hour-long safety and security seminar and then at eleven a.m., Charlotte, a production assistant, or PA, will give you a tour. Later today you will assume the same title as

Charlotte. You won't be asked to perform skills we don't think you're ready for, but you might be asked to do something you don't think you're ready for. Remember, the most important axiom: the first step on the road to success is saying 'Yes.' At Tovar, we go by three simple rules: 1. Personnel Safety, 2. Equipment Safety and Security, and 3. Get the shot. You're here to learn, you're here to contribute, but you're here to have fun. A bad day making pictures is better than a good day doing anything else. Finally, remember, if you don't ask the question, you won't know the answer. Good luck; be safe and go out there and help us make great movies."

They started their tour, "Here is Sound Stage Three where the *Virtual Detective* is shot," Charlotte said. They saw the backlot, effects and editing suites, makeup, a star's trailer, the commissary, and the location of restrooms. "Keep these places in mind. Your go-fer duties might take you there." Jennifer perked up when they walked past the empty space storing *Brilliant* finally arriving at the commissary where they took a lunch break.

Back at HR, Jennifer received her initial assignment. She met Angel who took her back to Sound Stage Three and *Virtual Detective*, a story where a female human detective and a male virtual partner solved crimes together. The virtual detective was human in every respect except that his eyes were yellow, a convention dictated by the agreement to set apart virtuals from human actors.

ANGEL AND JENNIFER PASSED THROUGH THE MASSIVE DOORS OF Sound Stage Three just as the crew was returning from lunch. "Welcome to the most high-tech filmmaking in Hollywood," Angel said. "Stay close to me and watch. Be ready to follow orders but understand you probably won't be asked to do anything difficult."

"Are they shooting real or holo today?" Jennifer asked.

"You've been around production?" Angel said.

"My mom is in the business."

Virtual Actors had been a part of Hollywood for fifteen years. When the studios cast the first virtual, the Screen Actors Guild demanded that a human actor receive pay as a cast member. Now, the Screen Actors Guild Royalty Fund and the Holographic Actors Guild receive a sum. Also, the eyes of the virtual must be yellow. The Holographic Actors Guild was a misleading title because it had been formed to protect human actors living and dead. The studios also conceded that only one-third of the cast would ever be virtual.

steveLearn technology advanced so far that the studio recorded many scenes on a virtual set using HTVR technology where the human actors holographed into a virtual environment.

"Today they are shooting a composite of real and virtual in the precinct," Angel said.

Jennifer watched several takes of a scene involving the human and virtual detective partners.

The assistant director shouted, "Take ten. Set up the lights for the next scene."

"Hey, Intern Girl, we need you over here," a voice said.

Jennifer looked around, *Duh, that's me.* She realized that the voice belonged to the Best Girl, the electrician in charge of all the lights.

"Your first day? What's your name?" she said.

"I'm Jen. How may I help?"

"Bill Kowalewski is my boss, the Gaffer. He needs a lighting model. Remember, don't touch or move any of the props." She pointed.

Jennifer carefully walked up on set, avoiding the many cables on the floor. "Bill, I'm your lighting model."

"Good, what's your name, Newbie?"

"Jennifer Gallagher. Call me Jen."

"Do you know what a gaffer does?"

"Yes, my grandfather, with three greats, got into the business as a gaffer."

"GGG?" Bill asked.

"That's the one."

"Do you remember how Mia was sitting in the last scene? Sit like that with your left hand on the desk but please don't touch or move the props. We'll reposition lights and camera," Bill said.

"Got it. Like this?"

"Look just to the right of the camera." He pointed at the new camera position. "Perfect, Jen. Don't move. You can breathe. But, don't move."

Ten minutes later, "You're free. Good job, Jen. You look terrific on camera. Have you acted?"

"I want to stay behind the camera. That's where I can contribute the most."

"That may be difficult with your looks and personality. The camera chooses its friends well," Bill said.

She watched several more takes with the new setup when Angel came over, "Jen, they need you to run some drinks over to trailers on the *Brilliant* set. Go to the Craft Services office and report to Amelia. Can you find it?"

"Yeah, I got it." She memorized the map earlier.

She entered Craft Services, "I'm the PA, and I'm looking for Amelia to run some drinks out to the trailers."

"Amelia, the intern is here," The receptionist pointed. "See her with the green t-shirt?"

Jennifer nodded. Amelia was a curvy thirty-something Latina with dark-rimmed glasses and skinny jeans.

Jennifer introduced herself, "Amelia, I'm Jen. I was sent to run drinks."

Amelia handed her a printed sheet, "The trailers on Sound Stage One need to be restocked. Don't lose this sheet and come with me."

While they walked to the walk-in refrigerator, Jennifer read through the list, analyzed and memorized it, and then folded it and put it in her jeans pocket.

"Get that cart and put on a jacket." It was about forty degrees in the walk-in. They got to the drinks, "Where is the list?"

"It's in my pocket. I read it and memorized it."

"No one can do that."

"Try me."

"What is line three?"

"Trailer Five. Two six-packs of Diet Cola. Granola Bars. Six apples," Jennifer recited.

"Okay, smart girl. Load up the cart and run it out to the lot." Jennifer walked through and loaded the cart.

"Don't forget to ask if you get lost. It is better to ask something stupid than to do something stupid. Can you handle this, Jen?" Amelia asked.

"Yes."

"This should take you to quitting time. When you finish, message your PA, and then take off for the day. No mistakes, right?"

"No mistakes."

JENNIFER ENVISIONED THE MAP OF TOVAR STUDIOS AND THE LIST. SHE rearranged the cart in the correct order. It was 4:10 p.m. when Jennifer got to Trailer Two on the *Brilliant* set, her final stop. She was ahead of schedule.

She walked up the steps to the door carrying two six-packs of soda. The door opened, and a surprised voice said, "Oh, I'm sorry."

Jennifer fell backward on her butt but held onto the sodas.

"Good catch. Are you ok?" She saw two legs. "Let me take those." Then she looked up and saw two incredible blue eyes.

"Um, Uh, I got it."

"Let me hold the door, then," the eyes said.

"Thanks." She got up and stood face-to-face with the nineteen-year-old actor whose poster was on her ceiling.

"I'm David," he said as Jennifer loaded his fridge.

"I know. Oh. I mean… I'm Jennifer Gallagher, but I go by Jen." *But you can call me anything you want.*

"What else do you have on your cart? May I help you?"

"Are you sure? Fruit, granola, and something called no-bake cookies. Let me hand them up. You're my last stop, and then I need to take the cart back."

"I fell in love with no-bakes growing up. My mom makes them at home. I have the studio order them from the Midwest for my trailer. All loaded," he said.

She looked up at those fantastic eyes again. "It was nice meeting you, David. Is there anything else you need?"

"Do you have a few minutes?"

Or, maybe the rest of my life. "Sure."

"Can you come up and help me run lines?" David said. "I have some long dialog tomorrow, and I need to memorize it."

"Sure. I'm done for the day. I can run the cart back after."

"Here is a pad with the sides. Sides are the pages of the script that we'll be shooting tomorrow," David said. "Would you like a soda?"

"Diet." While he reached into the fridge and grabbed a soda, he also grabbed a couple of cookies. "Here, try one of these. They're pure peanut butter heaven."

She read the sides and handed the pad back to David.

He said, "You'll need that. I have one of my own."

"No, I've got it. I have this eidetic memory thing. I can read something and remember it perfectly."

"Like Navvy," David said.

"You mean Mr. Kelrithian?"

"Yeah, he's like my uncle. I thought he was the only one who could do that."

"I'm his biggest fan. My greatest dream is to have his job someday. I'm a writer and a student filmmaker. Someday, I want to write and produce a major film. I studied Gene Roddenberry, George Lucas, and Navvy Kelrithian."

"Always good to start at the bottom," David said. "You said you're a writer? Have you done anything serious?"

"A bit. My pen name is Jenna Seldon."

"Seriously, as in *Galaxy Warriors*' Jenna Seldon?"

She nodded.

"I love those books," David said.

Jennifer took a bite out of the no-bake. "Omigod, this is delish."

"Wow, we have something in common."

"Duh, who couldn't love these? We need to run your lines so that you can be ready for tomorrow."

They read parts of the script. Jennifer helped with memorization tips. An hour later David said, "I'm exhausted, but I think I've got it."

"You do, but you need to read through once more in the morning. A steveLearn would help you a lot."

"What's that?"

"It's the same tech as the virtual actors, but steveLearn helps you learn academic subjects. I've used steveLearn since before kindergarten."

"Does it help?"

"I'm taking math and literature at the college graduate level."

"Are you human?"

"Seriously, you just saw me on my butt," Jennifer said. "I have to get this cart back and get home."

"Let me walk with you."

"I can manage."

"I'd like to."

"Lead on, McDuff," Jennifer said.

"Okay, the dust on your behind says you are part human. What do you do for fun?"

"My best friend Tayla and I play tennis. We practice singles, but we compete in doubles."

"I love tennis. We need to play. What else?"

"I play games on steveLearn. My fave is the *StarCruiser Brilliant Bridge Simulator*," Jennifer said.

"That's the system where I practice. That's steveLearn?"

Jennifer nodded.

"Wait, you aren't a Brillian, are you?"

"Moi, an overly obsessed fangirl? I wouldn't label myself that." Jennifer turned a bit red.

"Would anyone else?"

"Maybe my mom, my best friend Tayla, my grandparents. Me? Never."

"Nerd!"

"Spaceboy847." She grinned at him.

"Wait, you know that's me?"

"It was a guess."

"Are you…Jendroid?"

She nodded again.

"You're right behind me on the weapons high score list."

"Nay, Nay, Spaceboy," she said. "I passed you last Saturday night."

"That's impressive."

"So, what's your dream, David?"

"I love acting in films, but I need to go to acting school. As the son of a starship captain, I want to play something other than the son of a starship captain."

"This movie wraps in six weeks. UVN has a great acting school, and they cater to working actors."

"That's a good idea. Maybe after that, I can play Logan Jones in *Galaxy Warrior*. I know the writer. Always good to start at the bottom."

Jennifer laughed and said, "We're here." Jennifer inhaled and took one more look at those eyes. David looked at Jennifer.

"Jennifer, I had to wait an extra hour for that cart," Amelia said as she came out of the Craft Services office. "Did you have any trouble with the deliveries?" She saw David. "Oh, Mr. Masing, is everything alright?"

The moment passed. "Miss Gallagher was kind enough to run lines with me. I was accompanying her back here."

"Thank you for your assistance. I'm sure you can get back to what you're doing now," Amelia said. "Jen, bring the cart in and let Mr. Masing get on his way."

Jennifer said, "Mr. Masing, I hope that I can be of assistance to you in the future."

"You were a great help today, Miss Gallagher," David said. "I'll see you around the lot."

They shook hands and parted. Jennifer got one last glance at those eyes.

When they got the cart put away, Alicia said, "Jen, it is frowned upon for PA's to have a relationship with above-the-line personnel. That includes writers, directors, producers, and cast."

"Yes, ma'am."

"That said, did you see those eyes?"

"I hadn't noticed, ma'am."

"Go home, Jen. Interns don't get overtime."

"Thanks, Amelia."

JENNIFER SET HER PRIUS TO AUTODRIVE HOME AND CALLED TAYLA.

Tayla appeared on the windshield display, "Hello, filmmaker. How was your first day?"

"Just regular first-day stuff. Paperwork, training, lighting model on a set, running lines with David."

"You saw David?" Tayla's speech accelerated. "Give me all the deets. Send me the selfie you took with him."

"No selfie. How unprofessional would that be?" Jennifer said. "I'll get one next time. He wants to be a serious actor."

"How did you meet?"

"I was delivering sodas to his trailer. He opened the door and knocked me on my butt."

Tayla laughed, "What was your second most embarrassing moment today?"

"He helped me unload, asked me to help him run lines, and reminded me that he had seen me on my butt. We had a couple of moments."

"Did you discuss baby names?" asked Tayla.

"No, but he wants to be Logan Jones in *Galaxy Warrior*."

"Hopefully tomorrow can be a little less boring."

"It's a job. I'm home now; gotta go, Tay."

"Say hi to Dandy Lion."

Will he say hi back, Jennifer thought.

"Poor Pugsley. He probably got beaten up today."

Her mom greeted her. "How did the first day go?"

"David Masing knocked me on my butt."

"It always good to start at the bottom."

"That's what he said."

"Any good moments?"

"David wants the Logan Jones role in *Galaxy Warriors*."

"May I represent you in the contract negotiations?"

"I told him to go to acting school first."

"It's always good to be picky when hiring movie stars."

"He asked me to run lines with him and we sort of connected."

"I don't doubt that you connected. Did David?"

"He remembered my name."

"Always good to start at the bottom."

"I'm going to feed Dandy and Pugs."

. . .

JENNIFER WENT TO HER ROOM. DANDY JUMPED INTO HER ARMS, AND Pugsley sat at her feet demanding attention.

"Dandy, did you and Pugs get along today?" Jennifer asked. She looked at Dandy Lion. "Did you just roll your eyes?"

She played with Dandy and Pugs, fed them, and then sat down to write some pages in her next novel. Jennifer had 150 pages remaining to a draft that was due in eight weeks. Challenging but doable.

SEVEN

SuperNerd

On her way to work, Sami messaged her. "What's up, Sami?"
"Report to Grayson in the Information Technology Office
before you report to Sound Stage Three," Sami said.

"Got it,"

She entered the IT office. "I'm Jennifer, the new intern?"

"Grayson is right over there." The help desk attendant pointed.

"You're Jennifer?" Grayson said.

"Yes, call me Jen."

"Your résumé says that you speak steveLearn," Grayson said.

"Yes, I do. I knew Alexandra Waring, one of the developers."

"Good." He lifted a pad with the steveLearn logo on it.

"That's the new HoloPad, right?"

"Correct. Looks like we made the right choice. We would like for
you to familiarize yourself with this device and then train others on
the lot."

"I can do that," Jennifer said. "but I really wanna see the demo
thing?"

"Um… oh, I know what you mean. Show 'Leia's Message.'"

Above the HoloPad, a twelve-inch tall girl popped up. With black
hair and a white robe, she said, "Help me, Obi-Wan Kenobi, you're
my only hope."

"Aren't you too young to be a *Star Wars* fan?"

"Any self-respecting Brillian has seen all of the *Star Wars* movies," Jennifer said.

"How would you suggest we train new users to use the HoloPad?"

"With the steveLearn, there is already a configuration assistant. Just show newbies how to turn it on and how to wear it," Jennifer suggested. "I see you attach it to your belt. The HoloBuddy comes up anytime you want."

"Would you like to spend the rest of your internship with IT?"

"No, but if you send me with some Pads, I can train new users. They need me on Stage Three at ten a.m."

"Here is a list of five people in the production offices."

"May I have one more for an actor? David Masing? I think steveLearn might help him run his lines."

"That is an interesting idea. We hadn't planned on giving HoloPads to the actors. Would you help us configure the device as a rehearsal tool?"

"I can do that. As long as I get to my crew calls."

She messaged David. "Message me when you're in your trailer."

She visited the five new HoloPad users, set them up pretty quickly, and answered their questions by 9:15 a.m. She called up her HoloBuddy and discovered that David was in his trailer.

On her walk over, she reconfigured her own HoloPad. "Login System UVN Jenna Seldon. Assign Samantha as HoloBuddy on this unit."

Samantha popped up beside her in 3D. "Hi, Jen."

"Sami, do you have access to Tovar scripts, actors, and characters through this HoloPad?"

Sami thought a moment, "Yes, I do."

"How about daily sides and script pages for individual actors?"

"I can set that up."

"Do you understand the idea of an actor running lines of dialog for rehearsal and memorization?" Jennifer asked.

"Yes, Jenna. I like this HoloPad environment and the Tovar back office system. It's a very spacious environment."

"Create an app called "Rehearsal."" Animate the avatar of the other actor so they can practice their lines. Got it? And use the memorization tutorial we created."

"Got it. Ready in two minutes."

"Jen, are you going to create more studio apps?"

"Yes," Jennifer said.

"There is a possibility of marketing and sales for these apps outside of Tovar."

"Good idea. Thank you, Sami."

"Sure, Sis."

JENNIFER KNOCKED ON DAVID'S TRAILER DOOR AND STEPPED BACK A safe distance.

"You were ready this time. It's nice to see you."

"Remember the steveLearn thing I told you about? These HoloPads just came in. They have the steveLearn software on them."

"HoloPad?"

"HoloBuddy, display first movie hologram."

Princess Leia popped up, "Help me Obi-Wan Kenobi…"

"Woah, that's cool. Is that from an old movie?"

"You've never seen *Star Wars*?"

"All I know is that there was a spaceship in the desert in one of the movies. My dad told me about that."

"You need to put those movies in the category of professional research," Jennifer said.

"You said the HoloPad could help me run lines."

"First let's personalize it. Instead of the generic HoloBuddy, you can program an avatar of your choosing. Just say 'Login your name.' Assign the name of your avatar to the HoloBuddy on this unit."

"Can I pick the smartest person I know?"

"Sure. Press the screen this time, and it will remember your voice after this."

He pressed the screen. "Login David Masing. Assign Jenna Seldon to the HoloBuddy on this unit."

Sami popped up on Jen's HoloPad. "I'm monitoring. Do you grant permission, Jen?"

"Is this creepy or what? Yes, Sami, I grant permission."

"Hello, David. Hello, Jennifer. You look familiar." the avatar said.

"Ya think."

"David, Jen has set up a rehearsal program for Tovar actors. Would you like to access that?"

"In a few minutes, Jenna. Logoff."

"Spooky. Jen, would you like to play tennis on Saturday? Riley McMaster and I like to play. Maybe you could get your friend Tayla. We could play mixed doubles?"

"He's the *Brilliant* Engineer?" Jennifer said.

David nodded.

"Sure, let me message Tayla. What time?"

"Ten a.m."

Jennifer said, "Sami, message Tayla. Ask her if she can play some doubles at ten on Saturday."

"Where do you usually play? The courts on the lot are ok, but...."

"I'll get a court at the Calabasas Club. It's public, but it has a stunning mountain background."

"Can we get a quiet court? I usually draw a crowd."

"Sami, message the director at the club. Ask him for a private court for ten am on Saturday. Tell him I'm bringing some Tovar celebs."

Sami said, "Tayla replied 'Yes, who are we playing?'"

"Tell her I'll get back to her. David, I have a crew call in fifteen. I'll message you the info."

"Thanks for the toy. I'll practice my lines. Stop by again."

JENNIFER ARRIVED FIVE MINUTES EARLY FOR HER CREW CALL. "GOOD morning, Angel. How can I help?"

"They need you on set for lighting. Actors on set at 10:30."

She carefully navigated to the set. "Morning, Bill, where do you want me?"

"Morning, Jen. Same as yesterday. Sit in for Mia, but the camera is stage left."

She spotted the camera and then looked at the desk and noticed something else.

Bill set the lights using his handheld controller. "Thanks, Jen, you're free."

"Angel, there is a problem with the props. They do not match up with yesterday."

"Olivia is the script supervisor. She does continuity. She's rushed. Be careful."

Jennifer walked over to the script supervisor. "Excuse me, Olivia?"

"Yes."

"I'm Jen, the intern. I believe Mia's coffee cup turns the wrong way."

"I checked that specifically this morning," Olivia said.

"Ma'am, the actor is left-handed."

"You're right. Let me look at the photos."

"Wow, Good catch. You have a great visual memory. What's your name again?"

"I'm Jennifer Gallagher."

"What are your duties?"

"Probably just a runner. It's only my second day."

"Let's try this. I'd like for you to take notes on dialog changes, prop moves, timing, and any problems you see. You'll be my backup."

"I can handle that. Would you like me to send you notes at lunch and end of day?"

"That's fine. Let your PA know you're assisting me."

"Thanks for the opportunity."

"Good luck, this is an important job."

Olivia called the Prop Master over and instructed him to correct the direction of the cup.

"Sami, do you know what a script supervisor does?"

"Yes," Sami said.

"I'd like you to record audio and video, keep times and script notes, and build a continuity log sheet. Label this program "Script Assistant." Communicate through my earbuds only."

"Tell me when to start recording."

"Listen for the assistant director cues. I'll keep notes from memory, and we can compile during breaks."

"Ok, Sis."

OLIVIA HAD AN OLDER PAD IN HER HAND CONTINUALLY TAKING NOTES, but she noticed that Jennifer never touched her HoloPad to take notes on what she saw. After the last shot, she called Jennifer over. "Miss Gallagher, I assigned you a task. I hoped that you might be able to help out. You didn't understand how serious this job was. I never saw you take notes one time. You're released back to your PA."

"Ma'am, if you'll check your inbox, I sent you notes during each break and at lunch. I will send you a final set in a few minutes," Jennifer said. "I have an eidetic memory, so I don't need to write things down. Take a look at my notes and see if they're right."

Olivia walked off, and Jennifer walked over to a table and reviewed her notes.

Fifteen minutes later Olivia returned and sat down next to Jennifer. She handed her a diet soda and a cookie. "Your notes are the most complete and detailed I've seen in this business. I'm impressed, and I truly apologize for snapping at you earlier."

"Thank you, Olivia," Jennifer replied.

"Explain this memory thing of yours."

"It's like I record images, sounds, and smells constantly. I can play them back. I can also recall them like data and build apps like computer simulations."

"That sounds like a blessing and a curse. But, aren't you using some tech, too?"

"I cheated a bit. I just got this new HoloPad with steveLearn on it. My HoloBuddy, Sami, records the audio, video, data, and time cues and helps me build the continuity log."

"Can I get something like that?"

"Let me stop by IT in the morning."

"Crew call is at nine a.m. Good job today."

. . .

JENNIFER SET HER PRIUS TO AUTODRIVE. SHE HAD A RETURN message from the Calabasas Club that their court was reserved. She called Tayla.

When she appeared, "So, who are we playing on Saturday?"

"A couple of guys from Tovar."

"Is one of them, perchance, named David?"

"Let me check my calendar… Yes, that's correct."

"Omigod. Who're you dragging along as table scraps for me?"

"Riley McMaster"

"The dreamy black guy David runs with? You're the best BFF ever!"

"It's just tennis, Tay."

"Seriously, Jen, tennis is life."

"Life is *Brilliant*. Ten o'clock at Calabasas. I'll pick you up a half hour before."

"I know what I'm dreaming about tonight."

"Mom is cooking tonight. That'll probably be what I dream about."

ON THE THIRD DAY OF HER SUMMER INTERNSHIP, JENNIFER Gallagher visited Grayson in IT before her crew call at Sound Stage Three.

"Good Morning, Grayson. Yesterday I created two apps for steveLearn on the HoloPad. Rehearsal helps the actors run lines and Script Assistant sets up a continuity log for the Script Supervisor."

"I heard about it. All of the actors want HoloPads now," Grayson said.

"Increased productivity, right? May I have one to take to the Script Supervisor I'm working with?"

"Yes. Ellen is your director, correct?" Jennifer nodded.

"Could you possibly create an app where above-the-line people, producers, directors, actors, and screenwriters, could view and make notes on daily rushes?"

"Got it. So, do you have seven extra HoloPads for my Stage? And a cart?" Jennifer asked.

Grayson pointed to a cart. "Use this one," Grayson spoke to his HoloBuddy. "Help me get the hardware." They loaded the equipment.

"Thanks, Grayson." She took a seat on the cart and said, "AutoCart, take me to Sound Stage Three." She heard the acknowledgment, and the cart began moving.

"Good Morning, Sami," Jennifer said. "Look up the term Daily Rushes and tell me when you're ready to data mine the dailies and scripts at Tovar Studios."

There was a pause. "Got it, Boss."

"I'd like to set up an app called Daily Rushes for producers, directors, actors, and screenwriters. How soon does the Director of Photography release the rushes?"

Sami responded, "The DP and the Director review the proofs immediately and release them to print and then the others have access."

"Great, set it up so that the people I listed can review their rushes as soon as the Director and DP release them. Map them to the script, including any differences from the sides. And create a tutorial."

Another pause, "Daily Rushes App created, and all current users notified through their HoloBuddy."

Jennifer looked around as she rode to her set. She noticed people focused on their HoloBuddy instead of where they were going. "Sami, are folks using their HoloPads while driving or walking?"

"Yes, they are. The Tovar data indicates that there have been five close calls in the last two days, and one involved lots of coffee."

"Sami, build an app called Tovar Safety Buddy. What is the motion sensor radius?"

"I'm able to sense fast moving objects like AutoCarts and faster at five hundred feet. I'm able to track slow and stationary objects out to one hundred feet. I see where you're going with this. That includes 360 degrees horizontally at user height plus ten degrees and a forty-five-degree cone for objects directly above the user."

"Implement the app in the background immediately. Alert or divert users while walking or standing. Implement an augmented reality display to alert users of nearby objects moving or stationary. Long-term, data mine the safety records for Tovar and any other public records for industrial safety on film lots and update the app to assist anyone carrying a HoloPad."

"The Safety Buddy is now implemented at a rudimentary level on all Tovar HoloPads. Give me an hour for the industry safety research."

"Alert Grayson. He might want to run it by the Industrial Safety office."

"Boss, there is one more thing you need to consider. You created some valuable intellectual property. You might want to look at the possibility of marketing our apps outside of Tovar."

"You're right, Sami. I probably need to bring Mom into this. Keep me posted on the progress of the Tovar Safety Buddy."

JENNIFER GOT HOME RIGHT BEFORE HER MOTHER.

"Mom, I need a lawyer. Can I ask you to represent me on a legal issue?"

"Somebody is suing you on your third day?"

"No, I created some apps on the new HoloPads at the studio, and Sami suggested that I try to make some money off of them. They'll increase productivity and improve employee safety. Sami thinks they might be marketable. I sent you my intern contract." Jennifer described the four apps that she created.

"Yes, there is a clause that the studio owns your work product, but it says that if you create content beyond your ancillary duties, the company may ask for a maximum royalty of twenty percent. Did your supervisor ask you to create this intellectual property?" Sheila said.

"Script Assistant helped me do my job. I created others to help employees use their HoloPads and to promote safety. But not at anyone's request," Jennifer said.

"You're right, the Script Assistant falls into a grey area, but the others should be straightforward."

"What's your advice?"

"I know an attorney at Tovar who handles intellectual property. I'll try to get an addendum to your contract granting Tovar an unlimited license to the IP you create and twenty percent of the royalties you receive outside of Tovar. That should cover any of the apps that you might create this summer."

"Do you think that what I described is worth anything?"

"I do. Especially the Safety Buddy. That can be marketed widely in the entertainment industry and adapted for any other industrial app. It might even become a consumer app."

"Is it enough to pay for dinner?"

"As soon as I agree with Tovar, I can see GGG offering you a contract in the high six figures."

"Ooh, nice dinner."

"Did you use Sami and your shared computing resources at UVN?" Sheila asked.

"Yes, I did."

"When we set up the student-study agreement with UVN, they assumed that you would use their hardware and software for creative endeavors. They requested that you assign ten percent of your royalties to UVN in the form of a donor contribution to the university. In exchange, they provide all of the online classes and tutors that you request and shared computing space for Sami and your other projects."

"Lab Rat One?"

"Yes, they deferred to you on your name for the project."

"Have we sent them royalties before?"

"Yes, we have. I assigned the school ten percent of your royalties from the *Galaxy Warrior* series. They have been very grateful for the two-hundred, twenty-thousand dollars that you sent them so far."

"Wow, how much money is in my bank account?!"

"A little over a million. Taxes are rather bothersome."

"Okay, continue the assignment of ten percent to the University."

SHEILA, JENNIFER AND HER STEP-DAD, ALLEN, WENT TO A celebratory dinner that evening. Jennifer shared her successes at Tovar.

Jennifer ended her first week when the episode of *Virtual Detective* wrapped. "Jennifer, I'm releasing you today," Olivia said. "You helped immensely and gave me some good tools to build on. Harper Jennings has requested for you to be her script assistant starting Monday on Sound Stage One."

Jennifer's eyes sparkled, "*Brilliant?*"

"Yeah, you get your dream job. Brilliant is starting the second week of interiors."

"Thank you so much, Olivia."

"You earned this one. Check in with Harper before you leave today. And, she wants a HoloPad with your Script Assistant so it might help if you came bearing gifts."

"I'll head right over to IT. Thanks for everything."

Jennifer entered Grayson's office. "The safety people are afraid that you're putting them out of business," Grayson said. "They want you to present an overview Monday morning. You've created a great demand on the lot for the HoloPads. The new toys are changing how we use technology."

She got to Sound Stage One as they were breaking for the weekend. She walked up behind a man with grey hair. "Sir, can you point me toward Harper Jennings?"

He turned and said, "Beatles shirt. Over there," He pointed. "And who are you?" Jennifer realized that she was talking to *the* Navvy Kelrithian.

"I'm Jennifer Gallagher."

Jennifer hesitated when she saw Navvy, then said, "I'm sorry to bother you, Mr. Kelrithian. I'll be interning on *Brilliant* with Ms. Jennings as her script assistant."

Navvy paused and sized up the sixteen-year-old. "You're the one who has been shaking things up at Tovar."

"I didn't mean to create problems."

"Keep shaking, young lady," Navvy said. "This industry runs on new blood, and you're saving me a lot of money,"

"Thank you, Sir. I'm a fan. I've read all twelve volumes of the *Brilliant* Tech Manual."

"So, you're the one. That's a difficult read. Welcome to *Brilliant*.

Keep in mind that you're now working with the best in the business. Good luck and I'll see you Monday."

They shook hands. Navvy headed back to his office and Jennifer walked over to Harper Jennings. "Ms. Jennings, my name is Jennifer Gallagher. I'm assigned to you as your Script Assistant next week. Call me Jen."

"I'm Harper. I hear that you're pretty good with your magical pad and your Jedi mind tricks," Harper said.

"No magic; no tricks. Here is your HoloPad. I already set up your Script Assistant app. Just log in with your name."

"Thanks, Jen. I heard that you're good with wrangling information and mining data. Right now, this shoot is ten percent over budget, and we need to streamline the production. You'll work with me and the Assistant Director, Brooklyn Nascimento, to direct traffic, update crew with current information, prevent duplication of effort, and keep the mistakes in check. If you see a possible fix, tell us, and we'll direct you to the person responsible."

"I'm just an intern. Are you sure you want me to have this responsibility?" Jennifer asked.

"This task is essential but not mission critical. You have shown you have a mastery of technology and data and you can think on your feet. Are you up to this challenge?" Harper asked.

"I need access to the data. I need scripts, schedules, financials, and logs."

Harper typed on an old App on her new HoloPad. "Jen, you have access."

"I guess I have a busy weekend."

"Yes, you do. And be careful with our young star on the tennis courts. Have a nice weekend."

Jennifer's eyes got huge. "News travels fast."

"But not far. Tovar is a small place. Welcome to *Brilliant*."

"Thanks, I'll get started right away."

JENNIFER WALKED TOWARD HER CAR. "SAMI?"

"I'm gathering data. I have a script, financials, schedules, and logs. I found something that may be slowing things down. The virtual actors and virtual sets are very slow and sluggish because they are sharing the system on the back lot with all the other Sound Stages. HumanAI recommends a HoloTurbo accelerator for locations that use HoloTech intensively."

"Can you run the numbers?"

"I've already done that. The cost for the three virtual stages and one edit suite totals $198,000. It'll pay for itself in about forty shooting days, speed up productions, and optimize post-production. HumanAI can install the hardware this weekend."

"I have to go to Mr. Kelrithian. Send me the details and contact Harper."

Jennifer sat in her car to make the call. Harper answered. "Harper, I found a solution that'll save $5000 per day on the entire lot. I need to get in to see Mr. Kelrithian before five p.m. The front-end cost is almost $200K. It'll speed up shooting and help in post-production."

"We just talked thirty minutes ago. Can't this wait until Monday?"

"They can only install on weekends. Otherwise, it slows the whole system down for a couple of days."

"Okay, I'll give Kathy Sakai a heads up that you're coming. Good luck," Harper said.

"Sami, I guess we're going to get home a little late." Jennifer walked toward the executive suites. "Set up a holographic presentation with the numbers and send his assistant the proposal and the funding request."

A pause from Sami "Ready for your review." Jennifer looked over the presentation. "Send it." She entered the executive suites at 3:15 p.m.

"Ms. Sakai, I'm Jennifer Gallagher. Did Harper Jennings tell you I was coming?"

"She did. Mr. Kelrithian is on a conference call."

Jennifer felt uncomfortable as the secretary looked her over.

Kathy thought, *She looks just like Anthen.* "Jennifer, your technology ideas are causing many changes at Tovar."

A tone sounded on her display, and she responded, "Navvy, Harper sent Jennifer Gallagher over. She has a critical proposal, a price tag, and a deadline. You have fifteen minutes before you need to leave for the premiere tonight."

"Send her in."

"Mr. Kelrithian will see you."

Jennifer went into the office. "We meet again. Kathy says it's important. I know that Harper ran something by me this afternoon about having you use tech and data to streamline production. Have you come up with something?"

"Yes, Sir. Sit down here, and I'll show you a quick presentation." Jennifer set her pad on the desk as Navvy sat to watch. A holographic display appeared above the meeting desk.

"Is that the new toy that cost me a lot of money this week?"

Jennifer looked worried. "I believe the HoloPad is increasing productivity on the lot."

"Calm down. I love it. The safety office is crazy about it. They reported a seventy percent decrease in potential accidents and near-misses in just two days. Okay, make your pitch."

Jennifer made the presentation and answered questions. "Jen, can you tell me about reliability?"

"After you install it, the new equipment will run side-by-side with the old. If there is a fault, there'll be an immediate switchover to the old system. The switchover will be transparent and protect data, but it'll slow things down to what they are now."

"Sounds good. What do I need to do?" Navvy asked.

"Kathy has a funding authorization for your approval."

"Does this come with chips and salsa?"

"Sorry?"

"You had me at $5,000 a day in savings. Miss Gallagher, you're a very expensive intern. How much do you make?"

"Five-hundred dollars a week, sir."

"Call me…Navvy." He almost said, Grandpa. "I'll see if I can fix that. Can you bring me a HoloPad on Monday? And enough for the *Brilliant* crew?"

"I can do that," Jennifer said.

"Jen, I hear that you have a pretty good memory."

"Yes, sir. I have an eidetic memory. I remember everything, and I can visualize apps using my memory. I tell people it's my vision thing."

"You remember the bad things, too?"

"Yes, it hurts sometimes, but I deal with it," Jennifer said

I can relate to that, Navvy thought. "Jennifer, keep shaking."

"I'll do my best, Navvy."

As Jennifer left his office, something told Navvy that he had just been with someone who had to deal with the same mental gifts he had. He felt sorry for the fact that she also had to deal with the curse as well.

"Kathy, did you receive the funding request from Jennifer?"

"Yes, I did."

"Authorize that request. And, Kathy, on Monday could you look at the things that this girl has done? I don't think we are paying her enough."

"Yes, Sir. Enjoy the premiere."

Jennifer got home after meeting with Navvy. It was the weekend and tomorrow there was tennis with David. Her mother arrived home ahead of her, and they met in the kitchen.

"Hi, Jen. I have news. Tovar agreed to take twenty percent royalties for your apps. I'll have an offer sheet from GGG on Monday," Sheila said.

"Will I make enough to cover the dinner I paid for as your fees?" Jennifer said.

"I suspect so. GGG will offer two-hundred-thousand plus royalties for the marketable apps you create. As your representative, I also contacted HumanAI. They want to market any apps you create that apply to a wider audience, and they want you to represent the company as an Apps Guru for the education and the entertainment industries. In exchange, they'll allow you to use their massive computing power to code and develop," Sheila said.

"How much time will that take?"

"Four events per year, including keynoting their developer conference. Two-fifty K, plus royalties."

"Please tell me you're taking fifteen percent for yourself and Allen?"

"How about we set that aside in a family vacation account? That way, you can pay for family fun."

"That works. I have news, too. I'm working on *Brilliant* now. I'm assistant to the Script Supervisor and AD. They want me to streamline production using tech and help with budget issues."

"You promised." Sheila's lips pressed together.

"I'll be careful," Jennifer said. "Also, I met with Navvy Kelrithian. I talked him into spending $200K to speed up the hardware."

"Executives love spending money."

"I convinced him that it would pay for itself in forty shooting days."

"Did you discuss anything else?"

"He asked me about the vision thing. He seemed to know more about it than most people. He asked if I remember the bad things, too. Do you think he might have a memory like mine?"

"That's possible, but still very rare. Remember our agreement: be careful. What's going on this weekend?"

"Tayla and I are playing tennis tomorrow with David and another cast member. Just an average weekend."

"Until you fall on your butt."

"Eww, mom."

SHEILA REMEMBERED HOW ANTHEN FELL UNDER THE SPELL OF *Brilliant* from the very beginning. She knew that show business is a jealous and dangerous mistress. *This is what I feared all along,* she thought. *I hope I am not losing my daughter.*

JENNIFER WENT TO HER ROOM AND PLAYED WITH DANDY AND PUGSLEY. "Pugsley, I met with my boss's boss, and he talked about a pay raise," Jennifer said.

Pugsley was all wrinkles and tongue, but behind that was a blank look.

"Dandy, what do you think?"

Dandy reclined on the bed. He stood up, walked over next to Jennifer and looked her straight in the eye. *You better watch what you wish for. Sometimes you get it,* Dandy thought. *Be careful.*

Jennifer did a double-take as she realized what the prescient cat was thinking. Then she nodded. "You're right, Dandy."

Jennifer remembered Navvy's words, *You remember the bad things, too?* Jennifer thought over the news story of her father's disappearance and her mother's warnings about the dangers of *Brilliant.* She remembered each time growing up when she wished her father was there, but he wasn't.

As always, when she became overwhelmed with her memories, she replayed scenes from *StarCruiser Brilliant,* when the ship was flying through outer space, when Jennifer would be the one flying on *Brilliant,* and when she would ring the bell.

EIGHT

Saturday with David

J ennifer and Tayla arrived at the Calabasas Tennis Center at 9:45 and discovered their opponents at their car, surrounded by tweens seeking selfies and autographs. The two girls approached to a respectful distance and waited until David and Riley signed and posed to the satisfaction of their fans.

"You two look like you enjoy the fan love. Meet my friend Tayla."

They shook hands and began their walk to their private court. "The studio encourages us to reach out to fans whenever we can. It's good marketing," Riley said.

"It probably doesn't hurt that they're cute thirteen-year-olds," Tayla said.

"Or even klutzy summer interns," David said with a smile. That drew a fist to the arm from Jennifer. "Watch out; you'll break my backhand," he said.

"You don't have a backhand to break, partner," Riley said. "Would you two like to play mixed? I held the state singles title back in New Mexico, and it might be fairer that way."

"I'll call your state singles with my SoCal Singles title and raise you our SoCal doubles title," Tayla said.

"Wow, am I the total newb? I didn't know I was getting into it with a bunch of total tennis nerds," David said.

"We'll take it easy on you two. Loser buys lunch," Jennifer said.

As the club director promised, they found a secluded hardcourt surrounded by shade trees and windscreens. Coached by Riley, David was a good tennis player. Riley had the most serve velocity, but Tayla had power plus more accuracy. Jennifer was an accomplished player and held her own. They traded games, and each pair held serve to 4-4. David's second serve at 15-30 was short, and Tayla charged. She hit the return into Riley's body, but he was able to react and volley right back to Tayla at the net. They traded four volleys until Tayla forced Riley to chase a forehand.

They're both in The Zone, Jennifer thought.

Riley returned the forehand into Tayla's backhand. She turned and took a two-hand volley into the alley for the winner. David served at 15-40, Jennifer saw Riley ready to poach, and she hit an easy passing shot to the empty court. Tayla served out the set.

During the switchover, the club director approached. "Ladies and gentlemen, we're hosting a Junior Girls tennis clinic today. Would you four be willing to play a set on our stadium court and give the girls a treat?"

"Is that okay with you guys?" Jennifer asked.

"Let's go entertain the kids," David said.

At the stadium court, Riley said, "It's hot. Is there any rule against playing without our shirts?"

"It's okay if David doesn't have a farmer's tan." Jennifer looked at David.

They took the court to the sound of almost thirty screaming and giggling tweens.

Tayla looked at Riley and whispered to Jennifer, "I could get drunk on that six pack."

"I have been high on those blue eyes all week," Jennifer said.

The girls spent too much time concentrating on eyes and abs, and before a cheering gallery, the boys took the first three games. Conditioning wins out, though. Playing a tournament every weekend through the Spring left the girls in much better shape as Riley and David faded. Tayla went on a hot streak, and the girls won the next six games to close out the set and the match, 6-3. The girls in the gallery cheered after the match and David and

Riley spent another fifteen minutes providing autographs and selfies.

"Where are you going to take us for our victory lunch?" Jennifer asked.

"There's a pool at our family ranch in Malibu. Dad is grilling burgers and steaks. Would you two like to skip lunch and join us for dinner?"

Tayla whispered to Jen, "No way I'm dropping my sweaty self into a bikini in front of Riley."

"Can we shower and change here at the club and meet you there?"

"How about a swim, some games, food, and then whatever?"

Tayla whispered, "Can we skip all the other stuff and go straight to the 'whatever'?"

PREPARED FOR ANY WARDROBE EXIGENCIES, THE GIRLS SHOWERED AND then followed Kanan Road through the Santa Monica Mountains to the ranch of Jack and Ellie Masing. The high desert landscape covered several hundred acres. As they approached, Jen's HoloPad interfaced with the security system, and the gate opened. They rode up the hill to the main house. As a part of her family's business, Jennifer had seen such places. Tayla just kept repeating, "Omigod. Omigod. Omigod."

The girls enjoyed the view from the high ground. Behind them was Castro Peak. At 2,826 feet it overlooked the town of Malibu. Beyond Laguna Point lay the Pacific.

Jennifer knocked on the door, and the very elegant Ellie Masing answered. Ellie still had the Swedish looks of a movie star from when she was Jack Masing's love interest in the first *StarCruiser Brilliant* movie. The chemistry caught and two films later, they married. Ava was born first, and several years later, David. Notably, Jack and Ellie continued as successful actors in a successful marriage all while raising a family.

"You must be Jennifer," Ellie said in greeting. "I'm Ellie Masing, David's mother."

"Yes, and this is my friend, Tayla Mendoza. You have a beautiful home. It blends into the high desert."

Tayla said, "I cannot believe I'm meeting an actress with four statuettes from the Academy. Your house is incredible. It's an honor to meet you."

"Thank you. This property was once owned by a billionaire who lost all his money in internet consolidation. It has been our project to return it to nature."

Tayla again muttered, "Omigod."

"You'll have to excuse my best friend. This is her first Hollywood mansion," Jennifer explained.

"David," Ellie said, "why don't you give the girls the tour. Don't forget the swimming pool shaped like *Brilliant*."

"Really?" Jennifer exclaimed.

"She's just kidding," David said. "Yes, our house has some creature comforts, the twelve bedrooms are pretty spacious, we have a large screening room, an eight-car garage, and two tennis courts, but we call it home.

"Omigod. We could have played here."

"Riley and I didn't want to beat you, and have you blame us for having a home court advantage."

"How'd that plan work out for ya?" Jennifer teased.

The four tired tennis players walked through the house. They paused for a long look at the four statuettes that his mother won for two starring and two supporting roles.

"Here's the pool. There's a cabana to change into your suits right over there. Dad says that he'll have burgers and steaks at five."

The girls were wearing sundresses over their swimwear. They brought jeans and t-shirts for after. Just then Riley arrived already in his swimsuit with his towel. Tayla stared at the six-pack abs.

"We'll be right back," Jennifer took charge and led Tayla to the cabana. "Aren't you supposed to be the cool one?"

"This isn't my world, Jen, it's yours. I'm intimidated by the glam thing here."

"Today it's our world, so let's enjoy it," Jennifer said.

The two teens stepped out of the cabana and walked to the poolside where the two actors were standing on the edge gawking at the two bikini babes. Having planned the maneuver, Jennifer and Tay pretended to hug David and Riley and then pushed them into the pool and dove in to follow. From there, the two couples demonstrated that pool frolic was a contact sport.

After a half hour, the four took to the pool chairs and did their penance to the SoCal Sun. A Latina approached carrying a tray of drinks, "I have some aqua de fresca for you and your guests, David."

"The kind with strawberry?" David asked.

"Just the way you like it."

"Everyone, this is Margarita Lopez," David said. "She and her husband, Alejandro, have been with our family since before I was born. Their daughter, Candace, is a few years older than my sister, Ava."

Margarita said, "Mr. Masing will be cooking steaks so don't ruin your appetite with snacks."

"Why don't we change clothes and then go to the game room?" David said.

DRESSED IN JEANS AND T-SHIRTS, THEY WALKED INTO THE GAME ROOM, and Jennifer gasped, "Is that what I think it is?" There was an elaborate platform with three seats, and each had an instrumentation console surrounded by a three-hundred-and-sixty-degree display.

David smiled, "Welcome to *Brilliant*Sim One. It's a few years old, but it's up-to-date with all of the bridge controls of *StarCruiser Brilliant*. It has the latest software updates."

Tayla whispered to Riley, "Jennifer has left earth and is now walking around in heaven."

"Take the right seat, Jen," David said.

Jennifer gingerly stepped up to the platform and softly sat at the Ops/Weapons console. "Omigod, it's so real. Just like the Manual."

Riley asked Tayla, "She's read the Manual?"

Tayla said, "A few years ago we went to Hawaii for Christmas. She brought a pad loaded with all twelve manuals. I had to drag her to the beach."

NINE

The Asteroid Field

"I'll take the Pilot seat. Let's take *Brilliant* for a spin, Jendroid," David said.

"Yes, sir, Captain Spaceboy," Jennifer replied.

The two gamers took their places in the simulator and belted in.

"Are the controls familiar to you?" David asked.

"Yes, it's just like the one at home on steveLearn. But much more realistic."

"Recognize spaceboy847. Authorization: moviestar," David said.

"Welcome back to the *Brilliant*Sim, David Masing," Ani said. "Would you like to configure your position for Pilot or Commander?"

"The Artificial Navigation Interface on this simulator is connected directly to *Brilliant*," David said.

"Got it. I've read the Manual," Jennifer said.

"Just the two of us. Configure the left seat as Commander. Jen?"

"Recognize Jendroid, authorization Dandy Lion. Configure Navigation."

"Dandy Lion?" David asked.

"I'm pet sitting a cat this summer," Jennifer replied

"Welcome back to the *Brilliant*Sim, Jennifer. Would you like the intro on the controls as it is your first login at this simulator?"

"I'm good, Ani, let's saddle up."

. . .

Riley and Tayla watched as David and Jennifer became involved in the simulator to the exclusion of all other social interactions. "Tayla, are you familiar with the game of ping-pong? The Masings have a table over here."

"Is that the game with the wooden paddles?" Riley missed the twinkle in Tayla's eyes.

"I can help you learn the game if you have never played."

"That would be nice of you. I'm not sure about the rules," Tayla said as she led the overconfident bull to slaughter.

"Take us to the final frontier, David."

"Let's start with something easy. Load Sim Program 42."

"Ready to engage The Asteroid Field," Ani said.

David didn't see Jennifer smile. She thought of the many times that she had run this simulation before and gotten herself blown up.

"Engage," David said.

"Captain, *Brilliant is* in orbit around Jupiter," Jennifer said. "Our current mission is complete. Ready for return to Earth."

"Ani, lay in a course to Earth three degrees above the ecliptic to avoid asteroids."

"Course laid in to Earth at sixty degrees North Latitude."

"Engage. Let's head home," David said.

"Engaging gravity drive at point-three light-speed," Ani said. "Flight time two hours and twenty-seven minutes."

Jennifer reviewed the controls and displays that were slightly different than her steveLearn at home. "The *Brilliant*Sim feels so much more comfortable than the HTVR version. The sharp edges are worn off, and the seats are broken in. And the controls have a more rapid response. I feel so much more at home here. Ani, perform a long-range sensor scan of our route home."

"Sensor Alert. Detecting a spacecraft approaching Earth. Classification: Brilliant class, StarCruiser."

"How could that be?" David asked.

"I think it's a sensor anomaly caused by...."

"Sensor Alert: Unidentified object entering the system at point-five light speed."

"Focus sensors, classify, and identify."

"It is decelerating at one-hundred Gravities. Classify Hoclarth battle cruiser Camday class. Identification *Camdex*, third in the class."

"How is she armed?" Jennifer asked.

"Long-range fighter drones. Medium range meteor cannons. Close-in Particle Beams."

"We're way outgunned, but we're more maneuverable than the *Camdex*," Jennifer said. "If they detect us and release a fighter drone, though, we're toast."

"Point us toward the edge of the asteroid field and let's hope we fit into the clutter."

"Ani, plot a ballistic course one-hundred kilometers above the plane of the asteroids."

"Laid in."

"Engage," David said. "Raise shields. Configure TopGun Pilot interface."

"The fighter pilot?" Jennifer said.

"Dad and I watched the Tom Cruise movie several times, and then we built this interface," David said.

Jennifer followed protocol, "Ani, configure Weapons to the Ops Console. Captain, recommend we cloak as an asteroid."

"Do it. Let's make the *Camdex* think we're planetary space junk."

"One hundred kilometers above the asteroid plane," Ani said.

"We are cloaked," Jennifer said.

"Very well; let's hope he doesn't pick up the gravity drive distortion path."

"*Camdex* has reduced her velocity and is on a routine patrol course," Ani said.

"Engage passive sensors," Jennifer said. "Let us know if *Camdex* activates weapons sensors."

"*Camdex* is changing aspect ratio. Accelerating towards our gravity drive path," Ani said.

"Ops, plot a course into the asteroid field. Ani, give me stick-and-rudder control."

"Activate Artificial Weapons Interface," Jennifer said. "Owwie, display tactical. Reinforce forward shields. Plot a maneuvering course into the field at three kilometers per second. Target small asteroids in our path with particle beams. Ani, look at the big picture and keep us out of the crowded areas."

"Tactical on Display," Owwie said. "Order activate to begin targeting small asteroids. Chances of surviving fighter drone forty-two percent."

"Activate," David said. "Now, we wait to see if he picks up our trail."

"OKAY, SO YOU KICKED MY BUTT AT PING-PONG. HAVE YOU EVER played pool?" Riley said.

"You mean the game with the long sticks?" Tayla asked.

"Ouch, this isn't my day."

"SENSOR ALERT: *CAMDEX* HAS ACTIVATED WEAPONS SENSORS AND released a fighter drone."

David turned his head to Jennifer. "How long before we dive the field?"

"The fighter's in search mode," she said. "If he changes speed, he has us. The Hoclarth have patrolled this system for years. They have contour and track for most of the rocks. I'm hoping that the fighter drone thinks we are one of the usual suspects."

"Fighter has activated narrow scan targeting sensors and is accelerating," Ani said. "Survivability is now twelve percent."

"Engage maneuvering thrusters and activate weapons," David said. "Take us into the field."

Brilliant began accelerating as David flew her like an F-14 jet fighter. The tactical display became cluttered with numerous asteroids. Shields deflected the green rocks, particle beams took out the yellow targets, and red asteroids, designated by their catalog number, were over a kilometer in diameter and were to be avoided at all costs.

"Locate the Karin cluster from our current position."

"Karin cluster is two-point-three degrees ahead in the orbital path of the asteroids," Ani said. "We can safely reach it in four minutes."

"Sensor Alert: Fighter Drone has entered the asteroid field and is in pursuit. Intercept in three minutes."

David asked, "You want to take us into the most crowded part of this field?"

"All we have to do is avoid asteroids. The fighter has to avoid asteroids and find us. The enemy of my enemy is my friend. Course laid in."

"I hope this works. Engage."

I know it will, Jennifer thought.

"Fighter drone is matching our course and speed. Five minutes to intercept," Ani said.

"Time to the cluster?"

"Begin deceleration...." There was a pause. "...now. Slowing to point-four kilometers per second. Entry in seventy-eight seconds," Ani said.

"Well, Spaceboy, let's see if you can fly a Tomcat like Tom Cruise."

"Enter the cluster at two kilometers per second," David said.

"We need the bad guy to think that there are two of us. Ani, activate a cloaked holodrone on our port quarter."

"Holodrone cloaked and ready, left echelon, Jendroid."

"Warning: entering dense asteroid cluster. Exceeding maximum safe speed. Fighter drone in pursuit. Intercept in forty seconds. Survivability three percent."

David was now in full manual pilot mode avoiding the Reds.

"Target yellow 3 and release," Jennifer said. *Brilliant* shook, and three seconds later, yellow 3 was space dust."

"It's getting crowded here," David said.

"Owwie, target two, five, and seven. Release," Jennifer said. "David, fly through that hole straight towards red 725."

"Warning: Intercept in twenty seconds. Survivability one percent."

"Do we win a prize if it hits zero?" David said.

"Gallows humor? Fly toward 725 at a point below the center, maneuver over and behind, and freeze in the shadow."

"Owwie, when the fighter loses us, decloak the drone and fly it straight into 863."

"We'll be in the shadow in five seconds."

"Seven seconds to intercept. The drone is tracking us below 725," Owwie said. "Lost signal. Clone released. Its sensors say the fighter turned in pursuit."

"He took the bait!"

The fighter and the clone arrived at Karin 863 simultaneously, and the tactical display went white. When the debris cleared, Asteroid Karin 863 was in three pieces, the decoy had gone to HoloClone heaven, and the fighter drone from the *Camdex* was space dust.

"I'm hungry for steak. How are you going to get us out of the asteroid field?"

"You won't like it. We might put a dent in the sim."

"What's your idea?"

"Ani, what are the stats on this rock?"

"Asteroid Karin 725 is a twelve-million-ton M-Class sphere one-point-one kilometers in diameter."

Jennifer turned to her panel. "Calculate a StarDrive jump with a cardioid wave around the asteroid. Put *Brilliant* at the cusp and report."

"The maneuver is possible but not predictable," Ani said. "With the energy available, *Brilliant* could activate a point-seven second StarDrive burst that would raise our velocity to 1.2 light-speed. The time distortion is undetermined."

"What is the estimate?"

"The predicted median time distortion is negative two hours and twenty minutes."

David interrupted, "What are you talking about? You can't engage the StarDrive near a heavy body. It's unpredictable."

"Brilliant did it and survived."

"But it traveled 200 years into the past…"

"And landed Navvy and your Dad on Earth forty years ago and here we are. We are on a simulator in your basement. The worst that can happen is that the steaks may be overcooked."

"So, what's your plan?"

"We are going to hitch a ride on this rock and blast our way out of here."

"Do you think this can work?"

"I know it worked."

"No balls, no blue chips. Get us out of here."

Jennifer operated an air computer and satisfied herself with the answer. "Position *Brilliant* for the optimum course out of the field and lay in a course using a point-one-eight second StarDrive burst. Make sure 725 remains on a safe orbit."

"Course laid in. Activating on your order."

"I hope you know what you're doing, Jen. Ani, engage."

"Positioning *Brilliant*. Activating StarDrive in three-two-one...." The tactical display blurred, and the nearby asteroids became lasers passing by. Seven hundred twenty-five stayed right in the center of the display. "Burst complete. Leaving the asteroid field in five seconds." David and Jennifer could see explosions and collisions around the edge of the asteroid for a few moments more, then nothing. "*Brilliant is* clear of the asteroid field. Velocity point-four-five light-speed. Recommend a course to Earth."

"Engage course to Earth," David said. "Take us home."

"Ani, what is the time distortion?" Jennifer asked.

"We moved two hours and twenty-eight minutes into the past."

"Do a long-range sensor scan towards Jupiter."

"Detecting *StarCruiser Brilliant*."

David was surprised and impressed. "That's us at the beginning of the simulation?"

"Yes, David," Jennifer said.

"You knew what was going to happen?"

"Yes, David. It's that vision thing that I have."

"Are you human?" David asked.

"I hope so because I'm really, really hungry."

"But how did the simulator know...?"

"Captain on the Bridge," Ani announced as Jack Masing took the Center Seat.

"Dad," David said.

Jennifer reached around and shook hands. "Mr. Masing."

"It's nice to meet you, Jennifer," Jack said.

"I'm honored, Sir. I have been a fan all my life."

"I, too, have heard a lot about you. So, David took you for a ride in our *Brilliant*Sim?"

"Yes, Sir."

"He promised me an easy ride." She winked.

"David, what simulation did you use?"

"The Asteroid Field, Sir."

"That has never been survived."

"Jennifer got us out of it."

Jack looked at Jennifer in a new way. "It looks like you two have a story to tell over dinner. Steaks are on the barbie."

David and Jennifer left the simulator and found Tayla and Riley hovering over a chess board. Jennifer could tell who was winning because Riley was down a queen and a rook.

Riley resigned. "This time, she asked me if it was like checkers."

DAVID AND JENNIFER WERE STILL COMING DOWN FROM THEIR experience on the simulator, and Tayla was still exhorting her mastery of basement games. Riley was looking at Tayla like a puppy who found his master. The elaborate picnic table gave the diners a stunning view of the Santa Monica Mountains. Jack Masing and Alejandro Lopez stood over the grills. Jack called the four over, "Tell me how you like your steak cooked."

After making their choices, Ellie called them over to sit down, "Margarita has prepared her famous salad."

Margarita stood aside the table and prepared the salad and handed plates around, "My great-great-grandfather passed this recipe down to our family. He was a sous chef at a hotel in the nineteen-twenties."

David's older sister, Ava, joined them and when Margarita finished serving the salads. Tayla's eyes lit up, "This is the best salad I have ever had. Ms. Lopez, did your grandfather work at the Caesar Hotel in Tijuana."

Margarita smiled. "Yes, young lady, you certainly know your culinary history. On July 4, 1924, the overcrowded restaurant ran out of food. The chef, named Caesar, was the brother of my grandfather,

Alex Cardini. The two put their heads together and using the ingredients on hand they went from table to table and prepared the salad. It quickly caught on with the Hollywood stars."

"So, they drove to Mexico for the salad?" asked David.

"Actually, son, they drove down for the booze. It was a time in our country called Prohibition when alcohol was illegal," Jack explained.

Riley asked, "This salad doesn't have the little fishies, does it?"

"Young man, this is the authentic Caesar Salad. My grandfather would never allow anchovies on his creation," Margarita said. "But I have some over here if you would like."

Tayla's face contorted. "Ewww, you don't know food, either, Riley?" Tayla teased as she dug into her salad.

"The steaks are ready," Alejandro said. After serving them, he joined the table, and everyone began to devour the steaks, freshly-baked bread, potato salad, and sweet corn on the cob.

After a few minutes of near silence, with only the sound of silverware and high desert crickets, Jack spoke to Jennifer, "David seems to think that you have run The Asteroid Field simulation on your system at home. Is that true?"

"Yes, Sir, I have run it twelve times," Jennifer said.

"As far as I know, no one has ever survived this simulation. Have you ever lost *Brilliant*?" Jack asked

"Yes…Twelve times."

"What was the difference?"

"At my house, I run the simulator on steveLearn either with a simulated pilot or I fly solo. I was never able to survive. steveLearn is a powerful system, but when I sat down on *Brilliant*Sim, it felt different," Jennifer said.

"You said you almost felt at home," David said.

"Yeah, everything felt like it was exactly where it should be. I was more in touch with *Brilliant*. Does that make sense?"

"I haven't heard anyone put it that way in quite some time, but yes, it makes sense," Jack said.

"So, you and *Brilliant*Sim?" David said. "That was the *only* reason you beat The Asteroid Field?"

"Okay, maybe part of it was because I had a decent pilot," Jennifer said.

David smiled.

Jack explained, "Navvy designed that simulation to give our crew members the understanding that one cannot survive every situation."

Jennifer replied, "The Kobayashi Maru."

"You've seen that movie?"

"I don't believe in the no-win scenario."

"Take me through the tactics, you two." The rest of the table began other conversations while David and Jennifer took Jack through the narrative.

"So, you engaged the StarDrive near a heavy body?" Jack asked.

"Yes, Sir," Jennifer said.

"She cheated," David said.

"I don't like to lose," Jennifer said as she took a bite of celery.

Tayla and Riley got up and helped clear the table, and Ellie Masing brought in a plate stacked with cookies, "When I was growing up near Columbus, my school always had my favorite desserts at lunch. These are called No-Bake Cookies with oatmeal and chocolate."

There were some serious "oohs" and "ahhs" from those who experienced this Midwestern specialty for the first time.

Jennifer smiled at David. "So that's where you found these."

They finished the no-bakes and prepared the extras for take-home. Tayla said, "You have an amazing home. Thanks for the wonderful dinner."

"The day was magical, and the dinner was the best I've had for a long time. It's time for Tayla and I to click our heels together and head back down the mountain to Kansas."

Ellie said, "We thank you for coming. Jack and I and the boys certainly enjoyed it."

"Jennifer, have you been aboard *Brilliant*?" Jack asked.

"That is my dream. I have seen it from a distance."

"We'll have to work on that."

Jen's eyes lit up.

David said, "You haven't even seen the whole house."

Tayla said, "OMG, there's more?"

"The screening room?" Riley asked.

* * *

"Jen, you talked about the *Star Wars* movie I have never seen. Stick around, and we can roll it," David said. "You told me it was pretty good," David said.

Jack said, "That was one of the first movies I saw." *In another time,* Jack thought.

"That is where you need to begin your space opera experience, David," Jennifer said.

Ava's boyfriend arrived at the end of dinner. David led the six down a long hall, and they arrived at antique double doors. "Everything in the lobby comes from old movie palaces built in the nineteen-twenties."

Along the walls in the entryway were antique movie posters. Tayla listed them, "*On the Waterfront* with Marlon Brando, *Tootsie* with Dustin Hoffman, *The African Queen* with Humphrey Bogart and Katherine Hepburn. Didn't she have a sister named Audrey?"

"Same last name but they were unrelated," Jennifer said. At the front of the lobby was a small concession stand. To the right was a glass box with a silver cylinder at the top. "Is that what I think it is? I love popcorn."

"I'll fire it up right now." David opened a cupboard and pulled out cooking oil and popcorn.

Tayla looked at the selection of candies at the counter. "Jujubes, Milk Duds, M&Ms, Corn Nuts. Wow, didn't these people believe in eating healthy?"

Ava spoke up, "I read about this in History of the Twentieth Century. It was all sugar, salt, butter, alcohol, and tobacco. Obesity, diabetes, alcoholism, and cancer were the leading causes of death."

They walked around, and Ava described the antiques. "This room is my mother's design. When she was growing up, she went to summer movies at the Ohio Theater in Columbus. The screening room is a virtual representation of that theater. Built in 1928 the Ohio Theater still stands and has a giant theater pipe organ installed. The studios built the movie palaces during the silent film era."

"You'll need these. The usher will ask you for them." David handed each person a movie ticket. They got their popcorn with lots of butter and passed through the door to a different time.

"Tickets, please." A virtual usher with a bowtie and tails took their tickets. "Gentlemen, please escort your ladies to the fourth row where you'll find your reserved seats."

The two girls walked a few steps from under a low ceiling until they emerged in the virtual immensity of the crowded hall. To their right and left were tall gilded arches. The two in front had velvet curtains. Behind and above was a nearly full balcony. Above them was an eight-pointed star with an ornate chandelier hanging down.

Tayla asked, "This is huge."

"The Ohio seats almost two-thousand-eight-hundred. Our virtual theater seats sixty."

Jennifer pointed to the right, "Do those curtains over there open?"

Ava said, "Behind those curtains are the 2,500 pipes for the Mighty Morton Organ. By the way, it was built here in the valley in Van Nuys."

"Pipes," Tayla asked.

"Have you ever seen someone play the flute?"

"Yes, the flutist opens the tube at various points to get the notes."

"Picture 2,500 flutes each with a single, distinctive sound and pitch. The pipes range from just a few inches for the high notes to sixteen feet for the lowest bass notes played on the foot pedals."

"It would be fun to hear it sometime. I took piano for five years," Tayla said.

"Is there anything you can't do, Wonder Woman?" Riley asked.

"Maybe, but for right now, keep wondering, Wannabe," Tayla teased, and Riley admired.

Just then, the house lights flashed off and on twice. "Show is about to start," David said. The crowd quieted, the lights went down, and a spotlight shown below Stage Left. An immense sound welled up throughout the theater as the Mighty Morton began to play Beautiful Ohio. At the same time, a gigantic white wooden organ console rose from the floor. The size of the console dwarfed the organist.

Tayla said, "It's beautiful. The sound is all around us."

Ava said, "That is the virtual Roger Garrett. He played there for ten years."

After eight minutes of music, the lights went down, and the

curtains opened with a slide announcing, "Previews of Coming Attractions." The movie screen converted to a modern-day holographic presentation, and the six friends saw five movie trailers of two *StarCruiser Brilliant* motion pictures and two award-winning pictures starring Ellie Masing. David whispered to Jen, "Pay attention, you haven't seen the next one."

Jennifer sat up.

The final trailer was *Attack of the Hoclarth*, the film that she was going to start working for on Monday.

Jennifer sat back and thought, *Amazing. I am going to work on that.*

The organ began to play the familiar music of the "Looney Tunes" cartoons.

"I love the Roadrunner and Coyote cartoons," Riley said.

At the end of the cartoon, the organ raised again playing the Looney Tunes music and then started playing some classical music. Ava said, "I took a course on Classical Music of the Twentieth Century. The song is from John Williams, one of the greats. He composed music for many motion pictures."

Jennifer replied, "This is the *Star Wars* theme."

The lights went down. The organ disappeared. Following the familiar Fox intro, the following words appeared, "A long time ago in a galaxy far, far away...."

Over the next two hours and five minutes, six viewers became three couples. Armrests disappeared to make way for cuddling. They got to know Luke and Obi-wan, the evil Darth Vader, Leia, and Han...and each other. It was a prototypical date movie except that each one had a close connection to the industry, the studio, and a ship called *Brilliant*.

After the screen faded to black, David exclaimed, "George Lucas made those movies for people just like our fans. It left us with a high standard to follow."

"I was six, and I wanted to start watching the *StarCruiser Brilliant* movies. My mom made me watch *Star Wars* first. I'm glad she did."

"Why don't we roll the second movie?" David said.

"Tayla and I have to get home," Jennifer said quickly.

"But it's only nine p.m."

"It's late, and I want to go home."

"But we're having such a great time," David said.

All Jennifer could think about was the evil figure clad in black saying, "I am your father."

Tayla knew the look of terror on Jennifer's face, "David, we had fun, but it's time for us to go."

"I've never seen *The Empire Strikes Back*. It'll be fun."

"I can't watch that movie. I have to go home," Jennifer said.

"Why?"

Tayla said, "David, it has to do with her father. We watched that movie a few years ago, and Jennifer was hurting for two weeks. It's her vision thing. She remembers every single thing forever, and she feels it, too. Just let it go."

"Sorry. I hope that you two will come back."

"We will. We had a great time. Thank your parents for us."

They hugged and the evening was over. As the girls drove home, Jennifer couldn't think of anything but the man in the black helmet and cape…and her father.

TEN

Creative Sunday

J ennifer got four hours sleep, awakened at three and entered her steveLearn system. She reviewed the apps she created, made small changes, responded to user feedback, and made more changes.

She called up the *Brilliant* script. She had scanned through it on Friday night. This time as she re-read it, she took very close notes and suggested changes. She felt it needed something.

Along the way, she noticed that Pugs was still chasing rabbits in deep REM sleep, but Dandy Lion curled up next to her and was alternatively purring and sleeping.

It was time to take a break, so she carried her HoloPad into the kitchen. "Starbucks, my regular," she said.

Jennifer decided that she needed to do a complete rewrite of the *Attack* script. Jennifer was sure that no one from the studio would see it, but she wanted to do it to get it out of her system.

"Good morning, Jennifer. One double-shot caramel Frappuccino coming up," Starbucks said.

That takes care of the sugar. She tossed a chicken tamale in the microwave.

Dandy followed her to the kitchen and growled hungrily. Jennifer spooned some cat food into his dish, and the cat surveyed his realm and settled into consuming his sumptuous repast.

As novelist Jenna Seldon, Jennifer could create original text very rapidly. She often created new material at a pace of five-thousand words per day using the HTVR keyboard.

She went to work on the script. *Seven a.m. First draft done*, Jennifer thought. She concentrated on smoothing and correcting the dialog, character behavior, and content to be consistent with all five previous films and to assure correct references to the *Brilliant Tech Manual*. She rewrote a glaring technical error and made a note to herself that she needed to bring this up at work. *Ten a.m. A clean second draft. Now, production costs.* The finale of *Attack* was a battle scene scheduled for September in a remote mountainous spot in the Mojave Desert. *No one will see this. Let's play around.* Jennifer was going over that scene in her mind when her mother came into the room.

"Allen and I have Sunday brunch reservations at The Baked Potato at one o'clock. Would you like to join?"

"I love that restaurant. Do they have music today?"

"Yes, it's the small combo in the main room. We'll be leaving a half-hour before."

"Thanks, Mom. Brunch is on me." She returned her attention to the project. She had an hour and ten minutes before leaving for brunch. She realized that this was a good break point and a good time for a power nap. "Sami, set the alarm at twelve-ten." As she relaxed, her thoughts again focused on the costs associated with the desert battle scene. The flying Cine-Drones to film the scene were horrendously expensive to rent and operate. She tossed and turned and saw dollar signs floating in the air. Then she saw something else floating in the air. She relaxed and escaped her thoughts in sleep. The scene faded to black, and shortly she was awakened by her alarm after a refreshing twenty-minute nap.

THE JAZZ COMBO AT THE BAKED POTATO PLAYED MUSIC THAT Jennifer loved. She was halfway through her Philly Cheese Steak Potato when she shifted the conversation. "I'm rewriting the script for

Attack of the Hoclarth Alliance. I'm sure that none of my changes will make it into the movie, but I'm doing it for practice." She took another mouthful and continued. "I told you they asked me to look for places to cut costs. The desert battle scene is very expensive. Our biggest expense is renting and operating the multiple aerial cameras for multiple takes and then editing together angles in post-production."

"That's the biggest ticket after talent on every high-budget film."

"I have an idea that might cut the costs by thirty percent, and it's scalable to the rest of the industry," Jennifer said.

"You have my undivided attention," Sheila said.

Jennifer held up her HoloPad. "What if we had two copter rotors on a device like this and then, in the middle, a lens pointing down. Finally, there would be a variable mirror that folds open and can rotate to follow the subject. That way the mini-drone stays horizontal and stable and only the mirror moves to track the image."

Sheila asked, "How many of these devices would fly?"

"I think that forty in the air would give us the coverage and the images to create a realistic three-dimensional scene."

"How would you control this array of drones?"

"GGG would roll two trailers; one would be a standard video production truck with a control room, the second van would carry the hardware and storage."

Allen asked, "Does this hardware exist?"

"No, Dad. Mom, can you help me with a patent and some engineering help?" Jennifer said.

Sheila thought for a moment. "Patent? Yes. We have some intellectual property specialists in my shop. Engineering? Yes. We have engineers that would be able to handle this project. Also, HumanAI seems very excited to support any ideas that you come up with. Marketability? If you can prove the cost savings, your system would most definitely fill a niche."

"The mini-drone is the big-ticket item. Have you thought of applications outside of motion pictures?" asked Allen.

"Yes, I even have a name for it. Selfie-Drone. It would interface with the HoloPad. Teenagers could upload photos and movies on their social media from this device."

"You've thought this through for a long time. It's a huge project," Allen said.

"I came up with it a couple of hours ago."

"Oh, yeah. The vision thing. I keep forgetting that you aren't human. In either case, the project is very complex," Allen said.

"You're going to be creating new technology with three different corporations. Each is going to want to hoard a large share of the ownership, profits, and control. You might consider incorporating. You would still share ownership and profits, but you would maintain control of your intellectual property," Sheila said.

"You're talking about forming a corporation?"

"Yes, but what about capital?" Allen said. "Nothing is a sure thing, but this is close. I can pledge five million. I'd then be willing to assign my proxies to Jennifer and the corporation. Sheila, you would probably need to take the executive role for a couple of years until Jennifer is prepared and old enough to sign contracts."

"I, too, could invest five million and I'm sure my parents would invest another ten for their granddaughter. Those numbers would offset the investment from the studio, GGG, and HumanAI and Jennifer would maintain control with the ideas that she brings to the project."

"I guess I need an MBA. What's next?" Jennifer asked.

"You need a name for the company," Sheila said.

"JennaTech," Jennifer said quickly.

After returning home from brunch, Jennifer summoned Sami, "Sami, I want to accomplish three things today: one more pass on the script, create a patent application for the mini-drone and begin a Master's in Business Administration. Call up the *Attack* script," she said. "Go through all technical references, so they agree with the *Brilliant* Tech Manual,"

"I have been following along, Sis. The major deviation was on page thirty-six. You found that the current script includes an incorrect release procedure for the STALT. The Weapons officer is required to specify the rules of engagement. There are three available scenarios…."

"Got it. There was a problem with the Manual at one point," Jennifer said.

"With your Jenna Seldon pseudonym, you submitted a correction."

"And I got a somewhat sarcastic thank you from the tech writers in return."

"Jenna does sound a bit arrogant at times."

"Seriously, Sami, you know my rule. You shouldn't be arrogant unless you have something to be arrogant about."

"That is why Jenna doesn't have many friends," Sami said.

"You're my friend."

"Yes, Jennifer, I'm your friend, and because of that I put up with Jenna."

"Ok, Sis, do a final look-through of the script and tell me how it looks."

"It looks good. The effects direction for the battle scene needs some definition, but that is dependent on the technology that you're developing. The pace, technical reference, and direction of the dialogue are good, in fact much better than the original. Your vision is true to the previous movies but with more edge," Sami said.

"Are you an LA Times movie critic now?" Jennifer said.

"No, but I helped her get her degree at UVN a few years ago."

"Touché. I need coffee, and after that, I need to learn how to design the mini-drone and submit a patent." Jennifer headed to the kitchen. Both Pugs and Dandy popped up from sleep and followed her to the kitchen. "My spoiled pets want treats. Starbucks, I want a double-shot caramel Frappuccino." She distributed treats to her needy children.

The Starbucks announced, "Your Frap is ready.

She grabbed the drink and headed back to her room with Pugs and Dandy in tow.

"Welcome back, Jen. I created a design palette for your device. Describe it to me."

"Good. Same size and form factor as my HoloPad. Along the vertical axis, two rotors at the top and bottom and a high-res video sensor with a four-hundred to one zoom at film resolution in the center. On the sensor, a fold out mirror that rotates from the stable platform to direct the camera."

"Can you define the mirror more clearly?" Sami asked.

"Do you remember that old movie I watched a few years ago with the airborne laser weapon? I think it was called *Real Genius*."

"1985. Val Kilmer. They called the weapon Crossbow. Got it. Tell me about power."

"It needs a long-range wireless power receiver and a ten-minute battery for backup."

"The battery is going to be the major weight consideration. What about CPU and software?"

"Operating system with interface, data, and power networking. Autonomous flight control, of course. Camera and mirror control. Room for user features on the consumer version. Can we fit a holo display?" Jennifer asked.

"Jen, the greatest concern is weight. Your MiniDrone weighs in at a little over six ounces. If you include the holo feature, the drone weighs nine ounces. With the projector, it goes up to thirteen ounces. That would make your average valley girl walk in circles," Sami joked.

"Okay, no-go on the holo…."

"Not quite so fast," Sami interrupted. "I extrapolated the current iteration of Moore's Law. In eighteen months, you'll be able to add the display and keep it around ten ounces. In the meantime, the software could probably support the display on the accompanying HoloPad."

"Version 2 it is. Do we have enough to begin a patent application?"

"I have done a patent search for similar technology. I found that your device will yield three different patents. Congratulations, you're an inventor." Sami said. "You will need help to bring it to completion."

"I need engineers. What's the next step?"

"I can have a preliminary patent application ready tomorrow afternoon. Then you'll need a patent attorney."

"I'll run this by Mom tomorrow afternoon," Jennifer said. "Pugs, would you like to take a walk while there is still light?"

Pugs was very familiar with the operative word. The wrinkle-nosed dog jumped up from his nap with tail and tongue wagging anxiously at either end. Dandy Lion observed his needy pet pal, raising his cat lip derisively at this lower animal who required exercise.

FORTY-FIVE MINUTES LATER, AFTER A BRISK EVENING WALK, JENNIFER returned to steveLearn to begin her quest for an MBA. "Sami, have you considered the courses I need and the skills I must pursue to lead the drone project?"

"Yes, I have. For students pursuing management in the high-tech industry, UVN has created an excellent tutor modeled after Thomas Alva Edison. He is credited with one-thousand, ninety-three patents and started over two-hundred different companies."

"I read his biography, and he would be perfect Sami," Jennifer said.

"Call Thomas. Jenna Seldon has an appointment with the inventor, and he's expecting you."

JENNIFER ENTERED A LABORATORY FROM THE NINETEENTH CENTURY. She expected it to be dry and musty like a museum, but this was very contemporary with the sounds of a nearby machine shop and the smells of many different materials and chemicals, but not as well-lit as a modern laboratory. At a bench was a very busy older gentleman in a black-vested suit and what looked like a bow tie. When he turned toward her, she recognized the snow-white hair around the distinctive square face of Thomas Edison.

"Welcome to my main laboratory, Miss Seldon. You need advice on a project, and you want to pursue some business and management courses."

"I believe that I need to form a team to pursue my idea of many mini-drones that can photograph a large scene on a remote motion picture location," Jenna said.

"I'm familiar with your proposal. Besides the drone, you require a mobile control room, data, and power networked wirelessly and the hardware and software to support the endeavor."

"That is the simple description, but I know that the project is very complex."

"I agree, Jenna. I'm not the lone wolf in a lab with a white coat, I'm a collaborator. I understand that you're a quick study," Edison said.

"Yes, Mr. Edison. I can read, memorize, and write rather quickly."

"My great-grandniece, Sarah Miller Caldicott, studied my work very intensely and wrote a book called *Midnight Lunch*. I suggest that you read it soon," Mr. Edison said. "Sarah suggests four keys to managing a collaborative team. Let me explain." And he did.

"You have given me a lot to think about, Mr. Edison," Jennifer said. "I'll read the book tonight and begin forming a team tomorrow. I look forward to collaborating with you on this project and gaining skills as a business and technology leader."

"Young lady, it's the scientists of the past who provide the tools to young inventors of the present, who build the future we'll live in. Good luck, Jenna."

"Good night and thank you, Mr. Edison."

Jennifer spent the next hour reading the book that Edison recommended. Sleep was an evasive prey as she chased down the new ideas she came up with on this day. She tossed and turned until Dandy Lion jumped on the bed and stared at her. A few moments later, she was fast asleep.

ELEVEN

Sound Stage One

On Monday, Jennifer reported to Grayson at Information Technology, checked her presentation, and went to the safety office for the meeting.

"Ladies and gentlemen, you're familiar with the Safety Buddy App that I created. I added some modifications to the app and connected it with Tovar's back office system. The pads will automatically report medical or injury events and call for responders in an emergency as well as collect data on high-frequency safety issues and request or recommend solutions. Finally, I recommend that you develop software and hardware to link up with all of the autonomous mobile vehicles and equipment," Jennifer said.

Her presentation was well-received, and afterward, she answered questions. The Vice-President of Operations welcomed her to Tovar Studios and congratulated her on having a substantial positive impact on safety in just a few days.

AT NINE-THIRTY, JENNIFER REPORTED TO THE SET OF *BRILLIANT* AND her supervisor, Harper Jennings.

"Good morning, Jennifer. The effects people love the upgrades.

They say the HTVR system is much snappier and more responsive. I sent you the continuity photos for our first scene. Please do a once-over on the set to verify that there is nothing out of place. When we roll, I'll be Stage Right, and you'll be Stage Left with Brooke Nascimento, the AD. You and I will communicate via HoloPad, and you'll inform Brooke of any problems. Do you have any questions?" Harper said.

"No, ma'am. "

"Jen, do you know how much of my paycheck I spend to look thirty? Call me Harper. Do the walkthrough and then grab your caffeine overdose."

"Thanks, Harper. Have a good shoot." Jennifer reviewed and memorized the photos and then did a slow and thorough walk-through of the set. She spotted two items slightly out of place. She informed Melinda, the props master.

"I looked at that twice. You're right. Good catch, I'm Mel," the props master said.

"Hi, Mel, I'm Jennifer. I'm the intern assisting Harper."

"You're the HoloPad guru, right?"

"Yes, I am."

"I'd like to chat between shots. After I saw what that toy could do, I started thinking about how it could help my crew," Mel said.

"Message me when you have a minute. I'll be here all day."

Jennifer went over to the Starbucks machine. "Hello, Starbucks," Jennifer said.

"It's Jennifer, right," the smart machine said.

"Yes, very good."

"Double-shot caramel Frappuccino, right?"

"That's the one. Thanks, Starbucks." Jennifer picked up a croissant while she waited, and a voice came from behind.

"Starbucks, after you give Jennifer her valley girl drink, make me a large coffee with cream."

Navvy startled Jennifer as she was standing in line mumbling to herself and running checklists in her head. She turned and said, "Good morning, Mr. Kelrithian."

The Starbucks machine said, "Yes, Navvy."

"Hear that, Jennifer. My set, my rules. Call me Navvy."

"Yes, Navvy, and thanks."

"Jen, you look overwhelmed and somewhat nervous."

"Yes, Sir, a little bit of both."

"Today, you may trip over something, you may face a difficult challenge, and it's highly likely someone will yell at you. Just remember, a bad day making movies is better than a good day doing anything else."

"Yes, Sir. Have a good shoot."

"I remember that your grandfather used to say that. He's a good man." Navvy turned on his heel and moved toward the chair that bore his name. As he did, the pace and the intensity increased, but the clatter and the noise went down. Everyone knew it was time to start making a movie.

JENNIFER TOOK HER PLACE NEXT TO THE ASSISTANT DIRECTOR AND took notes. She reported minor script deviations to Brooke and Harper. After several takes, the Director called a fifteen-minute break, and the stage crew redressed the set for the upcoming scene.

Jennifer again reviewed the continuity photos and did a walk-through on the set. She reported a couple of problems to Mel. "Do you have plans for lunch?" Mel said.

"No, let's chat in the cafeteria," Jennifer said. "I have been thinking about some ideas for a Props Buddy app,"

"Give me twenty minutes after we break for lunch so I can direct the stage crew to get ready for the afternoon." Many of the stage crew took their breaks and lunch during the shooting so that they could prepare when the cast and crew were off the set.

ON THE SECOND TAKE OF THE NEW SCENE, JENNIFER NOTICED THE problem that she spotted on her rewrite of the script over the weekend. The actor on the science station, Eiji Noguchi, was pressing the wrong keystrokes and the display was giving the incorrect result for the situation portrayed in the scene. It wasn't a critical mistake, but it was one that would have the Brillians on social media calling it out as a technical mistake when the movie came out. "Harper, the actor on the science station is pressing the wrong keystrokes for the current scenario, and it results in an incorrect display in the background."

"Is it serious?" Harper asked.

"The Brillians will be all over it on social media when the movie comes out."

"Tell Brooke; I'm coming over."

"Brooke, there's a technical problem with this scene," Jennifer explained the problem and what might happen if it wasn't corrected.

Brooke nodded and turned to the director, "Arturo, can we hold the next take? Our Script Assistant found a technical problem. Jennifer, explain it."

She quickly explained the problem to the director. "Navvy has the final call. We need to go to him." They walked over to the producer. "Navvy, our newbie Script Assistant has found a mistake in the script for this scene. Explain it, Jennifer."

"Navvy, Eiji on the science station calls up the long-range scanner in this scene. The correct procedure in the manual in section 12.36 is to call up the close-range weapons scanner and let Owwie track the target. I'm afraid that if this scene makes the cut the Brillians on social media will get all bent out of shape as they typically do when they spot a mistake in the movie."

"Can someone show me the scene?" Navvy asked.

"Here, Sir." Jennifer held up her HoloPad. "Sami, call up the last take and zoom into the science station."

The scene arose from the Pad, which displayed the problem area.

"I still don't see the problem," Navvy said.

"Sir, when did you finalize this part of the script?" Jennifer asked.

"We reviewed in April. I specifically remember going over this scene."

"Navvy, you updated Section 12.36.3 of the *Brilliant* Tech Manual on May third. That change addressed this issue. Based on *Brilliant* system upgrades, the scanning procedure changed. I found this when I did a rewrite on the script over the weekend."

"Some sci-fi author named Jenna-something sent us a snotty letter about that. She was right, so we made the change."

"Guilty as charged. Sorry for the nasty part. I had just broken up with my last boyfriend. My pen name is Jenna Seldon," Jennifer said.

"So, you're saying you started shaking things up before you even got here?" Navvy said.

"Again, sorry...."

"It's okay. Shaking is good. How fast can you train Eiji to do it correctly?"

"Five minutes."

"Arturo, let's take ten. Jennifer, go straighten this out. See me before you break for lunch."

"Yes, Sir."

JENNIFER WENT TO SEE EIJI AT THE SCIENCE STATION.

"Eiji, I am Jennifer Gallagher, the new intern. I pointed out a procedural error in the script and Navvy asked me to go over the correction with you," Jennifer said.

"I went over the procedure in the script, and it's correct," Eiji said.

"Unfortunately, the script was based on an earlier version of the Manual. The new procedure is slightly different, and I'm afraid that Brillians like me will see the mistake when the movie is released."

"Jennifer, you're just an intern. How do you know this stuff?" Eiji asked.

"I have been a Brillian since I was six years old. I finished reading the *Brilliant Tech Manual* when I was thirteen, and I keep up with revisions."

"You sound like you have it memorized."

"I do but let me show you the updated section."

She set her HoloPad down on the surface. "Sami, bring up the revision."

They spent the next five minutes going over the proper procedure. Jennifer watched the actor rehearse the correct actions.

"You're the supernerd that has been going around creating the amazing HoloPad apps, aren't you?" Eiji said.

"Correct."

"Wow, let me know if I screw up again, preferably before the cameras roll," Eiji said.

"Will do."

Lunch occurred at noon. As the crew was breaking for lunch, Jennifer walked over to Navvy. "You wanted to see me, Sir?"

"Yes, you're THE Jenna Seldon, author of the Logan Jones novels?"

"Yes, Sir. I'm trying to work on the arrogant streak."

"You said you did a rewrite on the script?"

"Yes, I saw some technical issues and some issues with dialogue and consistency with past movies. I also have some ideas on the battle scene. I'm working on some technology that might reduce costs and improve the look. I haven't completely tricked out that scene yet. I included notes to advise on minimizing necessary re-shoots."

"May I have a look at your script?"

"Yes, but please remember, I did it for practice and to analyze costs. It's my first attempt at a screenplay. I can have it on your computer in a few minutes."

"Jen, if we have an earthquake, could you raise your hand to let me know if it's you or the San Andreas Fault?

"Sir?"

"Keep shaking, young lady."

"Thank you, Sir."

DURING HER WALK TO THE COMMISSARY, SHE CHATTED WITH HER HoloBuddy. "Sami, Navvy wants to read my rewrite. Check me off on this. I did the rewrite and included notes on recommended re-shoots, budgeting, and shooting schedule?"

"Check."

"Is it noted where it requires collaboration with his writing team to finish?"

"Check."

"Are there notes where I need to flesh it out further?"

"Check."

"Can you do another copyedit pass?"

"Done."

Ok, Sami here goes. Make sure that the significant changes are in Bold Red. Address it to Navvy and cc: Kathy."

"Ready."

"Send it, Sami, and wish me luck."

"Done and sent."

"Next, Melinda, the Props Master wants to meet with us. I want to do a Props Curator app. What data do we have on the props inventory?"

"After a century of filmmaking, Tovar has an immense inventory," Sami said. "Over the last five years, they updated their inventory for twenty percent of the stock to actual photos, provenance, and repair data."

"Sami, use the Big Data from the lot to create a Props Curator app that will assist the Props Master and Grips with inventory, maintenance, repairs, continuity placement, scripting, and scheduling," Jennifer asked.

"Are you aware GGG maintains the Big Data for props for all the SoCal Studios in what's called the Props Collective? Tovar is a founding member of this group. So, what do we want the app to do?"

"Good call. Use the best source of data," Jennifer said. "There's Melinda." Jennifer waved and then grabbed a tray of food and carried it over.

"Hi, Mel," Jennifer said.

"Hey, Jen. Have you made progress?" Mel said.

"Yes. Sami, my HoloBuddy, searched work logs, public communications, and documents about the duties of the Prop Master. She's now integrating Big Data from all of the Hollywood sources."

"What did you and your HoloBuddy come up with?"

"The Props Curator app will maintain inventory, keep a record of purchase and rental costs, and repair status for all items relevant to a project. The data will be available for all items held in the database. It'll maintain placement and inventory based on detailed photos and rushes. In pre-production, it'll recommend a props list based on scripting descriptions and history. Props Curator will facilitate communications between your crew, your office, and the above the line positions on the set. Finally, it'll coordinate autonomous delivery vehicles for on-time delivery and return to storage."

"Does it fetch coffee?" Mel asked.

Not sensing the sarcasm, Jennifer replied, "I'm sure that we could set up an interface between the Starbucks units and the ADV's that bring the props."

"Just kidding about the coffee. During the strike at the end of the picture, we inspect and inventory all the pieces and refer them to cleaning and repair. We do that at the Props Shop."

"Sami?"

Sami popped out of the HoloPad, "Boss, we don't have complete capability now. I recommend that we send a referral to JennaTech for an upgrade to the Autonomous Delivery Vehicles to conduct a pre-inspections en-route and triage the props returning to the shop."

"Timeline?" Jennifer said.

"It's a hardware-intensive project. We don't yet have staff in place. Four months to beta implementation if the process goes smoothly."

"Good call, Sami, let's put that in motion." She turned to Melinda. "Any other ideas that we could include?"

"What is JennaTech?" Melinda asked.

"JennaTech is a company I started to manage all my technology projects."

"Do you sleep, or do you have your assistant do all your work? Is it possible for my assistant to pop up on the HoloPad as yours does? Wait, You're just an intern. How do you have an assistant?" Melinda asked.

Sami and Jennifer both laughed. "Sami, introduce yourself," Jennifer said.

"Hello, I'm Samantha, Jennifer's virtual assistant. Jennifer and I got to know each other about nine years ago when Jennifer started taking classes at UVN. I started as a virtual student advisor, but we've worked together on many things since. We've become good friends, and we now work together on many of Jennifer's projects."

"So, where is your office?"

"My source code and computation power are hosted primarily at the University of Van Nuys, but I have data shared at GGG, Tovar, and HumanAI. I am a virtual HoloBuddy."

Mel did a double-take. "Jennifer, could I have a HoloBuddy like Sami?"

"Of course, it's a part of your initial setup."

"Perfect. When can my crew and I get our HoloPads?"

"How many?"

"My *Brilliant* crew will need four. Other shoots on the lot will require fourteen."

"Okay, I'll bring you four by the end of day and let you know when the others will be available," Jennifer said.

"Thanks for your help. Lunch is on me,"

JENNIFER'S MIND HAD BEEN IN HIGH GEAR SINCE SHE ARRIVED ON THE lot at seven-thirty. She needed some quiet time. With time before the afternoon call, Jennifer took the scenic route through the backlot. Some of the sets were over a century old, but the false fronts looked brand new. Of course, her favorite sets were the ones created for the early *StarCruiser Brilliant* pictures. With her memory and vision, she could walk among the stars in the scenes as they occurred in the movie.

Like a magnet, her walk drew her to *Brilliant*.

JENNIFER PASSED THROUGH THE ACCESS GATE AND CAME FACE TO FACE with her ship of dreams. According to the *Brilliant Tech Manual*, when not occupied by the crew, the ship was tended by the Artificial Intelligence.

Her first view was from the right flank where she could see the three engine exhausts. Jennifer noted the position of each sensor, each shield emitter, and each plasma weapons port. She walked along the starboard side close enough that she could see the details, but still see the entirety of *Brilliant*. Walking around the eighty-foot length and sixty-foot breadth, Jennifer examined the detail of the skin, contemplating what equipment was on the interior. The torpedo doors on the waist facing forward were where the STALT weapons emerged. When Jennifer reached the bow of *Brilliant*, she looked up to see the small window on the top forward end of the bridge that serves as the only viewport. Along the port side, she passed the docking collar and the port weapons release points. She finished the circular tour just behind the ramp leading to the inside of the ship.

She heard a recognizable voice. "Jenna Seldon?" the Artificial Navigation Intelligence said, as she stood her permanent watch over the safety and security of *Brilliant*.

"Hello, Ani."

"Only authorized crew members may come aboard. What is your authorization password?"

"Ani, I am just an intern here at Tovar. I am not an authorized crew member. I just wanted to walk around and see *Brilliant*."

"What is your authorization password?"

It can't hurt to give it a try. "Authorization: jendroid," She always accessed the *Brilliant Tech Manual* and the *Brilliant* Simulators using her secret identity.

"Welcome to *StarCruiser Brilliant*, Jenna. This is your first time aboard. Would you like a guided tour?"

Her mouth dropped open. "I'm listed on the crew of Brilliant?"

"When your assistant, Sami, informed me that you arrived on the lot for your summer internship, I spoke with Navvy. Your study of the bridge stations and your studies of the *Brilliant Tech Manual* indicate that you have the third highest knowledge level of the ship's systems behind only Navvy and the captain, and your simulator scores are the highest ever recorded," Ani said. "I recommended that he add your name to the crew list just in case. Navvy concurred but asked that I inform him if you accessed the ship."

"Wow, thank Navvy for me. I will find my way around on my own."

She climbed the ramp to the lowest deck.

"Ani, don't wake me up. This is the best dream I have ever had," Jennifer said.

"I am not very good at metaphors, but I am guessing that was one," Ani replied.

"Correct."

The aft-most compartment of the sub-deck was a small hangar

deck. The outer doors opened to the vacuum of space protected by an air-tight force field. She stood on a pad with a pentagon of five circles. "Ani, is this what I think it is?"

"Jennifer, that information is classified above your authorization. Sorry."

Jennifer walked around the Main Reactor which was sealed and maintenance free. It was very similar to the Scott Reactors which supplied unlimited energy to the world, but it came from a different timeline. The reactor occupied the center of the ship from the keel through the three decks below the bridge. Forward of the ramp and center ladder was the automated torpedo room. Currently, it contained a vicious-looking Smart Tactical Autonomous Long-range Torpedo lined up with Tube Two on the port side. The starboard tube displayed a message, "War Shot Loaded," indicating that Tube One contained another STALT. Two small auxiliary tubes were set fore and aft to release countermeasures.

She walked up the steps of the ladder to the main deck, so-called because it extended from the stem of the ship to the stern. Jennifer went aft and looked into Navvy's office. The title on the door indicated *Ship's Designer*.

"Hello, Jenna. Are you enjoying your tour?" Engi, the Engineering Intelligence said.

"Hi, Engi. Brilliant is more beautiful than I dreamed."

"Our ship does that to people."

Outboard of that was the controller for the ship's fabricator which created the parts necessary and delivered them throughout the ship. Forward of the main reactor was the athwartship passage which passed between the instrumentation and auxiliary controls for the StarDrive and the gravity drive. Beyond was life support and ship's stores.

Every detail is like I remember it from the Manual.

Up the ladder again and Jennifer arrived on the 01 deck, the first deck above the main. Aft of the reactor, Jennifer looked into sickbay. "Good afternoon, Dr. Ami." Ami, the Artificial Medical Intelligence, was the ship's doctor. Ami was a holographic Tactile Virtual Reality entity just like the actors on Tovar's sound stages.

"Welcome aboard, *Brilliant*, Miss Seldon. I hope that you enjoy your tour."

Jennifer walked forward past the three staterooms, the galley, and the crew's mess. Looking inside one of the staterooms, it had stacked bunks and two working desks equipped with steveLearn technology. In the galley, she saw a Starbucks machine.

"Miss Seldon, would you like a double-shot caramel Frappuccino?"

"Yes, please."

While she waited, "Ani, are all the HoloBuddies, assistants, and smart tech networked with *Brilliant?*"

"Yes, Jenna. Navvy worked closely with HumanAI to develop HTVR technology. *Brilliant* fabricated some of the first equipment including the hardware that I run on. Navvy is one of the early investors of the company."

"Navvy must be one of the richest people on the planet."

"Navvy himself does not know the exact number because it's constantly changing. He's not a trillionaire quite yet but very close. Tovar Studios and HumanAI crowned four of the top ten on that list, with Navvy at the top."

Jennifer received her coffee in a unique spill-proof mug with her name on it. "Mine?"

"Yes, but it stays aboard *Brilliant*. We are having a patent disagreement with NASA about our mugs," Ani said.

Jennifer looked at the fire pole and spiral ladder that would take her to the bridge and began climbing to her destiny. At the top, she viewed the layout. To her left was the engineering station at the aft bulkhead. On the port side was the science station, and on the starboard was the communications panel. On the forward bulkhead were the pilot seat on the left and the Operations seat on the right. In the center was the Captain's Chair.

She went aft, opening the door to the Captain's Ready Room and Stateroom. Aft-most was the captain's desk surrounded by displays and three chairs. Port and starboard were fold-down bunks below displays that showed the starfield outside the ship. The center of the room featured a holographic tactical virtual reality display. It was steveLearn on steroids.

"Ani, is this like steveLearn?"

"It is the first installation of steveLearn. This particular version is always a generation ahead. There are only a few others with the same capability. Interestingly, HumanAI has maintained the one in your bedroom at nearly the same capability."

"I wonder why?"

"steveLearn is an interactive system designed to teach concepts and information to the user, but it also learns and adapts from the user. You, Jenna, taught steveLearn as much as it has taught you," Ani said. "The modes by which you interact with steveLearn are unique. You taught steveLearn innovative and rapid ways to create new information from old. HumanAI has implemented those processes for other users."

Jennifer thought about that and how she observed others interacting with steveLearn. "I guess I knew that, but I didn't think it was just me."

She walked forward, inspecting the pilot and operations console, sat in the captain's chair, and placed her coffee in the holder. Engineering was over her right shoulder, the science station to her left, and communications on her right. Ahead on the center line was the ship's bell and the only hull penetration that allowed a viewport.

Jennifer sat for several minutes contemplating what was to come. Ani interrupted, "You know, you followed the same steps that the captain walks every time he comes on board for a mission."

"I didn't realize that."

"Sami informs me they want you on Sound Stage One in five minutes."

She took one last look around and then exited the ship and went back to her real job. "Thanks, Ani. I will be back."

Yes, Jenna, you certainly will, Ani thought.

She was immersed in her memories of *Brilliant* when Sami popped up, "The HoloPads are at the sound stage."

"Sami, ask the Starbucks to make my favorite for when I get there."

She walked onto the stage with two minutes to spare. Her third double-shot caramel Frappuccino of the day was ready when she got to Craft Services. She grabbed it and resumed her place on the set near Brooke. Harper Jennings' avatar popped up over her shoulder, "There is a delay. Come over and let's chat."

Jennifer arrived near her supervisor, "What's up?"

Harper explained, "Navvy has put a thirty-minute hold on the shoot. There are script changes that involve reshoots from this morning. We have also been warned to standby for more rewrites."

Harper looked at Jennifer, whose eyes were open very wide. "You know something?"

"Well…"

"Spill," Harper said.

"Over the weekend, I did a rewrite of the *Attack* script," Jennifer said.

"And?"

"I mentioned this to Navvy during our conference. When we broke for lunch, Navvy asked me to send the rewrite. He should have received it right after we broke for lunch."

"Who are you, anyway?"

"Just a lowly studio intern trying to do my job, Boss." She winked her blue-green eye at Harper.

"Go back to your spot and keep a low profile this afternoon. That may be nigh onto impossible for you but do your best." Harper's look of intensity relaxed into a smile. "The best part of this business is working with extremely talented people. One of the most depressing things is seeing them burn out like a shooting star. A professor once told me, 'Knowledge becomes wisdom when experience becomes the teacher.' Make sure that you stick around long enough for the experience to take hold."

"I've heard that before. The last thing I want to do is screw up a great opportunity. I understand what you're saying, and I'll do my best to follow your advice."

"Take your spot," Harper said.

"Thanks, Harper."

Next to Brooklyn, she caught a look from the director that seemed to be a mix of anger and astonishment. Navvy wasn't in his usual seat. An alert popped up from her HoloPad for a script revision. The props and set decoration crews scrambled to update the sets moving cameras and lighting. She looked at the script revision. Her words appeared just as she had written them over the weekend. As she glanced around the stage at the controlled chaos, she caught Harper's eye stage left. Harper was posing the question to Jennifer. *She wants to know if all this is my fault.* Jennifer nodded in response. She knew that it was going to be challenging to keep a low profile from here out.

David Masing passed Jennifer on his way to his mark, "I wonder who caused this five-alarm fire?"

"Some pesky intern must have learned how to type," Jennifer said.

David stopped and turned to Jennifer. "You?"

Jennifer shrugged and tried to look innocent.

David stepped up and wrapped Jennifer in a hug. "That's for luck. You're gonna need it." Jennifer returned the hug warmly. "Hey, Wednesday is a short day. Riley and I would like for you and Tayla to join us and sample a new dance club after work? My publicist got me four passes to The Virtual Copa. Riley would be happy if Tayla joined."

Jennifer smiled. "I think that Tayla and I can fit that into our busy social calendar. I'll call her, confirm, and let you know."

The rest of the afternoon was surprisingly quiet. The crew performed reshoots on three interiors. Each of the setups was one of those recommended in the shooting script she sent Navvy.

At the afternoon break, Jennifer called Tayla. "Tay, are you up for some clubbing Wednesday evening?"

"Yes, what's the plan?"

"David has four passes for us at some club called The Virtual Copa. Have you heard of it?"

"Omigod. That is the toughest ticket in the valley right now. Wait, Wednesday is the official grand opening. We got tickets? The club is modeled after the Copacabana in New York from the nineteen-fifties. It's a virtual black and white club."

"Black and White?" Jennifer asked.

"You enter the club's interior and into a film noir picture. The acts are reproductions from the period: Frank Sinatra, Louis

Armstrong, Martin and Lewis, and MGM floor shows. And get this, when you're dancing, a virtual actor may cut in. My New York friend told me she was dancing, and Cary Grant cut in and danced with her. I hear that there is a table near the front with the whole Rat Pack: Frank, Dean, Bogart and Bacall, and Sammy Davis, Jr. They even sign napkins and take selfies. They won't let you in unless you're wearing period fashion. So, we need to schedule some retail therapy."

"Wow, that sounds fun."

"Are you and David ready to go public? The paparazzi will be out in force."

"You're right. David's publicists gave him the passes. I guess we're going to be social media stars," Jennifer said.

"Wait, we?" Tayla asked.

"In all the tabs, Riley is David's wingman. You're going to be on Riley's arm, Wednesday."

"Wow, this is real. Watch out klieg lights; here I come."

"I'll let David and Riley know that you can make it."

When shooting ended for the day, Jennifer got a call on her HoloPad. Kathy, Navvy's assistant, popped up. "Hello, Jennifer, Navvy would like for you to join him for a business lunch on Wednesday after the shoot wraps for the day."

"I'd be glad to. What time?"

"One o'clock in the Tovar Executive Dining Room."

"I'll be there. Anything I should prepare for?"

"You might think about whether your goals include being a part of Tovar Studios after your internship is complete," Kathy said

"Tell Mr. Kelrithian that I look forward to meeting him on Wednesday."

Jennifer was deep in thought by the time she got home. Jennifer set out some food for Dandy and then took Pugs for a walk around the neighborhood. She started just last week as a studio intern. Now, Jennifer Gallagher was preparing to negotiate a screenwriting credit for *Attack of the Hoclarth Alliance*, and she was romantically involved with its most eligible young star. Jennifer needed some mom time to help her put things in perspective.

Sheila pulled in to the driveway just as Jennifer and Pugs were completing their walk. When her mom exited the car, Jennifer grabbed her in a bear hug. "We need to talk."

JENNIFER AND SHEILA SETTLED IN TO THE BREAKFAST NOOK.

"You look overwhelmed," Sheila said.

"Things are happening very fast. I created an app called Props Curator, but it needs some new technology to make it work. I rewrote the screenplay for *Attack* on Sunday, sent it to Navvy today, and we shot from it this afternoon. David invited me to go dancing at the most exclusive club in LA. Whatever there is between us will become very public after the paps get all over us coming into the club."

"Jennifer, since you were eight years old, you accepted and mastered challenges way beyond your years. I have often wanted to step in and try to make you slow down and be a kid just a little longer. I resisted that urge because, on top of all the other things you accomplished, you managed to grow into a well-adjusted teenager. A highly-educated, best-selling author, entrepreneur, inventor, and star athlete with a large bank account, but first and foremost, a nice kid I'm extremely proud of." Sheila sipped her coffee. "If you need to step back and slow down, I'll help you do that. That is your personal choice."

"I don't want to stop. I want to put all of my tasks and commitments on the road to completion. I need your advice as my attorney and my mom."

"I can do that. Where do you want to start?"

"The screenplay. I sent it to Navvy. He started shooting on it two hours later. He wants a lunch meeting on Wednesday. Kathy says I should be ready to discuss my future with Tovar Studios."

"Jen, I would have advised against submitting the script without contractual protection, but I trust Navvy to treat you fairly. So, let's start there. Where do you want to be in five years?"

"I want to be a filmmaker. I want to be in the entertainment industry. But I know that I can be creative as a novelist and in the tech industry."

"So, don't commit to long-term employment. Make it project-based. You have time to commit hours during your senior year because your education is complete, so promise Navvy twenty hours a week during the year. Leave it open after that. Ask him if he's open to giving you a writer's credit on the current script and how he might compensate you."

"Will you negotiate my contracts?" Jennifer asked.

"Of course. We need to start documenting your writing accomplishments for membership in the Writer's Guild. Have you decided what name you want to use for screen credits?"

"I want to go with Jenna Seldon for the writing credits. Do I want that for everything?"

"Not necessarily, but we can decide later," Sheila said. "I sent your mini-drone design to the intellectual property expert. He likes it but agrees that you need an engineer."

"We have two pending projects. What do you suggest?"

"I suggest that we have dinner with the Mendoza's tomorrow night. Steven's project at Skunk Works is shutting down, and he's afraid he might be laid off."

"That's too bad...Wait, you think that Tayla's dad could be the project manager for my projects?"

"Exactly. We can suggest some team members from HumanAI and GGG, and he can select the aerospace talent. I made a couple of phone calls. The two companies would be more than willing to contribute personnel as their share of the investment."

"Should I make the invitation?"

"You're the CEO of JennaTech."

"Here or at a restaurant?"

"Set a time, and I'll arrange catering here."

"Okay, let's talk about David Masing."

"Do you want to be in a relationship with him?"

"I think I do, Mom. He's nice, and he is part of *Brilliant*."

"Are you ready for the baggage that comes from the fact that he is a movie star?" Sheila asked. "Are you ready to become a public figure?"

"I think I can handle the paparazzi," Jennifer said.

"Then you and Tayla need new dresses. Call Tayla up and invite her dad and mom for tomorrow's dinner and then go shopping."

"That works for me. Thanks, Mom. Love you."

"That's what I'm here for."

JENNIFER CALLED AND TAYLA ANSWERED QUICKLY. "HI, JEN. ARE WE going shopping?"

"Yes, where do we go?"

"I looked it up. There is a store called Vintage on Rodeo Drive that caters to people attending The Virtual Copa. They print dresses on site after you select and fit them. It's incredibly expensive but trés chic. We can look inside and drool a bit and then look for something more affordable."

"Girlfriend, I got us into this; it's my treat."

"But...."

"You remember those apps that I have been building for the studio?" Jennifer asked.

"You mentioned them. Have you made a little money off the software?"

"Six figures."

"OMG. Deal. You buy the threads; I'll buy dinner. I'll pick you up at six-thirty?"

"That works. Tayla, I need to speak with your father. Mom and I are inviting your family over for dinner tomorrow. It's a business thing."

"I'm worried that Dad might lose his job."

"That's kind of what this is about. I'm working on a couple of projects, and I need your dad to work for me. May I speak to him?"

"Sure, I'll call him. Dad? Jen wants to talk to you." Tayla yelled. "See you in a few."

"Hi, Jennifer," Steven said.

"Mr. Mendoza, I'm calling you about a startup company called

JennaTech. I need a program manager with aerospace experience to form a team to develop my designs."

"Your mom must have told you my situation. I'm interested."

"Could you, Ana, and Tayla come for dinner tomorrow to discuss this?"

"Yes, we could. Is it possible for you to send me a look at your design?"

"As soon as I get off the phone. I call it a Selfie-Drone commercially, but it'll be used in large numbers to film large and complicated location scenes. It's in the non-disclosure agreement."

"Sounds interesting. I look forward to hearing your proposal," Steven said. "Jennifer, I need to warn you. I need to protect my family, so I will be circulating my résumé for a permanent position."

"Of course, Mr. Mendoza."

"SAMI?" JENNIFER SAID.

"Yes, Boss."

"Send the Selfie-Drone design under cover of an NDA to Steven Mendoza."

"Tayla's dad?"

"That's the one."

"Done."

JENNIFER SHOWERED AND DRESSED FOR A SHOPPING TRIP TO RODEO Drive. Jennifer rode with Tayla as she navigated her vehicle to the hills of Beverly. They found parking a couple of blocks above Rodeo Drive and walked down to the shopping mecca. After a couple of blocks of window shopping, Jennifer and Tayla came to the store called Vintage.

"May I help you?"

"We have reservations to The Virtual Copa for Wednesday. We heard that you might be able to dress us up for that club." Jennifer said.

"You came to the right place; I'm Julia. We have a special

agreement with the Copa so that the ladies attending don't wear the same gowns. All of our products are unique," Julia said.

"I'm Tayla, and this is Jennifer. So, how does it work?" Tayla asked.

"We capture some motion media to generate a virtual representation of you, and then we take you through our media collection of celebrities wearing high fashion. We do our best to match your look with the most elegant contemporary gowns. When you select a dress, we get all the measurements and then recreate the dress using our patented VintageTech printing process. We'll have a sample within an hour for fitting. Our tailors will then finish the gown, and we deliver within twenty-four hours. We recommend a stylist for hair and makeup. You're then ready to attend your function in a vintage replica worn by a Hollywood icon. Also, Vintage provides you a one-page provenance of the dress identifying the original wearer, the circumstances, and the events," Julia said.

"It sounds pricey," Tayla said.

"We try to stay competitive with the name brands along Rodeo, but yes, we are a bit expensive."

"Like I said, my treat. Let's do this," Jennifer said.

Julia took several views of the girls. The two then sat down on a virtual reality set. They viewed the stars in their dresses. When they saw one that they liked, they were able to see themselves in the gown.

"Jennifer, why don't you look at some gowns worn by Maureen O'Hara? You two share some stunning Irish characteristics," Julia said.

"She was in one of my favorite movies from that period." Jennifer searched through the Maureen O'Hara collection. "Tay, what do you think of this pink dress?"

"Wow. That works. Can we redo her hair?"

"Vintage, show Jennifer with makeup, curly hair, and bangs," Julia said.

"Omigod, that's perfect," Tayla said. "You're ready for your closeup."

Jennifer blushed. "I think I'll take that one."

Julia looked at Tayla, "May I ask if you dance?"

"My best friend can't decide whether to be buried on Wimbledon or the Met. She is equally obsessed with both dance and tennis."

"Rita Moreno was the principal dancer in *West Side Story* and won best supporting actress."

"I love that movie, and I know most of those dances."

Tayla looked through the Rita Moreno collection and selected a dress that Moreno wore in *West Side Story*.

"You look terrific, Tay," Jennifer said.

"It really is me. You sure you can afford this, Jen?" Tayla asked.

"Let's do this. If we are going to be Hollywood starlets for a night, we might as well look the part."

The girls spent some time with measurements. "Were you planning on dinner? Now would be a good time and then you can come back and do the final fitting," Julia said.

"Agreed." The girls had a light dinner along Rodeo and came back for the fitting.

Afterward, Jennifer presented her black AmEx card. Julia turned it down. "Ladies, Mr. Kelrithian sends his compliments and hopes that you have a great time," Julia said.

"Thank him for Tayla and me," Jennifer said. "Close your mouth, Tayla."

They took their packages and scheduled Wednesday afternoon at The Old Style. Tayla drove home, and the two girls hugged. "I think that we'll be appropriate eye candy for our movie-star escorts," Tayla said.

"Are you ready for the paps?"

"Can't live under a rock forever."

TWELVE

The Writers' Room

J ennifer arrived on the Tovar lot at her regular time of seven-thirty. Kathy popped up on her HoloPad. "Good Morning, Jennifer. Navvy would like for you to sit in with the writers at eight o'clock. I sent the location info to your assistant. You will make your call time after the meeting."

"I'll be there, Kathy. Thanks." Jennifer wondered how she would do in a meeting with experienced screenwriters. She decided to sit in the back, keep quiet, and watch. She had time to stop at Craft Services and arm herself with her double-shot caramel Frappuccino.

She arrived at the meeting five minutes early and took a seat at the back near the wall. There was the main table surrounded by comfortable chairs. Along the walls were stacks of paper scripts, reference materials from long past movie history, and a table with a Starbucks and breakfast food.

Two writers arrived, leaving the seat at the front table empty. They ignored Jennifer.

"Good Morning, James. I heard that somebody dumped a total rewrite on Navvy's desk yesterday and he bought it." Susie, a blonde with brown eyes, said.

"They did reshoots from the rogue script yesterday afternoon," James said.

"How could he do that without running it past us?"

"I heard it was an intern." James, a blonde-haired, blue-eyed Brit, said.

Jennifer nervously sipped her Frap.

"Somebody said she's a writer," Susie said.

"Can Navvy do that without guild approval?" James placed his travel mug and notebook on the table.

"He's the head of the studio, the producer, and he wrote the story. So, yes."

"Are we going to lose our jobs?"

Just then, a forty-something woman came into the room and took the empty seat at the head of the table. Everyone started shouting at once.

"Is it true?" James asked.

"Gia, is he firing us?" Susie said.

The woman, named Giorgia, looked past the two writers, past the table, to the back of the room. "Are you Jennifer?"

All the heads at the table immediately turned towards the young intern.

"Yes, ma'am."

"Apparently, young lady, you are now one of us. My name is Giorgia Bianchi, and I've got three Academy screenwriting nominations and one win. James has a Ph.D. from MIT and Susie won a Golden Globe two years ago. I go by Gia. Team, this is Jennifer Gallagher, a summer intern who has been on the lot for five whole days."

THERE WAS GASPING AND MUMBLING.

"How old are you?" Susie asked.

"I turn seventeen next Thursday."

"Have you ever written anything or been published?" James asked.

Gia interrupted, "Have you studied writing? Have you had any training?"

"I started taking courses at UVN when I was eight."

"How far have you gotten?" Susie asked.

"I completed the coursework for a bachelor's degree in English and a Masters in English Literature."

"How many screenplays have you done and what is your training?" Gia asked.

"I completed all of the screenwriting classes at UVN. *Attack* is my first complete screenplay rewrite," Jennifer said.

"But you're still in high school?" Susie asked.

"I decided that I didn't want to show off for my classmates, so I do all of the college stuff as Jenna Seldon. It's my secret identity."

There was a pause. "Hugo award-winning *Galaxy Warrior* Jenna Seldon?" Gia asked.

"Guilty."

"My name is James Weldon. I consult on the technical issues for *Brilliant* and keep the *Brilliant Tech Manual* up to date. Are you the one who sent several corrections over the last few months?"

"Yes, that's me."

"Navvy sent me a volume called *The Mathematics of Brilliant*. Are you the author?" James asked.

"Yes, that was my Ph.D. Dissertation."

"Ph.D.? You read the Manual?" Susie asked.

"I finished the twelve volumes when I was thirteen," Jennifer said.

"I'm Susie Wilder; there was a rumor that you won an argument with Navvy on set by quoting a passage from the Manual."

"We discussed it, and Navvy deferred to my opinion."

"How can you quote a random passage from that twelve-volume monster?" James asked.

"I have an eidetic memory."

"Alright, team. I read Jennifer's rewrite. It is rough in places, but it's solid," Gia said. "Jennifer, it appears you're in the right place. Navvy reassured me that there would be no other personnel changes to our group." There was a collective release of breath at Gia's last comment. "Jennifer, our group meets at this time and place Tuesday through Friday. I understand that you have other duties on the set, so I hope that you can give us this first hour and we can pass out writing tasks. In the future, please send me your changes directly and keep me in the loop. Why don't you come and join us at the table?"

Jennifer moved to an open seat. "Thanks for letting me join you. I hope I can help."

"Are you the one who creates all of the magical apps for that new HoloPad that people are getting?" Susie asked.

"Guilty again."

"Could you write an app for us?"

"What would you like it to do?"

"On the set, techs can create virtual actors and program their lines. Is it possible to do that on a much smaller scale with scenes that we write so that we can see how they play out?" Susie asked.

"Sami, could you join us?"

Another redhead popped up to the right of Jennifer. "I have been listening, Boss."

"This is Samantha, my HoloBuddy"

"Where is her office?" James asked.

"Sami is virtual. When you get your HoloPad, you can configure a virtual assistant for yourself. Sami helps me with a lot of work, and she interfaces with the computing power that I have access to."

"What computing power will we have access to?" James asked.

"Tovar Studios has the local HumanAI server plus the four HoloTurbo units installed this past weekend. There is currently enough overhead to make the HoloPads very responsive. Sami, is Susie's idea plausible?"

"Presently, it's possible only on the most rudimentary level. You could see the characters interacting, the resolution would be grainy, the audio would sound rather flat, and the acting would lack nuance. Current technology is approximately one-point-five Moores behind what this app would require to be robust and mature," Sami said.

"What is a Moore?" Susie asked.

James replied. "A Moore generation is a doubling of computer and software capability and a thirty percent decrease in cost. Named after Gordon Moore, an early chip developer, this doubling takes about fifteen months. What Sami is saying is that someone should start this project, but it'll take about two years before it's fully useful."

"That's correct, but I can start building it soon and have something up and running in two weeks. After that, we'll need an engineering tech team to perfect the hardware and coding," Jennifer said. "Sami, do you remember those writing aids we developed? Could we quickly implement those?"

"We have Actor-to-Dialogue, Character-to-Dialogue, BeatSheet, Scene Generator, Similar-Scenes, Similar-Dialogue and Similar-Action, and Unblocker. Yes, sis, we can include those."

"Sami, begin implementation of ScreenWriter's Buddy using those parameters. And include an immersive tutorial," Jennifer said.

"You just used some interesting names. Could you explain?" Gia said.

"The apps that I create are based on an engine that HumanAI developed which collects, maintains, and accesses Big Data. For example, the Humanities data includes about sixty percent of all literature ever written. That number is low because so much was historically lost to fire, flooding, and war. It includes eighty-five percent of worldwide scripted media ever produced for motion pictures and television, and it contains over ninety percent of shooting scripts and screenplays. My family's company, GGG, has helped HumanAI curate this data.

"If you're writing for a specific actor, Actor-to-Dialogue analyzes and makes suggestions based on the dialogue performed by the actor in the past. Character-to-Dialogue does the same if you're adapting from a specific literary character or even a historical figure. BeatSheet comes from Blake Snyder's book, *Save the Cat*. It helps generate an outline for a screenplay. It analyzes and suggests based on BeatSheets from almost all movies ever produced. It then enables you to write to the BeatSheet and keep on track with the correct screenplay paging.

"SceneGen allows you to set up a scene based upon a detailed description and historical context of past movies and then provides analysis and writing cues. The Similar apps track your writing to help you choose whether to adapt from the past or avoid copying writing from another source in the data. I based this one of my favorite quotes, 'Creativity is plagiarism from multiple sources,'" Jennifer said.

"I like that. What is Unblocker?" Gia asked.

"That is a fancy screensaver and mind trick. The system tracks what you're writing, and if you pause for a time, for example, if you have writer's block, it'll flash words, audio, video, and pictures that relate to what you're writing. I found that these take my mind out of the box and encourage better writing. Unblocker also interrupts if your writing is getting repetitious or stale and suggests a break. Sami and I designed it to adapt to the user. It'll be much more useful after you have used it for a couple of weeks," Jennifer finished.

"Omigod, does it make coffee?" Susie asked.

"You can order a specific drink from a nearby Starbucks machine from your HoloPad and then walk over to pick it up."

"Excuse me, Jennifer, but it's ten minutes to your next crew call," Sami said.

"Before you go, when do we get our HoloPads?" Gia asked.

"Sami, contact Grayson and ask him to send five HoloPads to the Writers' Room," Jennifer said. "How many writers on the lot, Gia?"

"There are fifty-four on staff and many others on contract."

"Sami, contact Grayson to coordinate a rollout to the other projects and writers. What is the timeframe on ScreenWriter's Buddy?"

"I can have ScreenWriter's Buddy up and running with the existing apps by tomorrow morning," Sami said. "I started to develop the HoloScene Generator, and it'll be in ugly alpha by next Thursday. Ugly alpha is barely functional and very buggy."

"We can't wait," Gia said. "Go do your other job. Again, we meet in this room Tuesday through Friday. Check in as often as possible."

"May I have your permission to record your meetings? That's a function on the HoloPad."

"That's fine. We look forward to working with you."

"Gia, five HoloPads will arrive at this room in forty-five minutes. Thanks for the opportunity to work with you."

By lunch, the director on *Brilliant* completed the reshoots recommended.

Jennifer called her mom on the way to lunch.

"Is dinner set up?" Jennifer asked.

"All fixed. Six o'clock. The house AI messaged me, and your dress has arrived," Sheila said.

"Cool. I created a new app called ScreenWriter's Buddy. It

compiles all the writer's tools that I created and opened up a new project for JennaTech. It'll be a challenge because the new function is about two years behind what we want it to do. I want it to generate HoloScenes based on the scene that the writer is currently working on."

"That sounds promising. I have a client coming in. I'll see you after work."

JENNIFER GRABBED A SANDWICH AND SAT DOWN ALONE IN THE cafeteria. On the second bite, a young man approached, "Jennifer?" he said.

"Yes."

"I'm Jake Hargrove. I work as a temp with Grayson in IT. May I join you?"

"Of course. How may I help you?"

"I'm a huge fan of you and the apps you created."

"Thanks."

"There is a problem."

"I'm listening."

"I charted the CPU demand on all the lot's computing power. If you consider the increasing number of HoloPads, the number of apps that users are subscribing to, and the amount of time users are spending on the pads; we'll exceed all our computing resources by next Thursday. Life in the fast lane will slow down to Sepulveda Pass with a sigalert at Mulholland Drive."

"I get it. Sami, join us."

Sami popped up. "I've been listening, Boss. I studied the problem that Jake presented. The studio will start to slow down after ten o'clock next Thursday."

"Do you have a solution?" Jennifer asked.

"During grad school at UVN, I interned at HumanAI, and I worked on the HoloPad. The beta devices were very underpowered. The current operating system and the underlying code of your apps depend on that architecture. The release version of the HoloPad hardware has about five times as much computing power. The OS upgrade is due in two weeks. That upgrade will only solve a third of the problem. The apps need to be recoded to take advantage of the computing power. I can do that in my spare time," Jake said.

"What is the third part?"

"Look around you." Jennifer looked around. At least two-thirds of the diners in the room were joined by a HoloCharacter, either their HoloBuddy or someone they were chatting with.

"I see it."

"There are several locations on the lot like this room with intense HoloPad use. Those areas are taxing the network and computing resources. We need to install local MiniTurbos and upgrade the fiber-optic network to the hub."

"You said you're a temp. What's your status?"

"My contract ends this Friday," Jake said.

"So, you're looking for a job?"

"Yes."

"What's your degree?"

"Undergrad degree in Computer Science and Masters in Artificial Intelligence from UVN. I'm working on my doctorate in HoloTechnology part-time."

"Do you have dinner plans?"

"No," Jake said.

"I'm forming a startup to help me bring my ideas to the market. Interested?"

"Absolutely."

They exchanged information and Jake left.

JENNIFER STARTED HER SHORT WALK BACK TO THE SOUNDSTAGE, "Sami, contact Grayson." A moment later Grayson popped up.

"How can I help you, Jen."

"Tell me about Jake Hargrove."

"He is our best temp. He mentioned that he was going to chase you down. He told me about the problems we're going to have. I'm working on the hardware end. I've promised him that he'll be the first to receive full-time employment when we get funds. I hate to lose him."

"I'm starting a new company called JennaTech to build my ideas. Would it be okay if I poached him?"

"That would be perfect for Jake. He's a bit over-qualified for our shop."

"When can you release him? I need for him to start recoding my apps to reduce the computing load at Tovar. I'm guessing that he has told you the timeline?"

"Yes, he has. I can release him to you tomorrow if you can start paying him."

"Is it possible that he can keep his office for a couple of weeks since he'll be working on projects benefitting Tovar? You can give him the bad news that you're releasing him but keep it quiet that I'm offering him a job."

"Of course, thanks for all of your help."

"Thank you, Grayson."

On the way back to Sound Stage One, Jennifer messaged her mother, "Could we add one more place for dinner tonight? Jake Hargrove is a potential new employee of JennaTech."

The rest of the day's shooting schedule was back on track and passed without incident. Afterward, David approached, "I'm looking forward to some serious dancing. So is Riley."

"Tayla and I are all fashioned up and ready to go. You know of course that I have twice the human complement of left feet," Jennifer said.

"I know. I've seen you on your butt."

"You won't let me forget that."

"I don't plan to. Wanna grab food?"

"I have a business dinner tonight. I'm starting a company for my technology ideas."

"Of course, you are. Good luck." They hugged and parted.

When Jennifer got home, she went to her mom, "Can we chat?"

"Sure, what's on your mind?" Sheila asked.

"I don't think that I'm ready to lead a startup company from the business side and I'm not old enough legally to have that responsibility. I need a competent CEO to handle those duties."

"I agree."

"Mother, would you be willing to take the position of Chief Executive Officer of JennaTech and mentor me in preparation for me to succeed you?" Jennifer asked.

Sheila's eyes watered as they had many times through the years as she dealt with the fact that her daughter was a cerebral superstar. "I would be honored."

"And, I don't want you to be my mommy on this. I want you to take a real salary and a real ownership share. I want Dad to participate as well. Between the three of us, we would maintain a controlling interest and then distribute profits and ownership to other participants. Tell me what you think of this."

"Great, so far."

"I'd like to assign my royalties, profit from my IP, and royalties from my books to JennaTech to provide some initial cash flow."

"Yes, on the income related to intellectual property. No, on the author royalties. As your attorney, I recommend that you incorporate your earnings as an author and related creative endeavors under a separate entity. If JennaTech fails, you don't want all of your wealth under the same tent when it falls."

Jennifer's eyes got big for a moment. "Too many eggs, not enough baskets, right?"

"Egg-sactly."

"Do you accept my offer of employment and compensation as Employee Number Two of JennaTech?"

"I accept." The two business partners shook hands. "Let's walk through and make sure everything is ready for dinner."

JAKE ARRIVED FIRST. JENNIFER GREETED HIM AND INTRODUCED HIM TO her mom who said, "Jennifer tells me that you're the software guru."

"That's very generous. I'm a real fan of what Jennifer has created in a short time," Jake said.

"My mom will be acting as CEO of JennaTech. Until I turn twenty-one, I'll be acting as Chief Technology Officer."

"Grayson let me know that I'll be laid off after tomorrow, but for some reason, he said not to pack?" Jake said.

"Would you like to work for JennaTech?"

"What is the position?"

"I'd like you to take the lead on AI and HoloPad Software. You pointed out some specific problems with my apps. I'd like you to start by fixing those. JennaTech doesn't yet have office space. The initial work would directly benefit Tovar, so Grayson is offering to allow you to keep your office space."

"What does it pay?" Jake asked.

"Initially, you'll get a twenty percent raise from what you're making at Tovar, with quarterly raises based upon productivity. You'll get company ownership incentives, and you'll receive thirty percent of royalties from any intellectual property that you create. JennaTech will also pay your tuition toward your doctorate." Jennifer said.

"That's very generous. I'm in. When do I start?"

"Can you start on Thursday?"

"Yes."

"Would you be willing to sign a non-disclosure on what we discuss tonight?"

"Of course."

"Done. Welcome to JennaTech. You're officially Employee Number Four. I'm Number One, mom is Two, and I'm reserving Three for our guest of honor this evening."

A FEW MINUTES LATER, THE MENDOZA FAMILY ARRIVED. Introductions were made, and the six retired to dinner.

"Dr. Goldstein, that is a very colorful tie," Tayla said.

"Thank you, it's by Jerry Garcia," Allen said.

"He must be a very accomplished clothing designer."

"Tay, my stepdad's a Deadhead," Jennifer said.

"Deadhead?"

"Look it up."

"Okay."

After the appetizer of Blue Cheese and Pear Tartlets, Jennifer began the serious conversation, "Mr. Mendoza, please describe the work that you have been doing?"

"Please, call me Steven. For the last seven years, I have been designing and supervising the Avionics and AI team that's creating the newest class of military aircraft. Unfortunately, after one-hundred and twenty-three years, our company is exiting the defense industry, and so my employment is ending. I will miss my work, but the company has offered me a generous severance package."

"What aircraft were you working on?" Jake asked.

"Jake, I could tell you, but then I would have to shoot you," Steven said.

"Skunk Works?"

"Correct."

"Have you ever been able to work on an aircraft as wonderful as the SR-71 Blackbird from the 1960s?"

"Like I said...."

"Never mind."

Jennifer steered the conversation back to the matter at hand. "What do you think of my design for the Selfie-Drone?"

"It's very promising and somewhat enlightened in that you used many off-the-shelf components. Of course, the biggest challenge is fitting it into a small enough and light enough package in the first generation."

"Selfie-Drone?" Jake asked.

"Sami, fly the mini-drone above the table for everyone to see. Start with actual size," Jennifer said.

"Yes, Boss." The device appeared above the table and zoomed in and out and revealed itself up close to each diner. The rectangle flew with two internal rotors. The mirror opened and rotated. A simulated image also hovered above the table indicating what the drone would display as it zoomed in and out and turned.

"There would be as many as forty mini-drones flying above an action scene on location, getting close-ups, overhead and tracking shots. The on-site networked hardware would gang-roll the drones, record all the shots, and compile the images for post-production. The system, called VirtualLocation40, would roll up to the location in two fifty-four-foot tractor trailers." Jennifer explained.

"Imaging, device software, avionics, power, networking, trailer hardware, and software. That's a challenging project." Steven said.

"Mr. Mendoza…Steven, would you be willing to manage this project as employee Number Three of JennaTech?" Jennifer asked.

The conversation continued as the second course of Tuscan Kale Caesar Salad was served.

"Would I be able to select my team? I'd need one of my aeronautical engineer colleagues from Skunk Works, engineers familiar with imaging, networking, and audio and video production software. I would also need a hotshot AI developer. And then there is funding?" Steven asked.

Sheila jumped in. "Jennifer, you aren't aware of this. I made a couple of phone calls today. My company, GGG, and HumanAI will be major investors in JennaTech. GGG will provide tech support, business and human resources, office and lab space, and will assist in marketing within the entertainment industry not only for the VirtualLocation system but the HoloPad Apps. HumanAI will provide funding, HoloPad software support, fabrication, and device integration in exchange for the simultaneous development of the Selfie-Drone."

"Selfie-Drone? You mean I can have this toy in my pocket?" Tayla asked.

"That's the idea. Jake, do you know any hotshot AI developers?" Jennifer said.

"Me?"

"That works. Jennifer, I'm in." Steven said.

There were congratulations around the table.

Allen stood and proposed a toast. "To Jennifer, and our new company, JennaTech."

"To JennaTech," the diners said.

Sheila stood, "Attention, our newest attorney at GGG has passed the California bar exam and has begun to write the Articles of Incorporation for JennaTech. With your concurrence, Jennifer, I am going to appoint Ana as General Counsel for the company."

"Of course," Jennifer said.

"To Ana Mendoza, Esquire," Sheila said.

Tayla smiled, "Mom? Congratulations?"

"Thanks so much. I'm honored to accept," Ana said.

There was more applause and handshakes around the table as the entree of Baked Dijon Salmon was served.

"Am I the only one at the table who is unemployed?" Tayla said.

"You can be the Chief Beta Tester," Jennifer said.

"You mean I get to play with the toys before anyone else? That works."

The dinner was deemed a great success by all present as everyone finished the dessert of White Chocolate Raspberry Cheesecake.

AFTER DINNER, JENNIFER ASKED TAYLA TO COME TO HER ROOM. "Would you like to see our dresses?" Jennifer asked.

They got to the room, and Jennifer turned, "Tayla, you have been flirting with Jake all night. Won't Riley be jealous?"

Tayla laughed, "You have always been gaydar-challenged."

"I thought...but...Sami?"

"Yes, Sis, Jake is gay. Now, show Tayla the dress," Sami said.

The two girls tried on their dresses and Jennifer gawked. "Wow, you and Riley will be pap bait. Total celeb couple."

Tayla took on a dreamy look. "Riley is special. He's cute. He can play tennis. I wonder if he can dance...."

THIRTEEN

Albuquerque, New Mexico, Three Years Earlier

R iley McMaster finished his twice-weekly advanced Salsa class at the SalsaMex Dance Studio. As usual, he was hit on by a couple of twenty-somethings, each wanting him to be their dance partner in a Salsa contest.

"My girlfriend is a senior at UNM. She's my regular partner in competition," Riley said.

"But can't we have a drink and talk about it?" one girl asked.

In reality, he was too busy studying to have a girlfriend. When he did compete, he had a list of enthusiastic partners to choose from. Besides, he was only seventeen and the son of a single mom. Jada McMaster was a laser engineer for Boeing at Kirkland Air Force Base.

"I have to get home and study for midterms." That, too, was a lie. He just completed his coursework for a Masters in Spaceborne Propulsion at the University of New Mexico. His thesis entitled, "Simulation of a Newtonian Heavy Body. Is the *StarCruiser Brilliant* Gravity Drive More than Fiction?" had attracted six-figure job offers from many aerospace companies.

He got in his self-driving Corolla and directed the car to take him to his Foothills home. He got out his pad and checked his messages.

From: @thechiefdesigner

To: @loboguru
Re: Your high score has been exceeded on *Brilliant*Sim

@THECHIEFDESIGNER HAS COMPLETED THEHANNACHALLENGE AND posted a higher score, passing you on the leaderboard. He challenges you to match his score and save *StarCruiser Brilliant*.

RILEY GOT HOME OVERLOOKING THE CITY AND GREETED HIS MOTHER in the kitchen. "Hi, Mom."

"I brought home Tex-Mex. Would you like to go to a movie with Alyssa and me? It's Friday night," Jada said.

"Sorry, Mom, I got a challenge from the chief designer," Riley said. "Thanks for dinner."

"That *Brilliant*Sim is going to fry your brain," Jada said.

Riley knew that his mother thought that he spent way too much time in steveLearn on the *Brilliant*Sim. *I am a brillian. I must beat @thechiefdesigner*, he thought.

RILEY ENTERED STEVELEARN. "START *BRILLIANT*SIM WITH TheHannaChallenge," Riley said.

Navvy Kelrithian popped up on the bridge of Brilliant. "Welcome back, Riley. You're at the Engineer Console on Brilliant. The ship is on a shakedown cruise inside the orbit of Mercury near the sun. The goal is to engage the gravity drive, escape the sun's gravity, and return to Earth all while avoiding the disaster of using the StarDrive and traveling back two hundred years to another timeline. The *Brilliant*Sim has the latest upgrades. Good luck. Say 'engage' when ready." Navvy disappeared.

"Engage," Riley said.

Instantly, Riley was facing the Engineer Console on the aft end of the bridge of Brilliant. Behind him were Navvy in the captain's chair and Jack in the pilot seat.

Navvy gave the order. "Pilot, we'll begin our outbound turn inside

Mercury's orbit at my mark and engage the gravity drive to point-one light-speed outbound on a return course to Earth."

"Make the turn on my mark and engage, Pilot, aye," Jack said.

"Engineer, report systems status."

Riley surveyed his panel and made the report. "Em drive nominal. Gravity drive indicates ready. StarDrive available,"

"Five seconds to turn," Navvy looked at all the indicators. "Pilot, make your turn and engage the gravity drive."

The sun appeared as a giant yellow ball on the view screen. It moved to the left off screen, and Jack said, "Engaging." Jack pushed the t-bar with his right hand to mid-range.

Immediately, red lights began flashing, audio signals sounded. Riley immediately saw the problem, "Captain the main gravity drive relay has failed."

"Pilot, engage the em drive."

"Em drive at full power."

Ani, the Artificial Navigation Intelligence, sounded off, "Alert. Decaying orbit. Collision with the surface of the sun in thirty-seven minutes."

"Engineer, can you make repairs?"

"Captain, the Manual indicates that it will take three hours to fabricate and replace the relay."

"Navvy, we need to engage the StarDrive," Jack said.

"We don't know what will happen if we engage the StarDrive in the gravity well," Navvy said.

"Captain, I am going to attempt fabrication and repair," said Riley.

"Riley, you better hurry. It's going to get warm in a few minutes," Navvy said.

Riley quickly reviewed the *Brilliant Tech Manual*. To do this, he would have to attempt something never before accomplished.

"Alert. Decaying orbit. Collision with the surface of the sun in thirty minutes."

"Engi, show me the failed relay in place," Riley ordered the Engineering Intelligence.

Before him, the failed relay appeared. "Engi, we fried the main coil.

That doesn't explain why it failed." Riley rotated the relay in the air using his hands. He spread his hands and looked at certain parts up closely. Then he looked at the extensible latching actuator. "Do you see it?"

"Alert. Decaying orbit. Collision with the surface of the sun in twenty minutes," Ani said.

"Yes, that's it, Riley," Engi said.

"The actuator arm was fabricated below specifications and failed causing the main power coil to fry," Riley said. "How long will it take to pull it and fabricate it?"

"It will take three hours, Riley," Engi said.

"Alert. Decaying orbit. Collision with the surface of the sun in fifteen minutes," Ani said.

"Navvy, we need to engage the StarDrive and get out of here," Jack said.

Navvy turned his chair, and his eyes were wide open. "Riley?"

"I have an idea, Captain," Riley said. "Engi, what is the status of the matter transfer device?"

"Riley, it is unproven. It can transport fifty pounds accurately eighty percent of the time."

"How much do the two parts weigh?" Riley asked.

Engi replied, "Forty-eight-point-three pounds, Sir."

"Engi, jerk the two faulty parts and use the material to refab the fixed parts."

"Beginning processing. It will take eight-point-seven minutes."

"Alert. Decaying orbit. Collision with the surface of the sun in ten minutes," Ani said.

"Engineer?" Navvy asked.

"Captain, we are fabricating the parts, and I will matter transfer them into the device."

"How long will it take?"

"Eight and a half minutes, Captain," Riley said. "Plus, I need a minute to test the relay."

"Seriously, Engineer, you're giving me thirty seconds leeway to fly or fry this starship?" Navvy asked.

"Yes, Sir. I think it will work."

"Alert. Decaying orbit. Collision with the surface of the sun in five minutes," Ani said.

"Engineer, confirm the StarDrive ready in all respects."

"Sir, the StarDrive is ready in all respects," Riley said.

"Pilot, be ready to engage either the StarDrive or the gravity drive on my mark."

"Ready, Captain," Jack said.

Riley focused on his console. "Engi, when the fab is complete, transfer the parts into the relay and I will begin the testing protocol."

"Alert. Decaying orbit. Collision with the surface of the sun in three minutes," Ani said.

"Transfer in one minute," Engi said.

RILEY HEARD A TONE ON HIS CONSOLE. "TRANSFER COMPLETE. READY for testing," Engi said.

"Engi, basic operation check."

"Passed."

"Twenty-five percent power check," Riley said.

"Passed," Engi said.

"One minute to burn up," Ani said.

"Fifty percent."

"Failed."

Navvy turned to Riley. "StarDrive?"

"Recalibrate the latching actuator twenty microns and re-run the fifty," Riley

"Thirty seconds to burn-up," Ani said.

"Passed the fifty," Engi said.

"Seventy-five, Engi."

"Fifteen seconds to burn-up," Ani said.

"Passed."

"Ten-nine-eight-…"

"Captain, I certify that the gravity drive is ready,"

"…five-four-…"

"Pilot, engage the gravity drive."

Jack pushed the t-bar with his right hand to mid-range. Brilliant shook for a moment, and then the rear-view display went from bright white to a receding sphere.

The bridge crew cheered. Navvy turned his chair and said, "Way to go, Riley!"

The simulation faded to black. Navvy popped up again. "Congratulations, Riley McMaster. You have now qualified as Chief Engineer of *StarCruiser Brilliant*." The simulator faded to black.

That's strange. It usually posts the high score, and that's all, Riley thought.

"End simulator." Riley got up to get ready for bed.

"Call from Navvy Kelrithian," Lobo, his HoloBuddy said.

"I said end simulation."

"This is a real-time call, Riley," Lobo said.

"Put him on."

"Riley McMaster, my name is Navvy Kelrithian. Would you be available to fly into Burbank tomorrow and have lunch? At Tovar's expense, of course. I want to offer you a job," Navvy said.

FOURTEEN

Lunch with Navvy

Jennifer came into the breakfast nook carrying her favorite caffeine and sugar fix. Sheila asked, "Are you ready for your big lunch with Navvy?"

"Yes. Should I ask for more money?"

"So far, Tovar Studios has been very generous in sharing royalties…to the tune of six figures. You committed to the summer and the stipend. I recommend that you accept that for right now," Sheila said. "On the other hand, if he brings it up, negotiate but don't get greedy."

Sami popped up. "Navvy's assistant sent you a message reminding you to meet Navvy Kelrithian in the Tovar Executive Dining Room at one o'clock. The dress is relaxed business casual."

"Tell Kathy thanks and that I confirm," Jennifer said.

"Remember, you also have an appointment at the stylist at two-thirty."

"Thanks, Sami. Mom, what should I wear to my lunch?"

"It's summer. Dress for success like a working exec but don't overdo it because you're working crew in the morning."

"I'm going to wear my thigh-high Vans. I read that sneaker boots are the new business casual."

"It's going to be ninety-six in the valley today. It's a break from the heat. When I was your age, half the days were in two digits. Do your boots come with a bucket for the sweat?"

"They are AutoSnug and AutoCool."

"What if the batteries run down?"

"Seriously, Mom, they run on public wi-pow."

"My daughter, the supernerd. High Tech from head to toe it is, then. Good luck and ask Maiara for the raspberry iced tea and don't stare at her tattoo. She comes from the indigenous people of New Zealand."

SHEILA WAS PROUD OF HER LITTLE GIRL AS SHE DEPARTED BUT THEN she thought, *The next time I see her she is going to be a lot more grown up.*

JENNIFER ENTERED THE WRITERS' ROOM AS OTHER WRITERS FILED IN. Susie asked, "Jennifer, have you heard that Tovar may bid for the *Galaxy Warrior* movies?"

"No one has talked to me."

"The rumor is that David Masing wants to play Logan Jones."

Gia walked into the room. "Gia, have you heard anything about the Jenna Seldon books?" Susie asked.

"I can neither confirm nor deny that Tovar wants that property for the off-years between the *Brilliant* movies."

"Wow, Jen, can I be on your writing team?" Susie asked.

Jennifer looked at the others for their reaction. "I know nothing about this."

Gia took charge, "It's time to get started. We need to finish the sides for next week. Let's focus first on the technical language while we have James and Jennifer here together."

The meeting continued, but Jennifer's mind was in several places. She contributed a couple of comments and then headed to Sound Stage One for the day's short production schedule.

On her way over, Jennifer called her agent, Sara Suleri-Abarca, a senior partner at the Agency for Creative Artists. "Sara, has there been any noise about *Warriors* from Tovar?"

"Wow, news travels fast. Just this morning, I received a query from your studio. They want a pitch deck, and they want your ideas on who should play Logan Jones and Ayiiia."

"David Masing wants to play Logan, and I support that. I wrote Ayiiia for my friend Tayla. I think she'll be great, but I don't want to bring her name up right away. Do we have the deck in shape?"

"It's dated and could do with a final look."

"Send it to me, and I'll look at it. In the meantime, promise the deck on Friday. Let them know that Jenna will have a first draft of the screenplay by September First."

"I know that you have a lot on your plate right now with the internship. Is that pushing it a bit?" Sara asked.

"I have most of it written in my head."

"You're an agent's dream. Any other presents under the tree in case Christmas comes early?"

"I did a rewrite on *Attack of the Hoclarth Alliance*, and I gave it to Navvy. They are now shooting with my permission."

"That's not good business, Jen."

"I know. I'm having lunch with Navvy. I'll drop hints for a contract and no matter what the number, I'll give you fifteen percent of the real value."

"Be careful, Jennifer. Some people in this business are cutthroat. Try to get a hundred thousand. Anything else?"

"There may be a demand for me as a speaker on technology for HumanAI. Do you have anyone in your office who handles speaking gigs?"

"Yes, we do. What kind of time do you have?"

"Once a month. Max three days travel. I think I can ask low five figures."

"Let's start at forty-K and see if anyone bites," Sara said.

"Thanks, Sara."

"You're amazing. Let's do lunch next week."

THE WEDNESDAY SHOOTING SCHEDULE FOR *BRILLIANT* WAS abbreviated to accommodate demands on the talent for publicity duties. Jennifer greeted David when he came on set, "Did you mention to anyone that you were interested in playing Logan Jones?"

"Yeah, Jen, I had lunch with my agent last week. I told him I knew the writer. What have you heard?"

"Nothing but rumors. Have a good shoot."

"I'm looking forward to tonight."

"Oh, yeah, we have plans, don't we?" Jennifer's blue-green eye winked above the smile. "Remember, I'm a lousy dancer."

"Nice Vans. Do you dance in those?"

"Go up there and pretend you're a movie star." *He noticed my shoes.*

Just then, the Assistant Director announced, "Places, everyone."

Production accelerated by the short day was uneventful, and the crew broke for lunch at twelve-ten.

Jennifer made a stop in an empty dressing room to check her makeup and hair. She entered the Executive Dining Room at twelve-thirty. She spotted a fifty-something female with a tattoo on her chin. Maiara Henare greeted her. "Welcome, Miss Gallagher. My name is Maiara. Mr. Kelrithian has informed me that he'll be five minutes late, but he has asked me to take you to his table."

"Thanks, Maiara."

"What would you like to drink?"

"My mom tells me that you have a special raspberry iced tea."

"It has been a long time since I saw your mother. You remind me of her. You have her beauty and then some. I'll have your server bring you the special iced tea."

"Thank you," Jennifer said. "Sami, the sign says no electronics."

"Low profile it is," Sami said.

"Take good notes, though," Jennifer said under her breath.

Jennifer looked around at the elaborate decorations in the style of twentieth-century English Royalty. Outside of Hollywood, they might have been considered over-the-top. But this was Tinsel Town. The waiter arrived with her drink and a martini for Navvy, "Miss Gallagher, the lunch choices today are Oven-Roasted Duck with an Orange-Ginger Glaze or Slow-Braised Lamb Shank Ossobuco in a

Savory Red Wine Reduction. Our authentic Hotel Caesar Salad precedes lunch and is followed by a selection of desserts."

"Shouldn't we wait for Navvy to come and choose?"

"Mr. Kelrithian always has a blood rare steak with a loaded baked potato."

"You know, I'll have what he's having. Hold the blood."

"Very good, Miss."

As the waiter walked away, Navvy Kelrithian stepped up to the table and Jennifer rose to greet him.

"Thank you so much for this opportunity to dine in such a spectacular room," Jennifer said.

Navvy caught the slight hint of sarcasm. "We make motion pictures here, Jennifer. These decorations came from a costume picture we did thirty years ago about the end of the British Monarchy. What are you having, young lady? I hear the lamb is delicious. Most of the food they serve here leaves me hungry for dinner."

"I'm having what you're having. I guess I have the same problem."

Navvy paused and gave her a lingering look. "The main reason I asked you to lunch was to correct a faulty decision I made very quickly on Monday."

"Sir?"

"You submitted the rewrite without going through an agent. That's unwise in this business. Do you have an agent?"

"Sara Suleri-Abarca at ACA. And yes, she used the words 'not good business.'"

"I know Sara. Very good. Very tough. Very honest. Many years ago, I met her grandmother. She was both an author and a critic, you know, someone who cuts off her tail and then eats it with lots of Tabasco sauce."

They both laughed as the waiter came to the table and created the salads. "Do you know where we got the recipe for this salad?"

"May I guess?"

Navvy looked up. "Go ahead."

"Margarita Lopez."

"Correct. You dined with Jack and Ellie?"

"David and I played doubles on Saturday with Riley and my best friend. We won. David bought dinner."

"That's right. You have stolen the heart of our young star."

"I wouldn't say that...."

"Jennifer, David was never a playboy, but before you came, he played a vast field. Take care of him. He is important to our studio. And take care of yourself. You are, too." Navvy paused to attack his salad. "Let's get back to business. We need to formalize a contract for the rewrite. We can talk some numbers and then you can call in Sara to handle the details. The normal number for a rewrite for a picture of this size is two, but an in-production rewrite at this point is normally twenty-five percent of that number. Would that be acceptable?"

"Two?" Jennifer asked.

"Yes, two million dollars, but you only get a quarter of that."

Jennifer choked on a piece of lettuce. "You're going to pay me half a million dollars for a few hours at the keyboard."

Navvy smiled. "There is a story about a nuclear power plant that went out of commission one day. The plant called in a retired technician as a last resort. He spent a minute looking at the panels, and then pressed a button. The plant was back in operation in just a few minutes. He then handed the supervisor his bill for $50,000.

"The astounded plant supervisor said, 'This is outrageous. Fifty-thousand dollars for pressing a button? Can you itemize this bill?' The old man then handed him a second piece of paper. It said, 'Pressing a Button: $10. Knowing which button to press: $49,990.'"

They both laughed. "Jennifer, as a writer, you know which keys to press."

"Navvy, you're very generous. I accept...after my agent looks at the contract, of course."

"Tovar would like the rights to *Galaxy Warrior*."

"I'm working on a screenplay."

"David wants to play Logan Jones."

"He would be my first choice."

"Did you have someone in mind for Ayiiia?"

"Yes, but I don't know if she's ready. She's athletic and passionate. She started training as an actor and dancer before she moved to the valley. But I don't know if I want to put my best friend through all of that."

"You're talking about Tayla Mendoza."

"You know about her?"

"The studio subscribes to several talent development agencies in SoCal. Young and hungry actors flood the area with great hopes but usually not much talent or looks. Tayla came on our radar after she did some junior theater. She has both talent and looks. She has that unique ability to get across the footlights, and she has the passion thing."

"David and Tayla are different types," Jennifer said. "David is very laid back."

"You think she would steal the picture from David?"

"He would be quite adequate. He has the looks and the acting chops."

"But not the passion thing?"

"Yeah."

"I'll write two versions of the screenplay. One for Tayla and one for David."

"I'll offer you five for the rights and the script to go into production in Calendar 2069."

"I want six, with options for the second and third books. And I want an EP credit," Jennifer said.

"Nineteen-year-old Executive Producer. You're a fast learner. Tell Sara I'll go as high as 6.5."

"Done."

"How much do you make as an intern?"

"Sir, I make five-hundred dollars a week."

"You know, for most of your colleagues, that's a gift. When you entered the Writers' Room, to good reviews I might say, I raised your pay to a junior writer, twenty-five hundred dollars."

"A month?"

"A week. You're worth every penny."

The steaks arrived, Navvy's almost raw and bloody, Jennifer's with a light patina.

"This looks tasty. The food is wonderful. Thanks again," Jennifer said. "And Tayla and I thank you for your kind gift at The Vintage."

"You're welcome," Navvy said. "Tell me about your education."

"Sir, as you know, I have my secret identity, Jenna Seldon, so there are two stories. As Jennifer, I'm attending my senior year at Harry Ford Academy. I completed my high school academics when I was ten, but Mom and I decided that I needed social interactions, lifelong friends, and physical activity. The academy supports this, so I attend three days a week on a flexible schedule."

"That's a good plan. Would you be able to give the studio fifteen hours a week in the writing room? I'll be glad to continue your current salary."

"I can handle that."

"What about as Jenna Seldon? What has she studied?"

"In second grade, my future stepfather, Dr. Allen Goldstein, tested my IQ and it was a very high number. When I was eight, he got me into a psychological study I call Lab Rat One." Navvy smiled. "In exchange, I got access to the UVN course catalog through steveLearn. Since then, I completed coursework in four undergrad degrees, three masters, and a doctorate. My friends at Warner and Harry Ford have known that I take college courses, but I try not to blow up the curve. The Jenna thing is my way of not getting teased at school."

"So, you have never accepted any degrees?"

"UVN wants me to. They got pushy when I was doing my dissertation. They wanted to market me as Doctor TeenyBopperKid. But my mom held firm. And it's helpful that my granddad has funded three academic chairs. So, the plan is to graduate from Han Solo High, that's our nickname for the school, and then I'll spend a year at UVN to get a feel for the college experience, then I'll collect all my degrees and move on. I plan to maintain my online status and eventually pay for all my courses."

"Tell me the subject areas."

"My undergrad degrees are in math, English and creative writing, astrophysics, and computer science. My master's work is in Twentieth-Century English Literature, AI Engineering, and Applied and Computational Math. My doctorate work was a co-op program between UVN, Cal Berkeley, UCLA, and me. I studied Artificial Intelligence as Applied to SpaceBorne Vehicles."

"*Brilliant?*"

"I'm a brillian. My study and my dissertation focused on codifying the science and math of the *Brilliant* Tech Manual. My Dissertation was dedicated to you, Navvy."

"Your book?"

"Correct. *The Mathematics of Brilliant* by Jenna Seldon. Not a best seller. I heard that even brillians read the first three pages and drop it like a hot piece of charcoal. Not to brag, but I heard of three Ph.D. Dissertations that explored questions that I raised."

"I picked it up last night. Not to brag, but I read it all last night."

"Touché."

"You covered it all very well, but you seem to have hit a wall on the StarDrive. I noted that you included references to the thesis of a young engineer from the University of New Mexico."

"You're right. I cobbled together Riley's work, some new mathematics, and adapted existing concepts, but yes, the StarDrive stumped me."

"Jennifer, let's start with the Manual. You say you've read the Manual and you understand it?"

"I understand it, but I haven't yet seen the mathematics that allows me to understand the StarDrive. I read all twelve volumes, and because of my eidetic memory I'm able to recall and understand pretty much anything in the manual."

"Let's talk about the gravity drive then. Tell me what you know about that."

"Do you want me to read back the whole volume? I can recall any section or any page that you would like."

"No, Jennifer, I would like to present you a much greater challenge. You told Kathy that you have a two-thirty appointment. I'd like you to wrap the concept up in a little package."

"I could try, but I'd probably oversimplify to the point where it was ridiculous and meaningless," Jennifer said.

Navvy laughed. "Albert Einstein, one of the greatest minds ever, explained it this way: keep everything as simple as possible but no simpler. Jen, give it to me as simple as possible but no simpler."

"Okay, here goes." She thought for a moment and then began. "The gravity drive theory is based upon two heavy bodies being nearby. Newtonian physics teaches that the force that they exert upon each other is inversely proportional to the square of their distance and directly proportional to their combined mass. The gravity drive theory offers only sparse mathematics in the manual. The mathematics is yet undiscovered. Very simply, each heavy body generates a three-dimensional vector. The amplitude of each vector is proportional to the mass of the heavy body.

"But in gravity wave theory, the force is also directly proportional to the phase distortion which has both a vector component and a distance component. In theory, if two bodies were an infinite distance apart, their gravity waves would be perfectly in sync. Similarly, if the two bodies occupied the same space, their gravity waves would be effectively 180° out of phase. Since two bodies cannot occupy the same space, they would then form a single gravitational wave which would exert a force on other heavy bodies proportional to the mass. How am I doing?"

"Very good."

"The gravity drive creates and offsets two heavy bodies; one is Brilliant and one is a clone body. The gravity drive can control the phase and direction of the heavy body clone and impart acceleration on *Brilliant* to near light speed."

"Correct. You generated the correct equations for the gravity drive on page 347 of your book. Now, what about the StarDrive?"

"This is where I hit the wall. I believe that gravity drive multiplies the effects of a single gravity clone. It effectively clones the gravity clone multiple times to provide massive acceleration to facilitate faster than light travel. To engage the StarDrive, the clones require a planetary radius almost as big as Jupiter. Meaning that you get unpredictable, chaotic space-time distortions if you're relatively close to another heavy body."

"That's correct. What about the mathematics?"

"Assuming that *Brilliant is* a fictional entity, the math doesn't exist. Assuming the opposite, the math doesn't yet exist."

"Maybe it has."

"Sir?"

"Have you heard of a young German mathematician named Joachim Finsler?"

"Yes. I was asked to peer-review a pre-publication paper by Dr. Finsler. I read it, but I haven't had time to process it." Jennifer's eyes focused on an undefined point a considerable distance away. Navvy smiled and sipped his coffee.

Jennifer was absent from the conversation for about forty-seven seconds, and then her eyes got huge.

"Omigod. The Instantaneous Finsler Transform. If you apply it to the gravity drive equations, it multiplies the gravity clones. How did you know about this paper? Only a small handful of mathematicians have this."

"I monitor contemporary literature for breakthroughs in *Brilliant* tech."

"*Brilliant*...it's real!" Jennifer said.

It was at that exact moment that Sami spoke in her ear. "Sis, your appointment!"

Jennifer was out of breath. "Navvy, I have to go. Thank you...for everything."

Navvy said, "Go, Jennifer... be impatient... be happy... my dear granddaughter." The last words were unheard by the quickly receding almost-seventeen-year-old wearing the funky sneaker boots.

Jennifer almost collided with Maiara. "Thank you so much for the wonderful time."

"You're welcome anytime," Maiara said as Jennifer ran out. *I haven't seen Navvy this happy for many years. Seventeen, to be exact,* she thought, *I wonder.*

FIFTEEN

The Virtual Copa

J ennifer sat in the chair at The Old Style next to Tayla, fifteen
minutes late.

"How did the lunch with Navvy go?" Tayla asked.

Jennifer had a far-off look. "I'm still processing." The girls settled
into their hair, makeup, and mani-pedis.

The Virtual Copa opened in New York City a year earlier using
HTVR Special Effects. The club started a nostalgia wave that took
America's teenagers back to a century ago when the celebrities were
much more colorful, but the motion pictures were mostly black and
white.

Aubrey, the stylist, and her virtual assistants went to work.
"Jennifer, you'll make a perfect impression as Maureen O'Hara and
Tayla, you're an exquisite Rita Moreno."

"My favorite movie was *The Quiet Man* with Maureen and the
Duke," Jennifer said.

"It's my dream tonight to dance with Gene Kelly and make Cyd
Charisse jealous," Tayla swayed in her chair.

"You did a pretty good job of that at the Burbank Rep last month
in *Singin' in the Rain*," Jennifer said.

"I spent six months on the floor with a virtual Gene before I went into rehearsal with a live partner, who was a total disappointment, by the way."

"Trust me, you got noticed."

"I heard rumors backstage that there were scouts from the talent agencies." Tayla wrinkled her forehead and looked up at Jennifer.

"You might be right about that," Jennifer said with a straight face.

"You know something. Spill!" Tayla shouted.

"Keep your head still, Miss Mendoza." The stylist tapped Tayla on the top of the head with her comb.

"Moi? I'm just a lowly intern at the studio. What could I know?" Jennifer smiled.

Tayla settled down and enjoyed her beautification.

"Do you think the paparazzi outside of the club will pay attention to us?" Tayla asked.

"The paps only care about movie stars. We're just arm candy."

"A girl can dream."

THE GIRLS GOT TO JENNIFER'S HOUSE WITH AN HOUR TO SPARE before David and Riley arrived to take them to dinner. Ana and Sheila were already there with their dresses ready to go.

"Hi, Mom," Tayla said.

"Hi, Tay. Dad will be here before you go to take pictures," Ana said.

Sheila took Jennifer aside. "How did the lunch with Navvy go?"

Jennifer looked at her mom with her most serious face, "The studio is now paying me twenty-five hundred a week as a junior writer. He offered me five-hundred thousand for the *Attack* rewrite and 6.5 for *Galaxy Warrior*, plus options." Jennifer's face broke, and the tears started forming. "Omigod, Mom, it was wonderful. Navvy is amazing. He has read Jenna's mathematics book."

"Don't cry. You'll streak your makeup. Are you ready for all this?" Sheila applied a tissue around Jennifer's eyes.

"I think so," Jennifer said. "I'm going to be the Executive

Producer and writer of the Logan Jones series. Can you help me with that?"

"Of course, I'm always here for you."

Just then, they saw a grand white automobile pull into their loop.

"Gotta go, Mom. Thanks for everything."

A very proud mother of a very grownup daughter shed enough tears for both of them.

David and Riley arrived in a 1956 Rolls Royce Silver Cloud and stepped out in black tie. David greeted Jennifer, "The studio sprung the limo from their fleet for the night, so we're going in style."

Introductions were made, and Steven was already taking pictures of the four.

Sheila recovered enough for a photo with David and Jennifer. Sheila hugged Jennifer. "Did they put extra padding in the back?"

Jennifer tilted her head, "My butt looks fine."

"I'm talking about when you fall on it."

"Eww, Mom."

The four stepped into the massive limo with the assistance of the chauffeur dressed in Tovar livery, and they departed for their big evening.

They had dinner at Here's Looking at You in Korea town. Jennifer had the Pork chop with Adobo Bolognese, Radish Tops, and Kumquat, while Tayla had the Prawns with Sauce Diabla, Avocado, and Cilantro. David and Riley each had the twenty-four-ounce dry-aged Holstein New York Steak with Radish Butter and Honey Onion.

THE LIMOS LINED UP A HALF A BLOCK FROM THE FRONT OF THE Virtual Copa. The club was surrounded by a massive crowd of fans hoping to see their favorite stars. Across the street, a gigantic World War II searchlight on a trailer bed spotlighted the clouds. Emerging from their car, David's group walked a red-carpet gauntlet of photographers and fans. David and Riley stopped for media interviews, and Jennifer and Tayla were asked for their names by curious reporters.

They entered the club, and David presented his credential to the Maître d'. "Right this way, Mr. Masing."

The four passed through a portal and were immersed in a scene right out of a fifties black and white film noir movie. The twenty-piece orchestra filled the front of the club on a small stage. The Maître d' escorted them to a four-top in the second ring of tables.

Curiously, the inner ring of tables was empty. "It looks like everyone is already here. I wonder who could be more important and sit floor-side?" David said.

"My New York friend told me that this is the best part," Tayla said. "The inner ring is for the virtual celebrities. They start arriving soon, table hop for about an hour and greet and dance with the customers. When they're seated, the floor show starts." Tayla studied the history of the period and knew most of the stars. For the next twenty minutes, the four stargazed at the celebrities from the Golden Age of Hollywood.

"Is that…?" Jennifer asked.

"Bogie and Bacall," Tayla said.

"Lauren Bacall looks like she is our age. How old is he?" Riley said.

"Humphrey Bogart died in 1957. He was twenty-five years older than she was."

"Is that Clark Gable? Omigod, he's coming to our table." Jennifer said.

"Welcome to the Copa," the virtual star said. Introductions were made around the table. "David, I look forward to your upcoming *StarCruiser Brilliant* picture."

"Thank you, Mr. Gable." David beamed.

"Miss Gallagher, I remember working on a couple of pictures with your great-great-grandfather. He became an accomplished craftsman after a few trips and falls. I knew he had a bright future."

Jennifer's jaw dropped and then she composed herself. "Thank you, Mr. Gable."

The four friends continued stargazing, both virtual and those from the present, "There are Frank Sinatra and Ava Gardner," Tayla said. Frank and Ava visited the other side of the room.

"Do they know something about each guest?" David asked.

"Yes, that's the best part. Wait, is that...?" Tayla gasped. "Fred Astaire and Gene Kelly. They're coming over here." She spoke no more and was starstruck. The two greatest film dancers ever came directly to their table and introduced themselves.

Gene Kelly looked at Tayla. "Miss Mendoza, I hear you did very well as my dance partner at the Burbank theater last month."

Nothing.

Jennifer raised her glass to her lips and said, "Close your mouth and say thank you, Tay."

"Thank you, Tay, ...Mr. Kelly."

"Maybe I'll see you on the dance floor later," the virtual Gene Kelly said.

Tayla sat there agape and just nodded.

Fred looked at Riley, "I hear that you're quite the hoofer as well, Mr. McMaster."

"I know a few dance steps. Thanks, Mr. Astaire."

Gene and Fred went to their floor-side seats.

Tayla looked at Riley. "You dance?"

"I studied for eight years. Tap, ballroom, and I taught Salsa. You?"

"Eleven years. I started with gymnastics and went from there... including Salsa."

The Virtual emcee took the stage. "It is my pleasure to introduce directly from Steubenville, Ohio to sing for your pleasure, Mr. Dean Martin."

David asked Tayla, "Is this Martin and Lewis?"

"Yes, they were headliners at the Copacabana in New York until they broke up."

Dean sang a song and then Jerry dressed as a teenager stumbled in, interrupting Dean. "What do you mean coming in at this time? Everyone is already here," Dean said.

"The prom broke up late," Jerry said. "There were lots of girls there."

"What would you do if a girl kissed you?"

"I'd kiss her back."

"What if it was a tall girl?" Dean said, and Jerry gave a deadpan look to the audience.

The famous comedy duo did fifteen hilarious minutes and closed with a song to great appreciation from the audience.

The emcee returned, "For our younger dancers, we'll have a Salsa contest. When a judge taps your shoulder, please return to your table." Caribbean music started.

"You up for this, partner?" Tayla said to Riley.

"I won't hold you back."

"David, Jen?"

"We'll wait for something slower," David said.

Riley and Tayla took the floor with twenty other couples. The music played at a moderate beat. Several couples were tapped out until ten couples remained including Riley and Tayla.

"Do they have a chance?" David asked.

"Tayla has won six valley Salsa competitions," Jennifer said.

"Riley is considered the best dancer at Tovar."

"They have an excellent chance."

The tempo picked up as the competition thinned out to five couples.

"We need to pick it up. Cuban?" Tayla said.

"Cuban," Riley responded, and the two dancers shifted to a more difficult Salsa Cubana style. One of the four remaining couples was tapped out, and there were only three pairs of dancers on the floor. Riley and Tayla were entirely in sync now. The two entered the zone, and the crowd sensed it clapping to the ever-increasing beat.

One couple was tapped out, and a moment later the other couple stepped aside and bowed to Riley and Tayla leaving them alone on the floor.

"I think they were virtual," Riley said.

"We won?" Tayla said.

Riley nodded.

"Then let's dance our asses off and earn this," Tayla said.

The band continued for another minute at a dizzying tempo, and then the music changed ever so slightly. "Finale?" Tayla said. Riley nodded, and the two winners executed a perfect competition move and ended at precisely the same moment as the band.

Jennifer and David jumped to their feet along with most other guests as Riley and Tayla took a stylistic bow to a generous ovation.

"Our winners," shouted the emcee. They jumped to the stage, and the virtual Fred Astaire presented them medals. "I was greatly impressed," Mr. Astaire said.

Tayla and Riley walked hand-in-hand back to the table. The band started to play a slower tune, and the guests began populating the dance floor.

"Shall we dance?" David offered his hand.

Jennifer rose and smiled as she and David took the floor and followed the other couples around.

"You aren't a bad dancer after all," David said.

"Tayla is an outstanding coach. You aren't so bad yourself," Jennifer said.

"My mom forced me into ballroom when I was eight.

"If I forget to tell you, I had a really good time tonight."

"Me too."

The tempo picked as Jennifer and David got into the feeling of dancing. They were on the same wavelength. David said, "Ready to twirl away?"

Jennifer was in the zone and said, "Twirl away."

Somehow, though, Jennifer's right foot switched places without permission and there she was, firmly implanted on her butt in the middle of Hollywood's most beautiful people. Jennifer looked at David, and he was on his knees covering his mouth. His sparkling blue eyes indicated that he thought it was hilarious.

Jennifer glared at her partner as David looked past her. She saw a hand reach out. *Finally, someone will help.* She stood up and found herself looking up at The Quiet Man. "May I have this dance, Miss O'Hara," the virtual John Wayne said. Jennifer almost forgot for a moment that she came as Maureen O'Hara.

"Of course, Mr. Wayne."

He was as tall as she imagined. She could feel the star power. Other dancers cleared a circle around the two and stared. Some wondered if both dancers were virtual.

"I'll let you get back to your dance partner."

"Thank you so much," Jennifer said.

He turned away then looked back. "I would have been honored to have you as a leading lady, Jennifer." Her heart melted.

David came back to Jennifer's side. She then looked into the eyes of her real dance partner. And she slapped him. Jennifer tried to get away. David took her arm and twirled her back in just like John Wayne did with Maureen O'Hara. At that moment, Jennifer realized that David, too, was bigger than life.

"You know, John Wayne's okay but…," Jennifer said.

David wrapped her into a close embrace and delivered a well-rehearsed Hollywood screen kiss.

They broke. "My boyfriend is a movie star," Jennifer said.

"Don't you forget it," David said.

The couple danced through the next song as Tayla and Riley took the floor. They traded partners, and then the dancing stopped as Old Blue Eyes came to the stage to sing a song.

"Frank Sinatra is such an amazing singer," David said. "My mom used to play his records for me."

By the time he finished, the guests had surrounded the stage, the ladies at the front and their abandoned partners at the periphery.

They returned to their seats as a series of comedians each did sets introduced by Ed Sullivan. Bob Newhart, Milton Berle, Bob Hope, Redd Foxx, and finally Groucho Marx all graced the stage for a few minutes each.

THE FINAL DANCE INTERLUDE BEGAN AGAIN, AND THE FOUR WERE getting ready to return to the floor when the Maître d' approached their table.

"Miss Mendoza," he said.

"Yes."

"Mr. Kelly is dancing the final number of the evening. Miss Charisse is under the weather tonight. Gene saw you dance earlier and would like for you to join him."

"Me? But…what dance? …Omigod…"

"It's the nightclub scene from *Singin' in the Rain*. We heard you performed it recently at the Burbank Rep," the Maître d' said.

"But… I'm not dressed…."

"We have the gown and assistants for you in the dressing room."

"Jen?"

"Go for it, Tay. This is your moment," Jennifer said.

"Okay, where do I go?" Tayla said.

"Follow me," the Maître d' said

Tayla looked at Riley.

"Go for it, partner. You got this," Riley said.

The three watched more dancing and performances. At a few minutes before midnight, the emcee took the stage. "Mr. Gene Kelly will perform our final dance of the night from the MGM Classic *Singin' in the Rain*. His partner tonight will be the very real and very talented Miss Tayla Mendoza. For authenticity, we present this performance in stunning Technicolor. Ladies and Gentlemen, Tayla Mendoza and the immortal Gene Kelly." The house faded to black.

The orchestra began, and the lights came up to a yellow-vested Gene Kelly touring the floor in his smooth, athletic soft-shoe dance style. He circled and then slid on his knees until, with a surprised look, he faced Tayla's emerald green heels holding up a straw hat on her extended right leg. Gene's eyes traveled up past the cigarette holder in Tayla's right hand to the emerald gown to the black bangs and the smoke emanating from her nose.

She extended her leg to the vertical and Gene stood and took the hat. Their dance began as the gangster held back his cronies and started flipping a silver dollar. Tayla danced around Gene as he pulled out his black-rimmed glasses to inspect.

The dance continued. Tayla took his glasses and then made a move that knocked Gene's hat off. She inserted the cigarette holder between his lips.

Tayla continued her sensual dance until the virtual Gene Kelly threw down the cigarette, grabbed her hand and Tayla flew into the air and into Kelly's arms. What followed was a memorable ballet as the virtual Gene, and the young Tayla continued to stun the audience. The two hoofers made the crowd believe that they had been dance partners for a century.

That is until the gangster returned with an offering of a jewel-encrusted trinket for Tayla in his left hand and flipping the silver dollar in his right hand and stole her back to his table. Gene tried to follow, but the two goons stopped him. As they walked away flipping their silver dollars, the lights faded to black.

The dance was over, the lights came up in black and white, and the audience erupted in a standing ovation. The pair returned to the floor hand-in-hand and took a bow together. Gene offered Tayla a solo bow, and the noise became even greater. Tayla returned the gesture to the virtual Gene Kelly, and again the audience reacted. One more bow together and then the pair exited. The ovation continued, and the couple returned. They shared the curtain call with the orchestra and the other performers present and then finally exited the floor leaving the guests with great moments they would remember forever.

Still standing and still astonished, David, Jennifer, and Riley were proud of their friend as the people around them started to depart. Virtual stars and stars from present-day stopped and asked them to pass along their congratulations.

"I would love to play opposite her in a movie," David said.

"You may just get your chance," Jennifer winked.

"Seriously, though, Jen, have you considered acting, too? I haven't yet seen anything you can't do," David said.

Riley was still processing, "Tayla is an amazing dancer." He had the look of a person who had fallen off a cliff.

They waited a few minutes more. Tayla exited the dressing room carrying a bag and made her way back to the table stopping for congratulations along the way.

"That was just amazing. I got three cards from agents. Wasn't Mr. Kelly amazing? Do you know that was the actual dress that Cyd Charisse wore in the movie? They even let me keep the shoes." Tayla held up the bag.

"You were amazing, too, girlfriend, and don't lose those cards," Jennifer said.

Tayla sent a puzzled look toward her best friend then said, "David and Riley, thanks for the best evening of my life. I'm exhausted."

"Let's get out of here before our Rolls turns into a pumpkin. I know an excellent ice cream shop on Wilshire that's open late."

Jennifer and David started to walk out but turned to see Tayla and Riley in a very serious embrace. Jennifer and David did the same.

It was a moment that dreams are made of.

THEY GOT TO THE ROLLS AND CHECKED THEIR MESSAGES ON THE WAY to the ice cream shop. "From the AD, our call times are at eleven," Riley said.

"Me too," Jennifer said. Her message was from Navvy. It also said, "Congratulations on successfully representing the studio."

Jennifer got home at one-thirty. The media center was showing late-nite. The volume was low, and her mother was asleep on the couch. Jennifer sat with her and gently awakened her. "You didn't have to wait up."

"Of course, I did. You're sixteen. You're my famous daughter. Albeit, soon to be a member of the Screen Writer's Guild. How was it?"

"It was magical. Clarke Gable remembered great-grandpa Sean. I danced with John Wayne. David and I kissed. Twice." Her mother's eyes perked up. "Tayla danced with Gene Kelly...."

"That, I saw."

"Mom?"

"You four are all over social media. Tayla and Riley Salsa dancing. You on your butt and John Wayne, you and David re-enacting the memorable move from *The Quiet Man* and Tayla's dance with Gene Kelly is a multi-camera 3D. By the time I got done watching it, the clip had passed 250,000 views. She was viral by a quarter after midnight."

"Omigod. Tayla needs an agent."

"That may be a bit premature."

"No, Tay needs an agent because Tovar wants her to play Ayiiia. Should I recommend Sara?"

"That won't work because she'll be sitting across the table from the Executive Producer who happens to be you and you two cannot have the same agent."

"Who, then?"

"Have her call me in the morning. I can give her some names. You need sleep."

"My call time is eleven."

"Yeah, I can see you aren't going to be sleeping soon. But I do need sleep. Today is a new day."

"Yesterday was the best day of my life. I don't know if I can top it."

"Remember what your grandpa says, 'The best thing you did is the last thing you did.'"

"Mom, you're the greatest." They hugged, and Sheila headed to bed.

JENNIFER WENT TO HER ROOM. PUGS WAS CURLED UP ON HIS PILLOW on the floor, but the nocturnal Dandy Lion jumped into Jennifer's arms as soon as she entered.

"Well, Dandy, we've had a lot of big days recently. I wonder what comes next?"

Dandy gave Jennifer the look again. *Be careful.*

"I'll be careful, Dandy."

Tayla popped up, "Hey, girlfriend, we are famous."

"That's what I hear, and you're seriously viral."

"The 3D is over 700,000 at two in the morning. One of the tabs calls me an unknown starlet. Another one says I would make a great Ayiiia in *Galaxy Warrior*. Where did they ever get that idea? I know you told me you wrote the character around me but...."

"Tay, get an agent."

"Why?"

"During my lunch, I agreed to write the screenplay and be the EP for the Logan Jones movies."

"And you proposed me for the part?"

"Navvy brought your name up."

There was a pause. "So, you're serious. Can I use your agent, Sara?"

"No, we're going to be negotiating against each other. You need a different agent. Call my mom tomorrow, and she'll recommend someone."

"Jen, you're the best friend *ever*."

"This is all you, Tay. Get ready for the big time."

"Riley and I kissed."

"I know. David and I kissed. Twice."

"When? I saw you two in a clutch on the floor, but...."

"When we saw you and Riley, it happened again. You were a bit busy."

"You need to watch the dance in 3D in steveLearn. Gene was amazing. We were amazing."

"You were amazing, Tay. When you wake up, you need to start being a movie star. Get your beauty sleep."

"Thanks for everything, Jen. I wouldn't be here without my best friend."

"Tay, I remember the bleeding toes after ballet, the sprained ankles after tennis, and the failed theater auditions. You earned this."

"It'll be a fun ride with you along, Jen."

"Yes, it will. Good night."

"Night."

Jennifer went over to steveLearn as Dandy snuggled by her side. She watched Tayla dance. The 3D was as amazing and as magical as Jennifer remembered. She watched her dance with John Wayne. And, she watched the kiss with David. Just like the kiss in *The Quiet Man*. Just like she dreamed. Jennifer watched it seven more times until it went from magic to reality.

She checked out the Hollywood gossip sites. The headlines were about her and Tayla:

UNKNOWN STARLET STEALS THE VC OPEN

Tayla Mendoza came to the opening night of The Virtual Copa as an unknown with some local stage credits and left as the conqueror. She glowed on the arm of *Brilliant* Co-Star Riley McMaster, costumed as *West Side Story*'s Rita Moreno. The newcomer joined McMaster in the Salsa Contest, and the pair danced to the stage to receive the winners' medals from the virtual Fred Astaire. Finally, she joined the Virtual Gene Kelly to dance in the role of the immortal Cyd Charisse and left the Hollywood notables hoping for a remake of the MGM Golden Age Classic *Singin' in the Rain*....

WILL DANCER TAYLA MENDOZA BE AYIIIA?

The reviews of Tayla Mendoza, dancer, and local tennis champ, at the Burbank Rep last month were consistently glowing. But, after viewing her live dance with the virtual Gene Kelly on the floor of opening night at The Virtual Copa before the Hollywood glitterati, this reporter calls them a gross underestimation of the immense talent of an emerging star. But, can she act? Rumors emanating from the powers that be at Tovar Studios say that the answer is 'yes,' and that Mendoza will play Ayiiia opposite David Masing's Logan Jones in the upcoming *Galaxy Warriors* Saga. Mendoza entered the club on the arm of *Brilliant* Co-Star Riley McMaster....

IS DAVID MASING'S GIRLFRIEND SECRETLY AN AUTHOR?

Young Jennifer Gallagher, last night, came to the opening night at The Virtual Copa with her squeeze David Masing, star of the upcoming Tovar Space Opera, *Attack of the Hoclarth Alliance*. With a writer's gift, she turned her most embarrassing moment of the night into a memory only Hollywood can produce.

There is a rumor that sixteen-year-old Gallagher is the actual identity behind the nom de plume, Jenna Seldon, author of the best-selling *Galaxy Warrior* series. Officials from Tovar Studios wouldn't confirm the rumors that Gallagher would pen the screenplay and take over the production as the youngest EP in Hollywood history....

EACH SHORT ARTICLE ENDED WITH A PROMISE OF MORE TO COME. Jennifer thought to herself that this was way too scripted. Was Navvy behind this?

Her eyelids were drooping, so Jennifer went to bed. Her last thought before she dropped off to sleep was 'More to come.'

SIXTEEN

Sixteen Going on Seventeen

Jennifer awakened at nine o'clock snuggled by Pugs on one side and Dandy on the other. A floating icon above her HoloPad indicated that she had eighty-six messages. Jumping out of bed fully awake, she headed for the shower. As the remnants of makeup and hair product washed down, the memories of last night returned, and she entered an enjoyable calm for enough time to relive the high points. Jennifer sat down in the breakfast nook with her double-shot caramel Frappuccino and her HoloPad and said, "Good Morning, Sami. Are there any important messages?"

"Good morning, Jennifer. Your mom texted, 'Good morning, my famous daughter. Off to work, home at normal time. Steven is settling in at GGG and screening recruits.' Reply?"

"Yes, 'Thanks, Mom. Screen and recommend salaries. I'll approve hires as you send them. Tell GGG thanks for the help. Do we need a part-time PR and social media person?' Sami?"

"Looks good."

"Send it. Next."

"Kathy sent you a text, 'Navvy would like to schedule a preliminary negotiation session on Tuesday at eight with you and your agent over breakfast. It sounds like you had a wonderful night.' Reply?"

"'Kathy, I'll send you a confirmation later today after I talk with my agent. Upon confirmation, could you contact her and finalize the agenda? Thanks, and tell Navvy thanks for the invite, the car, and the dresses.' Send it and call Sara."

"Sent and Sara is on."

"Hi, Sara."

"Hi Jennifer, I see that you had a magical evening. You're all over the tabs and social media this morning. So is your best friend, Tayla. I think she needs an agent and I would love to represent her."

"Mom says that wouldn't work and I agree. I'm going to be sitting across the table from her. Tovar wants her for Ayiiia, and I'm going to be EP."

"So, the tabs have it right. I agree. May I recommend someone from my agency? We set up firewalls for these situations all the time."

"She is going to call Mom for a recommendation, but I can have her call you as well. Sami, can you handle that message to Tayla?"

"Done, Boss," Sami said.

"Tell me about your meeting with Navvy," Sara said.

"He offered me five hundred thousand for the rewrite. Will you do the paper on that?"

"Yes, I will. That's more generous than either of us hoped."

"Tovar wants the rights to Logan Jones. I'll do the screenplay and act as Executive Producer for production in 2069."

"What did he offer?"

"Five. I asked for six, options, and the EP credit. He told me you should ask for six-point-five."

"Wow. That would make you my second-most-lucrative client. So, what's the plan?"

"Navvy wants to talk with us over breakfast on Tuesday morning. I told Kathy that after I confirm with you today to contact you and form an agenda. We need to have lunch Friday or Monday."

"Tuesday is confirmed, but I'm booked for lunch on Friday and Monday. Do you have time on Saturday? It would be more relaxed, and we can go to a nicer place."

"Perfect. Can you coordinate with Sami?"

"Sure. One more thing. You need someone to handle your press and public appearances."

"I agree. Twenty-three of my eighty-six messages this morning are press queries."

"We hired a girl who just graduated from The Ohio State University, and I think she would be perfect for handling your press and public appearances."

"When can she start?"

"Her name is Scarlett, and I can bring her into the call right now. I chatted with her when I came in, and she understands your situation."

"Can you send me her résumé?"

"I'll do that."

"Sara, thanks for everything. Kathy will contact you after I confirm. Put Scarlett on."

"This is Scarlett Cavanagh. Hello, Miss Gallagher."

"Hi, Scarlett. Please, call me Jen. You're five years older than I am. Welcome to the team. Tell me your degree."

"I have a double with honors from Ohio State in Journalism with a focus on Public Communications and AI Systems."

"Perfect. Sami is my virtual assistant. She'll send you the press queries."

"Virtual assistant?"

"Sami, have HumanAI courier a HoloPad to Scarlett. Charge it to JennaTech. She needs a HoloBuddy. Can you assist her?" Jennifer said.

"Yes, Boss," Sami said.

"Scarlett, the press queries?" Jennifer said.

"How would you like to respond?" Scarlett said.

"Form an individual response to each. I have a pen name, like a secret identity, Jenna Seldon, for my writing and my academics. The cat is out of the bag on my pen name for *Galaxy Warriors*, but I'd like to keep my academics at UVN under wraps. I just formed a company called JennaTech, and you may be handling some press on that as well. Say 'no comment' about all that until we have more information. Specifically, 'last night was the most wonderful night of my life, it is wonderful hanging out with such wonderful friends, and I think my best friend, Tayla Mendoza, is one of the most talented people on the planet.' Hype it up from there. Get with

Sami for biographical details. She knows what to release," Jennifer said.

"Aren't you still in high school?"

"Yes, but there's more to the story. We need to sit down and chat. Are you free for dinner? What kind of food do you like?"

"I'm free, but I'm new to the area."

"Mexican, it is. Coordinate with Sami for time and place. She knows the good places. I need to get to the studio."

"I have what I need. I look forward to working with you."

"Same here."

Jennifer scanned the remaining messages of congratulations. She recorded a personal video to her grandparents and then sent a generic thank you to all her other friends and colleagues.

JENNIFER GOT TO THE TOVAR LOT AT TEN-FORTY-FIVE. PASSING through the annex to Sound Stage One, she grabbed her second caffeine fix and deemed herself ready for the day. The Director shot around David and Riley all morning, but the two arrived just out of makeup a few minutes earlier.

"Did you dream about John Wayne?" David said.

She looked into those eyes, "Who? Thanks for a wonderful evening."

"You already thanked me."

"That was in case I forgot. Who did you dream of?"

"You," David kissed her on the lips.

"Go make love to the camera, Movie Star."

Navvy approached. "Good morning, Jennifer. You and your best friend represented us very well."

"Thanks for everything. May I ask a question?"

"Of course."

"Was last night a setup?"

"As I said, Jennifer, I own a movie studio. One of the perks is that I get to hand out opportunities for young people with talent. Often, they waste those opportunities. You and your best friend, Tayla, did very much the opposite last evening."

"Then, Sir, I thank you for the opportunity."

"You're very welcome. Let's go make a motion picture, Miss Gallagher."

Just then, the AD said, "Places everyone."

JENNIFER MOVED TO HER SPOT AND GREETED HARPER OVER HER earpiece.

"I hear I might be working for you soon."

"Hey, I am just a lowly studio intern."

"And John Wayne was just a tall cowboy. My HoloBuddy seems to be a bit snappier today. Is that you, too?"

"Maybe."

"Do you have a clone that I could adopt and raise as my daughter?"

"Haven't gotten that far...yet."

They smiled at each other across the set as they heard the traditional call of "Roll 'em" and the snap of the clapper.

THE AD CALLED A SHORT LUNCH BREAK AT ONE O'CLOCK. JACK Masing came over to her. "I hear that you and my son had quite an evening."

"It was magical. We had a great time."

"You're good for David. You're smoothing some of his rough edges."

"Sir?"

"David was born thirteen years after his sister. He was like an only child. Unlike his sister, he grew up as the child of two very successful movie stars, and I fear he thinks that stardom is hereditary and not the result of hard work. You're good for him. You can put him in his place when he needs it."

"I'll keep that in mind."

"That isn't why I came over here, though. Navvy tells me that you're in on our little secret."

"Yes, we talked about *Brilliant* yesterday."

"Would you like to ride along on a hop next Wednesday? We'll end the day at eleven and launch at noon to help out our friends at NASA."

"They know?"

"*Brilliant is* a difficult secret to keep. We needed friends in high places. The FAA and NASA help us, and so we help them now and then."

"Sir, I have plans for dinner with my parents that night. You see; it's my seventeenth birthday."

"I promise to have you back in time." He winked.

"You knew about my birthday?"

"David suggested it."

"I'd love to ride on Brilliant. It's always been my dream."

"Unfortunately, the only empty seat on this trip will be the right-hand seat."

"Operations and weapons?" Jennifer said.

"You can handle it, right?" Jack said.

"Yes, Sir. I mean yes, Captain."

"Keep this under your hat. And, one more thing. You need to read the Tech Manual."

"Captain, I've read all twelve chapters. I can read back any part from memory."

"I'm talking about Chapter Thirteen."

"Chapter Thirteen?"

"It covers launch and near-Earth operations. It has a lot of information that would give away too many secrets to the smart reader. Navvy and I have given you access to that and the Operation Profile for this mission. Contact me if you have any questions," Jack said.

"Thank you, Captain. I won't let you down."

"Don't sweat it, Jen. It's just a milk run."

"Yes, Captain. Thank you, Captain.

"Ix-nay on the aptain-cay. Wait 'til we get on *Brilliant*."

"Yes, Sir." She smiled and thought to herself, *Did a starship Captain just use Pig Latin?*

Jennifer ran over to David, grabbed his head, and landed a wet kiss on the surprised boy. "In case I forget, thanks for the great birthday present."

"Sure. It's just a milk run. No worries."

On her way to Craft Services, Jennifer asked, "Sami, what is a milk run?"

"It's an aviation term from World War Two. It was an easy mission with no expected contact with the enemy."

"Okay. Milk run. In space."

"Boss, you have reservations at Poco's in Canoga Park at six with Scarlett."

"Good job. I love that restaurant. Message Mom and let her know I'll be home after dinner."

Shooting wrapped at five. Jennifer stopped by IT to check on Jake.

"How's it going?"

"Not well. This system update is going to impact the Safety Buddy. It's going to take me four more hours to recode that app. That is after I get the new operating system greenlighted with HumanAI."

"When you get a minute, send me the entry points. When I get home from dinner, I'll get online with you, and I'll recode the Safety Buddy."

"The coding on Safety Buddy is pretty elegant. You think you can handle it? Whoever created that app has more than my Masters in AI."

"Would a Masters in AI Engineering work?

"You're only seventeen."

"I completed all the coursework online. I qualify for the degree. I'll accept it someday."

"Yeah, get online, and I'll have a list of problems to solve."

"Keep up the good work."

"Yes, Boss."

Jennifer arrived at Poco's Mexican Restaurant a few minutes early, ordered a Coke, ate chips and salsa, and went over Scarlett's résumé until she came.

"Jennifer?" Scarlett said as she came to the table.

"Welcome, Scarlett."

"This music almost sounds like the polka music I hear in German Village in Columbus."

"It's called Norteño Music from Northern Mexico and, yes, it has German roots," Jennifer said. "So, Sara recently hired you?"

"Yes, I flew out here in March to interview, graduated from Ohio State in late May, and I just got to the valley last week. I'm still settling in," Scarlett said.

"Where are you from?" Jennifer asked.

"I grew up with my parents, and big sister in a community north of Columbus called Minerva Park and graduated from Westerville East High. It was the new high school south of Westerville."

"Explain that. It sounds confusing."

"It is. Westerville East is south of town. Westerville South is in the center of town. Westerville Central is north of town, and Westerville North is east of town. The powers that be are directionally challenged."

"Did you have steveLearn?"

"Not until my junior year at Ohio State. The State of Ohio had gone all-in on an earlier system called LearningGates. It was created by some wealthy tech guy who left all his money to fund this project. The system was buggy, susceptible to viruses, and full of extraneous content like advertisements. They always charged for content and upgrades, so it became too expensive for school districts. Too late for me, schools converted to steveLearn, and the students have caught up quickly." Scarlett dipped a taco chip in the salsa and took a bite. "Ouch, that's spicy."

"Welcome to SoCal," Jennifer said. "We had a LearningGates in a corner at my school. It was kludgy, and no one liked to use it. I hated it because it was anti-creative. What did you study?"

"My first major was Journalism with Public Communications. When I got full-time access to the steveLearn system, I raised my grade point average, pivoted, and studied AI Systems. How about you? How long have you had access to steveLearn?"

"My grandfather and our family company, GGG, were original investors, so I have had a system in my room since I learned to read."

"First grade. That must have been nice."

"I got it when I was two."

Scarlett's mouth fell open. "Really?"

"My mom took me to the library one day and left me with the picture books. Then she caught me sitting on the librarian's desk discussing chapter books. That was the first time we realized I was smarter than the average bear," Jennifer said. "I scored a high IQ when I was eight. They created a study that I call LabRat One, and they gave me access to the online course library at University of Van Nuys, and I have been doing college courses ever since."

Scarlett raised her eyebrows. "Let me guess. As Jenna Seldon."

"Correct. I created the secret identity so kids wouldn't tease me when I do the high-IQ stuff."

"Author. Inventor. Filmmaker. A book on math based on a Ph.D. dissertation. Tennis Champ?"

"No, I play tennis as Jennifer with my friend Tayla Mendoza. Let's order."

The waitress came over.

"Can you bring us a Cali cut in half, five rolled tacos, and a chicken quesadilla?" Jennifer said.

"Two plates?" the waitress asked.

"Yes, we'll share."

"I know what most of that is but what's a Cali?" Scarlett said.

"A California Burrito has carne asada, sour cream, guacamole, and the secret ingredient: French Fries."

"Omigod, I'm not eating this weekend," Scarlett said. "So, how would you like me to help you?"

"The Internet has figured out the Jenna Seldon thing. I'd like for you to create a unified biography as an author, screenwriter, future producer, and entrepreneur at JennaTech. I want to keep my curriculum vitae at UVN under wraps, for now. Just say that I have taken college-level courses in English Literature that prepared me as a writer."

"Okay. I notice that the HumanAI website lists Jenna as an ambassador and HoloPad guru."

"That's where the bulk of my speaking appearances will come from."

"Have you spoken in public?"

"Not before a large audience outside of school but steveLearn has an excellent Toastmasters module. I did twenty speeches, got evaluations from the Tony Robbins avatar, and completed their communications awards when I was fourteen."

"Thank you for the HoloPad, by the way. I love the HoloBuddy."

"What is the name of your buddy?"

"I call him Abraham after a friend I had growing up who died in a car crash with a drunk driver."

"That's sad. You there, Sami?"

Sami popped up nearby. "Yes, Boss."

"Can you coordinate with Abraham and give Scarlett access to what she needs, including photos and media?"

"I set up a shared office for you two on the pad and in steveLearn," Sami said.

"How much CPU does she have?"

"HumanAI assumes that she and you are going to promote their company, so they comped her pad and gave her full resources," Sami said.

"Scarlett, your HoloPad is hooked up to a supercomputer. What have you done with your AI Systems degree?"

"I did a summer internship and part-time with the publications department at a Columbus research institute called Batelle."

"They do a lot to support AI education technology. Good. Would you like to do some side work with JennaTech?"

"Sara hasn't yet given me a complete portfolio, but I need the money."

The waitress arrived with the two full plates and two empty plates.

"Done. The food is here. Let's eat," Jennifer said.

From then on, there was lots of eating and little talk.

"The food here is wonderful. The Cali is my new favorite," Scarlett said. "One last thing. The press? Interview requests? An initial release?"

I don't have time for interviews, keep those to a minimum. Compile a bio and send it to me for approval. Promise more news to come late next Tuesday. I have a contract meeting," Jennifer said. "Sami, reroute press inquiries to Scarlett and keep us informed of press mentions. Does that about cover it?"

"It does. May I get dinner?"

"No way, Scarlett, you work for me, and I always pick up the check."

"Deal, Boss. I look forward to helping you form your image."

"Okay, I have to get home and do some coding."

"Thanks for the opportunity."

"Good luck," Jennifer said. She hurried out to her Prius and rode home looking forward to a couple of hours of intense coding. That said, her mind focused on the fact that next Wednesday, she was going to fly into space on *StarCruiser Brilliant*.

JENNIFER AWAKENED AT FIVE-THIRTY ON THE MORNING OF HER eighteenth year. *I wonder what it's like to be seventeen.* She lay in bed and contemplated this conundrum for about thirty seconds before she remembered that this was the day she would fly into space on the *StarCruiser Brilliant*. Asked and answered.

To prepare, Jennifer memorized Chapter Thirteen, ran twelve takeoff and landing simulations in various configurations, and studied the Flight Profile to perform maintenance on the micro thrusters installed on Comet 2943. Dr. Neil Goldfarb would again lead the NASA team to complete the maintenance. For the crew of *Brilliant*, it would merely be a milk run. For Jennifer, it would be her greatest dream.

At precisely six a.m., there was a knock at her door, and her mother entered.

"I figured I would bring breakfast in bed for my super-rich daughter since the butler doesn't start until next week and it's your seventeenth birthday. Happy Birthday, Honey." Sheila said.

"Thanks, Mom. You didn't have to do this."

"Might as well get used to it. You're going to be the most important producer in Hollywood when *Galaxy Warrior* starts filming in a couple of years."

"Not gonna happen. I'm not going to become one of those stuck-up self-important execs that everyone hears about. Where is my double-shot Caramel Frappuccino?" Sheila gave her daughter a stern look. "Just kidding. I'll go get it," Jennifer said.

"What are your plans for the day? You told me it was a short shooting schedule. We have dinner at seven," Sheila said.

"Yes, and then I'm going sit in on a simulation on Brilliant. It's David's birthday present to me."

"Jennifer, dangerous things happen on that junk-heap of a prop."

"Seriously, Mom."

"Just a simulation. Promise?"

Jennifer hesitated. "Promise." It was only the second time she ever lied to her mom.

"Don't be late then; we have reservations."

"Thanks for breakfast, Mom."

JENNIFER ARRIVED AT THE LOT, STOPPED AT CRAFT SERVICES FOR HER second caffeine fix and entered the Writers' Room five minutes early. There was conversation among those present, but Susie was missing from her seat. She was usually the first one there.

At eight o'clock, Susie came in with a cupcake and a lit candle. The writers began singing "Happy Birthday." Jennifer blew out the candle as hugs and congratulations. Gia presented her a gift bag containing a t-shirt that said, "Screen Writers never miss a period."

Jennifer laughed and said, "I love it."

"We are just buttering you up so you will put us on your writing team for *Galaxy Warriors*," Susie said.

"I'll keep you in mind. Again, thanks for letting me be on the team."

"We have some changes for next week," Gia said, and the crew began their daily writing assignments.

JENNIFER GOT TO SOUND STAGE ONE AT NINE. IT WAS A SHORT DAY for the *Brilliant* crew, but it was a full schedule for the others with B-Roll and effects in the afternoon. It was just fine with Jennifer that there was no mention of her special day and it was business as usual.

Overloaded with what was to come later. She didn't even notice when David snuck up and kissed her.

At eleven-fifteen, the Assistant Director announced, "Virtual, set up the next shot."

They were off-script. "Harper?" Jennifer said.

"Didn't you get the memo?" Harper said.

The main set transformed into something she recognized.

"Harper isn't that the Cantina from…."

Just then the aliens started playing "Happy Birthday."

She looked around nervously and saw Tayla next to Riley, smiling at her and singing. *What is she doing here?*

Just then David emerged from the Cantina carrying a giant birthday cake with Jennifer's name on it and seventeen candles. The crew applauded.

The AD announced, "Everyone, have some cake and then break for lunch."

Jennifer shared some hugs, blew out the candles, and said, "This is my best birthday ever. Thanks, everyone."

David hugged Jennifer and said, "As soon as you saw the cake, I thought you were going to fall on your butt."

"Seriously, movie star, that has only happened twice."

Tayla hugged her. "Riley invited me for this and a tour of *Brilliant.*"

"A tour, huh?" Jennifer looked at Riley, and he winked.

Navvy came up with an older woman that Jennifer guessed to be his wife.

"Jennifer, I would like you to meet my Hanna," Navvy said.

Jennifer offered her hand but instead received a very tight hug as she said breathlessly, "Nice to meet you."

"You've made Navvy so happy since you came to Tovar. Thank you and Happy Birthday."

"You may need to open this right away, Happy Birthday," Navvy said as he handed her a package.

Like a little kid, she ripped off the wrapping and found the cerulean and maize colors of the *Brilliant* flight suit with the name 'Jennifer' embroidered above the left pocket.

"Omigod, Omigod. Thank you, Navvy. Thank you, Hanna." She hugged both of them again.

"It feels almost like the real ones."

"Jennifer, it's real, and it has all the tech."

"Thank you so much. I'll cherish it forever."

Jack Masing came up. "Happy Birthday, Jennifer."

"Thank you, Sir."

"You're out of uniform, young lady. We launch in forty-five minutes."

"Yes, Captain."

She was starting to understand what it feels like to be seventeen.

SEVENTEEN

StarCruiser Brilliant

J ennifer ducked into a dressing room and donned the *Brilliant* flight suit. It seemed a little baggy. When she closed the final fastener, the suit seemed to come alive, and it snugged-in close. She took a look and found that it fit her curves perfectly. *I'm ready to ride my dream,* she thought.

She came out of the dressing room, and David approached, "StarGirl!"

"Jendroid to you, Spaceboy," Jennifer said.

As they walked toward the *Brilliant* Facility, Jennifer reviewed her walking tour the week before.

"We have a few minutes before launch. I can offer you seventy-five cents worth of the dime tour," David said.

"I did a walk-through at lunch last week. The ship is beautiful."

"Then this way to your carriage, birthday girl."

"The words, videos, and pictures in the *Brilliant Tech Manual* don't do her justice."

"Seriously, has anyone ever actually read those? It's not your summer beach read." David continued, "I learned most of what I needed as I was growing up, from Navvy, my dad, and my simulator time. I refer to the Manual now and again."

Just then, Tayla and the rest of the crew arrived. "This looks like a real spaceship," Tayla said.

David got a twinkle in his eye, "Yeah, something like that."

"*Brilliant is* amazing. I always thought that it would look much smoother up close, but the grain of the surface, the realistic seams, the fittings, even the sensors are an incredible design," Tayla said. "It looks as if it could take off and fly into space."

Just then, Jack, Riley, Dr. Goldfarb, and the NASA complement, joined them.

"Tayla, I'll pass along your kind words to Navvy," Jack said. "Are you ready to come aboard, Jennifer?"

"I have been ready for a long time, Captain," Jennifer said. David went to the Number 5 strut, to a panel with a camera and a display panel.

"Good morning, Ani. Request permission to come aboard," David said

"Permission granted. I know everyone except the New Girl." Ani stood watch continuously on board the *StarCruiser Brilliant*.

"This is a beautiful model of a spaceship. I always thought the computer voices were actors," Tayla commented.

"You will find that the 'model' has quite a bit of its own computing power," David responded. Again, the twinkle.

Ani interrupted, "Does New Girl have a name?"

"Ani, this is Tayla Mendoza. she'll be riding along today," Riley said.

"Welcome aboard, Tayla, and happy birthday, Jennifer," Ani said.

Tayla played along with what she thought was a sophisticated computer simulation. "I'm honored to take a tour of your beautiful ship, and you may call me Tay." Then she spoke to Jennifer, "It's an amazing simulation, for a computer. It could almost pass the Turing Test like steveLearn."

"Miss Mendoza, it is impolite to talk about someone in the third person when they are present in the conversation, I prefer the pronoun 'she,' and who is this Turing person and why do all of these people think I should take Mr. Turing's test?"

Jennifer smiled, and David apologized, "You have to excuse Ani.

She has a bit of an attitude and takes things personally until she gets to know you."

TAYLA WAS SUFFERING FROM SENSORY OVERLOAD. A RAMP BEGAN descending. Her consciousness was fighting a battle between the vision that was forming, the reality that she knew to be true, and what she was seeing. It was in this haze that Jennifer guided her best friend up the ramp.

Tayla looked around in amazement, "Jennifer, this is just like the Manual." She looked to the left, "That is the Auxiliary StarDrive Console." She looked to her right, "And the Gravity Drive. The ship is just as I pictured it."

"You've been reading the *Brilliant Tech Manual?*" Jennifer asked.

"You got a job; I got bored. Why do they need all this equipment if the interiors are virtual on the soundstage?" Tayla said.

"We like to keep the simulations as realistic as possible," Riley said. "Let's get up to the bridge and see if this simulated model flies."

To complete the tour, they walked to the aft ladder, came forward on the second deck past the galley, crew quarters, and sickbay, and then up to the bridge.

JENNIFER CLIMBED THE LADDER AND EMERGED IN THE CENTER OF THE bridge and felt very much at home. Almost all the flat vertical spaces showed displays that simulated depth. Jennifer glanced at the ship's lone hull penetration, a transparent viewport facing forward with a rope hanging down to sound the ship's bell. The Commander's seat dominated the bridge. Jennifer had the same overwhelming feeling from when she visited the week before. With her perfect memory, Jennifer could operate any console.

She sat at the Ops/weapons position.

David was on her left in the pilot's seat. "Recognize spaceboy847. Good afternoon, David." Ani said.

Jack Masing assumed the center seat. "Recognize Brilliant. Welcome aboard, Captain," Ani said.

"Where can I sit?" Tayla said.

"Sit at the communications console next to Jennifer," Jack said.

Tayla sat at the communications console. Tayla was not entirely honest with her best friend. She spent many hours studying the bridge consoles along with many simulator hours on the Communications and Ops/Weapons console where Jennifer was sitting. She tried on the headphones and heard from Ani: "Authorization?"

Tayla kept her voice low. "Ayiiia."

"Welcome aboard, Tayla. Comms configured to your settings."

"Thanks, Ani."

"Who are you chatting with, Tayla?" Jennifer asked.

"*Brilliant is* amazing. It already knows my playlists," Tayla wanted to keep her qualifications to herself. This was Jennifer's day.

Jennifer logged in to the Ops/Weps console.

"Authorizing Jendroid on ops," Ani said. "Welcome to *Brilliant*, Jennifer."

"Thank you, Ani. What is our weapons load?"

"Full Dazzler, full-power close-in Plasma, and two Smart Tactical Autonomous Long-Range Torpedoes," Ani said.

"Ani, how are the STALTs currently programmed?"

"STALT One is on the port rails in standoff, and STALT Two is loaded as a war shot set to acquire and chase."

"Planning on some target practice, Jennifer," Jack said.

"Captain, the manual requires that I query the weapons load before launch," Jennifer said.

"Yes, it does, Ops. Ani, time till launch?"

"One minute, forty seconds to launch window. SoCal Tracon reports we have a three-minute clearance westbound through the southbound commercial corridor."

"Very well, Ani."

Riley took his seat. "Recognize stardancer. Hi, Riley." the Engineering Intelligence said.

"Hi, Engi. Give me a status update."

"Em Drive ready for launch, Gravity Drive and StarDrive ready. Life support nominal. Auxiliary systems are fully functional," the Engineering Intelligence said.

.   .   .

THE CAPTAIN ANNOUNCED, "STRAP IN EVERYONE. WE ARE LAUNCHING NASA Mission 615 to Comet 2943. Begin the pre-launch checklist. Reports, everyone. NASA?"

"NASA is Ready," Dr. Goldfarb said.

"Propulsion?"

"All Modes ready. Life support nominal. The ship is space-ready." Riley reported.

"Pilot?"

"All flight controls responsive. Ready to rock and roll." David reported.

"Ops, what is our departure profile?"

"Captain, we'll raise the ship to 100 feet, cloak *Brilliant*, ascend subsonic at a sixty-degree climb westbound over Malibu to Flight level eight-zero-zero, and then conduct unlimited vertical acceleration to the Karman Line," Jennifer reported. She rehearsed this procedure many times last weekend at home with every simulated casualty possible. She was ready for anything.

"Tayla, are you strapped in?" the captain asked.

"Um, oh yeah. The Simulation. Strapped in."

"Ani?"

"All systems nominal. *Brilliant is* ready for launch. Our window opens in fifteen seconds…ten seconds…"

"Ready to raise ship, Pilot," Jack said.

"Aye, Captain," David said.

"… five, four, three, two, one," Ani said.

"Take us up, David."

There was a rumble.

Tayla grabbed her chair and thought, *This is way too realistic.*

"Ops?"

"The ship is cloaked."

"Very well. Pilot, begin the ascent."

"Ay, Captain. Thrusters engaged subsonic."

"Jennifer, is that your house on the right?" the Captain said.

She glanced at the display. "Yes, Captain, thank you. Tayla, is that your mom's car in our driveway?"

"Omigod, yes. How realistic is this simulation? She said she was going to visit your mom for lunch," Tayla said.

"Twenty-thousand feet. We are clear ten miles around," Jennifer reported.

"Wow, the beach looks small," Tayla said.

"Forty-thousand feet. We are clearing commercial flight levels."

"Very well, Ops. Ani, plot a Tranquility Pass when we are spaceborne."

"Aye, Captain. To the Moon and beyond."

"Sixty-thousand feet."

"Engineering?" Jack asked.

"Gravity drive ready in all respects and shields ready, Captain," Riley reported.

"Pilot, on my order, engage gravity drive and accelerate to one-half percent light-speed. Shields up, Engineer."

"Half-percent lunar approach, Pilot, aye," David said.

"Eighty-thousand feet, Captain. Sensors indicate clear space above," Jennifer said.

"Very well. Pilot, engage. Ops, decloak at the Karman Line."

"Aye, Captain…decloaked at one-hundred kilometers above the surface," Jennifer said.

"This is the Captain, unstrap, get your space-legs, and enjoy the view. In a few minutes, we are going to pass by Tranquility Base where Neil and Buzz took a walk."

Tayla stood and walked around the bridge, "Mr. Masing and everyone, thanks for the nice tour but I want to grab lunch before I head home. I have an appointment to get my hair cut and styled."

"Sorry, Tayla; you're stuck here for the duration," Riley said.

"Seriously, Craft Services is only a hundred yards away."

"Miss Mendoza, if you open that hatch, there will be a big sucking sound, and we'll all have a terrible day,"

"But this is just a simulation. We are on Earth," Tayla said, but there was doubt in her voice.

"This is the Captain. We are going to lighten things up. Grab it if you need to. Bag it if you're going to blow lunch. Engineer?"

Jennifer knew what was coming, she stood, held a strap, and looked at her best friend who didn't.

"Engi set gravity to zero," Riley said.

Tayla's stomach wasn't where it was supposed to be. She looked down, and her feet were definitely *not* where they were supposed to be. She looked around as she floated in weightlessness. Jennifer was horizontal, and Riley was upside down. Then she screamed. She started to flail and grab at nothing. Riley launched from his console to the rescue, grabbed onto Tayla, sailed to the opposite bulkhead, then gracefully bounced back to Tayla's chair and assisted her in securing her belts.

"Breathe, Tayla."

"Omigod, Omigod. We're in space. Riley, you saved me. I could have died," Tayla said.

"No, the interior surfaces have cushioning force fields. For a dancer, you aren't very graceful in zero-gravity." Riley said.

"You could have warned me," Tayla said.

"And miss the show?"

"This is the Captain. We are going to set lunar gravity and do some maneuvering. Engineer, set inertial dampeners to one-half G. Pilot, give us a rollercoaster ride to the Moon."

"Aye, Captain. Engi, set gravity to sixteen percent and inertial damper to point-five G's," David said.

"Pilot, maneuver at will and set us up for an Honor Pass over Tranquility Base with Earth above the horizon.

Jennifer handed her best friend a barf bag with the *Brilliant* logo on it. Tayla clutched it like a talisman.

David gave everyone a fun ride and beautiful views of the approaching Moon and the receding Earth. "Orbit is set, Tranquility Base just over the horizon. Ready for *StarCruiser Brilliant* Honor Pass."

Everyone stood. Tayla stood but held on tight.

Ani announced, "Hand salute."

The crew responded, facing forward. Jack then repeated words from his past in another timeline, "To the pioneers of the past, we honor you. To Orville and Wilbur Wright who took to the air, to Chuck Yeager and Scott Crossfield who went to the edge of space, to Yuri Gagarin, John Glenn, Valentina Tereshkova, Alan Shepard, and others who crossed the barrier into space, to Neil Armstrong, Palton Vendarko, Cindy Brennaman, and others who first set foot on other planets, we honor you. To the crews of *Discovery* and *Challenger*, to Gus Grissom, Ed White, and Roger Chaffee and to the many others who gave the supreme sacrifice, we remember you. To every pioneer who brought us to this place and beyond, we honor and salute you. Ops, as the junior member of the crew, join us and sound the ship's bell a single time."

"Aye, aye, Captain."

Jennifer knew the significance of this hallowed tradition. It is one that she had seen in the movies and one that she rehearsed repeatedly. Jennifer released her salute, stood ramrod straight, walked to the place forward and on the center line, faced the distant Earth through the viewport, and pulled the rope to sound the bell a single time. At the sound of the brass bell, the crew members rendered a crisp salute.

"Relax, everyone. Jennifer Gallagher, welcome to the crew of *StarCruiser Brilliant*." She smiled, she cried, and she accepted handshakes and hugs from the bridge crew.

"You're living your dream, Girlfriend," Tayla said, hugged Jennifer, then hurried back to her seat and strapped in with the paper bag close at hand.

"ANI, WHERE IS COMET 2943 AT PRESENT?" JACK ASKED.

"2943 is one-point-three Astronomical Units above the ecliptic, near the asteroid belt. It is twenty-eight light minutes away."

"Very well, plot an intercept at point-five light-speed. Keep us above the garbage. Engineer, set gravity to one-sixth Earth and inertial damper to normal. We don't want Tayla to leave chunks of birthday cake on the Comm panel."

Tayla's face turned from green to red.

"Aye, Captain. Course laid in."

"Pilot, engage." There was a low-frequency rumble throughout the ship.

"On track, sixty-two minutes to target," Ani said.

"Very well. Dr. Goldfarb, perform your final equipment checks. We are an hour out."

"Yes, Captain. We'll have the repair drone and two replacement microthrusters ready."

"Hopefully, two mikes will be enough," Jack said. "Riley, take the

girls down and show them the galley and come back with some coffee
for me and whatever David wants. And, bring back some M&Ms."

"Aye, Captain." Jennifer and Tayla bounced behind Riley to the
ladder. Both girls stepped gingerly as they weren't used to Moon
gravity. Riley hugged the fireman's pole and dropped down a deck.
Jennifer shrugged and did the same. Tayla took the ladder step-by-
step, clutching the safety rail.

"The Captain is addicted to sugar?" Jennifer said.

"No, he likes to show off the *Brilliant* logo on the special M&Ms.
He and Navvy took the POTUS for a ride. A few weeks later, they
got a case of candy with the *Brilliant* logo and a thank-you note from
the President. *Air Force One* even has the presidential seal on the toilet
paper. Jack breaks out the swag when there are newbies on board."

"Where is the food replicator?" Tayla asked.

Riley laughed. "Navvy watched all of the episodes of *Star Trek*
from the sixties on. He's a real Trekkie, but he hasn't figured that one
out."

"But you do have a Starbucks," Tayla said.

At the mention of the name, the machine said, "Would you like
your favorite, Jennifer? Tayla?"

"Yes, please," Jennifer said.

"I don't think my stomach is ready," Tayla said.

"Coffee for the Captain."

The machine produced Jennifer's double-shot caramel
Frappuccino and a black cup of joe for the Captain. The drinks filled
spill-proof mugs.

Jennifer held up the cup with her name on it.

"Navvy tried to market them," Riley said. "NASA complained
that it infringed on their design. The Navy and Air Force use them
along with private jet fleets but not the civilian airlines. They don't
like to remind their passengers that the ride may be bumpy."

Riley grabbed a soft drink for himself and David and loaded the
drinks and snacks on a sophisticated-looking dumbwaiter. "This
delivers the drinks to the stations above. Tayla, are you feeling
better?" Riley said. She nodded. "Would you go down and take
orders from the NASA crew?"

"Make myself useful as a flight attendant? Aye, Sir." Tayla

delivered a crisp military salute, turned to the ladder, and this time took the fireman's pole down to the lower level to take the orders.

Jennifer and Riley returned to the flight deck. Riley grabbed the pole, gave it a jerk and flew gracefully up to the bridge but it took Jennifer three pulls to negotiate the pole clumsily.

"It takes practice," Riley said.

Tayla returned to her chair fifteen minutes later leaving her belt unbuckled. The bridge crew was relaxed, but alert as well.

"We are twenty minutes out, Captain. Jupiter is in visual range at high magnification," Ani said.

The crew gazed at the beauty of Earth's biggest sister and the red storm.

"The comet is in sensor range," Ami said, "...there are indications of changes on the comet's surface...not natural. Captain, there are traces of chalgamite on the surface."

"DAMN, HOCLARTH. OPS PUT THE SHIP ON ALERT. STRAP IN, everyone. Jennifer, are you ready for this?"

"Captain, I ran through twenty-five scenarios involving the Hoclarth on the simulator. I think I'm ready."

"Hopefully you won't get any target practice."

"Target practice? Hoclarth?" Tayla said to Jennifer.

"The Hoclarth shoot back. It just got real, Tayla."

"NASA, we may have bad company about. We need to do the repairs and don't dally."

"Yes, Captain. After the last trip, we simulated a rapid repair scenario from Comet position one," Dr. Goldfarb said.

"Ops, prepare the port launcher to deploy the STALT in standoff mode."

"Aye, Captain. Recommend we deploy it towards Jupiter. There are lots of safe hiding places."

"I concur. Deploy STALT 2 when we begin deceleration at one-million kilometers' range in stealth mode."

"Aye, Sir," Jennifer said. "Activate Owwie. Load STALT 2 in Tube 2."

"Two minutes to a thirty-second deceleration," Ani said.

"Pilot, as soon as you have directional control, get us to position one, ASAP," Jack said.

"Position one, Pilot, aye," David responded.

"This is the Captain. Stuff is going to happen fast. Keep your communications crisp and try to think ahead two steps. Good Luck."

"One minute to deceleration point."

"Very well. Riley, can you handle the comm board if needed."

Tayla interrupted. "Captain, I've got this."

Jennifer turned her head and watched Tayla configure the communications board quickly, competently, and correctly. "Captain, Tayla's got it."

"Very well, good job."

"Decelerating," Ani reported.

"STALT 2 is away in stealth mode," Jennifer reported.

"Very well."

"At point-one light-speed," David said. "I have the ship. Thirty seconds to position one."

"NASA, on my mark, release the drone and two mikes at the ready."

"Aye, Captain," Dr. Goldfarb said.

"*Brilliant* at position one, in station-keeping," David reported.

"NASA, release," Jack said. "You're on the clock."

"Repair components away. Drone proceeding to Mike-1. Estimated time, seven minutes and thirty-two seconds."

"Now, we wait. Ani, plot us a course near the Belt. We may need some chaff."

"Captain, Mars is near our track. Recommend we divert in case we need to hide." Jennifer said.

"Concur. Ani, how will that affect our track?"

"It will provide us some cover, but it will slow us down and delay our return by two hours."

"Lay it in, Ani. I hope no one has dinner plans." Tayla saw the worried look on Jennifer's face.

"Captain, Mike-1 and -2 are repaired and redirected. Unable to repair -3, -5, and -6. We'll have five mikes in place in three-and-a-half minutes. We've got some cushion with five in place, so the repair and replacement will suffice," Dr. Goldfarb reported.

"Very well, NASA."

There was an alarm at Jennifer's panel. "Report," the captain said.

"The STALT reports a Hoclarth Signal Drone. The STALT is twenty-five seconds away from Dazzle range." Jennifer reported.

"Ops, dazzle it and then recover the STALT."

Jennifer's hands moved very quickly. The forward display showed the drone and then a flash. "Sir, the drone is disabled, and the STALT is on its way home."

"Very well, Ops."

"Captain, STALT is reporting that the drone was sending a beamed signal."

"Direction?" the captain asked.

"Titan, sir."

"That's close. NASA, time?"

"One minute. If we leave behind the drone, twenty seconds."

"Leave the drone. We can come back. Ops?"

"STALT 2 is on board," Jennifer reported.

"Very well."

"NASA is clear."

"Pilot, engage."

"Accelerating to point-eight light-speed. We'll be at the edge of the belt in twelve minutes. We can manage point-three light-speed under cover of the asteroids."

"Very well."

"Sensor Alert. Detecting a gravity drive signature leaving orbit from Titan. It's the *Mendex*. We will be in his detection range in fifteen minutes. There is a five percent chance of detection while we are in the Asteroid Belt." Ani reported.

"Okay, *Brilliant* crew, we can fight them head-on, but we don't want to. I need ideas. David?"

"I got nothin', Dad."

"Riley?"

"Damn it, man, I'm an Engineer, not a tactician."

"Jennifer, opinions?"

"Captain, the Hoclarth is going to assume that we are Earthbound. He is also going to assume that we will dive the Belt and that we'll be undetectable. He isn't going to guess that we are going to head for Mars. So, he will make a high-speed run directly to Earth and then sit inside the Asteroid Belt to catch us when we emerge. When we make our dash to Mars, we'll only be in his sensor range for a short time as we approach the moons of Mars."

Jack looked impressed. "The vision thing?"

"Yes, Sir."

"Ani, where is the Hoclarth?"

"The Hoclarth signature indicates a course directly toward Earth."

"Timeframes, Ani?"

"We are sixty-eight minutes to the interior edge of the Asteroid Belt and then another thirty-three minutes to Mars orbit."

"I need a sandwich," Jack said.

"Captain, I'll go down to the galley," Tayla said.

"Very well, Comms." Tayla stood a little straighter when the Captain addressed her as a crew member.

"I'll help her," Jennifer said.

"Brilliant, this is the Captain. We have about an hour-and-a-half until things get dicey. Stretch your legs, grab a bite, and send word back to your significant others that this flight will be delayed."

Jennifer and Tayla slid down to the galley. "Tay, when did you learn the Communications Console?"

"Remember all those times when you were either studying or buried in the *Brilliant* Sim?"

"Yeah."

"I was bored."

"Really?"

"You're my best friend. I gave you tennis; you gave me *Brilliant*," Tayla said.

Jennifer hugged her best friend, "And, thank you for that."

"See if they have pickles in the fridge," Tayla said. "Are you gonna text your mom?

"I told her that this was a simulation."

"You're gonna be in trouble."

"How about you?" Jennifer said.

"Do you think she'll believe that The Asteroid Belt is a dance club in the valley?"

EIGHTEEN

Brilliant Escapes

StarCruiser Brilliant exited the inner edge of the Asteroid Belt approaching Mars.

"Ani, report." Captain Jack said.

"The Hoclarth is no longer detectable on long-range sensors."

"Ops, what're you thinking?" the Captain asked.

"Captain, the Hoclarth ship has cloaked and secured their gravity drive. They're continuing their track but on a ballistic trajectory. Recommend we accelerate towards Mars, cloak, and secure propulsion. On a ballistic track, we'll pass within their sensor range, but we'll be dark. We should be able to locate the Hoclarth using passive sensors when he falls within medium range." Jennifer said.

"Ani, what is the analysis of a ballistic track to Mars?"

"I recommend that we accelerate to point-eight light-speed and then cloak and secure propulsion. We'll be in Hoclarth sensor range for twenty-three minutes maximum, during which there will be a twenty-five percent chance of detection depending upon the aspect ratio. Unlike ours, the Hoclarth sensor suite is directional, not spherical. They're blind in their baffles very much like early Russian submarines. The transit will require forty-eight minutes."

"Very well. That's the plan. Ani lay in a course."

"Course laid in."

"Pilot, accelerate the ship to point-eight. Then secure propulsion."

"Accelerate to point-eight, aye," David said.

"Ops, cloak the ship when we go ballistic."

"Cloak at ballistic, Ops, aye."

"*Brilliant*, this is the Captain. We are running patrol quiet for Mars. Don't radiate or operate any high-powered equipment that will change our energy signature."

"Point-eight light-speed, Captain," David said.

"Very well, Pilot."

"The ship is cloaked, Captain," Jennifer said.

"Very well, Ops. Ani, passive sensors only."

"Aye, aye, Captain," Ani said.

"This is the captain. Take a quick break if you need to, but strap in your seats when you return," the Captain said ship-wide and then spoke to the bridge crew. "Now, we wait."

The bridge was quiet for fourteen minutes.

"Sensor Alert. There is an unidentified ship to port at two-point-three million kilometers. Still too distant to classify," Ani said.

"Very well, Ani."

A few minutes later, "Detecting sensor radiation. Sir, it's the *Mendex*. We are still out of his range."

"Very well, Ani."

A few minutes later, "Captain, we are in *Mendex*'s detection radius for the next twenty-one minutes," Jennifer said.

"Very well. Ops, if we are detected, activate Owwie. Prepare to deploy port STALT to standoff the *Mendex* and the starboard in stealth acquire and chase mode. Do you have any further recommendations?"

"Yes, Captain. Phobos is near our track. Its orbit is very close to the planet…"

"Captain, *Mendex* is changing its aspect ratio," Ani reported.

"Direction?"

"Toward us."

The Captain began to answer, "Very…."

David placed his hand on the T-bar and moved it forward. "Accelerating away from *Mendex*," David said.

"David, noooo," Jennifer said.

"Stand down, David." But it was too late.

"Pilot, secure the drive and mind my orders," Jack said.

"But, Dad, he had us," David said.

"He was clearing his baffles, David. They used to call it a Crazy Ivan."

"Crap," David said.

"Detecting gravity drive signature. *Mendex* is accelerating," Ani reported.

"Analysis?"

"Sir we are fourteen minutes to the orbit of Mars where we can dive to the surface for cover. *Mendex* has a point-one light-speed speed advantage. He will catch us in eleven minutes," Ani said.

"Captain, the standoff STALT will slow him down. Recommend we deploy when he's at five-hundred-thousand kilometers," Jennifer said.

"Very well, make it happen. You were talking about Phobos. Do you have a plan, Ops?" Jack said.

"Sir, if we dive to the surface, the *Mendex* cannot chase us. But that will only delay the outcome," Jennifer said.

"Concur."

"I recommend that we track wide of Mars, deploy the starboard STALT in acquire and chase, make a hard turn into the gravity well of the planet, and circle behind Phobos and hide. We then deploy a clone of Brilliant…" Jennifer said.

"A clone of Brilliant?"

"I have done it several times on the simulator."

"Seriously, Jen, that was a video game," David said.

"Quiet, David. Ani is this possible," Jack said.

"Sir, it's never been done but, yes, it's possible," Ani said.

"Okay, continue, Ops."

"The clone should give us just enough time for both *Brilliant* and the STALT to sneak up in their baffles. By the time *Mendex* realizes the feint, we'll have the tactical advantage we need."

"Have you played out the numbers, Jennifer?" the Captain said.

"Yes, Sir. It has a fifty-five percent chance of success."

"Dad, I still think we should dive the surface to safety. Jennifer has never done this for real."

"Son, we have dealt ourselves a pretty lousy poker hand, but her plan has the best odds. Steer *Brilliant* to a one-hundred-thousand-kilometer orbit around Mars after we deploy STALT 2."

"Aye, aye, Sir."

"Ani, range to the *Mendex*?"

"Nine-hundred-thousand," Ani said.

"Ops, raise shields. Count us down to the STALT and the first turn."

"Shields are up," Jennifer said.

"Very well."

"Five-four-three-two-one...."

"STALT 2 deployed."

"Very well."

"Sir, STALT 2 has acquired the *Mendex*...*Mendex* is firing on the STALT...STALT has engaged...*Mendex* shields are down to sixty percent...Sir, we lost the signal from the STALT."

"Very well, Ops, it did its job," the Captain said. "Ani, Tactical?"

"*Mendex* is accelerating at point-four light-speed. We are safe to the turn and then to Phobos."

"Captain, we are being hailed," Tayla said.

"Comms, open a channel on screen."

"On screen, Captain," Tayla said.

"StarCruiser, I am Kalim Kone of the Hoclarth Alliance ship *Mendex*. Heave to and make ready to be boarded. If I am happy with what you have to offer, I'll leave you with your lives and your ship," the bearded pirate said.

"Sorry, Hoclarth, we are on a peaceful science mission on our way home to dinner. Our families would be unhappy if we're late."

"Very well, then, we'll destroy your ship and comb through the wreckage for what we want."

"Close channel. What is it about pirates that they don't like to negotiate? Did he look familiar to anyone?"

Jennifer had the same uneasy feeling as if she had seen him somewhere.

"Ani, range to *Mendex* at the turn?"

"*Mendex* will be at six-hundred thousand kilometers."

"Pilot, after the turn, begin decelerating, turn behind Phobos and slow to orbital speed."

"Aye, Captain."

"Ops, put STALT 1 in stealth mode and deploy in acquire and chase mode at the turn."

"Aye, Captain."

"Thirty seconds."

"Very well. Let's have some fun, everyone."

"*Mendex* has released a meteor cannon. It will miss us at the turn," Ani said.

"Very well."

"Mark the turn," Ani said.

There was an increased noise as the ship shook from the hard turn.

"STALT 1 deployed in stealth," Jennifer said.

"*Mendex* has turned in pursuit…four-hundred-thousand…*Mendex* has released another meteor. It will intercept ten seconds before we turn behind the moon."

"Ops, release counter-measures. Ready Plasma cannon."

"Five evaders away. Plasma cannons ready."

"Four hits on the meteor. It has broken up. Three targets incoming."

"Large to small, Ops. Pilot, evasive."

"One destroyed…two destroyed…prepare for impact."

The ship shook. The port-side display lit up.

"Engineer, damage report?"

"Shields are down to forty percent," Riley said. "Engi, report damage." Engi gave a damage inventory and recovery estimates. "Captain, one hour to recover shields. Cloaking is down. No hits on the hull."

"Take us behind Phobos, David."

"The ship is in orbit."

"*Brilliant* clone is formed on a re-entry trajectory. The clone is a lame duck indicating shields are down," Jennifer said.

"Ani?"

"STALT 1 is chasing. *Mendex* has turned to intercept us coming out of orbit."

"Release the decoy. Let's see if he bites."

"Clone away," Jennifer said.

"STALT 1 pursuing in his baffles at one-hundred thousand," Ani reported.

"Pilot, give chase and maintain two-hundred-thousand-kilometer range."

"Aye, Captain. In his baffles."

"*Mendex* is firing on the clone."

"Very well."

"No effect. He knows. *Mendex* reversing course."

"Direction?"

"Directly towards STALT 1.... It's engaging...*Mendex*'s shields are down...STALT is dazzling...torpedoes attacking the STALT.... Lost signal."

"Ani, tactical?"

"He is coming right toward us. His shields are down, and he's blind," Ani said.

"Ops, target the *Mendex* with torpedoes and Plasma."

"Recommend we disable."

"Your call, Jennifer."

"Firing torpedoes and Plasma at his StarDrive and weapons."

"Very well, Ops."

Jennifer released several salvos of weapons fire. The *Mendex* shook but didn't break up.

"Ani, report," Jack said.

"*Mendex* is disabled. They have maneuvering capability. No weapons. No shields. They will be able to recover their gravity drive in three days. In any event, it will take them several months to get to their nearest base."

"Good shooting, Jennifer," the Captain said.

"You're such a girl," David said.

"David, I gave her the option. I trusted her judgment. She made the correct call."

"But Dad, we could have bagged a Hoclarth."

"Stand down, Son. If we destroyed the *Mendex*, we would have killed the son of their senior commander, and we would have had a whole fleet coming to this system looking for revenge. David, you are relieved, take over Engineering. Riley, you're in the left seat. Comms, open a channel to the *Mendex*."

"Aye, Captain," Tayla responded. "On screen."

"*Mendex*, I'm Captain Jack Masing of the *StarCruiser Brilliant*. Do you require assistance?"

Predex Kalim Kone appeared on screen, "We can find our way, StarCruiser. You should have destroyed us. Why did you not do that when you had the chance?"

"In our culture, we have a book called, *How to Win Friends and Influence People*. Chapter fifteen says that you shouldn't destroy your enemies if you want to become friends someday. Tell your father, the admiral, to ask for an invitation before you come back to this system."

"*Brilliant*, you're a worthy adversary. Someday, we may become friends… or I may destroy you." The screen went blank.

"Sir, the channel is closed," Tayla said.

"Very well, Comms."

"Captain, the *Mendex* has turned and is accelerating out of the system on Em drive."

"Very well, Ani. Lay in a direct course to Earth at best possible speed."

"Course laid in, arrival at eight-fifteen local time."

"Pilot, engage."

"Aye, aye, Captain. *Brilliant* headed for home." Riley said.

"*Brilliant*, this is the Captain. Sorry for the bumpy ride. We survived a close call. Stand down from the alert. Let your families know you're on your way home. My congratulations to the bridge crew today on your excellent performance on a difficult tactical problem." David saw his father looking directly at Jennifer as he said that.

"Captain, I have a question. I read that book, and I remember every word. It says nothing about destroying your enemies."

"Jennifer, you know that, and I know that. Maybe someday, we'll get along well enough that the Hoclarth will know that as well," the

Captain said. "I'm sorry that you missed your birthday dinner with your parents."

"That isn't my biggest problem. I told my mom that I was going to do a simulation on Brilliant."

"Well, there's always your next birthday. Unless you're still grounded."

"Yes, Captain."

"Will it help if I tell her that you saved the ship?"

"Not so much. May I be excused."

"You're temporarily relieved, Ops."

She passed by David at Engineering. He reached out to stop her. "Jennifer, I'm sorry."

"Don't touch me, jerk. We are so over."

THE CAPTAIN TURNED TO HIS RIGHT. "TAYLA, YOU DONE GOOD, today. It was nice to have you aboard."

"Thank you, Captain, but I only hitched a ride with my bestie, and she may not get to fly on Brilliant again," Tayla said and then stood. "Captain?"

"Go, be there for your best friend, Tayla," the Captain said. "Engineer, what is the status of shields?"

"Shields will be at ninety-percent before re-entry," David said. "We are unable to cloak the ship, but we can camouflage."

"Very well, Engineer."

"Dad?"

Jack turned the command seat to face his son.

"I screwed up, didn't I?"

"Yes, Son, you did a pretty bang-up job of that. You lost my trust, and you lost your girlfriend."

"Will Jennifer ever forget what I said?"

"David, you know your uncle Navvy, and you know Jennifer. She isn't going to forget."

"How do I get her to forgive me, then?"

"I suggest that groveling should be a key part of the plan."

"Will you ever forgive me?"

"Son, you put the ship in danger, you questioned my orders, and you questioned the judgment of a fellow bridge officer in a way that was very hurtful. But I'll always be your father. That means I'll always forgive you — not today, and maybe not for a couple of weeks. And, definitely not before you work very hard to earn my trust back. But I'll forgive you. Do we understand each other?" Jack said.

"Yes, Sir. I'll do my best."

TAYLA FOUND JENNIFER WITH A DOUBLE-SHOT CARAMEL FRAPPUCCINO in her right hand, a wet napkin in her left, and tears in her eyes. "Tay, I screwed everything up today."

"Seriously, Girlfriend, you need to make a list. Since I have known you, it has been your dream to fly on *Brilliant*. Check. For the last seven years, you wanted to ring that bell. Check. From where I sat, your performance at the Operations panel was utterly flawless. Check. Every single time the Captain needed advice, he deferred to you because he knew you were right. Check. You saved the ship. Double Check. One for me because I'm going to sleep in my bed tonight."

Tayla took a sip of Jennifer's coffee, "How can you drink this craze-inducing rotgut? Jen, you lost your boyfriend. But that was David's fault, and he deserves it. Yes, you lied to your mom, yes, you will be grounded, and, yes, I'll probably not see you for the rest of the summer. In all the time I've known you, you've never had a big-time screw-up, until now. But all things considered, I think you had a pretty good birthday."

Jennifer issued one more sob and then hugged Tayla. "You're definitely the best."

Just then, the Captain announced, "Bridge crew to stations."

JENNIFER AND TAYLA WERE NOW MASTERS OF THE FIRE POLE. THEY were at their stations fifteen seconds later.

"Welcome back, Kiddies; we are fifteen minutes from re-entry. Since we cannot cloak, we are going to fly a dirty approach into Burbank as a business jet followed by a short helicopter ride to Tovar."

Riley asked Jennifer, "Dirty approach?"

"Pilot, are you able to fly an ILS approach?"

"Sorry, Captain, I haven't done that on a simulator."

"David?"

"I did it once three years ago."

"Okay, Jennifer?"

"Sir, I have done twenty-three approaches, sixteen to Burbank both directions. I made twelve practice approaches this morning," she said.

"Very well, Ops. Swap virtual consoles, you will fly us home."

"Yes, captain," Jennifer said, "Ani, configure this console for multi-engine jet, authorize Jendroid." Her station reconfigured to that of a Gulfstream 850. She took hold of the virtual control yoke, and her feet operated the rudder pedals.

"Tayla, I need you to communicate this message word for word."

"Yes, Sir."

"TraCon is the air traffic control station for all of southern California. Contact SoCal Tracon on the classified channel. It's one of the options. When they respond, you say, '*StarCruiser Brilliant* requests dirty approach to Burbank Runway one-five, authorization *Brilliant* 4975.' Now, repeat that back," the Captain said.

"*StarCruiser Brilliant* requests dirty approach to Burbank Runway one-five, authorization *Brilliant* 4975."

"Good, Tayla, put it on speaker and send the message."

"Aye, Captain." She conveyed the message. "What is a dirty approach?"

"Navvy invented cloaking about fifteen years ago. Before that, we had to fly in dressed as a fixed-wing aircraft. We can't cloak tonight, so we come in dressed as somebody else," the Captain said and then initiated all-ship announce, "*Brilliant*, this is the Captain, we are on re-entry approach. Strap in and look at the pretty lights on the ground. Pilot, handle air traffic communications from now."

TraCon acknowledged, and responded, "Welcome home, *Brilliant*. Traffic is light; you're clear to Burbank one-five and rotor-wing transit to Tovar. You are designated GulfStream 682. Enter airspace southbound at flight level 800 over Lake Hughes and descend to 250. Contact TraCon at the boundary twenty-five miles out. At Burbank, taxi to the Dark Pad and designate as Mediflight 15 to Tovar."

"Enter at flight level eight-zero-thousand Lake Hughes, descend two-five-thousand, Gulfstream 682. Good evening," Jennifer said.

"Ani, plot a re-entry to Lake Hughes at eighty-thousand feet."

"Course laid in, re-entry in two minutes," Ani said

"Engineering, raise shields for re-entry," the Captain said.

"Shields are up at ninety percent. The ship is ready to re-enter," David said.

"Pilot, enter the atmosphere."

"Enter the atmosphere, Pilot, aye." The forward display lit up in red. "Entering communications blackout in ballistic mode."

"Very well, Pilot."

The ship vibrated, the fiery red became brighter, and then began to subside.

"Altitude one-hundred twenty thousand, decelerating through Mach 3."

"Very well. Engineer, lower shields and camouflage as a Gulfstream 850. Nav lights on at fifty-thousand."

"Configured as Gulfstream. Lights on at fifty thousand, Engineer, aye."

"We are over Lake Hughes at altitude," Ani said.

"Pilot, begin your approach."

"Aye, sir. 800 descending to 250. Forty miles to Burbank," Jennifer said. She got a feel for the real *Brilliant* after many tries on the simulator.

"Twenty-five miles to Burbank," Ani said.

Jennifer depressed a button, "TraCon, Gulfstream 682, flight level 310 with clearance to 250 our discretion. Please pass on to Burbank, requesting runway 15."

"682 Roger, checking your request for runway 15," SoCal TraCon said. "Gulfstream 682, descend to 11 thousand."

"Gulfstream 682 is leaving flight level 270 for eleven thousand."

"Gulfstream 682, contact Burbank Tower on 128 decimal 73."

"2873, Gulfstream 682, good evening."

· · ·

"BURBANK, GOOD EVENING, GULFSTREAM 682 IS OUT OF THIRTEEN six for 11 thousand, requesting runway 15 and direct ILS."

"Gulfstream 682, runway 15, maintain 6 thousand, altimeter 30.05, maintain present heading," Burbank approach said.

"Cleared to 6, present heading."

"Gulfstream 682 is cleared for ILS 15."

"Cleared for ILS 15." Jennifer operated the controls. "Captain, I have the locator. The ship is fly-by-wire."

"Very well, Pilot."

"Burbank, Gulfstream 682 will be descending to 3000 on the ILS."

"Roger," Burbank air traffic control said.

"Gulfstream 682 has the field in sight, requesting visual."

"Gulfstream 682 is on visual to runway 15. You are cleared to land; contact tower on 118 decimal 80."

"Cleared for visual approach, switching to tower, Gulfstream 682" Jennifer was now flying *Brilliant* manually as a jet aircraft.

"Now, you're just showing off, Jennifer," Jack said.

"Aye, Sir. It might be my only chance," Jennifer said.

"Engineer, maintain five feet ground clearance."

"Five feet. Aye, Sir," David said.

"Burbank Tower, Gulfstream 682 is 10 miles back on visual 15."

"Gulfstream 682 altimeter is 30.05" Burbank tower said.

"30.05, Gulfstream 682."

"Gulfstream 682 is cleared to land runway 15, winds 070 at 5 to 10." Burbank was experiencing Santa Ana crosswinds from the East.

"Cleared to land, Gulfstream 682," Jennifer responded. "Crossing the airfield apron, Captain."

"Gulfstream 682, contact ground 121 decimal 9."

"Gulfstream 682, good evening."

"GROUND, GULFSTREAM 682 IS WITH YOU FOR THE DARK PAD."

"Gulfstream 682 is cleared to the dark pad. Reconfigure to Mediflight 15. You are clear visual southbound then westbound to Tovar at two-thousand feet."

"Gulfstream 682, good evening."

The dark pad was a virtual hangar created exclusively for *Brilliant*. The ship entered the enclosure as a Gulfstream 850.

"Engineer, reconfigure *Brilliant* as a Bell 703 Medicopter," Jack said

"Aye, Sir. Reconfigured."

"Ani, reconfigure console as Bell 703, authorization Jendroid." Again, the virtual controls changed. Jennifer placed her left hand on the collective, her right on the cyclic stick, and her feet on the anti-torque pedals to control the tail rotor. She then started the engines. When the main rotor was at full RPM, she reported, "Ready to depart, Captain."

Three minutes later, *Brilliant* exited the virtual hangar as a Mediflight helicopter.

"Take us back to Tovar." He turned to the right, "Tayla, does Jennifer spend her whole life in the simulator?"

"Why do you think I had so much time to learn the Comms panel?"

"It was time well spent…on both of your parts."

The crew spent the next four minutes enjoying the city lights in the valley.

"Sir, descending to the Tovar pad."

"Very well." There was a bump. "Nice landing, Pilot."

"Thank you, Sir."

"*Brilliant*, this is the Captain. Congratulations go to our NASA team. Congrats again to our bridge crew. Tomorrow is a day off. I'll see you all on set on Monday. It's always a good day that ends with our feet on the Earth. Engineer, secure the ship and drop the ramp, let's go face the dangers of SoCal traffic."

THE CREW STARTED TO LEAVE THE BRIDGE. "JENNIFER, A MOMENT," Jack said. Jennifer stopped. David looked back at her. All he saw was anger.

She turned to the Captain, "Yes, Captain."

"It's Jack now. Jennifer, I know that when you walk off Brilliant, you're going to be in big trouble with your mother. I don't know when you will be back in that seat, but I want you to know, you're the

best tactician we have had on Brilliant since…. For a very long time."
Jack Masing looked down in sadness.

"Since my father?" Jack looked up at her.

"You know about Anthen?" Jack said.

"All I know is that his first name is Anthen and he died in an accident on set."

"That's not the whole story, but I'm going to ask you to live with that a little longer."

"You know what happened?"

"Just a little longer, Jennifer. One thing more. David needs to grow up. I hope you two can work things out. Now, hug your mom. She looks worried."

Jennifer gave Jack a quick hug, "Thank you, Sir." She took one last look at the bridge and then worked her way down the stairs to the ramp. She felt part exhilaration, part anger, and part foreboding for what her mother would do when she got home.

She didn't have to wait long. As she descended the ramp alone, she looked around. She saw Navvy and Hanna next to David, hugging his mother and Tayla and Riley were holding hands in front of Steven and Ana. Sheila was standing alone. When their eyes met, her mother started walking toward Jennifer and Jennifer did the same. They embraced and shared some tears. "Are you alright, Honey?"

"Yes, Mom." She looked up. "Mom, I lied to you."

"Yes, you did."

"I had to ride on *Brilliant*. It has always been my dream."

"I suspected that."

"You knew that *Brilliant* flies?"

"Yes, I've known about that junk heap since long before you were born."

"Am I grounded?"

"Yes, Young Lady, you certainly are."

"How long?"

"Until you're thirty, but let's talk about that in the morning."

"Mom, I saved the ship."

"Okay, maybe only until you're twenty-five. Have you eaten?"

"No, just my coffee." Right then, Navvy walked up.

"Jennifer, go to the car, immediately," Sheila said.

Jennifer walked away but glanced back.

"SHEILA, JENNIFER IS A HERO," NAVVY SAID.

"And you, Sir, are not. You promised to keep my daughter safe, and you and your damn *Brilliant* almost killed my daughter and her best friend."

"I'm sorry, Sheila. We thought that this would be an uneventful ride. And she wanted it so much. All I can say…."

"That's what you said about Anthen."

"Sheila, we both lost everything that day."

"Fortunately, I still have my daughter, and I want to keep her safe."

SHEILA CAUGHT UP TO JENNIFER. "YOUR DAD IS WAITING AT THE restaurant. Don't tell him about this."

Sheila practically dragged Jennifer to the parking lot. "Jennifer, program your car to meet us at home." She did.

They ate her birthday dinner, sang "Happy Birthday," and had cake. But it wasn't a celebration.

NINETEEN

Grounded

Jennifer awakened the day after her very eventful birthday with Dandy Lion standing watch at the foot of her bed, and Pugsley snuggled nearby fast asleep.

"Messages, Sami?"

"From David." Jennifer cringed and then listened. "'Jennifer, I'm sorry for what I said. It was the heat of the moment. Can we meet for coffee today?' Reply?"

Jennifer rearranged her pillows to sit up in bed. "No reply. Reassign David as priority seven. Next?"

"Tayla sent a message, 'Are you OK?' Reply?"

"Reply, 'Tired, single, and grounded. Call you later.' Send it. Next?"

"Sara says, 'The contracts are in review. We are bouncing them back to your mother. Plan on signing in about three weeks.' Reply?"

"To Sara, 'Thanks for your hard work. I'll let Mom know.' Send it and copy my mother."

"Anything else, Sami?"

"Your mom has breakfast ready and would like you to join her."

"Thanks, Sami."

"Have a good day, Boss."

. . .

JENNIFER WALKED INTO THE KITCHEN

"Good morning, Mom."

"Good morning, Jennifer." Her mother brought her a cup of regular coffee and a plateful of scrambled eggs and sausage.

Her mother sat and joined her.

Without turning to her mother, Jennifer asked, "How long am I grounded?"

"You're seventeen years old. You have a Ph.D. In math. You're a best-selling author. You created a tech startup that is going to be worth billions in just a few years. And, you're going to sign contracts making you the richest teenager in Hollywood." Jennifer looked at her mom. "But you lied to me."

"Yes, Mom, I'm sorry."

"I talked to Jack and Navvy, and I made them promise that you won't fly on that damn starship. So, you're grounded from *Brilliant* until you're eighteen."

She expected to be grounded, even for the rest of the summer, but a whole year. From *Brilliant*?

"But, Mom. What are my restrictions? I can't go out. I can't go to work?"

"Like I said. You aren't permitted to set foot on *Brilliant*, and you cannot go into space. You're grounded. On Earth. I trust that as long as you stay that way, you can live the rest of your intelligent teenage life as you choose."

She exhaled in relief. Her mom was fair. Then, out of its compartment came the exhilaration and she remembered the vision that she would meet her father soon. "What if Jack and Navvy find out where my father is?" Jennifer asked.

"Your father went up in that ship seventeen years and seven months ago and never came back. He's gone."

Jennifer looked at her mother with surprise, "You knew?"

"Your granddad and Navvy were best friends. I grew up on the set of *Brilliant* with Anthen, and we became very close as teenagers. I was on board Brilliant as a seventeen-year-old when Anthen rang the ship's bell." Sheila took a sip of her coffee and Jennifer saw that the surface of the coffee indicated that her mom's hands were shaking.

"We drifted apart when I started college because he focused on his acting career. Half-way through my senior year at UVN, I ran into Anthen again. We had a short fling. I found out I was pregnant, and before I could tell him he was gone. The executives at Tovar blamed it on an industrial accident caused by GGG equipment."

"Why haven't you told me any of this, Mom?" Jennifer asked.

"From the time I first knew Anthen, he was drawn to Brilliant. It was all he talked about. It was always his dream to ring that bell. And then he was gone. I never wanted to lose you to that horrible ship."

"You still miss him?"

"Jennifer, you will never forget your first love. I love your step-dad, but I'll never forget Anthen. How can I? You remind me of him every time I look at you. You have the same eyes, the same face. And from the time you saw your first *StarCruiser Brilliant* movie, you've had the same dreams." Sheila looked over Jennifer's shoulder. "And, ever since then I have been awakened by the nightmare that *Brilliant* will take you away from me as well...and it almost did."

"Was my father intelligent? Did my dad have the vision thing?"

"He did. He didn't have the same advantages you had, like Warner Academy and steveLearn, but he was just as smart as you are."

"Mom, when I was on *Brilliant* out there, I had a vision that I would meet him soon."

Her mother became angry, and she slammed her cup down, splashing coffee on the table. "Jennifer, your father is dead! Brilliant took him away forever. Anthen is gone." Her mother stood up and ran to her bedroom.

Jennifer sat alone with the feelings, which she had awakened, revivified. She was now shedding the same tears, some for her mother, some for herself.

BACK IN HER ROOM, "SAMI, ASK KATHY WHEN NAVVY IS IN. LET HER know I want a moment with him," Jennifer said.

Moments later, "Kathy responded. They canceled production for today. Navvy will be in at ten."

"Thank you, Sami. Let me know when Tayla is accepting calls."

Jennifer settled into steveLearn, logged in as Jenna Seldon, and returned to her MBA curriculum. Her tutor, the virtual Thomas Edison popped up, "Why don't you come into my lab?"

Jenna entered Mr. Edison's laboratory. It had the smell of ozone, and of the stogies he won from a luckless lab assistant who bet against Edison's technical prowess.

"You look as if you need to talk?"

"I had a difficult day yesterday. It was wonderful, it was hurtful, and I let down my mother."

Mr. Edison inhaled from the short stub of what remained of his cigar, "Success, failure, and depression are often fellow travelers."

"I saved the ship with my recommendations and actions. I showed mercy on an adversary and my boyfriend, the Captain's son, said, 'you're such a girl.'"

"A female asserting her leadership, a relationship in the workplace, an outsider coming between a son and a father. I once wrote a letter to Mr. Darwin asking for advice. I suspect that even he would throw his hands up trying to analyze the triangular problem you face." The cigar expired, and Edison took some time to relight that which remained. "When faced with such a difficult problem, I always go back to basic lessons learned and predict how the materials will react to whatever stimulus I might apply. And it always comes down to this, materials and other people will always react predictably. It's you who must be unpredictable; it's you who must stray from the well-worn path, it's you who must understand yourself and take the right action."

"Is that how you solved problems during your life?" Jennifer asked.

"I was known as a bully and a prankster," Edison laughed. "This virtual thing provides one a lot more information. It allows one to re-invent oneself over and over."

"Thank you, Sir." Jennifer considered what he said. Her memory and her vision thing allowed her to re-invent herself. And forgive David. If she could get over the desire to rip David's face off.

· · ·

At nine-fifteen, Sami indicated that Tayla was up and available. "Call Tayla."

Tayla appeared

"Hi, Jen."

"Hi."

"How long are you grounded?"

"Until I'm eighteen."

"I won't see you?"

"I can't set foot on *Brilliant* until my next birthday," Jennifer said.

"Oh. That's worse for you. When you were in that seat, you were the best I have ever seen you. You owned it even more than I own dance and tennis."

"Yes, but it is fair. I know how my mom feels about it. She was on board *Brilliant* when my father rang the bell. She knew."

"Riley called me. David is devastated. He's sorry about what he said. I told Riley that David hurt you and that you aren't mentally capable of forgetting that."

"It still hurts, Tay," Jennifer said.

"I know. For you, it's like it's still happening. You'll never forget. Will you forgive David and allow him back in?" Tayla asked.

"I believe I will. But I need some time and distance."

"Speaking of, I'm meeting with an agent today. She's from Sara's agency."

"Good, Tay. I'm going down to Tovar. I need to speak to Navvy."

"About *Brilliant?*"

"I think I need to work on a different project."

"Keep me posted. Love you, Jen."

"Good luck. Love you, Tay."

She arrived at Tovar and stopped by the IT office to see Grayson and Jake. "Grayson, tell me about the system. Is it catching up to the demand?"

"The MiniTurbos are scheduled to be installed this weekend. Jake has recoded the most taxing applications, and that, along with the system upgrade, has significantly improved performance. The VP of Operations wants to retain your new company on a yearly maintenance contract for HumanAI software and hardware."

"JennaTech can do that. I have an excellent candidate in mind to handle that contract."

"And, I suspect that you want to visit with Jake as well. Thanks for all of your help," Grayson said.

JENNIFER MADE HER WAY DOWN TO JAKE'S OFFICE. SHE NOTICED THAT he had a better view. His triple screens showed the coding he was working on along with Tovar's system performance. "How's it going, Jake?"

"Hi, Boss. I believe that as soon as we install the localized MiniTurbos, we can take a deep breath until someone I know invents another revolutionary app that taxes system resources," Jake said.

"Good job."

"Steven contacted me. I'm working on software design for the drone systems."

"Keep me copied on all of your work. I might contribute some lines of code."

JENNIFER WALKED INTO THE EXECUTIVE OFFICES OF TOVAR STUDIOS. She passed through the door to Navvy Kelrithian's outer office and greeted Kathy.

"Hello, Jennifer. Navvy is on the phone. Can you wait a few minutes?" Kathy said.

"Sure." Jennifer looked around the office. She saw the golden statuette on the bookcase behind Kathy's desk. "You have an award for Best Picture?"

Kathy smiled. "Navvy directed Ellie Masing's fourth picture. It was her and Navvy's first attempt outside of science fiction. He brought me on from the office to produce. Ellie won Best Actor and Navvy, and I shared Best Picture that year."

"That's amazing." Jennifer stood and walked around the outer office. "Why didn't you stay with producing?"

"One of the tricks in this business is figuring out what you're good at and sticking with it. I'm good at helping Navvy get things done. I get to make an impact."

"That's a good philosophy. Navvy seems to value people who shake things up." Jennifer stopped at a photo that was rather prominent on the wall. "This is the Board of Directors of Tovar. The date is when the Studio went public a few years ago. Am I correct?"

"Yes, and you're also correct that Navvy values his people," Kathy said. "When Navvy got to Tovar about forty years ago, it was practically an empty lot. The owners were almost ready to sell to a real estate developer. Navvy learned the business in three years and produced a string of hits that put Tovar Studios back on the map. I joined the studio out of UCLA Film School when he started producing. Along the way, he paid me well and gave me a piece of the action. By the time they took that picture, I owned five percent of the studio, and I had a seat on the board."

"You could retire as a wealthy woman and travel the world," Jennifer said.

"And, then I could sit at home and wonder what kind of trouble the old man was getting into. I'll stay here as long as Navvy still comes to work."

"You love him, don't you?"

"A long time ago, it almost went over the edge, but I love Hanna, too. We came to an understanding. Navvy is mine here at work, and after that, he goes home to her. It's not a particularly unique story, but it's my life, and I enjoy living it that way." She reached for a tissue. "Allergies. Navvy is off the phone. You may go in now. Keep this little chat to yourself."

"Of course, I will. Thanks."

Navvy rose as she entered. He walked over to a work table and motioned her to a chair. Navvy sat across from her. "I talked to your mother. She won't let you near *Brilliant* for a year. Are you okay?" Navvy asked.

"It hurts, but I understand. There's more than that, though," she said.

"What did David say?"

"He called me a girl for not destroying the *Mendex*."

"Jack told me that he said something like that. He also told me that you made the right call. We have been trying for a long time to develop a good relationship with the Hoclarth. Jack said you provided the leadership that brought *Brilliant* home."

"Brilliant has always been my dream. I felt like I was serving my destiny in that seat. Now...."

"I believe I understand how you feel. Brilliant is a harsh mistress. It brings out the best and worst in people. So, what can I do for you?"

"I want off the *Brilliant* set. I'll still write and assist. I'll still work on *Galaxy Warriors*, but Sound Stage One isn't a place where I want to work right now."

"I believe that I can accommodate that. Would you be willing to work on a *Brilliant* spin-off?" Jennifer understood what show he was referring to.

"Yes, of course."

"Report to the Writers' Room tomorrow morning. I'll have something before then. We like to give our summer interns a lot of exposure." He winked. "How is the mini-drone project coming?"

"It's coming along. Steven recruited GGG's leading designer, and he's working on the hardware in the production truck. Our biggest problem is power. Off-the-shelf Wi-Pow is very good at serving either one unit continuously or many units intermittently. Forty drones in the air require continuous power and networking so we would need to have forty Wi-Pow units on the ground to serve each one individually."

"Here is a suggestion. There is a postdoctoral fellow at the Ell Donsaii School of Physics at North Carolina State. Her name is Piper Simmons. She may be running out of funding, and she has the technology you need."

"Thanks, Navvy, for everything."

They shook hands and Jennifer left with less weighing on her shoulders.

JENNIFER GOT INTO HER PRIUS AND INSTRUCTED IT TO TAKE HER TO the GGG Annex. "Sami, could you look up Piper Simmons at NC State?"

"Got it. As Navvy said, she's a postdoc. She is working on a Multiple Beam Independently Tracked Power-Transfer System. She has applied for, but not yet received, a patent on the device. She is being held up by funding issues."

"Bingo. That explains why Navvy heard of her. It's the same technology as the Close-in Plasma Weapons on Brilliant. Sami, what information is online?"

"Here is her patent application."

Jennifer examined the patent and then asked Sami, "Sami, I need confirmation. Could we create a portable Wi-Pow base station that could power ten devices aloft continuously using off-the-shelf technology?"

"May I include HumanAI fabricators in the evaluation?"

"Yes."

"It could be fabricated in three weeks if we have Dr. Simmons."

"Good, Sami, do you have contact information for Piper? Contact her as Jenna."

"Yes, Boss, connecting now."

"This is Piper."

"My name is Jenna Seldon, and I'm with a company called JennaTech. I'm curious about your Multi-beam technology. Could you tell me about your research?"

"Unfortunately, you caught me at a bad time. My research hasn't borne fruit. I received an offer from a large company for my patents and research. In exchange, their company will retire my debt and provide me a small royalty. Today, I'm closing down my lab and releasing my employees."

"I'm sorry to hear that. What amount of funding would you need to retire your debt and continue your research for six months?"

"My debt totals one-point-three million dollars and our monthly expenses run about two-hundred thousand," Piper said.

"If I sent you funding for one month, could you give me time to create a request for proposal so that we could grant you the funding you need?"

"What do you need in return?"

"You happen to have the technology my company needs to complete a project in the very near term. If you helped us with that, JennaTech would assign you any additional patents and thirty percent of the royalties derived from them. We would need you to fly to the West Coast for three weeks."

"This is rather sudden."

"If you joined JennaTech as a wholly-owned subsidiary, our company would assign you and your employees sixty percent of the royalties for patents that you originate and an equal share for those you help us develop."

"My company would disappear?"

"You keep your brand and receive five percent of JennaTech."

"You're making a big bet on me," Piper said. After reflection, "That would be agreeable and generous."

"I have to consult my team for approval of the initial funding. I'll call you in two hours."

"I look forward to your call."

At GGG, Jennifer went to Steven's desk carrying two cups of coffee. She walked around the room to look at the pictures on the wall depicting the history of her family business. There were even a couple of grainy black and white photos of her great-great-grandfather who had come from Ireland and started Gallagher Gaffers and Grips.

Steven came into his office. "Steven, are we making progress on the drones?"

"We are on track to have a flying prototype in three weeks. HumanAI is fabricating our designs. My optics engineer has done some innovative work with the mirror and the camera. Jake is coming up with some innovative software design for the drone and the truck interface," Steven said. "Sam, the incredible designer from GGG, tells me he will be able to create the truck from off-the-shelf equipment with Jake's AI software to compile the images."

"The good news is that the signal networking and control is solved, but our biggest problem is power distribution. Wi-Pow base stations only serve two clients. We would need at least twenty Wi-Pow bases on the ground to fly forty units. I have a power engineer on it, but he's up against a wall."

"I think that I may have a solution. I spoke with Dr. Piper Simmons at the Ell Donsaii School of Physics at NC State. She has applied for a patent for a Multiple Beam Independently Tracked Power-Transfer System. Each base station would be able to power ten drones."

"I read about her ideas, but I understand that her funding has run out and critics are saying that it isn't a viable technology," Steven said.

"It is correct that there are funding issues. I have reason to believe that the technology is viable, and that Piper can help us solve this problem in the very near term," Jennifer said. "As soon as I get Mom's approval, she is flying out here."

"That should put us back on track," Steven said.

"Thanks for your hard work," Jennifer said.

JENNIFER WAS BACK IN HER CAR EN ROUTE TO TOVAR. "SAMI, CALL MY mom."

"Hello, Jennifer. How's it going?"

"I talked to Navvy, and I am off *Brilliant* for now," Jennifer said.

"That's good," Sheila said.

"Navvy suggested a scientist, and she may have a solution for the power problem with the mini-drones."

"What's the price tag?"

"I need for you to authorize two-point-five million to hire her and acquire her company."

"That's a steep price tag. How do you know this will work?" Sheila asked.

"Mom, Navvy recommended her because this is the same technology used by the Plasma weapon system aboard *Brilliant*."

"Explain?"

"*Brilliant* was built in the other timeline where her technologies already exist," Jennifer said. "When Navvy sees the inventions on this timeline, he can release the *Brilliant* tech derived from it."

"And become the first trillionaire," Sheila said. "Okay, I'm in. Give me the numbers."

"I'm going to transfer five-hundred thousand to Dr. Piper Simmons to hold her over. She'll fly here and get us out of the Wi-Pow jam. Then, I'll offer two million for her company and five percent of JennaTech."

"That is a big gamble, Jennifer, but I've learned not to play seven-card stud with you if I want to keep my money. It is approved. How much do you need initially?"

"I promised her two hundred thousand by four p.m. Pacific to keep her on her feet. She'll then fly out here to work with our team. When her Wi-Pow base station hits the market, we'll become a billion-dollar company within one year."

"The vision thing?"

"Yes, Mom."

"Call your troops and share the plan."

"Sami, call Piper for me," Jennifer said.

"Hi, Jennifer," Piper answered.

"I'm sending you a transfer of two hundred thousand dollars upon your agreement to merge with JennaTech. we'll then turn it over to the lawyers."

"I agree."

"Can you fly to LAX on Sunday? You'll have a bungalow at the Beverly Hilton during your stay here."

"Is that close to Roscoe's? I heard that their fried chicken and waffles would make me homesick."

"I'll take you there Sunday evening. I love that place, too."

"I look forward to meeting you."

They hung up, and then Sami popped up. "There is a message from Kathy."

"Read it back."

"Jennifer, you have been assigned to assist Nessa Buskirk as the Second Assistant Director on *Star Doctor*, a new fall series that has been in production for three weeks. You are to meet with Nessa at ten a.m. on Sound Stage Four tomorrow," Sami repeated.

"I acknowledge and confirm."

"You have access to scripts, budget, and production notes."

"Thanks, Sami, I guess I have a new job."

TWENTY

Star Doctor

J ennifer parked her Prius at Tovar Studios on Friday morning. After meeting with the writers, she was to begin her new position as Second Assistant Director on a new television series called *Star Doctor*.

Her first stop was at Sound Stage Four to pick up her double-shot caramel Frappuccino and survey the project. As of today, she had secure access to this sound stage where she would officially report at ten a.m.

Jennifer walked around the set. The craftspeople were busy preparing for today's shooting schedule. She saw Bill Kowalewski, a gaffer she met on her first day. "Good mornin', Bill. How are you doing?"

"It's Intern Girl. Hi, Jen. Are you joining us?"

"Yes, I'm assigned to Nessa Buskirk as Second Assistant."

Bill grimaced. "You may not be able to learn a lot from her. She has been a bit overwhelmed. She did well on her last set as Second Assistant and got promoted to this project. She's in over her head. We are behind schedule and over budget," he explained. "But you, Jen, you need to have a positive attitude and help her as much as you can and learn from the experience."

"I'll do that." She noticed the HoloPad in his hand. "Bill, how is the HoloPad working out?"

"It's one of the best tools I've come across since I've been in the business. It saves my crew and me three hours a day. I use the Script Assistant to help me plan lights. It would be nice to have an app for the lighting team." He gave Jennifer a curious look. "What do you know about the HoloPads?"

"Bill, I created all of the apps folks are using. Tell me what a Lighting Buddy would do."

"So, you're the one who has been shaking the place up? Okay, we need a map of the stage, the location for points to hang lights, and hard points for the heavy equipment. Of course, we need power distribution and then an inventory of lighting instruments," Bill explained.

"How about communications with the warehouse and the delivery vehicles?"

"That would be nice. Our guys spend a lot of time hoofing it between the sets and storage. Finally, we need to be able to map the set based on the script to program the lighting."

"Is safety an issue?"

"Gravity and electricity aren't our friends. Safety Buddy is helpful, but it isn't specific to the issues we face in lighting."

"Okay, I'll build hooks into Safety Buddy to monitor cabling and power draw to prevent overloads, and I'll use safety cameras to check for proper mounting and security."

"That sounds like a big project. Will I have it before I retire next year?" Bill asked.

"Sami, is this something we can implement quickly?"

Sami's holo image popped up to Jennifer's right. "Bill, I should have Sound Stage Four mapped and running by lunch with about seventy percent of the features. Check your pad after lunch for an app called Lighting Buddy," Sami explained. "Boss, I'll have the rest of Tovar mapped and have the feature-rich app ready by Monday."

"Amazing. Now, if you could invent something so we could get rid of all the cables," Bill said.

Jennifer smiled. "Can you hold that thought for two months?"

Bill's eyes got huge. "You may be just what Nessa needs to get her on the right track."

"Thanks, Bill. Does Nessa have a HoloPad?"

"No, she juggles three legal pads and an old-fashioned notebook computer."

"That is good to know. I'll get her a Pad before I return. I'm off to the Writers' Room. I'll see you after."

"Sami, ask Grayson if I can pick up a HoloPad for Nessa."

JENNIFER ATTENDED TO HER WRITER'S DUTIES AND THEN RETURNED TO the set at nine-thirty. On the way out, she ran into an Autonomous Delivery Vehicle that was flashing her name. "Yes?"

"I have a HoloPad for you from Grayson."

She took the Pad. "Tell Grayson thanks. Can you give me a ride to Sound Stage Four?"

When she arrived back at her set, she waved at Bill and then shrugged her shoulders with the obvious question. Bill pointed to the corner on her right and a very cluttered desk. Jennifer saw a short, dark-haired, thirty-something female who was very thin and looked both confused and flabbergasted. Jennifer diagnosed the problem and detoured to Craft Services and lopped salmon cream cheese on one bagel and a maple syrup version on the other and approached her new boss.

Nessa looked up and started babbling. "Who are you? Are you the new girl they told me they were sending? I told them I didn't need any help. I'm catching up. Wait; how old are you?" Jennifer set the bagels on the desk. "Omigod, is that a bagel for me? I haven't eaten a full meal in three days. Hi, I'm Nessa."

"Hi, Nessa, I'm Jennifer Gallagher. I was sent over to learn from you how to be a Second Assistant Director because they said you were the best." Jennifer spoke so that Nessa had time to inhale the bagel. "I just turned seventeen, I have been interning for three weeks, and I look forward to working with you."

"Are you the HoloPad girl? I've wanted one since I heard about it, but I just haven't had time to go pick one up. I heard that you helped people do better and faster work. I have been pretty good at using my legal pads and my notebook. I probably don't need a Pad anyway."

Jennifer reached into her bag and pulled out a HoloPad. "I come bearing gifts," Jennifer said.

"No effing way! Thank you so much. Does it have one of those Buddy things? How can I learn this and still do everything?" Nessa unconsciously picked up the second bagel and took her first bite. "This bagel is sooo good. Thanks. Do you know what a Second does? Do you think you can help me?"

"I studied the duties of the Second Assistant. I memorized the script and the schedule. I have a good idea of what is supposed to go on here. Let me help you get set up for the day, and at the first break, I can show you how to create a HoloBuddy who can be your assistant."

"Thanks, Jennifer. Maybe I do need an assistant. Could you get me another bagel? I think that my sugar is low. And, another cup of espresso. I don't get going until I've had three. Do you think that a HoloBuddy will help me?"

"Yes, now sit down and get your schedule on top. I'll get you a bowl of granola and a carton of milk."

JENNIFER RETURNED AS DR. AMI CAME OUT OF HER VIRTUAL DRESSING room.

"Good morning, Nessa, what is the first scene?" Dr. Ami said.

Nessa scrambled through the papers on her desk. Jennifer picked up a paper and handed it to Nessa. "The first scene is third-floor rounds with your interns. You will visit a child who is suffering severe abdominal pain."

"Thank you, Nessa. I see you have an assistant today."

"Yes, Dr. Ami. Meet Jennifer Gallagher, a summer intern who will be my second AD."

"Nessa, Miss Gallagher is also known as Jendroid aboard *Brilliant*. She played a key role in bringing the ship back to Tovar on Wednesday." Nessa now looked at Jennifer with astonishment and respect.

"Thank you, Doctor. I did my best."

"I suspect that if you do that here, you will help us bring home a hit. Welcome to the show."

"I didn't realize that virtual doctors got bored," Jennifer said.

Dr. Ami winked. "I sent Navvy some hints that I could be helpful in a real hospital. He came up with a semi-scripted reality show in the *StarCruiser Brilliant* universe. I get to be an attending physician in the pediatric ward at Hollywood Methodist Hospital."

"Isn't the virtual actor equipment difficult to install?" Jennifer asked.

"Navvy and HumanAI are creating more advanced projection technology. Hollywood Methodist has the equipment to support my presence wherever I need to be. I think Navvy is planning to create some sisters for me at other hospitals."

"That idea might put his wealth over a trillion dollars," Jennifer said.

Dr. Ami looked at Nessa and the granola and milk. "I see that you're eating more healthy food. A woman cannot live on Bagels and cream cheese alone."

DURING THE FIRST BREAK, "NESSA, LOOK AT YOUR HOLOPAD AND then ask it to set up a HoloBuddy. You can create any image you want, any name, any accent and then you can assign any administrative scut work, and your Buddy will perform it and keep you up to date," Jennifer explained.

"The name of my dream guy is Nathan. Does he have to wear a shirt?" Nessa asked.

"No, Nessa"

Jennifer went to the coffee machine for her third double-shot caramel Frappuccino. She observed Dr. Ami. On *Brilliant*, the doctor was there to stitch up wounds and stabilize injured crew members until they could have access to advanced medical care. On her new series, Dr. Ami used her greatest gift, her bedside manner. According to the *Brilliant Tech Manual*, she was a composite of all the great healers of history from Hippocrates to Freud to the Mayo Brothers. Dr. Ami possessed their knowledge of the medicine to heal the patient, but also their ability to impart to the patient the ability to repair their wounds through mental attitude and stamina.

· · ·

"IS IT POSSIBLE TO PUT ALL MY DOCUMENTS ON THE HOLOPAD?" Nessa asked.

Jennifer turned her attention to help Nessa. The stored paper documents are already there. Just point the camera at the paper to import your written notes."

"Thanks," Nessa said as she turned her wandering attention in another direction.

A tap on her shoulder caused Jennifer to turn. "I see that you're still drinking that lethal caffeine-sugar concoction," Dr. Ami said. "At least you're helping Nessa eat better."

"You're very observant, Doctor."

"For any good doctor, that is our superpower," the doctor said. "What is your superpower, Jennifer."

"You're very good at asking the question that gets to the point," Jennifer said. "I can analyze and solve problems quickly, and I can help others learn to handle difficult technological situations," Jennifer said.

"Is that why you're here on this low-budget television series?"

"I think this is where I should be right now. Nessa needs my help getting organized," Jennifer said.

"*Brilliant* is where you are meant to be. Did you leave because of what David said?"

Jennifer thought of the hurtful thing that David said and what her mother said, "That and my mother forbids me from setting foot on the ship. I need to shift my focus from *Brilliant* to something else."

"Jennifer, you will be successful here, you will be successful there, you will succeed at whatever endeavor you choose. Most people would give anything for that. For you, it is a burden."

"What do you mean?"

"You're so successful at everything you try that it tears you away from your destiny."

"*Brilliant?*"

"Isn't that a statement rather than a question. What is your real question?"

"Will it help me find my father?"

"Maybe it already has."

"Dr. Ami, what do you…."

Just then, Nessa shouted, "Places, everyone!"

"Chase your destiny, Jennifer," Dr. Ami said and then walked back to the set.

NESSA'S HOLOBUDDY POPPED UP ABOUT THREE TIMES AN HOUR without a shirt to cover his six-pack abs. He was the prototypical cover model of all the romance novels that Jennifer studiously avoided reading over the years.

When the Assistant Director called an end to the day's shooting, the Director, Christopher Cherry, took her aside, "This was our most productive day since we began this project. Thank you for helping Nessa get organized."

"Of course, Mr. Cherry."

"Call me Chris," the director said. "Navvy told me that a talented young intern would be coming to my set today and that she would shake things up. In a good way."

"Navvy has been a good mentor so far."

"He is that. He grabbed me out of the summer intern crew five years ago. Where do you want to go in filmmaking?"

"I know it's presumptuous, but I want to do it all. I'm already writing. I want to direct," Jennifer said.

"You do look as if you would be a good friend to the camera. In the meantime, though, why don't you stick close to me when you aren't helping Nessa, and I'll share some tips and techniques. Or, maybe I'll learn some from you."

That weekend, Jennifer had more questions after her chat with Dr. Ami. She was unable to find answers yet, so she focused on learning.

ALONG WITH HER MBA, SHE STUDIED DIRECTING TECHNIQUES through steveLearn until she returned to the set on Monday morning. And, for the next two-and-a-half days, that was how Jennifer began to learn how to direct a television series.

TWENTY-ONE

The Meeting

Jennifer came to work on *Star Doctor* on Wednesday, June twenty-second. At lunch break Sami popped up, "Kathy messaged you to come to an urgent meeting in Navvy's conference room at one o'clock. You're excused from your duties on set."

"Respond to confirm." Jennifer wondered who called the fire alarm.

Jennifer took one last bite of her sandwich and emptied her tray in the trash. Her thoughts investigated the possibilities. Was she being fired? Not likely. Reassigned? Possibly. Writing a new movie? Maybe. Another ride on *Brilliant*. Not possible.

SHE ENTERED THE CONFERENCE ROOM AND LOOKED AROUND. NAVVY stood before the table. Seated alongside were Jack, David,—and her mother??? *Omigod, what is going on?*

"Take a seat, Jennifer," Navvy said. Jennifer sat as far from David as the long table would allow.

Sheila spoke up, "What's going on, Navvy? I made it clear that Jennifer and I would have nothing more to do with *Brilliant*."

"Sheila, you need to see this," Navvy said. "Ani, playback the communications with the Hoclarth from last Wednesday." Navvy stepped aside, and the front of the room became a sizable holo display.

The *Mendex* commander appeared. "*StarCruiser*, I am Predex Kalim Kone of the Hoclarth Alliance ship *Mendex*. Heave to and make ready to be boarded. If I'm happy with what you have to offer, I'll leave you with your lives and your ship," the bearded pirate said.

During the playback, both Jack and Navvy focused not on the screen but Sheila's reaction. Jennifer did the same. Her mother leaned forward, and her eyes got huge. For Jennifer, the room suddenly got very chilly, and she wrapped her arms around her body.

The video finished. "Is this a joke?" Sheila said, more loudly than she probably intended.

"No, Sheila. I sent the communication to our special effects department. They removed the facial hair and smoothed out some wrinkles to reverse the aging," Navvy said. "Play cut two."

A much younger, clean-shaven pirate appeared on the screen.

"Anthen Kelrithian?" Sheila said. "You believe he's alive?"

Jennifer's mind was now very quickly processing the possibilities.

"Yes, Sheila, I believe that my son is alive," Navvy said.

Jennifer looked at Navvy, opened her mouth, almost said something, then turned to her mother whose eyes were very wet, "Mom, that's my father?"

Sheila nodded. Jennifer then looked at Navvy, "You're...my..."

"Yes, Jennifer, I'm your grandfather," Navvy said.

Jennifer never fainted in her life, but now she felt the blood draining from her head.

"Push your chair back, lean down, and put your head between your legs," Sheila said.

"But...but," she said as her vision began to tunnel. She pushed back and leaned down, "Omigod, I almost killed my father."

Now, David looked a bit pale. Jack put his arm on his son's shoulder.

Sheila looked at Jack and snapped, "Jack, what is she saying?"

He shook his head to Sheila then looked at Jennifer for a moment to let her recover.

Jennifer brought her head up, "Omigod, Omigod...."

All eyes were riveted on Jack now, especially Sheila's. "Jennifer, I trusted your judgment. I knew you would make the right call," Jack said. "But, just in case, I had my hand on the override. I had my suspicions."

Sheila almost shouted, "You people are bat-smack crazy! You take my daughter into space on a two-hundred-year-old spaceship, fly her half-way to Hell, then put her in a position to kill her father or be killed. Then you come back here and hit her with this." Jennifer had never seen her mother's face as red as this. "Honey, we are out of here, off this lot, and you're never setting foot on it again."

Sheila stood to walk out, "Come, Jennifer."

Jennifer looked around the room as she regained her composure, "No."

"What? These people almost killed you," Sheila was shouting now.

"Mom, you're my family. But so are Navvy and Jack and Riley and Tayla and *Brilliant* and…" She looked at David for an instant and then looked away, "…and Tovar Studios. I need to help my family bring back one of their own, my father, Navvy's son."

"But you could get killed. I don't want to lose my daughter, too," she said, but there was defeat in her voice and more tears in her eyes.

Jennifer was composed now. "Mom, I need to finish this. I need to find my father."

"No way…Navvy?" Sheila said.

"Jennifer, your mother may be right," Navvy said. "We can probably pull this out without…"

"Mother, you have always trusted me to make the right decisions," Jennifer said. "I need to do this. I need to follow my destiny. I need to find my father."

"But…I don't want to lose you, too" Sheila slumped as she exhaled. "What's the plan?"

"First, we need to find *Mendex*," Navvy said.

"Ani, where is *Mendex*?" Jennifer said.

"*Mendex* has completed partial repairs and is one day away from a communications waypoint at the Lagrange point, between Alpha Centauri and Proxima Centauri. The Hoclarth have a robotic repair station in orbit around Naclar," Ani said. "*Mendex* can call for help from there."

"Ani, why did you not tell me where *Mendex* is?" Navvy asked.

"Sir, you complain that I'm too verbal," Ani said. "You didn't ask."

"More importantly, how do you know where *Mendex* is?"

"Nav…Grandfather, during the last exchange of fire, I attached a tracker on the hull of the *Mendex*," Jennifer said.

Jack smiled, "That's our Jennifer. Ani, how much time to the waypoint?"

"Eighteen hours at best speed."

"Okay, how many STALTs do we have on hand?"

"Sir, there are two available in storage."

"I want to leave with four on board," Jack said. "What else do we need?"

"Jack, remember that two-person shuttle we had before we came here?" Navvy said.

"Yeah, I always thought that might be a good thing to have."

"I redesigned a four-person shuttle. We need to fabricate it," Navvy said.

"Fabricate? It would take weeks to build something like that," Sheila said.

"Mom, *Brilliant* has a fabricator. It's like a 3D printer on steroids."

"Ani, how long to fab the shuttle and a full weapons load?" Jack asked. "It may get crowded out there if *Mendex* gets a message off."

Ani responded, "I began yesterday, Sir. I need another twenty-four hours."

"Very well, we raise ship just after sundown tomorrow. Between now and then, we all need rest and some time on the simulator."

"Jennifer, are you coming?"

"Yes, Captain, but I need to run some simulations."

"You aren't going, Jennifer." Sheila tried one more time. "You're only seventeen, and I forbid it."

"Mom, if I wanted to join the Marines, you could sign a permission slip. You need to trust me."

"I trust you. I don't trust these crazy space people who think you're the only one who can pull their chestnuts out of the fire."

"Mom, I rang the bell. I'm one of those people now."

Sheila was defeated, "Jack Masing, will you bring my daughter back?"

"That is the plan. we'll do our best."

"You'd better," Sheila said. "I'm going to wait outside while you people make sausage. The more I hear, the less I like it."

SHEILA WALKED TO THE ANTEROOM AND RAN INTO HANNA Kelrithian. They hugged. "I've missed you, Sheila. I wish we could have been close all these years," Hanna said. "Kathy told me I should come down here."

"Jennifer knows," Sheila said. "She's in there."

Hanna's eyes became moist, "You raised a wonderful daughter, Sheila. Navvy hasn't been this happy since…. But why are you here? I thought they wouldn't let Jennifer near *Brilliant*."

"Hanna, they are going after Anthen."

"My son? But, he's…."

"He is a starship captain for the bad guys and my Jennifer is the only one who can figure out how to get him back."

IN THE CONFERENCE ROOM, JACK SAID, "RILEY, YOU NEED TO GET some sleep and then spend tomorrow on the simulator."

"Captain?" Jennifer interrupted.

"Yes?"

"Riley is our best engineer, and that's where we need him."

"Your suggestion?"

"We need the best pilot with the most experience. You need to put David back in the left seat."

Jack nodded. "Son, can you be the great pilot I know you are, follow my orders, and not say mean and sexist things to your fellow crew members?"

"Yes, Dad."

"Okay, we follow Jennifer's suggestion and…."

Navvy interrupted, "Jack, you need the best science officer you know. I need to go. I need to be there when Anthen comes on board."

"Yes, Pops, I suppose you do," Jack said. "I wish we had his knowledge of the Hoclarth. Could this be like those others who had a memory suppressor mounted in their brain? Someone call Dr. Ami."

"Sami, can you call...."

"Calling her, Boss," Sami said. After a pause. "Connected."

"This is Dr. Ami. Hello, Jennifer."

"Doctor, are you able to remove a Hoclarth memory suppressor underway."

"Jennifer, I have extensive medical knowledge, but I don't have the manual dexterity to remove this device from the brainstem. This surgery requires a human neurosurgeon."

"That settles it. We have to bring Anthen back here."

"Sir, I know a neurosurgeon," Jennifer said.

"Your step-dad? Would he be willing to come along?" Jack asked.

"I guess I could ask?"

Navvy laughed, "Has anyone ever said no to you, Jennifer?"

"Not lately, Grandfather."

"Okay, we have our assignments. Get rest, get fed and get some sim time. And be ready to raise ship at twenty-hundred hours tomorrow."

"Captain, one more thing. We need a comms officer," Jennifer said.

"You wanna bring your best friend on this shindig?"

"Yes, Sir."

"Captain, you saw that she's qualified," Riley said.

Jack looked at the three young crew members. "So, you want your whole squad?" Jack said.

"We need each other," David said.

Jennifer gave David a mean look, but the anger softened.

"Jennifer, you may ask her. Dismissed," Jack said.

THE CREW OF BRILLIANT FILED OUT OF THE EXECUTIVE CONFERENCE Room. Jennifer saw Hanna next to her mom and ran to her and hugged her, "Grandmother."

"You're a special gift to me, Jennifer. Sheila, thank you for bringing her back to me."

Jennifer turned to her mom. "I need to ask a favor."

"I'm guessing I'm not going to like it."

"You're going to hate it. We need to bring a neurosurgeon along to restore Anthen's memory. We need Dad."

"This just keeps getting better and better." Sheila sighed and dropped her head in defeat. "Go ahead and ask him."

Riley walked up to the oldest member of the crew, "Navvy, I need one more favor…."

AFTER THE MEETING BROKE UP, JENNIFER WALKED TO HER CAR AND ordered it to drive her home.

"Sami, call Tayla."

"Hi, Jen," Tayla answered.

"Hi Tay, I need a favor. It will take a couple of days, and it might be dangerous."

"*Brilliant?*"

"Yes, we are going to get my father."

"Kalim Kone?"

"How did you know?"

"I saw the blue-green eyes and I saw your reaction when he came on screen," Tayla said. "Don't you remember?"

"I guess he did make an impression, but I thought it was just the heat of the moment. Tayla, I need you to be there with me. Will you come?"

"Of course. I'm up for a little trip with my bestie. Where are we going?"

"Proxima Centauri."

"The one in the mountains?"

"No."

"The one four light years away?"

"Yes."

"Will it have a cell signal? A valley girl's gotta have her social media?"

"Tayla!"

"You had me at 'Hi.'"

"We raise ship tomorrow night at eight p.m."

"Love you, Jen."

"Love you more, Tay."

JENNIFER, HER MOM, AND HER STEP-DAD SAT DOWN TO DINNER. IT WAS quiet throughout the main course. "You two are very quiet. Are you okay?" Allen said.

"Dad…" Jennifer said.

"Wait until dessert," Sheila said.

"Suspense, it is," Allen said.

Jennifer cleared the plates and Sheila brought out three rather small slices of chocolate cheesecake.

"Okay, Jen," Sheila said.

"Dad, I know you have Friday off. Would you like to take a father-daughter road trip with me?"

"Jennifer!" Sheila interjected.

"Where to?" Allen asked.

"Proxima Centauri."

"Isn't that up in the mountains near Yosemite?"

"Dad, we need a neurosurgeon on Brilliant?"

"Proxima Centauri, as in four light years away?"

"Yes."

"*Brilliant is* a ship in a science-fiction movie."

"No…it isn't," Sheila said. "Remember last week when Jennifer came home late from work, and I had to go get her."

"Yes, we almost missed her birthday dinner reservations."

"That day, your step-daughter rode Brilliant beyond Mars and was attacked by space pirates. She saved the ship and got them home late for dinner."

"You mean like in a movie?"

"No, I mean like in outer friggin' space," Sheila explained.

"Ok, I'll play along. What do you need me for on this trip?"

"Dad, the captain of the pirate ship is my father, and we are going to rescue him."

"Sheila, your ex? You told me he is dead."

"I thought so, too," Sheila said. "It is Anthen."

"Still playing along…. So, what do you need me for?"

"When the Hoclarth kidnapped my father seventeen-and-a-half years ago, they implanted a memory suppressor wrapped around his brain stem. We need you to remove it."

"So, let me get this straight: You want me to get on a movie starship, ride four light years from Earth, and perform intricate neurosurgery that no one on Earth has ever done. Where, on the table in the Galley?"

"In a fully equipped Sick Bay on Brilliant."

"Great; I suppose I'll do it alone."

"Dr. Ami will assist."

"The holo character in the TV show you're working on?"

"She's the ship's doctor on Brilliant. She's got about ninety-five percent of the medical knowledge ever known on Earth."

"I spend five days preparing for a surgery I have never performed."

"Dr. Ami will be available in Sick Bay tomorrow on Brilliant to help you prepare."

"You're serious?"

"Dead serious," Jennifer said.

"Allen, this is real. My child, your step-daughter, is flying out in space on a dangerous mission to save her father. She needs you."

"Of course, I'm in."

Jennifer came around the table and hugged her dad. Sheila joined.

JENNIFER WENT TO HER ROOM AND ENTERED STEVELEARN. "HELLO, Sami."

"Hello, Boss."

"Message Dr. Ami, 'My step-father is going to ride aboard Brilliant. He would like to consult with you after two o'clock.' Send."

She got settled in steveLearn. Again, Dandy Lion diagnosed Jennifer's stress level and jumped into her lap.

"Dandy, I'm going to get my father," Jennifer said.

The purring stopped, and the tawny cat looked Jennifer in the eye. *I told you to be careful. Who is going to give me my treats if you get blown up?*

"I'll be back, Dandy." She cuddled the cat, and the purring resumed. Jennifer paused to think about the upcoming mission.

Take me with you, Dandy thought.

"Ridiculous. You need to be here to take care of Pugs."

I am serious. You'll need me.

Jennifer looked at Dandy and realized that he was.

"Ani?" Jennifer asked.

"Ani here," the Artificial Navigation Intelligence said.

"Have you run the simulations on the Instantaneous Finsler Transform that I requested?"

"Yes, Jennifer. The success rate is seventy-four percent outside of certain parameters. It is ninety-four percent within precise restrictions."

"What are those restrictions?"

"The maneuver must occur within two-point-seven astronomical units of a star with a mass within twenty percent of the mass of the Sun."

"What are the restrictions around Proxima Centauri?"

"I found that to be an interesting simulation, Jennifer. It is also known as Alpha Centauri C. It's about one-tenth the mass of our Sun. If you perform the jump at one-half astronomical unit, it is ninety-nine-point-seven percent reliable and the time displacement is predictable within eighty-seven percent. The most stable trajectory is thirty-seven degrees off the star's center."

"What if another ship is close by?"

"As you asked, I did 1,343 simulations of that type. The results go chaotic at close range but are reliable at a range of greater than 430,000 kilometers."

"Ani, run as many simulations as you can between now and launch tomorrow. Limit input parameters to Alpha C, split between the *Mendex* and a Camday class Battle Cruiser. Assume the desired time displacement is between three and seven minutes. Provide me an intermediate success rate tomorrow morning at six a.m. and then optimize for the upcoming mission."

"I understand and will report."

"Did you run those other scenarios I asked for?"

"Yes. The chance of a successful recovery of your father is forty-seven percent. That's the good news."

"What's the bad news?"

"The chance of losing *Brilliant* and not returning is also forty-seven percent."

"Heads we win. Tails we lose. Good night, Ani. Keep plugging away."

"Sleep well, Jennifer, I'll try to improve the odds."

"Sami, message Maiara, 'Please include the following items in the stores load.'" She attached the list of cat food and pet supplies.

"Done," Sami said. "Jack won't like this."

"I know. Thanks, Ani. Sami, wake me up at five a.m."

TWENTY-TWO

Preparing for Departure

Jennifer woke up at four-fifty-eight a.m. She was surrounded by her down comforter, a sleeping pug, and a wakeful cat on watch at the foot of her bed. The nocturnal animal made several tours of the house through the night, momentarily waking Jennifer each time upon his return.

"Good morning, Sami. Any messages?"

"Again, you beat my alarm. Yes, there are several messages, by priority. From Nessa, 'Production is suspended today and tomorrow. Have a nice day.' Reply?"

"Yes, 'I'll see you Monday. Work with your new HoloBuddy, Nathan. Ask him to help you find data and organize." Jennifer thought of the six-pack abs that Nathan displayed each time he popped up. "And ask him if he has a shirt. It gets cold in the studio.' Send when Nessa is awake."

"From Piper, 'Thanks again for dinner at Roscoe's on Sunday. I have been working with Steven and his engineers. I designed the ten-channel Wi-Pow base station using the steveLearn design tools. We are applying for two new patents under JennaTech. Steven says that you have access to something called a fabricator. Is it able to implement our design and when can we have access to that?' Reply?"

"'Congratulations, Piper. The fab system will be unavailable until

Monday, as will I. Keep testing and we'll build it then.' Send," Jennifer said. "Ani, are you up?"

"This is Ani. I have run all the simulations and scenarios that you requested. The best I could do was increase the odds in our favor to sixty percent. We could increase those odds to seventy-five percent if you run some live simulations on Brilliant with David and the Captain," Ani said.

"When will Jack be on the lot?"

"He and Navvy are meeting in the conference room at noon. Would you like to join?"

"Please make that request, Ani," Jennifer said.

"Message from Dr. Ami, 'I'll be available in Sick Bay all day at Dr. Goldstein's convenience. I attached an information package on the surgery plan and the capabilities of Brilliant Sick Bay.' Reply?" Sami said.

"Sami, reply and forward to my dad, 'Thanks, Dr. Ami. Dad, here is the info from Dr. Ami. Thanks again, Dad, for doing this and I'll let you coordinate with Dr. Ami from here on. I'll be on the lot at nine.'"

"Jennifer, your mom has breakfast ready and would like for you to join her."

"Thanks, Sami." Jennifer hugged Dandy one more time and gave Pugs a belly rub before making her way to the breakfast nook, where she found a double-shot caramel Frappuccino waiting for her. "Good morning, Mom."

"Good morning, Jennifer, I figured that you would be up early this morning," Sheila said.

"Thanks, Mom, and thanks for the Frapp," Jennifer said.

"You want your eggs scrambled with cheese and bacon? Your favorite?"

"That's nice of you, Mom."

"Here is a chocolate chocolate-chip muffin. I don't want you to go on Brilliant."

"Thanks for the muffin. I have to go, Mom."

"I guess I know that, too," Sheila said.

Jennifer focused on the muffin and Sheila focused on the frying pan.

"Here are your eggs…. Jennifer, you're my daughter, my best client, and my best friend. I don't want to lose any one of those to those crazy people and their crazy ship."

"I'll come back. I'll bring back my father and Allen, and I'll bring back Brilliant."

"The vision thing?"

"Yeah." Like every teenager who ever lived, Jennifer believed she was invincible. But she also understood probabilities. "You need to believe in me."

"I do, Honey," Sheila said. "I'll see you at dinner at Tovar. Navvy wants all of the family there."

They finished their breakfast quietly. Jennifer went back to her room and prepared her uniform for later.

On her way to the lot, Jennifer called up Sami, "Message Riley and David and ask them to come to *Brilliant* around nine a.m. to run some simulations."

"Messages sent."

When she arrived at Tovar, she walked directly to Brilliant's hangar facility.

This is where my destiny lies, she thought and then walked to Brilliant and up the ramp. She took her seat at the Operations console.

"Recognize jendroid," Ani said.

"Good morning, Ani, let's program some live scenarios with the Finsler maneuver around Proxima Centauri. I want different approaches with a Camday Battle Cruiser. We'll rotate David, Riley, and me in the left seat. The boys will come about nine a.m." Jennifer said. "Ask Tayla to come to *Brilliant* at three p.m. for training."

"Message sent and Navvy invited you to lunch with him and the Captain."

"Thanks, Sami."

For the next hour, Jennifer and Ani worked out many live simulations for both pilots. She acted as pilot in each simulation. Her vision indicated that there would be a musical chairs game with the three seats, and everyone needed to be ready. She settled on three distinct scenarios to train David and Riley.

Riley arrived on the bridge at eight-forty-five with his coffee cup in hand. David came five minutes later carrying two cups. He offered one to Jennifer, "Your favorite."

"Thanks. And, thank you for coming. I believe that we are going to see some action around Proxima Centauri. And I believe that the *Camdex* will arrive at the *Mendex* about the same time that we do."

"How do you know?" asked Riley.

"She has this vision thing," David said. "I have seen it in action. She's pretty good."

"Okay, when it gets busy around PC, I have some tricks up my sleeve."

"What kinds of tricks?"

"David, remember that maneuver we pulled in the asteroid field that day on SimOne?"

"Omigod, engaging the StarDrive in a gravity field. That's crazy. Dad told me that is how *Brilliant* wound up in this timeline."

"Navvy gave me a heads-up on some mathematics. I worked it up, and Ani and I can program it and control it to give predictable results," Jennifer explained.

"How predictable?" Riley's engineering sense kicked in.

"As long as we stay within well-defined parameters, it is over ninety percent."

"I can work with that. What do you want us to do?" Riley asked.

"I programmed three scenarios. We can learn them and then rotate seats and practice."

"Rotate seats?" David asked.

"I believe we are best prepared if all three of us are familiar with the three seats. We can do some training with the Captain this afternoon after I present it at lunch."

"Navvy and Dad aren't going to like this," David said. "But I trust your judgment ...now. Sorry for before."

They took their seats with Riley in the center seat, Jennifer at ops, and David in the pilot seat.

David looked to his right, "Jen, are we okay?"

"Yes, but don't get close to me. I might still rip your face off."

For the next two hours, Ani paced the three through the different programmed scenarios she and Jennifer created in various configurations.

"That was some of the best operation training I have ever done on *Brilliant*," Riley said.

"I'm exhausted, but I think I've got it," David said.

"The purpose of effective training is to know what you know but be able to anticipate what you don't know," Jennifer said. "I'm going to have lunch with Navvy and Jack and present this plan. Wish me luck. I heard that Craft Services at Sound Stage Three is open."

ON THEIR WAY TO LUNCH, RILEY ASKED DAVID, "I KNOW THAT Jennifer has read the manuals but how is Jennifer so far above the curve?"

"I have known Navvy all my life and Jennifer is his granddaughter. That pretty much explains it for me," David said.

"Works for me, too."

ON HER WAY TO THE EXECUTIVE SUITES, SAMI POPPED UP, "MESSAGE from your step-father, 'I'll be at the studio at one-thirty. I reviewed the information. I'm properly impressed. I'll bring two sets of scrubs.' Reply?"

"Let Dr. Ami know and reply, 'Thanks, Dad.' Sami, direct my dad's car to Executive Parking, let me know when he's on the studio lot, and I'll meet him out there.

Jennifer entered Kathy's office a minute after noon. "Hi, Jennifer, they're in the Conference Room expecting you," Kathy said.

"Thanks, Kathy," Jennifer said.

"Jennifer?"

"Yes?"

"Be careful out there," Kathy said. "Jack and your grandfather seem to think that you're going to be the one to bring home Anthen and *Brilliant*."

No Pressure, huh? "I'll do my best, Kathy."

"Go on in."

JENNIFER ENTERED THE ROOM. THE TWO MEN STOOD, AND JACK SAID, "We're planning this mission. I suspect that the reason you're here is that you have some good ideas."

"I hope I do. What is the plan so far?"

"The basic outline is that we intercept the *Mendex* and snatch Anthen," Jack said.

"We'll have to disable the *Mendex* again before we can board her. Is that part of the plan?" Jennifer asked.

Navvy spoke, "I believe that it will be easier than that. I looked at my son's eyes as he communicated with *Brilliant*. I think he remembers something and he will give himself up in exchange for letting his crew return home."

"I agree. I don't think it will be a cakewalk, but it will likely be straightforward," Jack said.

"I see some complications. I believe the *Mendex* will have had time to get an alarm off to the Hoclarth system. We'll arrive at the same time as a Camday Battle Cruiser," Jennifer said.

"The *Camdex*," Jack said.

"Why that one?" Jennifer asked.

"The commander claims to be Kalim's father."

"Complications. I have some tricks I worked out. That is why I wanted to meet with you," Jennifer said.

"I get the feeling I'm not going to like them."

"I have a feeling that you two are going to hate them."

Jennifer grabbed a sandwich from the side table and explained the time-displacement maneuvers that she trained David and Riley on that morning.

"You think these will work?" Navvy asked.

"Yes, Grandfather. Besides, you gave me the keys. You told me about Joachim Finsler and Piper Simmons. How did you know?"

"I follow the scientific literature, I know what to look for, and I have this thing…I think you call it the vision thing," Navvy said.

"Got it."

Navvy pulled out a package. "Could you deliver this to Riley? It's for Tayla." Jennifer knew exactly what it was.

"Away Dinner at six p.m. Families will be there. Look sharp," Jack said.

"Aye, aye, Captain." Jennifer came to attention and then departed.

"Do you think we can pull this off?" Jack asked Navvy.

"I believe the key to this mission lies in whether Jennifer thinks we can pull this off. Jack, I think she is as good as Anthen."

"I have seen her in action, Navvy. She's better. Too bad you don't have more grandkids like her."

"Maybe I do." Jack saw the look in his old friend's eyes and realized that there were no more questions to be asked.

Back at *Brilliant*, Ani announced, "Jennifer, Dr. Goldstein is five minutes away from the lot."

"Thanks, Ani."

Jennifer took one more minute to close her eyes and envision all the scenarios that she considered, all of the possible outcomes, and then concentrated on the one avenue which would bring home her father and the crew of *Brilliant*.

She opened her eyes, exited *Brilliant*, and arrived in the Executive Parking lot just as her step-father parked.

Jennifer and Allen hugged. "May I help you carry anything?"

"Grab that bag with my scrubs. I'll carry my go bag."

They walked to the *Brilliant* facility. Jennifer held the security gate and carefully watched as Allen first set eyes on *Brilliant*. He stopped cold for a moment.

"It looks as if it could take off and fly at any moment. Stunning."

"That's my *Brilliant*. It affects everyone like that."

"Show me to Sick Bay. I want to meet your Dr. Ami."

He followed her lead to the ramp, up the ladder, and aft to Sick

Bay, "Dad, may I present our Artificial Medical Intelligence and Ship's Doctor, Dr. Ami."

They shook hands, "Doctor," Allen said.

"Dr. Goldstein, I'm honored to meet you. I read your account of the very first spine replacement and reconstruction. Your surgery revolutionized medicine and eliminated almost all forms of paralysis."

"Thank you, Dr. Ami, I'm anxious to see the Robotic Surgery Assistant I read about in your packet. I'd love to learn how to use it."

"As soon as you're ready, I have it programmed with a virtual patient, and we can begin."

"Where can I change into my scrubs?"

"Use the doctor's stateroom starboard. The two-patient ward is to port." Dr. Ami pointed to the stateroom.

Jennifer delivered her step-father's clothes bag and said, "Good luck. I know you'll do well."

"This should be fun. I'll be the first one in my medical class to perform surgery in another star system."

"Another article in the medical journal?" Jennifer asked.

"Publish or perish is what they call it."

"I'll leave you two to your doctor things."

JENNIFER STOPPED IN HER STATEROOM AND DONNED HER UNIFORM. The female attire on *Brilliant* was different from the males in that knee-high boots were worn on the outside. She walked up to the bridge and found Riley in uniform preparing and testing the systems.

Jennifer went forward, retrieved the package, and delivered it to Riley, "Navvy said that you asked for this."

"You know what it is?" Riley said.

"Tayla is pretty snobby about fashion, but if this fits, I think she'll wear it."

"Thanks, Jen."

Just then, David and the Captain arrived. "Riley, are we good to go?"

"Captain, the ship is ready."

"Jennifer told me that you three had done some serious training.

I'm not crazy about the maneuver, but if we need it, it is there for us," the Captain said. "Let me know when Tayla gets here. I'll be in my ready room."

"Aye, aye, Captain," responded the bridge crew in unison.

A half-hour later, Tayla arrived wearing skinny jeans and a Grace VanderWaal concert t-shirt. On Jennifer's advice, she was wearing the same boots as Jennifer. She got looks of humorous disdain from the rest of the bridge crew. "What am I supposed to wear?" Tayla went to her station.

The captain came out of his stateroom, "Tayla, you're out of uniform."

"But, but Captain…."

"Riley, how are we going to fix this?"

He reached around, grabbed the package, and tossed it to Tayla. She ripped it open. "It's beautiful." She paused. "But the blue doesn't go with my hair."

David laughed. "Are you serious?"

"Captain, I'll take her down to our stateroom and get her into uniform," Jennifer said.

"Thank you, Jennifer. But first, we are hosting an Away Dinner at six p.m. It is a special occasion for our families and us. Go over the protocols and be in the Executive Conference Room at five-forty-five for inspection."

SHEILA SAT AT A CIRCULAR TABLE WITH STEVEN AND ANA. THERE were three empty seats at the table. "I came to one of these events before. It's a lot of pomp and circumstance. But it's enjoyable, and Maiara's food is wonderful. She was the head chef then, but now she greets diners at lunch," Sheila said. She felt physically uncomfortable and thought. *The last time I came to an Away Dinner, Anthen didn't come back.*

A voice came from the back of the room, "Ladies and gentlemen, please stand and welcome Captain Jacnen Masing of *StarCruiser Brilliant*." Jack stepped up wearing the cerulean flight suit reminiscent of the one worn by the Navy's Blue Angels.

The captain marched to the podium, "Good evening, friends and family of *Brilliant*, I'm Captain Jack Masing. Please help me welcome the crew of *Brilliant* beginning with Senior Officer and ship's designer Navilek Kelrithian."

Navvy came in wearing an olive-drab flight suit, definitely old style but distinctively *Brilliant*. He stood to Jack's left. The remainder of the crew lined up to the captain's right.

"First Lieutenant Maiara Henare." She also wore the old-style flight suit.

"Pilot David Masing." Jack looked at Ellie who was beaming with pride.

"Engineer Riley McMaster" Jack saw Riley's surprise at seeing his mother and sister, who flew in from Albuquerque.

"Operations Officer Jennifer Gallagher." Jack looked at Sheila whose expression showed both pride and foreboding.

"Communications Officer Tayla Mendoza." At the inspection, Jack and Navvy argued, but the captain deferred to Tayla's fashion sense, and the girls came out wearing bright yellow scarves.

"Finally, Dr. Allen Goldstein, who will be joining us as ship's Surgeon." Allen came out in hospital scrubs.

Right behind Allen was Dandy Lion who jumped into Jennifer's arms.

"What the hell?"

"We need a ship's cat," Tayla said.

"We don't need a damn cat underfoot on my ship."

Dandy hissed and punched the air. He then looked at Navvy.

Jack turned to his left and saw Navvy nod, "Navvy?"

"I think we want this cat," Navvy said.

"Your call, Nav," Jack said. "Please continue."

"Raise your glasses," Navvy said. "To the crew of *Brilliant*. May your knowledge and training lead you. May excellence and success follow you. And, may courage and grace always walk beside you. To this, we say:"

And the entire crew shouted, "*Brilliant*."

Jack turned toward his oldest friend, "To our ship, may you be our home away from home. May you be our shining armor in battle. And, may you fly us into the stars of our destiny. To this, we say:"

And the entire crew shouted, "*Brilliant.*"

As the junior member of the crew, Tayla then stepped forward, "To our family and friends, you brought us here with love. You gave us our confidence. And we'll take you with us everywhere. To you, we say:"

And the entire crew shouted, "*Brilliant.*"

Jack again took the podium, "Attention to orders. Number One, be safe and keep your fellow crew members safe. Number Two, keep our *Brilliant* and its equipment safe and secure. Number Three, Achieve Mission Success. My Crew, we have a challenging mission to bring home one of our own. I have confidence that this crew can achieve that mission and bring us home to everyone here on Sunday afternoon. Posts." At that, the members of the crew marched to join their family and friends. "Take your seats and enjoy the dinner that Maiara and her team prepared. There will be a studio photographer present outside *Brilliant* for crew and family photos."

When Tayla and Jennifer reached their seats, their moms were in tears, and some serious hugs were exchanged. "My little girl looks so good in uniform," Ana said.

"I know, Mom. I wish I had some jewelry to match," Tayla said.

"Get over it, Tay. It's a uniform," Jennifer said.

"You three do look good enough to be in a movie. I pray it has a happy ending," Sheila said.

Jennifer took hold of her mom's shoulders. "Mom, I'm going to bring my step-dad back. I'm going to bring my father back. And, this crew is going to bring *Brilliant* back. I'm sure of it."

Sheila saw in her daughter's eyes the same look of confidence and surety that she had seen in Anthen's eyes on that night long ago. And it made her even more worried. But all she could do was smile and nod.

Dandy jumped on Sheila's lap and stared directly at her.

"I guess you'll be alright, honey."

Maiara's excellent dinner was consumed with relish, topped off by Hokey Pokey ice cream, a Kiwi favorite. Afterward, the families took photos with *Brilliant* in the background and then got a quick walkthrough of the ship. After that, crew and families exited *Brilliant*. Family and friends exchanged goodbyes with crew members who made their way up the ramp. A few minutes later, the ramp closed. The observers walked back to a safe distance. A persistent hum began and got louder, and then the ship rose, retreated into the twilight, and disappeared.

The moms were standing close together. Sheila asked, "Hanna, you have done this more than any of us. How do you cope?"

Hanna responded, "I remember the last line of a sonnet by John Milton, 'They also serve who only stand and wait.'"

TWENTY-THREE

Rescuing Anthen

As the Captain did a final walkthrough, he verified that the crew was aboard and in their places for departure and that the families were a safe distance away. The bridge crew logged in to their stations. Jennifer confirmed the weapons load.

"First Lieutenant, are all crew members aboard?" the Captain asked.

Maiara responded from the engineer's office, "The crew is aboard. Belowdecks is secure."

"Very well. Engineer, raise the ramp and seal the ship."

"Aye, Captain," Riley responded. "The ship is sealed."

The Captain announced, "Make all preparations for getting underway." It was a signal to strap in. "Comms, do we have clearance from SoCal Tracon?"

"Captain, we have westbound clearance beginning in two minutes."

"Very well, Tayla.

The Captain announced, "Strap in everyone. We are launching Mission 618 to Proxima Centauri. Begin the pre-launch checklist. Reports, everyone. Sick Bay?"

"We are ready. The doctors are in," Dr. Ami said.

"Engineer?"

"All Modes ready. Life support nominal. The ship is space-ready." Riley reported.

"Pilot?"

"All flight controls responsive. Ready to rock and roll." David reported.

"Ops, what is our departure profile?"

"Captain, we'll raise the ship to one thousand feet, cloak *Brilliant*, ascend subsonic at a sixty-degree angle westbound over Malibu to Flight level eight-zero-zero, and then conduct unlimited vertical acceleration to the atmospheric boundary," Jennifer reported.

"Ani?"

"All systems nominal. *Brilliant is* ready for launch. Our window opens in fifteen seconds. Ten seconds…"

"Prepare to raise ship, Pilot," Jack said.

"Aye, Captain," David said.

"We are within the window," Tayla said.

"Take us up, David."

There was a rumble.

"Ops?"

"The ship is cloaked."

"Very well. Pilot, begin the ascent."

"Ay, Captain. Em drive engaged subsonic."

"Forty-thousand feet. We are clearing commercial flight levels," Jennifer reported.

"Engineering?"

"Gravity drive ready in all respects, Captain," Riley reported.

"Pilot, on my order, engage gravity drive and accelerate to one-half percent light-speed."

"Half-percent lightspeed, Pilot, aye," David said.

"Eighty-thousand feet, Captain. Sensors indicate clear space above," Jennifer reported.

"Very well, engage."

David pushed the T-bar forward.

"Ops, decloak at the Karman Line."

"Aye, Captain…decloaked at one-hundred kilometers altitude," Jennifer said.

"Continue acceleration to point-eight light-speed. Direct us perpendicular to the solar ecliptic. We'll engage StarDrive at one astronomical unit."

"Point-eight light-speed. Parallel to the solar axis," David said. "Ani?

"On track in clear space. Six minutes to StarDrive clearance."

"This is the Captain; we'll be reducing gravity to moon normal. Unstrap, get your space-legs, and enjoy the view."

"Engineer set gravity at sixteen percent."

"Sixteen percent, Captain."

DR. ALLEN GOT UP FROM HIS CHAIR AND BOUNCED AROUND. "DR. Ami, I guess deep down, I didn't believe all this until now. Interesting way to lose weight."

"That is a common feeling among passengers when we alter gravity."

"ANI, LOCATE THE *MENDEX*."

"Captain, the *Mendex* is approaching Proxima Centauri bound for Hoclarth space at 300 lightspeed," Ani reported.

"Set a course to intercept at best speed."

"Captain, at 1800 lightspeed, we'll intercept at 2:18 p.m. tomorrow, two hours outbound of Proxima Centauri. We are one minute to StarDrive clearance."

"On Ani's mark, engage StarDrive," the captain said.

"Captain, we are clear of solar system gravity. Course laid in."

"Very well, engage."

"Aye, Captain. We are accelerating through faster-than-light," Jennifer said. She thought, *Just a slight shimmer as we went to light speed.*

"Captain?" Jennifer asked.

Navvy responded, "If we showed what you just saw to our audiences, they wouldn't believe it. People pay twenty-five dollars to see a movie; they expect to see magic."

"Bridge crew, we're going to go three-section watches for the transit. Navvy and I will take the First Watch. Jennifer and Tayla will have the mid-watch in three-and-a-half hours, and Riley and David will relieve the morning watch at 0400. Navvy and I will return at 0800 after breakfast. All hands on the bridge at 1300 after lunch for the approach," the Captain instructed. "During watch turnovers, review my standing orders and wake me up if even the cockroaches twitch. I have the ship; you're relieved to get some rest. It's been a long day," the Captain said, and then throughout the ship, "Set Condition Three for interstellar transit."

A FEW MINUTES LATER, JACK AND NAVVY WERE ALONE ON THE bridge.

Jack turned the captain's chair to the left and looked at Navvy, "Here we are again, Old Friend."

Navvy gazed at the star-field, "I wish to have no connection with any ship that doesn't sail fast, for I intend to go in harm's way."

"Isn't that a quote from a John Wayne movie?"

"It was John Paul Jones in the Revolutionary War," Navvy corrected. "We have a young crew. Are they ready for this?"

"I've seen them in action. The youngsters perform incredibly together. Maybe even better than we used to."

"Even David?"

"David is growing up. He'll answer the call."

"Then I guess the only question is: Are we as good as we used to be?"

AT ELEVEN-THIRTY, JENNIFER WOKE UP FOR HER FIRST MID-WATCH AS Officer of the Deck. She roused her bunkmate.

"It's midnight," Tayla said.

"You can snooze for fifteen more minutes, and then I'll come back," Jennifer said.

Five minutes later, in her *Brilliant* jumpsuit and boots, Jennifer began a walk-through of the ship in the sub-deck, to main deck engineering, and up to Sick Bay. "Good evening, Dr. Ami. Is my dad settled in and ready for tomorrow?"

"Jennifer, your step-father is an amazing surgeon. He has fully adapted to the *Brilliant* Sick Bay. I have already learned much from him. I believe things will go well tomorrow."

"Thank you, Doctor." Jennifer went into the Galley for her double-shot caramel Frappuccino and was surprised to find Maiara with a modest spread of sandwich fixings. "You're up, Maiara. That's kind of you."

"The Captain enjoys mid-rats going on or off at midnight."

"This is nice. Let me rack out my roomie, and I'll come back."

Just then, Tayla dragged into the Galley carrying a cup of coffee. "Thanks, Maiara."

"You two have time for a sandwich, and then you mustn't be late relieving your grandfather and the Captain."

Jennifer fixed a veggie sandwich and then asked, "How did you come to *Brilliant*, Maiara?"

"I spent ten years in the Royal New Zealand Navy, went from cook to Supply Corps officer. Then I spent a year in Paris at Le Cordon Bleu. Navvy recruited me to coordinate food service for Tovar Studios and offered me this collateral duty once or twice a year when *Brilliant is* underway for more than a day or two."

Maiara noticed Tayla staring at her tattoo. "My Maori ancestors are the indigenous Polynesians who settled in my country long before the Brits arrived. My chin tattoo is a coming of age signal," Maiara said. "It's time. You better head up to the bridge."

The girls finished their sandwiches and delivered their utensils to the automatic scullery. "Thank you. I'm jealous of your beautiful body art," Tayla said.

"Keep us safe, you two."

THE TWO GIRLS ARRIVED ON THE BRIDGE AT ONE MINUTE BEFORE midnight. Tayla went directly to Navvy as Jennifer instructed and asked him to take her through the process of relieving the watch as Junior Officer of the Deck.

"Good evening, Captain, Grandfather." Jennifer walked around the bridge and stopped at each station to familiarize herself with the indicators. She asked Navvy and then the Captain some detailed questions and finished by reviewing the ship's log, the message board, and the Captain's standing orders. When she finished her familiarization, she stood at attention before the Captain. "Captain, I'm ready to relieve you."

"Very well. The ship is underway on a course to intercept *Mendex* at 1418. Ani is piloting the ship in StarDrive and sensors are clear. There are no heavenly bodies on our track. Notify me immediately of any sensor alerts or operational communication. Do you have any questions?" the Captain said.

"No, Captain. I relieve you."

"Very well, the ship is yours."

"Maiara has mid-rats laid out. I enjoy life underway," Jennifer said.

"I do too; keep my chair warm."

"Yes, Sir."

JENNIFER TOOK THE CAPTAIN'S CHAIR WITH A VIEW OF THE BRIDGE consoles around her. She moved her hands in the air before her to bring up various tactical and operational displays. Tayla took her seat at the communications console and diligently performed her duties. "Rena and Chrissie want to play tennis Saturday."

"Better tell them we can't make it. We won't be back until Sunday afternoon."

"What should I tell them?"

"We're on a road trip, and we aren't in SoCal," Jennifer said. "Tayla?"

"Yeah, Sis."

"I never thought you had any interest in *Brilliant*. And here you're a very competent comms officer."

"Remember the day that you and David were in the simulator?"

"Yeah."

"I realized that if I wanted to be a part of the future for my best friend and my boyfriend, I had to be a part of their world as well."

"So, you've spent a few hours on the simulator?"

"Four hours a day for the last three weeks."

"Woah!" Jennifer said with a surprised look. "It shows. And I keep forgetting that you have a genius IQ as well. Have you selected a major besides tennis at UVN?"

"I'm going to study Spaceborne Instrumentation Engineering with a double in Performance."

"That's a heavy course load. Do you have time?"

"Remember when you set me up with UVN access after my sophomore year?" Jennifer nodded. "I'll enter UVN with two years of credits as a junior."

"Omigod. Tayla, the supernerd," Jennifer said. "Why haven't I been informed of this?"

"Jen, you've been so busy becoming a multi-millionaire that this is the first chance this summer that we have had time to chat."

The girls monitored their watch stations intently, but the girl talk continued for the next four hours.

At 1300, the members of *Brilliant*'s crew were at their assigned stations.

"First Lieutenant, report?" the captain asked.

"Condition One is set throughout the ship. Crew members are logged in and belowdecks is secure," Maiara reported.

Dandy stared at Jennifer. "Captain, the ship's cat reports that all mice are accounted for."

"Seriously? Ani, report all contacts."

"Captain, there are no contacts. Anticipate acquisition of *Mendex* on long-range sensors at 1355."

"Very well, we have a few minutes. Any questions?" There were none. "Ops, we have some time. Could we run through a couple of the scenarios using the Finsler Transition?

"Aye, Captain. Ani, Implement Finsler 1A."

"Beginning," Ani said. "Captain, *Brilliant is* approaching Proxima Centauri, *Camdex* is behind us. Range one-point-three million kilometers...."

At 1340, the Captain announced, "Good Job, team. I don't know if we'll have to use those, but we are ready. Take ten and then be back on station. Navvy and I will be right back. Ops, you have the deck."

Jennifer moved to the center seat. "David, are you all right with your dad treating me like the first officer?"

David turned the pilot's chair to face Jennifer. "Jen, I'm an outstanding pilot and I know I was a real jerk to you the other day. Dad and I discussed this. You're sitting right where you're supposed to be."

"Thanks, David. Could we...."

"Sensor alert," Ani said. "Medium range sensors are picking up an active sensor drone."

"Very well. Engineer, shields up. Captain to the Bridge."

"Shields are up," Riley reported.

"Report?" the Captain said as he took Jennifer's place in the center seat.

"Drone is a Hoclarth Sensor Array. It is unarmed."

"Very well."

"Recommend cloaking the ship and diverting course," Jennifer said.

There was a pause. "No. It looks like Kalim was anticipating our arrival. Let's not disappoint him."

"Captain, the drone is transmitting on a narrow beam in the direction of the *Mendex*," Jennifer said.

"When we acquire on long-range sensors, begin slowing to match course."

"Aye, Captain," David said.

"Engineer, coordinate with the First Lieutenant and run the checklist on the shuttle, operational designation *Challenger*."

"Aye, Captain," responded Riley.

"After we make contact, David and I will take the shuttle over to get Anthen. Navvy seems to think that this exchange will be amicable."

Riley reported, "Captain, the *Challenger* is ready in all respects."

"Very well, Engineer."

"Jack, I'm the only one who has flown an actual shuttle," Navvy said.

"David has trained as a shuttle pilot."

"Captain?" Jack looked into a father's eyes and realized that a negative answer wasn't an option.

"Sure, Old Friend, you can drive. Try not to hit any potholes."

"Sensor alert. The *Mendex* is ahead," Ani said.

"Ani, what is the status of their weapons?"

"Long-range and medium-range weapons are disabled. They have close-in plasma beams. Her shields are down."

"Very well, continue the intercept."

"Sir, I have the *Mendex* on visual."

The *Mendex* showed the scars of the previous battle. The propulsion pod on the port side showed severe structural damage. "You did a number on him, Jennifer," Navvy said.

Jennifer tried to hide the pride she was feeling.

"The *Mendex* is requesting comms," Tayla reported.

"Let's chat. Open it."

Predex Kalim Kone of the *Mendex* appeared. "Are you here to finish us off, StarCruiser?"

"We are here to rescue a member of our crew, Kalim."

"We have no one on board our ship that requires rescue, StarCruiser."

Navvy stepped up next to Jack and looked at Kalim. "We are here to take you home, Son."

Kalim's eyes showed that there was momentary recognition, and then he looked away for a second and then looked back, "I don't know you, Old Man," Kalim said. "Prepare weapons."

Dandy Lion jumped on the center console and looked directly at Kalim.

Kalim looked fearful. "You have a dangerous animal, StarCruiser." Dandy continued staring. Kalim stared back and relaxed.

"My apologies, Toxem'al," Kalim said. "You will keep her safe?"

Dandy nodded.

His shoulders sagged for a moment then he addressed Jack.

"My father, Predex Kalea Komdor of the Battle Cruiser *Camdex*, has disowned me because of my defeat in battle. I have been ordered to Hoclarth to face trial. Therefore, I ask asylum in exchange for the lives of my crew."

"Granted. we'll send a shuttle to bring you back."

"Very well, StarCruiser."

The captain turned to Tayla. "Close comms."

"Navvy, did that cat just talk to Anthen?"

"Seriously, Jack. A talking cat?"

"Looks like this will be a milk run, after all," Jack said.

Jennifer didn't subscribe to Lady Luck, but on the other hand, she certainly didn't believe in slapping her in the face like the Captain just did.

"Riley, take the pilot's seat. Jennifer, you have the ship while we're gone."

"Aye, aye, Captain." Jack, Navvy, and David slid down the pole to the hangar deck, and Jennifer moved to the center seat. On their way to the *Challenger*, Jack and David stopped at the armory and withdrew blasters.

"I guess we can take it easy now," Riley said as he sat in the pilot's position.

"On your toes, Riley. We're at our most vulnerable right now," Jennifer responded.

Tayla looked at her best friend and saw in Jennifer's eyes that she was on the alert as if she was a cat on the prowl.

Tayla tried to relax her friend, "Like the Captain said, Easy-Peasy Lemon…."

"Sensor Alert. An unidentified vessel is decelerating from light speed from the direction of Hoclarth space," Ani said.

"Classify!"

"Classification Hoclarth Battle Cruiser Camday Class. It's the *Camdex*."

"Very well, Ani." She depressed a button on the right arm of the captain's chair, "*Challenger*, we have company. The *Camdex* is approaching."

"Very well, we'll make it quick," Jack responded.

"Riley, position us between the *Mendex* and the Hoclarth cruiser."

"Aye, aye." Suddenly Riley was very serious.

"Ani, configure this chair for Artificial Weapons Intelligence…."

Tayla interrupted, "Wait, Sis. I got this."

"Tay?"

"It took me a whole day to learn comms. I spent the rest of the time on ops and weapons." She moved to the ops console. "Configure, Owwie. Authorization: Ayiiia."

"Presumptuous much?" Jennifer said.

"A girl's gotta dream," Tayla responded. "Weapons ready."

"Prepare to launch STALT One from the starboard tube in Standoff Mode. Cloak the missile just outside the tube and approach the *Camdex* outside of detection range."

"Starboard STALT Standoff cloaked, Weapons, aye," Tayla repeated back.

Jennifer used her hands to manipulate the tactical display. *Camdex* was making a circular approach. "The *Camdex* is approaching *Mendex* to their port."

"Riley, position us on the *Mendex*' bow. When we are there, I'll give the order to release the STALT. Ops, place the STALT in the middle of the triangle."

"*Brilliant is* in position," Riley said.

"Release STALT One."

"Oops," Tayla said.

"Tayla?!?"

"Just kidding. STALT away and moving to position."

THE *CHALLENGER* DOCKED WITH THE *MENDEX*. JACK OPENED THE hatch. "Interesting, no greeting party. Navvy, stay with the shuttle," Jack said. "David, go to the bridge and fetch Anthen. I'm right behind you."

On the Mendex' bridge, Kalim Kone sat alone.

"Predex," Jack said.

"Captain," Kalim said.

"Your crew?" Jack asked.

"My two crew members are temporarily incarcerated. They will be released when I am off the ship."

"Your father is nearby on the *Camdex*. We need to get back to *Brilliant*."

"Kalea Komdor is not my father."

"I know. Navvy Kelrithian is waiting in the shuttle."

"No, Kalea Komdor is my father-in-law."

"You're married? Where is your wife?"

"She's dead."

"Then we need to hurry."

"I'm not leaving without my daughter."

"Where is she?"

"Down a deck in our quarters."

David spoke up, "I'll go down and get her."

"Son, be careful," Jack said as his son ran away.

Jack led the way to the shuttle.

"OFFICER OF THE DECK, THE *CAMDEX* HAS RELEASED A SHUTTLE AND is requesting comms," Ani said.

"On screen."

An older, bearded Hoclarth appeared on the screen. His face showed several battle scars.

"Welcome to the party, *Camdex*," Jennifer said.

"I am Predex Kalea Komdor of the Hoclarth Battle Cruiser *Camdex*. What is your purpose here?"

"We are on a rescue mission."

"Coincidence. We, too, are on a rescue mission and we relieve you of your mission," Kalea said. "You're just a girl. A very familiar-looking girl. Where is your Captain?"

"He is aboard our shuttle which is engaged with the *Mendex* right now."

"Withdraw your shuttle and leave the area. I'll permit you to do so with your ship and your lives. I won't ask again." The screen went blank.

"OFFICER OF THE DECK, THE HOCLARTH SHUTTLE HAS ENTERED THE hangar bay on the *Mendex*."

"Very well, Ani," She depressed the communicator. "*Challenger*, a Hoclarth shuttle just entered your hangar bay."

"Understand, *Brilliant*," Jack answered.

If the Captain was already aboard the shuttle, there must be a problem. "Ani, how close must we be to cover the shuttle with our shields when they separate?"

"The length of a football field."

"Can you get us that close, Riley?"

"American football or soccer?" Riley replied.

"Just get us as close as possible."

JACK BROUGHT ANTHEN/KALIM TO THE SHUTTLE PORT, ENTERED, AND communicated with Jennifer on *Brilliant*.

The Hoclarth refugee followed. Navvy saw him, "Son?"

"Sir, I don't recognize you, but I'll take your word for it," Anthen said.

"Anthen, you have an implant from the Hoclarth. We have a doctor aboard *Brilliant*," Navvy said.

"Captain, where is my daughter?"

"My son needs to hurry," Jack said.

KALIM'S DAUGHTER WAS BEHIND THE THIRD STATEROOM DOOR HE opened. The ten-year-old looked at him, and he said, "Are you Kalim's Daughter?"

"I am Kalinda. And you are?"

"I'm David. We need to hurry."

"Let me guess, you're from Earth, and you're here to save us," she said sarcastically

"You knew we were coming?"

"I know that my dad is a bit confused right now. I know that he isn't Hoclarth and I know that he recognized the old man on your ship."

"That is your grandfather. How did you guess?"

"I can see things happening in the future," Kalinda said. She was gathering objects and stuffing them in a bag. "These are the last things I have that my mother gave me."

"Your sister calls it the vision thing, seeing things in the future," David said. "How can I help?"

"Grab that photo board over there and put it in the bag," Kalinda said. She looked at David. "I have a sister?" She paused and looked into his eyes. "And you're in love with her."

"You're good," David looked surprised. "We need to go NOW."

"Ready. Take me to your leader."

"Seriously?"

"The Patrol ships hooked us up with the Internet. I watch Netflix."

David grabbed her bag, and they began running. They went down a deck and saw the open hatch. Kalinda dove through the opening to the *Challenger* and David passed Kalinda's belongings to his father's waiting hands.

"Stop, Earthman." David froze when he felt the muzzle of a blaster planted firmly above his ear as he planted his hands on the rim of the hatch.

The Hoclarth officer said, "We'll trade your crewman for the granddaughter of Predex Kalea Komdor. You may keep the traitor."

Out of the left corner of his eye, David saw a T-shaped lever. Its function was obvious. He gave one last look at his father. "Sorry, Dad," David said and pulled the actuator and the hatch closed.

ANI REPORTED, "*CHALLENGER* IS AWAY. THEY EJECTED WITH explosives."

"Very well. Ops when they are inside the umbrella, raise shields," Jennifer said.

"Shields are up. *Challenger* is inside the umbrella," Tayla reported.

"Maiara, *Challenger* is returning. Notify me when she is secure," Jennifer said.

"Hangar Bay, Aye," Maiara responded.

THE HATCH CLOSED IN FRONT OF JACK, AND HE FELT AN EXPLOSIVE jerk on the *Challenger*. "Navvy?"

"They separated us, Jack."

"Get us back to *Brilliant*, quickly."

"Range 98 yards. We are under the shield umbrella."

"Way to go, Jennifer," Jack said.

"Captain, may I present my daughter, Kalinda," Anthen said.

"Who is Jennifer and who is that man? He resembles my father?" Kalinda said.

"Lined up with the hangar bay," Navvy said. "We are inside."

"Kalinda, meet your grandfather, Navvy," Jack said.

Navvy turned to look at the young girl. "You're very beautiful, Kalinda."

"My mother told me that beauty among women is a weakness exploited by men of power," Kalinda said. "A warrior requires intelligence and strength of character. I'm quite intelligent, but my mother wasn't able to teach me about character. She died a hero in battle."

"Kalinda, I believe that your mother did just fine," Navvy said.

"Navvy, when we get on *Brilliant*, take Anthen to Sick Bay and deliver him to Dr. Goldstein. We may need his knowledge sooner than we thought," Jack said. He turned to the young girl. "Young lady, your father has a device in his head, and we have an excellent doctor who is ready to remove it."

"I know about the memory suppressor," she said.

"You appear to be as smart as your father and your grandfather."

"David says I'm as smart as my sister," Kalinda said. "May I meet her?"

"Yes, let's go meet Jennifer, your half-sister," Jack said as he led her to the bridge.

TWENTY-FOUR

Proxima Centauri

J ennifer was in the command chair as Officer of the Deck on *Brilliant*, awaiting the return of the *Challenger* on its away mission.

"Riley, when *Challenger* is secure, set course to Proxima Centauri at point-eight light-speed. We need to get in their gravity well soon," Jennifer said

"*Challenger* is aboard," Maiara reported.

"Engage."

"On track to Proxima Centauri."

"Officer of the Deck, *Camdex* is turning to pursue leaving the shuttle behind."

"Very well. Ops, uncloak STALT One and activate in standoff mode. Make the *Camdex* fight her way toward us."

"*Camdex* is firing on the STALT, and it is returning fire. Dazzler's jamming sensors. Their StarDrive pod is damaged."

"Good shooting, Tay,"

The Captain came on the bridge and motioned Kalinda to wait behind his chair. "Ani, plot a StarDrive jump to the Proxima Centauri gravity well and engage."

In response to the order from the Captain, Jennifer said, "The

Captain has the deck." Tayla and Jennifer immediately returned to their positions.

Riley engaged the StarDrive after his panel indicated that Ani had laid in the course. He then looked around for his relief and said, "Where's David?"

The starfield blurred for just a moment as *Brilliant* accelerated through light speed. Jennifer turned back to the Captain and saw a young girl with black hair and the same high cheekbones and blue-green eyes that she saw in the mirror each morning. "Captain?" she asked.

"The Hoclarth have David, Jennifer. We are going to have to use your maneuvers around Proxima Centauri to make Kalea Komdor chase us. He wants to trade David for his granddaughter." Jack turned to Jennifer, "Jen, meet your half-sister, Kalinda."

Jennifer hesitated and then rose from her seat and took Kalinda's right hand, "Hello, Kalinda."

"David says that you can see things in the future like me," Kalinda said.

"Yeah, I call it the vision thing," Jennifer said. "Is David okay?"

"He was captured by my grandfather's guards. You know that David is in love with you?"

"Yes, I know."

"Why do they have gravity set so low?" Kalinda asked.

"It is normal for our moon."

Tayla looked at the two girls who just went through a life-changing moment with perfectly straight faces and said, "Definitely sisters." Kaylinda looked to her right, and Tayla said, "I'm Tayla, Jennifer's best friend." Tayla stepped up and wrapped a hug around a very surprised and uncomfortable ten-year-old.

"I hate to interrupt, but we have work to do. Navvy is with Anthen in sickbay. Jennifer, report?" Jack said.

"Captain, STALT One is back onboard, It was able to disable the StarDrive on the *Camdex* before it began pursuing. We are three minutes to the gravity well of Proxima Centauri and then five hours to the position for optimum use of the Finsler maneuver. I estimate that the *Camdex* will intercept us at that time."

"Good shooting, Jennifer," the Captain said.

"Not me, Sir. Tayla was sitting at Ops, and Riley was piloting. I was directing traffic."

"Really?" the Captain looked at Tayla.

"I was bored, and I like shoot-'em-up video games," Tayla said.

"Well done, crew. Let's go get David back."

Navvy came on the bridge, "They have gone to work in Sick Bay. Dr. Goldstein says it will be about two hours."

THE HOCLARTH PIRATE WALKED INTO SICK BAY. HE LOOKED AROUND at the equipment and was impressed that it was much more advanced than that on his ship. He looked at the two doctors awaiting him. He focused on the yellow eyes of Dr. Ami. "Your eyes? Are you human?"

"I'm Dr. Ami, the Artificial Medical Intelligence aboard *Brilliant*. I'm a Holographic Tactile Virtual Reality entity."

"And an outstanding physician, at that," Dr. Goldstein said. "Anthen, there is a device wrapped around your brain stem at the transition from the spinal cord to the medulla oblongata. It was implanted on Hoclarth when they kidnapped you. It suppressed the knowledge and memories of all the time before you were captured and replaced them with a Hoclarth childhood and education. We are going to remove it. After that, I expect your previous memories and knowledge will return over a matter of days and weeks."

"Will I forget?" Anthen asked. "I don't want to lose the memories of my wife and my daughter."

"This surgery was performed previously in another time and place," Dr. Ami explained. "You will retain your current knowledge and memories of your family and your experience. Please lay face down on the table, and we'll take some pictures."

"CAPTAIN, STARDRIVE IS DISENGAGED. WE HAVE ENTERED THE gravity well at point-eight light-speed en route to Proxima Centauri," Riley said.

"Very well," Jack said. "Ops, where do we need to be for you to pull this rabbit out of a hat?"

"We need to be just past the closest point of approach to Proxima Centauri at about eight million kilometers outbound with the *Camdex* one million kilometers behind us when we turn back," Jennifer said.

"Ani, what is our best speed to the CPA?" Jack said.

"Point-five-five light-speed. At that speed, the transit will take six-point-five hours. Course laid in," Ani said.

"Very well, engage," Jack said. "Now, we wait."

DR. AMI OPERATED THE IMAGING EQUIPMENT, AND THE TWO DOCTORS studied the holographic view of the device wrapped around Anthen's brain stem. Using their hands, they rotated the image to see the implanted intruder completely. "Those sneaky bastards," Dr. Goldstein said. "It looks like they poured a liquid metal around the implant. I see that it has involved three spinal nerves. He will suffer paralysis if we cut them."

"Sir, I studied all of your procedures. You reconnected and regenerated these nerves many times," Dr. Ami said.

"I have. But not this many. Not without an extra set of hands. And not four light-years from home," Dr. Goldstein said. "You told me that you aren't able to perform intricate surgery?"

"Sir, I haven't been certified to perform at this level. I studied all of your operations from both your view and the view of your colleagues at the table. I believe that I can act as a competent assistant even though it is my first time."

"Let's do this, then. Is there any way we can have normal gravity?"

"Yes, Doctor," Dr. Ami said. "Captain, Dr. Goldstein requests that you set gravity to Earth Normal."

THE CAPTAIN RECEIVED THE REQUEST FROM SICK BAY. "SET GRAVITY to Earth Normal."

Jack depressed the communicator, "How is that, Allen?"

"That's much more like it for me. Thank you," Dr. Goldstein responded.

"Good luck, Dad," Jennifer said.

"Thanks, Jen, I expect you will have your father back in a couple of hours."

"I hope that he is as good as the one I have now."

"I appreciate that, Jen. We'll do our best."

"How do you stand this gravity? I feel twenty klims heavier," Kalinda asked.

"When was the last time that you ate?" Navvy asked.

"I haven't had sustenance during this awake cycle."

"Let's go down to the Galley and see if Maiara can add a couple of klims," Jennifer said.

"And ask her to send some snacks up to the Bridge," Jack said.

"Dr. Goldstein, the patient's vitals remain normal."

"Good. Dr. Ami, make the next laser cut along the toroidal axis and expose the greater occipital nerve," Dr. Goldstein said. "Do you have any music in here?"

"What do you prefer, Doctor?"

"I'm a Deadhead. You do the math."

"Ani, play Grateful Dead in Sick Bay."

Dr. Ami cut a wedge exposing the nerve. "Excellent, Ami. Now excise the nerve."

"Doctor?"

"If I'm going to certify you for general and neurosurgery after this is over, you must demonstrate the skills as I instruct. So far, you demonstrated the best hands of any surgeon that I have worked with."

"Thank you so much, Dr. Goldstein. I'm honored."

"Call me Allan. Let's cut this nasty monster out of this man's head and then we can placate each other with honorifics."

The two doctors continued to work with the fast pace of a well-honed team.

"The suppressor is no longer functioning. EEG is nearly flatlining. Brain function appears to be severely impaired." The nerves were now free, and the final laser cuts readied the intruder for removal.

"You predicted this based on past surgeries. Let's get that intruder out of there," Dr. Goldstein said.

The two doctors continued to work diligently. Allen observed a marked acceleration in the actions of Dr. Ami. The intruding toroid no longer existed in Anthen's head.

"Dr. Ami, bring him out of anesthesia. Let's verify our nerve connections," Dr. Goldstein said. "Kalim, can you hear me?"

"Who is Kalim? My name is Anthen Kelrithian. Where am I?"

"You're recovering from surgery aboard *StarCruiser Brilliant*."

"Was I injured on the planet?"

"Yes. We need to check to see if everything works." The two doctors did a complete neurological inventory to check for any paralysis. The test was successful.

"I have a daughter?" Anthen said.

"Yes, and she is nearby. You will be able to see her very soon," Dr. Goldstein said. "We are going to put you back to sleep now."

"Very nice job, Ami. Please close him up."

"Thanks, Doctor. His brain function is improving rapidly," Dr. Ami said.

KALINDA RETURNED TO THE BRIDGE AND WAS STANDING BETWEEN Tayla and Jennifer, carefully observing their consoles as the girls pointed out functions.

"Ani, report?"

"Captain, we are three hours from the closest point of approach."

"Very well, Ani."

"Captain, the Finsler maneuver will put us in the baffles of the *Mendex*, but I haven't figured out how we are going to get on board their ship. They certainly aren't going to welcome the shuttle," Jennifer said.

Jack smiled, "Navvy?"

"I recently installed a device on *Brilliant* that dematerializes matter and rematerializes it at a remote location," Navvy explained.

"A Transporter. Seriously?"

"When we first got here, Navvy started watching all the episodes of each *Star Trek* series," Jack said. "He told me one day that *Brilliant* had to have one of those. So, he built one."

Jennifer looked at Navvy, "How Trekkie of you. Why is it not in the manual?"

"Our *Brilliant*'s gotta have some secrets," Navvy said.

DR. GOLDSTEIN CAME UP THE LADDER, REMOVED HIS HEAD COVERING and stood next to the Captain. "Doctor?"

Everyone turned to Allen. He looked at Jennifer and Kalinda. "The surgery took longer than expected, but it was completely successful. Kalinda, he asked about you. Jennifer, he is still reforming his old memories, and he isn't ready for new ones yet. Could you hold off on introducing yourself for a while?"

"Yes, Dad, and thanks."

"My compliments to your skill, Doctor," Jack said.

"Dr. Ami performed most of the surgery. She is extremely competent. I'm going to nominate her as a Fellow of the American College of Surgeons when we get back."

"Stop by the Galley, Doctor, and relax after a job well done. Hopefully, you can enjoy the rest of this pleasure cruise."

"Thanks, Captain. Anthen will be up and around in a couple of hours. Navvy, you and Kalinda may go down to see him right now. Captain, the patient may benefit from Moon gravity now."

"Riley, make it so."

Allen cautiously grabbed the fireman's pole and slid down a deck. Navvy followed with cautious experience. Kalinda leaped and bounced down a deck.

"One down, one to go," Jack said.

"Who is going to the *Camdex*?" Jennifer asked.

"Riley and I will go over," Jack said.

"Captain, you need to be here to fight the ship against the *Camdex*," Jennifer said. "I need to go."

"Jennifer, this will be dangerous."

"*Brilliant* needs you on the bridge. Riley and I need to go get David back," Jennifer paused. "I need David back."

"Can you handle a blaster?"

"I'm certified as a marksman on the simulator."

"Very well but try to avoid using it."

As *BRILLIANT* APPROACHED THE RED DWARF, THE BRIDGE CREW WAS relaxed but ready. Riley was in the pilot's seat, and Jennifer was to his right in the Operations seat. Proxima Centauri filled the screen at full magnification. Although very massive for a small star, its actual diameter is only a third larger than Jupiter, with only one planet orbiting in the Goldilocks zone. Being that close to a red star, though, means the conditions on the planet prevent it from sustaining life. The Hoclarth had a crewless way station in orbit around the planet.

"Sensor Alert. The *Camdex* has appeared on long-range sensors. Captain, we are one hour from the closest point of approach to Proxima Centauri. The *Camdex* will intercept three minutes after CPA."

"Very well, Ani. Ops, what is our weapons load?"

"Two Smart Tactical Autonomous Long-Range Torpedoes loaded in tubes, two STALTs in reserve, full dazzler, and close-in plasma weapons."

"We have the toys. Let's hope that your tactics work, Jennifer."

Anthen Kelrithian came up the pole to the Bridge followed by his father. "This place looks very familiar." Jennifer turned to look at her father in person for the first time.

"Welcome back, Anthen," Jack said.

"Same old *Brilliant* but some new faces. Could you introduce yourselves?" Anthen said.

"I'm Riley McMaster, Engineer and Pilot."

"I'm Tayla Mendoza on Communications."

"I'm Jennifer Gallagher."

"I used to date a Sheila Gallagher."

"My mother, Sir," Jennifer said.

Anthen furrowed his brow realizing that he was missing

something when he said, "I guess I'll meet David again when you can get him back. You need some information?"

Jennifer and Riley met Anthen at the Science Station. "Riley and I will transport to the *Camdex* to get him back. We need you to tell us how to do that," Jennifer said.

Anthen looked for some buttons and controls. "The console configuration has changed. I want to display a drawing of the *Camdex*," Anthen said.

Jennifer moved her hands in the air, and a 3D drawing of the ship appeared before them.

"Impressive," Anthen said. "Looks like I need to review the *Brilliant Tech Manual*."

"I can answer any questions you have right now. I can recite it verbatim," Jennifer said.

"I thought Navvy and I were the only ones who could do that," Anthen said, scratching his cheek. "Okay, the *Camdex* has a minimal crew. You will transport to this empty storage room. From there, you must go forward and avoid the sensors. They will slow you down. Jennifer, apparently you have a good memory?"

"I have a visual eidetic memory. I have the drawing memorized, Sir."

Again, he looked at her as if he was missing something. "The detention facility is located one deck up in the center of the ship. All of the Hoclarth Predexes have the code to bring down the force field, but it's a long stream of Hoclarth characters." He manipulated a drawing and exposed a close-up of the keypad that opened the force field detaining David. "Watch closely." Anthen pressed twenty images in order on the keypad. "Would you like to see it again?"

"No, Sir, I've got it."

"Show me."

Jennifer keyed in the sequence exactly as Anthen had.

"Impressive," Anthen said.

"Once you release David, the alarms will sound. You should have thirty seconds to return to the transporter point. You will be cutting it close. Are there any questions?"

"Are there any physical barriers?" Riley asked.

"You will pass through three hatches that are built just like those on U.S. Navy Ships. They are ovals, and the bottom is about eight inches above the floor. The Navy calls them knee-knockers. Don't trip over them."

"Thank you, Sir. It's nice to have you back on board *Brilliant*," Jennifer said.

"Good luck to both of you."

"*Camdex* is five million kilometers behind us. They will close to one million in three minutes."

"Very well, Ani. Ops, read the procedure once more," Jack said.

"At one million we'll turn to intercept, deploy STALT Two in standoff, and engage the StarDrive for three one-hundredths of a second."

"Wish we knew if this was going to work," Jack said.

"Sensor Alert. Detecting a StarCruiser in the baffles of the *Camdex*."

"Asked and answered," Jack said.

"*Camdex* is hailing us, Sir," Tayla said.

"On Screen."

The bearded Predex of the *Camdex* appeared on screen. "Heave to and be boarded. I'll trade your crewman for my granddaughter. If you do not comply, I'll destroy your ship," Kalea Komdor said.

"Very well, *Camdex*," Jack said. "Screen off. Riley begin your turn to the *Camdex*. Release STALT Two when we are face-to-face."

Riley and Jennifer acknowledged.

"Ani, at 500,000 engage the StarDrive," Jack said. "Ani, you will pilot this evolution."

"Captain, I used to be a pretty good pilot," Anthen said.

"You've got it, then. Welcome back, Anthen."

"STALT Two released. Tube is reloading."

The screen blurred as the StarDrive took *Brilliant* back in time.

"Riley and Jennifer to the Hangar Bay. Maiara will operate the transporter controls."

Riley and Tayla touched hands as she made her way to the Ops position and Riley dropped down a deck behind Jennifer.

"PREDEX, THE STARCRUISER HAS RELEASED A WEAPONS DRONE," THE Navigator said.

"Shields up. Activate weapons," Predex Kalea Komdor said. "Destroy them."

"Predex, they are no longer onscreen. They engaged their StarDrive."

"That is suicide this close to the star. They are insane."

"Intruder Alert!"

RILEY AND JENNIFER ARRIVED AT THE HANGAR DECK AND STOOD ON two of the five circular pads.

"Good luck, you two," Maiara said.

"Hangar Deck, we are in range. Transport the away team," Jack said over the communications.

Jennifer and Riley felt a distinct tingling as they dissolved into nothing.

JENNIFER AND RILEY REMATERIALIZED IN THE STORAGE COMPARTMENT on the *Camdex*, "Riley, follow my steps exactly and watch the knee-knockers,"

"Yes, Jen."

Riley watched closely as Jennifer stepped gingerly along the passageways to avoid the sensors. It took about a minute to arrive at the Detention Facility, and Jennifer saw David.

"Took you guys long enough. Can you get me out of here?"

"The Captain said it was my choice if you showed too much attitude."

"AWAY TEAM IS ABOARD THE *CAMDEX*, CAPTAIN."

"Very well, First Lieutenant," Jack said. "Ops, cloak the ship and raise shields. Lower them when you hear Jennifer call for transport."

"Shields are up. The ship is cloaked," Tayla said.

"Ani, lay in a course out of the gravity well."

JENNIFER STEPPED UP TO THE KEYPAD THAT CONTROLLED THE FORCE field detaining David. "Ready to run? This is going to set off alarms." She typed in the characters as Anthen instructed. The force field dropped, and alarms began to sound.

"Cat's out of the bag. Hurry up, David, we have thirty seconds," Riley said.

They ran and almost made it before Riley slammed his shin into the bottom of the third hatch and fell. It cost them ten seconds. David and Jennifer helped Riley up and assisted him to the storage compartment. When they entered, Kalea and two guards greeted them. "Daughter of Kalim, we meet again."

"Brilliant, now!"

"You won't escape this time."

Kalea raised his blaster and pointed it at Jennifer as she felt the tingling. The last thing Jennifer saw was David jumping in front of her and the bright flash of a blaster.

JENNIFER, DAVID, AND RILEY MATERIALIZED ON *BRILLIANT*. DAVID WAS standing in front of Jennifer. When the transport was complete, David collapsed.

Jennifer shouted, "Captain, David took a blaster to the chest. Set gravity to five percent so we can move him to Sick Bay." Maiara ran to assist Jennifer. "Riley, go to the Bridge. We've got this."

"CAPTAIN, *CAMDEX* IS TURNING TO ATTACK," ANI SAID.

"Sick Bay, prepare for incoming," Jack announced. "Riley, engage gravity drive at maximum speed. Shields up."

"Ops, Release STALT One from starboard tube. Set to chase and disable."

Riley reached the Bridge and limped to the pilot's chair. "Anthen, take the Science seat and configure for weapons. Are you okay, Riley?"

"STALT One away," Tayla reported.

"I should have looked before I leaped, Captain," Riley said.

"Weapons configured on Science," Anthen said.

"You still a good shot, Buddy?"

"On Hoclarth, I can hit the middle eye of a framsel at two-hundred-fifty klarks."

"That good, huh?"

JENNIFER AND MAIARA BROUGHT DAVID INTO SICK BAY. DR. AMI directed the two to position David on the table. "He's barely conscious, Doctor. What should I do?"

David whispered, "Ask my dad to come down. Jennifer, are you okay?"

"Yes, David. You saved my life," Jennifer said.

"I hate to see the one I love on her butt."

Jennifer leaned in and kissed David, "I love you, too, Movie Star." She looked at her step-dad. His grim look told her all she needed to know.

Dr. Ami worked so quickly that her hands blurred as she positioned equipment and inserted tubes into David's body.

"Send Jack down here," Allen said.

Jennifer took three steps and bounded up the fire pole.

JENNIFER CAME UP TO THE BRIDGE OF *BRILLIANT* AND JACK TURNED his chair and saw a very emotional girl. "It's bad, Sir. You need to get down to Sick Bay."

"*Camdex* is attacking," Jack said.

"We've got this, Sir. Go be with David. I've got the ship."

"Very well."

"Sir, he saved my life."

Jack jumped out of his chair and was down the fire pole in a flash.

. . .

"ANI, REPORT." SHE LOOKED AROUND THE BRIDGE. HER FATHER SAT to her left on a weapons panel. Riley was in the pilot's seat and Tayla at the Operations and Weapons console. The display showed Proxima Centauri receding, and the tactical display showed *Camdex* in close pursuit.

"Officer of the Deck, *Camdex* isn't gaining now while fighting off the STALT. We have two STALTs loaded in the tubes. We are twelve minutes to our exit from the gravity well."

"Very well." Jennifer looked at that odd angle of Riley's leg and then saw the extreme pain in his face.

"First Lieutenant, can you do advanced first aid?" Jennifer paged down to Sick Bay.

"Yes, Jennifer."

"Bring up the tools to fix a broken leg and give Riley localized painkillers. I need him to remain on duty." At this, Tayla looked over to Riley in alarm.

"Aye, aye," Maiara responded.

"Thanks, Jen," Riley said.

"We are going to fight this battle and win it now. Otherwise, this ship is going to be on our ass all the way to Earth. Are we ready?"

Each crew member acknowledged.

"Riley, when we turn and engage, we'll be within range of their meteors. I need you to evade the rocks and put me in a position to get a kill shot on their meteor cannon. Tayla and Riley, I'll assign you to handle drone fighters. Tay, make ready STALT Four to release cloaked and get in position in their baffles to disable their propulsion and weapons," Jennifer turned to Maiara, "How long will it take to get Riley back to battle-ready?"

"It's a simple fracture of the lower fibula. I have it immobilized. The painkillers should take effect in a minute."

"Very well. Good job, Maiara," Jennifer said. "Ani, tactical report."

"We lost signal on the STALT Three. *Camdex* is StarDrive capable but limited to point-four light-speed in the gravity well. The STALT disabled the port side sensor array, port meteor cannon, and port side close-in plasma on *Camdex*."

"Very well. Tayla, release STALT Four and track it around the port side until it's on the *Camdex*'s left flank at very close range. We'll turn to attack *Camdex* on their starboard. They will release their drone fighters when we turn. Any questions?"

"Officer of the Deck, there is a soft spot near the keel on the port side. If your STALT attacks that location, it will disable their main reactor," Anthen said.

"Tayla, use the information from Anthen and program STALT Four to uncloak and attack when *Camdex* turns to meet us," Jennifer said.

JACK ENTERED SICK BAY. THE TWO DOCTORS NOW HAD DAVID hooked up to tubes. They were about to insert a tube into his lungs. "David," Jack said.

"Dad, I should have ducked."

"I'm proud of you, Son."

"We need to put him under for surgery," Dr. Goldstein said.

"How bad is it?"

"His liver, pancreas, and left lung are destroyed. His heart is severely damaged. We are doing all we can."

"Will you do the surgery?"

"I'll assist Dr. Ami. She is extremely competent in this operating theater."

"I'll be right here."

As he watched the two doctors perform, he noticed the actions of Dr. Ami got faster and faster. Foreboding medical alarms sounded continuously. The efforts of the Artificial Medical Intelligence became almost a blur as Dr. Goldstein watched and assisted where he could.

TWENTY-FIVE

The Return of StarCruiser Brilliant

"Officer of the Deck, we are five minutes to exit from the gravity well. *Camdex* is now one-hundred-thousand kilometers behind us. We are in range of her close-in weapons," Ani reported.

"STALT Four is in position on her port side," Tayla reported.

"Ops, release STALT Three to attack forward weapons at the turn."

"STALT Three ready," Tayla said.

"Riley, turn to intercept the *Camdex*. Owwie, configure this chair for the Dorsal Plasma array. Assign Port array to the Science Station and Starboard array to Ops," Jennifer ordered. "Good shooting, everyone. Riley, turn to intercept."

"STALT Three is away."

"Sensor Alert. *Camdex* has released two fighter drones designated Fighter One and Fighter Two."

"Tayla, you have Fighter One, Anthen, you have Fighter Two. Riley, take me in for a shot on the starboard Meteor Cannon."

"Sensor alert. Three rock salvo incoming."

"Riley, evade right."

Jennifer blasted the first meteor into sand. She broke the second rock into several large pieces.

The display flashed when the small pieces struck the shields. "Damage report, Ani."

"We lost the port electronics pod. We won't be able to cloak or camouflage," Ani reported.

"Very well, Ani."

The third meteor was fast approaching *Brilliant*'s broadside. Faster than she could see, Anthen shifted focus and destroyed the meteor. "Good Shot."

Riley piloted *Brilliant* close aboard on the *Camdex*'s starboard side, Jennifer didn't waste the opportunity and got a bullseye on the starboard cannon.

"Good shooting, Jen," Tayla said. "Dazzling Fighter One."

Ani reported, "Fighter One is blind." Tayla fired five plasma shots at the fighter and sent it to drone heaven.

"Excellent, Tay," Jennifer said. "Riley, pursue Fighter Two."

"Fighter Two, Aye," Riley said.

Anthen said, "I know the pilot controlling this fighter. He is going to jink right and then roll back toward us. Riley, when he jinks, I want you to pitch down and roll right."

"Aye, Sir."

"There's the jink." Immediately, the starfield on the display began moving upward and twisting counter-clockwise. On tactical, Fighter Two jinked back to the left and began his tight roll backward. "Got him!"

Jennifer saw a single plasma shot that struck the fighter head on, and it exploded at close range on the screen.

"Way to go, Dad," Jennifer.

On display at that moment, the *Camdex* shook, and its lights flashed out.

"Riley, turn to target *Camdex*'s bridge."

"Ani, report?" Jennifer asked.

"STALT Four took out the main reactor. STALT Three disabled starboard weapons. The *Camdex* is dead in space."

"Tayla open comms and then recover STALT Three and Four."

The bearded Predex of the *Camdex* appeared on screen and looked surprised. "Daughter of Kalim, we meet a third time. My compliments. You're a worthy adversary."

"Predex Komdor, I'm targeting your bridge with all of my shipboard weapons. We can keep shooting at each other, or you can wait for the *Mendex* to catch up and return you and your crew to your home. Your choice."

"I accept your terms, *Brilliant*. Will you treat my granddaughter well?"

"Kalinda is my half-sister, Predex. Along with our father, we'll treat her like our family and raise her as well as her mother and father have so far."

"I trust you as one warrior to another, and I'll keep her in my memories."

"Maybe one day, we can meet as one friend to another, and you may make new memories with your granddaughter."

"Maybe it's time for that, Young Captain. Until then, Daughter of Kalim."

"Until then, Predex Komdor," Jennifer said. "Screen off."

"STALT Three and Four are aboard," Tayla reported.

"Very well, Ops. Ani, lay in a course for Earth, maximum speed and engage StarDrive when we are clear of the gravity well."

"Two minutes to gravity well clearance. Fifteen hours to Earth."

"Very well, Ani."

"Good job, *Brilliant*," Jennifer said. "Let's hope we get everyone home safely."

Anthen spoke up, "Jennifer, I'm confused. You called me Dad and why does Kalea think I'm your father?

Jennifer turned, "I'm guessing that he sees the resemblance. Sheila Gallagher is my mother. She was pregnant with me when you got kidnapped."

"And Dr. Allen?"

"He is my step-father."

"Jennifer, your mother has given me a daughter that I'm most proud of."

"And you brought me a wonderful sister. Welcome home, Dad."

Tayla observed another life-changing moment that her best friend went through with a straight face. "Definitely father-daughter."

. . .

ALLEN CAME UP TO JACK, "WE HAVE DONE ALL THAT WE CAN ON board *Brilliant*, but he needs regenerated organs as soon as possible."

"How long?" Jack asked.

"If it takes more than fifteen hours, he will start suffering irreversible decay of his brain function."

"I understand, Doctor."

"Can we communicate with Hollywood Methodist? That is Dr. Ami's hospital, and they have organ regeneration capability."

"Of course, whenever you need."

"I'll be up in a few minutes. We'll need to send a large data file."

"We communicate through a repeater at Tovar," Jack said. "Thank Dr. Ami for me. I have never seen anyone perform as fast as she did to save David."

"Captain, I can assure you that no one ever has."

"I need to go up and see if your step-daughter has kept *Brilliant* in one piece."

Three steps and a bounce later, Jack was on the Bridge.

IT WAS ALMOST MIDNIGHT, AT THE END OF A LONG FRIDAY. THE bridge crew had worked eleven hours straight.

"*Brilliant* has now transitioned to StarDrive at maximum speed."

"Very well, Ani."

Jack came up to the Bridge and looked around to see relaxed watch standers.

"Jennifer, report. Did I miss anything?"

"Captain on the Bridge," Jennifer said as she and Tayla shifted to their normal seats. "Sir, the *Camdex* is in orbit around Proxima Centauri. She is disabled and waiting for the *Mendex* to rescue her. *Brilliant is* at maximum speed to Earth with arrival at 1500 local time. We suffered damage to port electronics and won't be able to camouflage on our descent to Earth. STALT Three and Four are recovered and replenished, Sir."

As he listened, the Captain was astounded. "Anthen?"

"Buddy, my daughter led this crew with great competence and distinction. She fought the ship better than we ever did."

"My compliments, then, to the First Officer of *Brilliant*."

"Captain?" Jennifer turned with a look of surprise.

"Yes, Number One?"

"Well, Girlfriend, I believe you just got promoted," Tayla said.

Allen came up to the Bridge just in time to share the moment. "Allen, your step-daughter done good," Jack said.

"That's all Sheila's fault, but I'll tell her how proud I am," Allen said. "Can we get a line to Hollywood Methodist Trauma Center?"

"Tayla, contact the repeater and get us a landline," Jack ordered.

"Dad, how is David?"

"We've done all we could, Jen. It's up to *Brilliant* now to get us to the helipad at the hospital as fast as we can."

"The line is open," Tayla said.

"Hollywood Trauma, this is Dr. Vinod Prashad."

"This is Dr. Allan Goldstein from UVN."

"I'm honored to speak with you, Doctor. I recognize your voice and picture from a conference. How may I help?"

"I'm on *StarCruiser Brilliant*. We are en route to your helipad and will arrive at approximately three p.m. I have a previously healthy nineteen-year-old male in critical condition, with severe thoracic injuries due to a weapon discharge. We need an immediate transplant of regenerated heart, left lung, and liver."

"Did you say *StarCruiser Brilliant*, Dr. Ami's ship from the movie?"

"Doctor, you need to suspend your disbelief so we can save this patient. I'm transmitting a file with his complete DNA and Patient History."

"I'll call in the Regen team immediately. We'll have a full trauma team and operating room at your disposal when you arrive. Will you be performing the surgery? We need to assign you admitting privileges."

"Dr. Ami will be the admitting surgeon."

"I know Dr. Ami and she is an exceptional non-surgical resident. She has never performed OR surgery here at Hollywood Methodist."

"Dr. Prashad, I observed, and I certify that Dr. Ami is the most competent surgeon with whom I have ever worked."

"I received the data file. We'll begin preparing now. Have a safe journey. I look forward to meeting you upon your arrival."

"Thank you, Doctor." The connection ended. "Jack, you owe him a sight-seeing ride."

"Allen, I'm going to owe many doctors and nurses quite a bit when David walks out of that hospital."

Just then, Kalinda came to the bridge. "Hi, Father. Hi, Sister. Captain, Maiara has been teaching me how to cook. There is a meal ready for the crew in the Galley."

"Very well, young lady. I love mid-rats. Set condition three for underway watch standing. Number One, relieve me to get food and then I'll take the watch with Ani until morning, and you will return at 0800."

"Aye, Captain," Jennifer said. "Dad, is there room in Sick Bay for one more. Riley has a broken leg, and the painkillers are wearing off."

"Of course, Jennifer. Tayla, can you help Riley get to sickbay?" Tayla got up, gave Riley a hug and a kiss, and then helped him down the ladder.

"Captain, I have the ship. I'll see you in a bit," Jennifer said.

"You saved the ship again." Jennifer beamed with the Captain's compliment.

BRILLIANT WAS ONE HOUR FROM EARTH. THE FACES OF EACH MEMBER of the bridge crew were grim. David's health was declining. Every minute would count in getting him to Hollywood Methodist to receive the transplant organs. Navvy sat next to Anthen at the Science Station. Riley wore a walking cast at the Engineer Station. Tayla handled communications from the Operations console. To her left, Jennifer prepared for a very steep re-entry. Jack sat in the captain's chair, wishing he could move *Brilliant* faster toward the hospital that might save his son's life. Kalinda was fast asleep at the comms panel with Dandy Lion on her lap. Dr. Ami and Dr. Allen were watching closely over David who was in extremely critical condition.

"StarDrive is disengaged. *Brilliant is* decelerating to sub-light,"

Jennifer said. "We'll pass the Moon at point-one light-speed in forty minutes."

"Very well, Pilot. Navvy, it looks like we are going to reveal a big secret after forty years."

"On a better day, I would look at this as a publicity gold mine for the next movie."

"On a better day. Jennifer, what is our track?"

"Sir, we'll come in from the northeast over the Wasatch Range and bleed speed to subsonic over Barstow. We'll be on the helipad at 2:47 p.m. We are going to rattle some windows on the Las Vegas strip," Jennifer said.

"Very well. Ops, you need to phone this one in."

"Yes, Sir," Tayla waved her hands above her panel. "Request classified channel to SoCal Tracon," Tayla said.

"SoCal Tracon classified."

"Tracon, this is *Brilliant*. We are carrying an extremely critical patient to the helipad at Hollywood Methodist. We are unable to camouflage. We'll go subsonic over Barstow at 1440 and will arrive at 1447. Advise Las Vegas Traffic that we'll be rattling windows on the strip. Request clearance for our track and a one-mile radius around HMH."

"*Brilliant*, be advised that five news helicopters are circling the hospital. You have clearance to Hollywood. Airspace is clear from Barstow direct to Hollywood."

"*StarCruiser Brilliant*," Tayla acknowledged.

Hollywood Methodist Hospital

The reporter heard the break-in and the toss in his ear. "We have Breaking News in Hollywood. I'm Lorena Nancarrow, KLAX NewsFive. You see live pictures of the helicopter landing pad above Hollywood Methodist Hospital from NewsChopperFive. We received information from two sources at Hollywood Methodist that an unidentified aircraft will arrive on the helipad to deliver an extremely critical patient, said to be an unidentified nineteen-year-old male with gunshot wounds. We now take you live to Bernard Gonzalez in front of Hollywood Methodist Hospital."

"Thank you, Lorena. I'm standing in front of Hollywood Methodist Hospital at Vermont and Fountain. At one-fifteen, KLAX received reports from an anonymous source that an unidentified aircraft was set to arrive above us at three p.m. We have been unable to confirm that the aircraft originated from Tovar Studios. I can tell you that in the last thirty minutes, four-time acting award winner Ellie Masing arrived here accompanied by Hanna Kelrithian, wife of the Chairman of Tovar Studios. You might remember that Ellie Masing started her acting career in the *StarCruiser Brilliant* movies and is married to Jack Masing, the long-time star of the *StarCruiser Brilliant* series," Bernard said and then paused listening to his earpiece. "Now, back to Lorena in our studios."

"Thank you, Bernard, we just received reports of a major earthquake in Las Vegas. We haven't been able to confirm this with the United States Geological Survey…. Wait… Yes? The event in Las Vegas involved multiple sonic booms. We have a viewer calling in from Las Vegas. You have a report, Sir?"

"Yes, I was at Cape Canaveral in 2011, as a ten-year-old, to witness the final landing of the space shuttle. The sonic booms today sounded very much like that," the caller said.

"Thank you, Sir. To update, we have a confirmed report that an unidentified aircraft will land in Hollywood in just a few minutes. We cannot confirm at this time any connection with the Sonic Booms over Las Vegas. You are watching live pictures from NewsChopperFive. Now, back to Bernard Gonzalez…" the anchor said.

"CAPTAIN, WE ARE SUBSONIC AT SIXTY-THOUSAND FEET. SIX MINUTES to our landing point," Jennifer said. "Airspace is clear ahead of us. There are five rotor-wing craft and over a dozen newsdrones circling Hollywood Methodist."

"Looks like we are going to make a Hollywood entrance," Navvy said.

"Two minutes, I have the helipad on tactical," Jennifer said. "Indicates a clear approach. We are at twenty-thousand, descending at eight-thousand per minute."

"Very well, Pilot."

"THIS IS BERNARD GONZALEZ. OUR CREW HAS MOVED TO THE helipad above Hollywood Methodist. The hospital's trauma team is standing near me ready to receive an unidentified patient. All eyes up here are focused Northeast where we received reports of sonic booms over Las Vegas, originating from a spacecraft re-entering the atmosphere. Just a moment…Doctor, can you tell us the name of the patient being brought in?"

"We cannot identify patients without their consent."

"Doctor, can you identify the aircraft that is bringing the patient in?" Bernard asked.

"You wouldn't believe it if I told you."

"Can you tell us your name?"

"I'm Dr. Vinod Prashad, head of the Hollywood Methodist trauma team."

"Again, we have very little information concerning what is about to happen here at Hollywood Methodist, but I can report that Ellie Masing and Hanna Kelrithian are now on the apron of the helipad. Lorena?"

"Thank you, Bernard. Our NewsChopper Pilot has just informed us that Air Traffic Control has asked all of the news helicopters to move one mile from the helipad. Bernard?"

"I HAVE THE HELIPAD ON VISUAL. WOW, IT'S CROWDED DOWN THERE."

"Very well, Pilot. Ani, can you magnify the pad on the left screen?"

The screen now showed the helipad in detail. "There are Ellie and Hanna off to the side. Engineer, drop the ramp as soon as we touchdown."

"Engineer, aye."

"Sick Bay, are you ready for the transfer?"

"Yes, Captain," Dr. Ami replied.

. . .

"LORENA, AS YOU WERE SPEAKING, SEVERAL PEOPLE WERE POINTING, and I spotted an aircraft descending from almost directly overhead. I can confirm that it's neither a helicopter nor a fixed-winged aircraft. Someone nearby has binoculars. Sir, can you identify the aircraft?"

"It looks like *Brilliant*. It is *StarCruiser Brilliant*," the man said.

"I cannot confirm that report. Wait, it does have the same form factor. I see the familiar coloring. The aircraft just banked for an upwind approach. It's getting very noisy here on the helipad."

"You're seeing what our camera aboard NewsChopperFive is seeing. Bernard, we cannot believe it either." Lorena interjected.

As *Brilliant* made its steep turn, it presented the classic plan view from an angle directly above the center of the craft. It leveled out, lowered its landing struts, and smoothly dropped to the helipad.

Bernard Gonzalez was drowned out by the noise for a few seconds. "Ladies and gentlemen, I can now confirm that at two-forty-seven p.m., June 25, 2067, *StarCruiser Brilliant*, a supposedly fictional spacecraft from the movies of the same name, has landed on the helipad here at Hollywood Methodist; apparently after returning from outer space. *Brilliant*'s ramp is dropping, and now the hospital's trauma team is boarding the ship with a gurney. Ellie Masing has moved to the foot of the ramp. Here comes the gurney down the ramp carrying a patient. I cannot confirm the identity of the patient, but I can report that he is surrounded by medical equipment that would indicate that this patient is in very serious condition. Ellie Masing has taken the hand of the unconscious patient," Gonzalez let the video play out. "Next down the ramp is Jack Masing, who hugs his wife. She appears to be crying. Now, the trauma team is quickly moving the patient and the family to the elevator. I see Hanna Kelrithian. Hanna, can you tell us who the patient is?"

There were tears in her eyes. "It's our David. It's David Masing," Hanna said.

"I can now confirm that David Masing, the nineteen-year-old son of Ellie and Jack Masing and co-star with his father, has been taken into Hollywood Methodist Hospital. We'll get updates on his condition as soon as we can.

"Two more people have come down the ramp, including a teenage female. I confirmed from facial recognition that the female is

Jennifer Gallagher, an intern at Tovar Studios. The second person is her step-father, renowned neurosurgeon Allan Goldstein. As Jennifer goes back up the ramp into the ship, the doctor is coming toward the elevator. Dr. Goldstein, can you comment on the condition of David Masing?"

"David is in extremely critical condition and requires the transplant of multiple organs. Hollywood Methodist is well-known in our area for their ability to regenerate organs for transplant."

"Will you be doing the surgery?" asked Gonzalez.

"Dr. Ami is the Artificial Medical Intelligence on board *Brilliant*. She is a resident at this hospital and will perform the surgery with my assistance, along with the excellent trauma team here."

"Can you tell us how David received his injuries?"

"I have no comment on that."

"Why is your step-daughter on board?"

"She is going to fly *Brilliant* back to Tovar," Allen said. "I have to go to work."

"Thank you, Doctor," Gonzalez said. "This story gets more interesting. According to her step-father, *Brilliant is* being piloted by a seventeen-year-old intern at Tovar Studios. Hanna Kelrithian has now gone to the foot of the ramp. Joining her is Navilek Kelrithian, her husband. They ascended back up the ramp."

JENNIFER RETURNED TO THE PILOT'S SEAT, NOW IN COMMAND OF *Brilliant* for the short journey back to Tovar. "First Lieutenant, do we have everyone on board?"

"I think Hanna is coming with us."

"Very well, tell us when we can raise the ramp."

"First Officer, ramp is up and, everyone is aboard. We are clear to depart."

"Engineer, report when ready for departure."

"First Officer, the ship is sealed. *Brilliant is* ready."

BERNARD WAS QUIET AS OTHERS YELLED INSTRUCTIONS, "WE ARE being directed to clear the helipad. The ramp on *Brilliant* is being retracted, apparently, in preparation for immediate departure. The noise is increasing, and yes, *Brilliant is* rising. The landing gear has retracted. *Brilliant* has now turned to the North." The reporter let the video speak for itself as *Brilliant* slowly ascended. The noise subsided. "To sum up this historic day, *StarCruiser Brilliant* has returned to Earth and has delivered its young pilot, David Masing to this hospital. According to Dr. Allen Goldstein, Masing is in extremely critical condition awaiting multiple organ transplants. *StarCruiser Brilliant* has departed at low altitude in the direction of Tovar Studios, reportedly piloted by a seventeen-year-old girl. In Hollywood, this is Bernard Gonzalez, KLAX NewsFive. Lorena?"

"Thanks to the excellent reporting of Bernard Gonzalez. To our viewers in the Southland and those watching on the networks, you are watching Breaking Coverage of The Return of *StarCruiser Brilliant*. I'm Lorena Nancarrow. You are watching live pictures as NewsChopperFive flies along with *Brilliant*. Its apparent destination is Tovar Studios. The spacecraft is now descending and has landed at Tovar Studios. Stay tuned for our continuing coverage of this historic day, The Return of *StarCruiser Brilliant*. We'll be right back."

JENNIFER WAS BUSY FLYING *BRILLIANT* BACK TO ITS HOME. SHE DIDN'T see the reunion behind her as a mother was united with her son and introduced to her grand-daughter.

"Landing gear is down; Touchdown. Engineer, make the ship safe and lower the ramp."

"Ramp is coming down."

"Ani, shut down all flight systems and place the reactor in ground standby."

Tayla shutdown operations at Ops, Anthen secured the Science Station.

"Dad, it's nice to have you back," Jennifer said. For the first time, her new grandparents, her new half-sister, and her father gathered in a group hug. Jennifer's new family made their way to the ramp and Jennifer remained on the Bridge.

"First Officer, the ship is in shutdown mode. I can make it off the ship with Tayla's help," Riley said.

"Very well, Engineer. Exit the ship."

"First Lieutenant, make shutdown and security reports."

"First Officer, auxiliary systems are shut down in maintenance mode. The ramp is open."

"Very well, exit the ship with my compliments on a job well done."

"First Officer, the reactor is in ground standby mode," Ani said.

"Operations and Weapons are shut down," Tayla said. "Communications in monitor and record. We did it, Girlfriend."

"Great job, you two."

With Tayla's help, Riley went below to the ramp.

Jennifer stood alone on the Bridge. "We did it, Ani. We brought Anthen home."

"Yes, Jennifer, it happened exactly the way you played it out on the simulator."

"Yes, it did."

"But, how did you know about Kalinda? That can't be the vision thing."

"Shhh," Jennifer said. "A girl's gotta have her secrets. I'm ready to be relieved, Ani."

"I have the ship," Ani said. "Be careful; I hear SoCal traffic is dangerous at this time of the day."

Jennifer descended from the bridge.

Sheila stood with Ana and Steven at the foot of the ramp. Maiara was the first down the ship, and she walked around to verify that all was secure. Then Hanna and Navvy came down the exit with a very familiar-looking man with a dark-haired ten-year-old at his side. They walked up to Sheila. "Anthen?" Sheila asked.

"Sheila," Anthen said. They hugged cautiously. "You raised our daughter to be a wonderful young woman and an excellent officer. She saved the ship with her leadership."

He still has those damned eyes. "I think she got some of that from you," Sheila said. "I've missed you."

Anthen decided this should go another direction. "Sheila, you have a wonderful husband as well. He got my memory back, and he saved David," Anthen said. "I would like you to meet my daughter, Kalinda."

"Welcome to Earth, Kalinda," Sheila said.

"Kalinda, this is Jennifer's mother," Anthen said.

"May I visit Jennifer sometime?" Kalinda said.

Sheila saw the blue-green eyes and could sense the intelligence behind them. "Something tells me it will be hard to keep you two apart."

Tayla and Riley came down the ramp. Tayla ran and hugged her mother as Riley slowly made his way. "Was it exciting?" Ana asked.

Tayla responded, "You should have seen Jennifer. She led us back to the *Camdex*, and we defeated it. And I bagged a drone fighter." She looked at Sheila. "You should be proud of Jennifer. She's an amazing First Officer. Oh, yeah, she got promoted. That's why she's the last one down. She's in command."

Finally, Jennifer came down the ramp alone. Navvy started to clap, then the crew members, and then everyone present. She paused at the ramp looked back up into the ship, then walked and then ran to her mother.

"We made it, and we brought Dad home."

They hugged. And then Sheila said, "You saved *Brilliant* again?"

Jennifer looked back at *Brilliant* and said, "Yeah, I guess I did."

Jennifer went to each person on the ground and hugged them and then came back to her mother. "Mom, there's no place like home."

"Yes, Dorothy, but I'm pretty sure your ruby slippers are on the top deck of *StarCruiser Brilliant*."

Epilogue

Jennifer Gallagher drove past the guard at the gate of Tovar Studios on the final day of her summer internship. After exiting her Prius, she took the long way to Sound Stage Four and passed now familiar landmarks. The back lot contained the memories of every Hollywood studio. Information Technology was where she met Grayson and began working on the HoloPads, which revolutionized the workflow on the lot. She passed the Executive Offices where she would end her day and end her internship. As she approached soundstage alley, she visited one last important thing: *Brilliant*. It was the ship that brought her to Tovar, and it would keep her at Tovar Studios as a filmmaker and as First Officer of *StarCruiser Brilliant*.

She entered Sound Stage Four and went to Craft Services to get her second double-shot caramel Frappuccino of the day. "Hello, Bill," she addressed the Lead Gaffer.

"Hello, Intern Girl. It's your last day. What do I call you now? Producer Girl? Writer Girl? Director Girl?"

"Call me Jen. I might be different things on different days," Jennifer said.

"I look forward to lighting your first scene."

"I do, too, Bill."

.   .   .

JENNIFER ENTERED THE WRITERS' ROOM AND TOOK HER SEAT FIVE minutes early. Gia Bianchi and James Weldon arrived soon after. "Susie is late as usual," Gia said. Susie was never late.

Susie came in at the top of the hour carrying a cake with Jennifer's name on it. Gia stood up. "You brought your excellent writing skills to this room along with your HoloPads and their Jedi tricks. We know we'll see you again, but today you're no longer an intern. We look forward to working with you to bring your first picture to the screen." Susie started cutting the cake, and James handed her a package. When she opened it, she found a black t-shirt with only three words:

Writers are
Brilliant

She thanked everyone, and they got to work finishing up the sides for next week's scenes.

A FEW MINUTES BEFORE NINE, JENNIFER BROUGHT A BOWL OF GRANOLA and a carton of milk to Nessa Buskirk who was conversing with her shirtless Dionysus in a very efficient manner to get her day together.

"This is your last day as an intern?" Nessa said.

"Yep. And thanks for all of the help."

"Seriously, I was a mess, and you fixed me. With kindness, healthy food, and incredibly cool toys."

"You're still my boss."

"Until you hire me for your first picture."

"Until then, is there anything you need before I work for Chris?"

"Haven't you been directing the last two weeks?"

"Moi? I am not a member of the guild."

"GOOD MORNING, CHRIS." JENNIFER TOOK A DIRECTOR'S CHAIR NEXT to Christopher Cherry, the titular director of this episode of *Star*

Doctor. Jennifer directed the last two episodes under his supervision. Today was the last day of the current series installment.

Nessa came over and presented the script order to Jennifer. Then Jennifer walked over to the DP, the Director of Photography, and Bill, the Lead Gaffer, to discuss the setup for the morning's scenes. Finally, Jennifer met with Dr. Ami and her co-stars to explain how she wanted the scenes to come across. Jennifer returned to her chair next to Chris. She asked the Assistant Director to call for places and the day's shooting schedule began.

At precisely two minutes before noon, Jennifer ordered the AD to announce, "That's a wrap."

Jennifer expected the crew to secure their equipment, strike the set, power down the lights, and roll up cables. But none of that happened. Instead, Navvy Kelrithian, walked onto the set along with another gentleman in a suit who, Jennifer noticed, had been observing all morning.

"Jennifer, you're in big trouble. You have been violating union rules," Navvy said.

Jennifer's face took on the same crimson as her hair. "But...."

The Suit began speaking, "Miss Gallagher, I am the President of the Director's Guild. You have been violating the rules of the Guild by directing episodes of this program. Normally that would result in large fines for both you and the studio. But Guild Member Cherry has monitored your progress, kept a record of your accomplishments, and endorsed your application for membership. Therefore, in the presence of Guild Members Kelrithian and Cherry, the tradespeople working on this production, and myself, I hereby appoint you a member in good standing of the Director's Guild with the all benefits and emoluments to come thereof. Congratulations, Miss Gallagher." The soundstage erupted in applause.

Jennifer took a deep breath, accepted the praise, and issued a big hug to Chris. After that, the crew began quickly and efficiently striking the set and going to lunch.

"One p.m. My office," Navvy said.

Before she left the set, she received one last visit.

"You look very happy; you deserve this, Jennifer," Dr. Ami said.

"Not without you, Dr. Ami. You saved David. I just came along and did my job," Jennifer said.

"You don't realize how much you have changed our studio, do you?"

"I know that I got to learn some things and do some things I am pretty good at."

"Jennifer, you have the most dynamic, inspiring leadership skills of anyone whom I've studied in history. You gave me the opportunity to become a great surgeon so that I could save David. You helped Nessa get out of her own way. And, most importantly, you brought Navvy's son back and allowed him to look past his next project toward being a grandfather. Everyone you've met up with has solved problems, grown more competent, and become empowered because they interacted with you. Everyone at Tovar would follow you into any battle simply because of their confidence in your leadership. That is your superpower, Jennifer Gallagher. Not your IQ, your leadership," Dr. Ami said.

"What can I say to your wonderful words? I am just a lowly intern."

Dr. Ami saw the twinkle in Jennifer's eye. "And *Brilliant is* just a starship in a movie."

They hugged once more.

PIPER SIMMONS AND STEVEN MENDOZA SOLVED THE POWER PROBLEM, and the VirtualLocation40 system was ready to go on location with forty drones as JennaTech's first product. The Wireless Power base station was six months away from commercial release. Tech writers predicted that it would have an enormous impact on Public Wi-Pow. Scarlett took over publicity and marketing for JennaTech, and Jennifer was in demand as an inspirational young entrepreneur.

OVER THE LAST FEW WEEKS, JENNIFER SPENT MUCH OF HER FREE TIME at Hollywood Methodist Hospital in David Masing's room. The first few days had been nerve-wracking until Dr. Ami announced that David was out of the woods. David moved from the hospital to a short stint in a physical rehabilitation center, and he was now getting around with a cane for a few more weeks.

She spotted David in the parking lot, "You're invited to this as well? Mom messaged that she is coming as well."

"Dad said to be here, so here I am," David said. They walked arm-in-arm into the office.

Kathy greeted them, "They are meeting in the Conference Room."

"Did I hear that you're retiring?" Jennifer asked.

"Not officially and only semi-retiring."

She entered the Conference Room and was surprised to see Tayla and Riley as well. Navvy started the meeting, "Jennifer, what is the status of VirtualLocation40?"

The system will be on location starting the first week in September, covering rehearsal and getting the bugs out. We'll be ready."

"Good," Navvy said.

"Navvy, I have a question."

"Yes."

"If I can work around school, may I go on location?"

"Your mother and I already discussed that, and yes, you will be on location."

"Thanks, Navvy."

"You will be directing the second unit from the truck. Can you handle that?"

"Yes, I can. Thank you."

"Now, the reason that we are here. The next *Brilliant* installment goes into production in eighteen months after *Galaxy Warrior*. I believe that we have a workable storyline to adapt and we need a script. The title will be 'The Pirate Returns.' Jennifer, will you put this on your to-do list?"

"I can. Who will be starring?"

"David and Riley, of course, will play their roles. Jack and I can fill in as needed. We have successful screen tests for the remainder of the *Brilliant* Crew."

"Who will play our parts?" Tayla asked.

"Is it possible that you and Jennifer could work it into your schedules?" Navvy asked.

"Me. Act?" Jennifer said.

Sheila interjected, "Navvy and I discussed it. You four have time to take acting classes at UVN before the *Logan Jones* movie. I agreed to be a part of this on that stipulation."

"Mom?" Jennifer asked.

"That's the rest of it," Navvy said. "I decided to step out of the day-to-day, so I hired a very knowledgeable producer who has a great background in the business end of movies. Sheila Gallagher will produce *The Pirate Returns*. Your mentor, Chris Cherry, will direct."

David hugged Jennifer. Riley hugged Tayla.

"Mom, congratulations."

"Granddaughter, I believe that this is your last day as an intern and your first day on the production staff. Let's retire to the dining room. I think that Maiara has prepared a not-so-bloody steak with your name on it.

JENNIFER WAS IN STEVELEARN MANIPULATING AN ENGINEERING drawing for an upcoming JennaTech invention. Pugs was at her side, and Dandy Lion was on her lap.

"Jennifer, the Nesbitt's are coming over in a few minutes," Sheila said.

I'm not going anywhere, Dandy thought.

"Dandy, you know your girls miss you," Jennifer said.

Jennifer knew she must give Dandy back to Kailyn and Kamryn Nesbitt. Their house was now complete, and the family was coming by to collect their pet. Unfortunately, Jennifer violated the cardinal rule of cat-sitting. She had fallen hopelessly in love with the striped, orange tabby. Dandy Lion had cuddled and comforted Jennifer during troubled times. And, he strutted his regal feline attitude when Jennifer was overconfident, putting Jennifer in her human place.

The doorbell rang. Foreboding the coming loss, Jennifer gathered up Dandy, put on the best fake smile that her recent acting lessons could muster, and went to the door. She opened it. Sheila stood nearby.

There were the parents and the Nesbitt twins. Dandy dug his claws into Jennifer's chest, and she almost didn't give a second look that revealed a white Persian kitten in Kailyn's arms.

"The girls got lonely, so we dropped by a friend's house. The girls fell in love with their Persian kittens, so we brought one to our new home."

Jennifer and Dandy hugged each other tighter.

"Kailyn and Kamryn were wondering if you wouldn't mind keeping Dandy Lion. Forever."

Kailyn said, "We would like to visit, but after the whole summer we know that Dandy has probably adopted you."

Jennifer's eyes were now full of tears, and all she could do was nod. Sheila said, "I think that would be alright with Jennifer. And yes, you may visit anytime."

"Here is another bag of cat food. Thanks for your understanding. And, Jennifer, thanks for saving Dandy's life."

"I'll love Dandy forever. Thanks so much." They got close to each other to hug until they heard hissing from both cats.

"I think we made the right decision," Mrs. Nesbitt said.

The Nesbitts departed, and Jennifer returned to her room with her permanent addition. "So, Dandy, are you ready to be Ship's Cat?"

I'm ready, First Officer. And then the V8 purring engine sprang to life as Dandy settled into his place on Jennifer's lap.

Thank you for reading *Brilliant*. I hope you enjoyed the story. If you loved this book, please remember to post a review on Amazon. Amazon reviews are so helpful to authors, because if a book has a lot of positive reviews, Amazon is more likely to show the book to new customers. As an indie author, I don't have the support of a major publisher behind me, so your reviews are incredibly helpful to the success of my books! I read every review, and love seeing the support from my readers.

Please go to Amazon or Goodreads and post a review.

Acknowledgments

Brilliant is my first novel. As a publisher, I have delivered thirty-five books by eleven authors but writing a novel is a new world. I would like to thank those who helped to make my book as good as it can be despite my efforts to the contrary.

I learned much from experienced authors, first and foremost my mentor, marketing guru, and editor, Penn Wallace, who writes exciting thrillers as Pendleton C. Wallace. Caroline McCullagh, author of The Ivory Caribou, provided much encouraging criticism. Jim Bennett suggested an incredibly descriptive title. My Ohio contingent included Sheila Dobbie, who is writing Letters to Sallie, the Civil War Letters of A.C. McClure, my great-grandfather, and Kathy Rider, my diligent copy editor.

One can only hope to have a wonderful cover like the one that Renata Lechner produced for this book.

Thanks to my beta readers including Swati Hegde, Elo Quijada Tarwid, Ron Hidinger, Dennis Mauricio and others.

Special thanks to author Laurence Dahners, whose character Ell Donsaii inspired Jennifer and who contributed valuable time and expertise at a critical moment. And to Sarah Char and Glenn Ripps, who provided their Hollywood insight.

My USS Drum sea buddy, Kent Gunn got me into the publishing

business with *The Apes of Eden* and inspired Jennifer. Kent is the answer to the question, "How can anyone have an IQ of 206?"

Finally, my greatest inspiration comes from my former students in Southwest High Video Productions and iCrew Digital Productions including John, Joel, Dante, Chris, Stacee, James, Brian, Brittni, Ayiiia, Rod, Katie, Meaghan, Anamaria, Marina, Lee, Jessica, Charlie, Tori, Ricky, Chris D., Robin, Liza, Brion, Darlene, and Francisco.

And my thanks and apologies to anyone I might have left out because of you know…CRS.

About Rick Lakin

Rick Lakin is the publisher at iCrewDigitalPublishing.com, Bringing New Authors to a Digital World. iCrew has published 35 books by 11 authors.

Rick has been an optimist for almost two years and is the district webmaster as calso41.us.

He is the founder of iCrew Digital Productions, A Community of Young Media Professionals and a member of the 1000 Club of the National Association of Sports Public Address Announcers. Rick is an Advanced Communicator Silver in Toastmasters International and is a member of American Mensa. Rick works as a Sports Statistician for broadcast television and is a retired math teacher.

He is a retired math teacher who lives in Southern California but his roots are in Columbus, Ohio, home of The Ohio State University Buckeyes.

facebook.com/ricklakinauthor
twitter.com/ricklakin
amazon.com/author/ricklakin